Ryan –
I hope you
enjoy reading my
book as much as
I enjoyed writing it!
Merry Christmas –
James A.

The Benefactor:

Truth Is Stranger Than Fiction

D1520767

ISBN: 1-4635-8229-3
ISBN-13: 9781463582296

The Benefactor:

Truth Is Stranger Than Fiction

A Novel

James A. Wynne

2011

Dedication

This book is dedicated to my loving wife, Marlene;

my inspiration and my motivation.

Chapter 1
Church

"Wake up, Edward! You're going to make us late for church."

His father was already to the bellowing stage.

What a way to begin a beautiful spring morning! Church!

"I'm coming, Father!" Edward was almost ready, but being late was part of the game. He did not want to seem overly anxious to attend Services—not today or any other day. He was having some issues with his faith. How could there be so much misery in Lower Manhattan? And without a doubt the richest man in the world would be sitting in church with them that very morning, turning a blind eye—as he always did—to the fact that such misery existed when he had the means, and the friends, to relieve some of the pain.

Edward had grown up on the Lower East Side of Manhattan, nowhere near a tenement, slum, or the Bowery. He grew up on 16th Street, off a little park called Stuyvesant Square. Named for Dutch governor Peter Stuyvesant, the square was surrounded by a real mix of the social classes—mostly middle and lower-middle class. But there were some truly destitute people, and there were some really rich people, too.

Edward's parents always told him that he had been a "miracle of modern science," as he was born almost two full months premature and yet had been an extremely healthy baby.

Both of his parents worked; they worked very hard. And between their two incomes they were able to put enough aside so that he could attend Columbia College. He graduated from Columbia in 1895. Columbia was in the process of relocating the entire school way uptown to Morningside Heights—from 49th Street!

Edward had graduated with a degree in law. He was planning to take the New York Bar Exam—one of these days. He just didn't know if that was what he really wanted to do. The idea of practicing law was exciting, if he could put it to good use; possibly use his knowledge to help some of the poorer people in New York City.

"Edward? We are leaving in two minutes." His mother's voice was gentle, but firm.

"I will meet you out on the stoop." How many times had he said that? He really didn't know, but it was too many to remember. The stoop referred to the short half flight of steps—usually concrete, brick, or fieldstone—that led up from the sidewalk to the main entrance of a brownstone. Almost as if by design, these were places for people to sit—whether to talk or just pass the day. On a nice spring or summer day, one could look straight down 16th Street and see a large portion of the neighborhood collected on their various stoops. Children played in the street in front of their house, under the watchful eye of a parent or grandparent.

In less than the prescribed two minutes, Edward met his parents on the sidewalk in front of their home.

"It's almost eleven o'clock, foolish boy! Why do you feel you must stay out so late with your friends?" This sounded like the start of a very familiar conversation; a conversation that his father seemed to love to re-visit at least several times a month. "Edward, I am not a Puritan! I spent some of my youth in the same manner—but only some of my youth, not all of it!"

They started to walk to church. "I am not that bad, Father, really! I only go out late on Friday and Saturday evenings, and I'm only a block away from home!"

And they were only a block away from church. "That's not the point!"

"And what is the point, sir?" There was, he had to admit, a certain tone in his voice that he hadn't meant to use, but was there nevertheless.

"The point is that you have yet to get on with your life!" His father's voice crescendoed as he finished that statement.

"Thomas!" His mother gently attempted to stall the inevitable. It was going to be spoken of; if not here and now, then over Sunday dinner.

"Elizabeth, don't take his side!"

"I'm not! Let's not have this discussion in the middle of Sixteenth Street, and in front of the neighbors."

"Fine. Fine."

But it wasn't fine. Thomas was wise enough to know that his wife's sense of decorum held sway when they were out in public. He didn't subscribe to the popular notion of "what would the neighbors say?" as a guide to his behavior, but he did respect the wishes of his wife.

But then again, it really didn't matter, for they had reached their destination.

St. George's Episcopal Church was one of the oldest parishes in New York City. The St. George Chapel was originally established by Trinity Church, on Wall Street, way back in 1749. The original St. George's was built at Beekman Place, but the membership soon outgrew the chapel. The church they were about to step into had been built in 1846, had a devastating fire that gutted the building in 1857, and was subsequently rebuilt. The church originally had matching spires on each of the front towers, but they were never replaced after the fire. The building was made of red stone, almost the same color as their brownstone home.

The small family walked through the front entrance doors and into the vestibule, or narthex, of the church. They were immediately greeted by organ music coming from above their heads, for the pipe organ was situated in the rear gallery. At the console was longtime organist and choirmaster, Homer Norris, a man known throughout the city for his keyboard abilities and his original compositions. He was meticulously playing a piece by Felix Mendelssohn, although the family didn't recognize it as such, trying as they were to find a seat before the prelude ended. The church was particularly packed for this Service, and arriving this close to the start of the processional meant they would have to sit closer to the front of the church than was their custom. Edward especially did not like sitting down front. It put him near the pews that held the wardens of the church—especially one. He felt that his place was in the back, under the balcony, with the other people of his class. Not that he believed in class distinction—he simply was not going to seem pretentious by sitting with the wealthy members of the congregation, even if he did have a college degree.

Mr. Norris transitioned into the opening hymn—the processional. Edward and his parents had yet to find an empty pew, and were aware that they were now in the center aisle of the nave and the choir would be processing in that same space in only a short time. Norris began the introduction of "O God, Our Help in Ages Past," a familiar hymn which nobody in the Episcopal tradition needed a hymnal to sing. Unfortunately for Edward, the empty pew his father had chosen was a mere two rows behind the wardens. They quickly entered the pew, knelt down for a few moments of preparatory prayer, and rose to their feet to join in with the congregation and choir on the first line of the hymn.

Even though Edward was ambivalent about his faith at this precise time, he did enjoy singing, especially in a crowded church. He had sung baritone in the Columbia College Choir, and had enjoyed the experience immensely. He read music well; it was almost a requirement for any well-rounded gentleman of the age. He also enjoyed getting to the last verse in the hymn, because he knew full well that Mr. Norris would take that opportunity to alter the harmonization of the tune and improvise on the hymn, which he was extraordinarily skilled at doing. People came from miles around just to hear him play a Service, let alone a concert.

The hymn ended and the congregation sat, ready for the rector to begin the liturgy. It was at this point that Edward usually found his mind wandering. This was the part of the service that was always the same. He remembered back to his Columbia days. From Columbia College on 49th Street to St. Bartholomew's Episcopal Church on 44th Street was only a few blocks, a brisk walk—except in the winter months, when temperatures often fell well below freezing. At first he was hesitant, but soon caved in to temptation when, in January 1890, he realized that St. Patrick's Cathedral was only a block away. It was the first time he had ever set foot inside a Roman Catholic church.

The cathedral was not all that much bigger than St. George's, but there was something almost ethereal about the interior. Of course, he noticed that the priests were saying the Mass in Latin—that was what really intrigued him—and he understood what they were saying, Latin being a requirement in the curriculum at Columbia. So, unlike the rest of the masses huddled together in that great edifice who mumbled along as best they could, Edward enjoyed the Mass from an intellectual point of view. But then it came to him: the Roman Catholic Mass was following the same order in the liturgy as his home parish of St. George's. How could the two denominations be so similar, and yet so different?

His curiosity took him to the Columbia College Library. He had forgotten about the fact that before the church he grew up in was called the Episcopal Church, it had long been known as the Anglican Church and/or the Church of England. His memory was jogged when he was reminded that it had been King Henry VIII and his desire for a divorce from his first wife, Catherine of Aragon, that had caused the rift between England and Rome. Henry promptly formed his own church, but it was, for all intents and purposes, still the same as the previous association.

He also found some writings about St. George's mother church, Trinity Church, at Wall Street. During the American Revolution, New York City was a stronghold of antirevolutionary sentiment, and no place was this felt more than in the Anglican churches—especially Trinity

Church. Even after the war was over bad feelings still existed, and the members of the Anglican parishes found that their ties to England and its king were a constant reminder of old wounds. When the Catholics decided to build a new, larger cathedral to replace the old St. Patrick's Cathedral on Mulberry Street, they chose a spot of land close to Columbia College to build on. Unfortunately, the Anglicans also had thoughts of building a new cathedral in the same area. Sentiments were so heatedly anti-English that the plans were changed and a new plot of land was purchased—this time as far away from civilization as one could get on Manhattan Island, all the way north in Morningside Heights. Edward was aware that this building, after countless delays in the construction process, was finally under way—but he found it somewhat ironic that the new cathedral would be neighbors with his alma mater, Columbia College.

Back at St. George's, Edward's daydreaming had taken him through the first fifteen minutes of the Service. The rector had sat down, and Mr. Norris was playing a short interlude. But then he stopped.

There was a sound—a musical sound. A voice—a rich, resonant baritone that filled the entire expanse of St. George's. The man sang without accompaniment of any kind—no organ, no choir—just him. This music was not Mozart, or Tallis, or Bach. It defied description. This man was in the St. George Choir, but Edward had never heard such a sound before. The man sang as if the lyrics and the notes came from his very soul, and that soul was a soul in profound pain.

Deep River...my home is over Jordan
Deep River, Lord...I long to cross over into campground.

What was the man singing about? Edward wondered. He could see confused looks on his parents' faces, and, looking around the congregation, he saw similar looks elsewhere. In fact, some of the expressions were more than confused; they looked angry. But why? He peered forward toward the place where the vestry was sitting. Some of the men fidgeted, but most seemed to take it well. Whoever this man was, or whatever had just happened, it made attendance in church this week memorable for Edward. The soloist continued:

Oh, don't you want to go, to that gospel feast
That promised land, where all is peace?

Edward wanted to turn around to see who was singing, but he knew that was frowned upon. Folks just did not turn around to look at the singers and musicians during church—it wasn't a performance, after all. With a few more lines of the song, the singer finished. There was complete and utter silence. Edward heard his mother exhale deeply. She then said quietly, "Well, that should raise some eyebrows."

What did she mean? Edward wondered. Did his mother know something about the man that Edward was not privy to? For that matter, did everyone else in the church know the same thing?

The dean of the parish rose from his chair. "I would like to thank Mr. Harry T. Burleigh, a member of our choir, for that beautiful musical offering. Mr. Burleigh has been a member of this choir for several years, but this is his first solo. I do hope there will be many more." And then he said, "And I also hope that there will be many more occasions when Mr. Burleigh enlightens us with more music from *his people*."

Did Edward understand what was just said? Was there a subtext hidden somewhere in there? What did the dean mean by "his people"?

Edward remained mystified by this event for the rest of the Service. His mother had to elbow him when it came time to receive the Eucharist. Suddenly, like thunder from above, Mr. Norris broke into a piece of Bach for the postlude. Edward leaped to his feet and quickly turned around, trying to peer through the rising incense to the choir loft. The church was filled with noise—and confusion. People were saying good morning to each other and shaking hands. His mother was talking with one of the neighbors, who had the equal misfortune to have arrived late and thus had to sit down front. But Edward wanted to know about this singer. Who was he? He took a step out into the center aisle and raised his hand over his eyes to try to block out the rays that were streaming in through the stained glass windows.

He felt a hand on his shoulder. "Pardon me, young man," a gentleman said from behind him. Edward turned to face the gentleman, and was instantly shocked to find that it was the one man he never wanted to have any contact with whatsoever who was now face-to-face with him. It was the richest man in the world, John Pierpont Morgan.

J. P. Morgan's face was a mere inch or two from his own. Edward didn't know what to do. Like a young schoolboy, Edward quickly looked for his parents, but they were otherwise engaged. He suddenly stuck out his right hand and said, "Good morning, Mr. Morgan...sir!"

"Morning? Why, it's practically the middle of the afternoon!"

"Is it?" Edward looked for words to keep the conversation lively. Even though he did not care for Morgan's approach to business, he did not want the most powerful man in New York to think poorly of him just because of a chance meeting at church. "Sir," Edward continued, being sure to pick his words carefully, "do you know of the singer we heard in the service today?"

"And why wouldn't I know of him? I'm a warden of this church, am I not? No one gets hired here unless we approve them first!"

Edward really didn't know that it worked quite like that. Maybe Morgan was just blowing smoke, he thought.

"So...did you..." Morgan stopped in mid-question. "I am sorry, young man, but I fear that I do not know who you are. If we are going to talk about music, or church politics, I should like to know just to whom it is that I am speaking."

"Quite right, sir. I am Edward Collier. My parents are Thomas and Elizabeth Collier of Sixteenth Street. They are standing directly over there. I am a lifelong member of this parish."

"Pleased to make your acquaintance, Mr. Collier," Morgan replied. "But how is it that you have been a lifelong member of the parish and I am just meeting you for the first time today?"

"Well," Edward said, blushing, "we usually sit in the back, under the choir loft."

"I see. Sat down front to see how the other half lives, is that it?" Morgan instantly sounded condescending.

"No...it's not like that. We were almost late for the Service, and this was one of the few open pews."

"Take no offense, Mr. Collier, I was simply making light of the situation."

"I am sorry, Mr. Morgan. I must admit, I am a bit flustered standing here talking with you."

"I am not the pope, young man, and despite what the *Herald* has been saying about me, it is he who is still the richest man in the world." Morgan chuckled a bit at his own sarcasm. "But about that singer. That is Harry Burleigh. Mr. Norris found him for us. Harry had been working for...wait a moment...oh yes, Dvořák, that's it...Anthony Dvořák, when he came to tour the U.S."

"Dvořák? Really?" Edward was impressed. He had gone to one of the Philharmonic's concerts when Dvořák was on tour.

"Dvořák hired Burleigh to help him research some of the songs of the Negroes. I think the song he sang this morning was one of those pieces."

"Really?"

"It has been said that he used some of Burleigh's work as the basis for that famous melody in his last symphony."

"From the New World?" Edward loved that work, especially the slow second movement, which featured an English horn solo. Was that the melody Morgan meant?

"Mr. Collier, you seem like an educated young man. Did you go to school?"

"Yes, Mr. Morgan. I graduated from Columbia College a few years back, with a degree in the law." Edward wanted that to sound as humble as it could, without making it sound like he was applying for a job.

"Lawyer, are you?" Morgan had raised a suspicious eyebrow.

"Not yet. I haven't taken the New York Bar Exam yet." Edward was embarrassed to even have to say it to the man. He then quickly added, "I'm not sure if I really want to practice law."

"And I can't say I blame you one bit, my boy." Morgan seemed almost jovial—so out of character from what Edward had read in the newspaper. "Lawyers are like cannibals. All they are good for is protecting what a man has, and if they aren't on that side, then they are trying to take it all away from you. Just look at that Roosevelt!"

Edward already knew that Morgan and Theodore Roosevelt were not political allies, although they were both Republicans. Roosevelt felt that the "robber barons" and their corporate trusts had the American economy in a choke hold. Even though the Roosevelt family once lived but a few short blocks from where they now stood, the similarity ended there.

"So did you want to meet Mr. Burleigh?"

Edward was somewhat shocked by this question"I would enjoy speaking to Mr. Burleigh, Mr. Morgan. If one of your assistants could set this in motion, I would be most appreciative of your kind thought."

"Nonsense! Let's go talk to him straightaway. Mind you, I'll not climb those stairs to the loft. If he won't come down, then you'll have to walk up there on your own."

Edward couldn't believe his ears. J. P. Morgan, the richest and most powerful man in the world, was personally arranging an introduction for him with a singer. Who else in the church was coming along? Edward quickly looked around. The church was almost empty now. His parents were still in their pew, but now they were standing alone, watching their son and the extremely important man he was engaged with in conversation.

Morgan and Edward started down the aisle toward the back of the church. Morgan looked up to the gallery and someone caught his eye. He raised his arm and gave a gesture that unmistakably meant, *Come down here.* But this was then followed by a frown. "I felt that he wouldn't come down. You'll just have to climb those stairs, my boy. Don't worry, he won't bite!"

In a morning filled with revelations, here was another. Harry Burleigh, a hired singer in the St. George's choir, refused to exit the choir loft when bid to do so by J. P. Morgan. Who was this man?

"I'll just leave you to it, Mr. Collier. My carriage is waiting for me outside." Morgan then extended his right hand again. "It was a pleasure to meet you, Mr. Collier. I hope that our paths cross again someday. Perhaps this can be accomplished if you choose to sit a little closer to the front on Sundays?"

As Edward grasped Morgan's hand firmly, he replied, "Thank you, sir. It was a pleasure meeting and speaking with you. I hope to see you again." Then Morgan turned and headed out the door.

Edward moved quickly to the staircase that led up to the choir loft. He had never had occasion to actually climb the stairs before, but he certainly knew just where they would take him. As he approached the top of the stairs he was greeted by a large Negro man. Edward assumed this was one of the caretakers of the church, because it was standard practice that black folk were not permitted to worship in an Episcopal church.

"Pardon me, my good man, but I am looking for a singer."

"This is where the singers are. Just who are you looking for?"

Edward felt a little put off. "Harry Burleigh."

"Well then, look no further, you've found him."

Edward was amazed, yet cautious. "But you're—"

"Black?"

"Well, yes...black!"

There was a moment of uncomfortable silence, and then Harry Burleigh's face lit up with a wide grin.

"Mr. Morgan send you up here?"

"Yes, he did. He didn't want to climb the stairs. He said I had to go myself."

Burleigh laughed. "And what was so special that made you have to come all the way up here?"

"It was your solo, your voice, that music. I have never heard music like that before." Edward realized he was close to carrying on, as his mother called it. "I'm sorry."

"That was one of the songs of my people. They're called spirituals."

Edward looked around the loft. Homer Norris was organizing his music at the organ console. Choir members were hanging up their robes and putting their sheet music away. The massive Jardine organ was just above his head. He looked at Burleigh again. "Thank you. I hope to hear you sing again very soon." Edward turned to walk back down the stairs.

"Mr. Morgan wanted me to come downstairs, but I couldn't come… not yet."

Edward looked back and saw the look of profound woe on Burleigh's face. "Why couldn't you come down?"

"I've been singing in this choir for quite a while, but church folks aren't used to a black man on Sunday. This was a big step today, but I think I'll just sit a spell before going out."

"But Mr. Morgan seems to like you."

"He likes me, all right! His was the deciding vote on the vestry that got me this job!"

"What? Really?"

"That's right! Mr. Norris, he suggested me to the vestry, and then there was a lot of discussion on the matter, but it was Mr. J. P. Morgan himself who made the final decision."

Edward thought back to the entry he had made in his journal just last night. In it, he wrote of the stagnant nature of life in 1898; how nothing really seemed to change. Now, he thought in retrospect, maybe things were changing after all.

Chapter 2
Sunday Dinner

When Edward walked back down the stairs he immediately made a right turn and reentered the sanctuary, looking for his parents. He did not see them in the now empty church, so he ventured out onto Stuyvesant Square, thinking they were waiting for him outside. Not finding them, he assumed they had started home without him. He smiled as he thought how his parents must have reacted when they realized he was talking with Morgan. He knew their Sunday dinner conversation was going to be very lively. His father would be covering all the major points in the development of his career and his mother would be cautious and caring.

Edward wasn't foolish enough to dismiss the entire event as something that could have been parlayed into some form of employment, but that really wasn't foremost in his mind.

When he reached the house he fairly bounded up the steps and through the front door. He removed his hat and hung it on the rack by the door. Sunday dinner at the Collier home was a formal affair. The two men wore their suits to the table, and his mother, with the addition of a large apron, was still in the long dress she had worn to church—including the petticoats. Luckily, however, the household was prosperous enough to afford a housekeeper, Mrs. Clara Watson, who had already been working on preparing the food.

Edward found his parents waiting for him in the dining room. His father was seated at the head of the table, napkin already tucked into the collar of his shirt. His mother had just brought in two bowls of vegetables from the kitchen when she saw her son. Edward moved to the sideboard and picked up a decanter of port that was sitting there. He poured the port into two crystal glasses that stood by the decanter. He gave one of the glasses to his father, and after taking a quick sip from the other, put it at his place on the table. His mother, although not involved with the temperance movement, did not drink any form of spirits. Edward sat in his seat, took his napkin, shook it out to his side, and then placed it across his lap—in stark contrast to his father's dining habit.

In addition to the formality in the room, there was also an unspoken tension that could have been carved with the same knife being used to cut the pork they would soon be eating. Edward knew the fireworks would begin very shortly.

"So, Edward, what did you and he talk about?" His mother had waited until dinner was on the table to ask him what had transpired in the church.

"Who, Mother?"

"You know very well of whom I am speaking, Edward. It's practically eating me alive!"

Edward cast an eye to the head of the table where his father, Thomas, was sitting. He, too, was waiting for an answer, but on another subject.

"Did he offer you a job, son?"

"No, he did not. Nor was I asking for one."

"Well, why not?" his father growled. "That was a perfect opportunity! He began the conversation, didn't he?"

"Yes, but it wasn't about me. Well, I suppose some of it was. It was mostly about Mr. Burleigh."

"Who, dear?" His mother feigned interest, now that the subject of career had been taken off the table.

"Mr. Burleigh, the man who sang the solo during the service." Edward took advantage of a brief silence at the table to take a sip of the port in front of him. "Did you know he was a Negro?"

Edward was not baiting his parents with this question. It was, as it seemed, a simple question. Edward's parents were strict, but were also very liberal in their social and political views. His mother's parents had both been abolitionists. They had known and worked side by side with Frederick Douglass. Edward had been raised in a household that was antislavery. It was a household that firmly upheld the idea of equality of the race; that whites were not necessarily more intelligent than blacks, but rather had far more opportunities afforded their race to make it seem that was so. As if to illustrate that point, Mrs. Watson, who shared the same skin tone as Harry Burleigh, entered from the kitchen with the roast pork and gravy. She then joined the family at the table for dinner.

"Ha!" was the only comment from his father.

"Well, this will really give those old biddies something to talk about." His mother seemed quite nonchalant about the situation. She turned to Mrs. Watson. "Clara, did you know that a Mr. Harry Burleigh, a man of color, is in the choir at St. George's? He's now a soloist."

"Oh, I've known about it for some time, Mrs. Collier. It's become public knowledge now, has it?"

"It was announced in church this morning, Clara," his father replied, his tone reflecting his cautiousness.

"I do hope there won't be any trouble in the church, Mr. Collier. I have heard that man sing, and I can say he has the voice of an angel, but…well, you know how funny folks can get."

"Don't worry, Clara," his father replied. "It's about time that place got shaken up a little bit. It's more than forty years since the war. Hasn't anybody learned anything yet?"

Edward's father was referring to, of course, the Civil War—and even though they lived in the North, that didn't mean that all felt the same as they did. There were a great many who felt there was a great intellectual divide between the races, or that the white race was, by nature, superior to the black race. And Charles Darwin wasn't helping the matter at all. His "survival of the fittest" manifesto just added fuel to the fire, and even if you didn't believe a word of his nonsense that man was descended from apes, you could certainly buy into the part that justified racial inequality.

"Father," Edward said, "both Mr. Morgan and Mr. Burleigh said it was a close decision to bring Mr. Burleigh to St. George's, but in the end it was Mr. Morgan's vote that allowed him to be hired."

"So, Morgan wants to take credit for that, does he?" His father was always skeptical when it came to J. P. Morgan, except of course if he were offering his son a job in one of his companies. That would be a good thing, as far as Thomas Collier was concerned. But politics—even church politics—was another thing entirely. "I am sorry, Clara, but I feel I must speak my mind here." Clara nodded. "I am not sure that I like the fact that Mr. Morgan is using a member of your race as a kind…well, as a kind of pawn."

"A pawn, Father?"

"Yes, a pawn, Edward! Just like in a game of chess."

Edward played chess. It was a gentleman's game. He was very well acquainted with the role of the pawn on the chessboard. There were more pawns than any other piece, and thus they were the least valuable to the game, or so it seemed. The pawn could be sacrificed so that the major pieces could gain an advantage. "So you think that Morgan is using the hiring of Mr. Burleigh as the means to a very different end? You think there is more to his motives than affording him the chance to perform on a larger, more public stage?"

"It is possible, my boy."

Edward also realized it was possible. Morgan could be ruthless at times. He hadn't come this far in the business world by letting other men dictate orders to him. He always bargained from a position of strength. He had advised presidents and Wall Street bankers. He had undercut some of the biggest giants in the railroad industry, including Jay Gould, to gain control over railroad holdings. He was not a man to be trifled with!

"Father, I have only just met both men today. I do not know what Mr. Morgan's intentions are. It was a very cordial conversation. And I really liked Mr. Burleigh. He is a man of great talent. So I think I will postpone any final decision on the matter until I have more time for thought and observation."

"Spoken like a true college man!" Thomas was about to lay out his final thoughts on the matter. "But I warn you that you, too, should not be caught up in his game, and also be used as a pawn."

"I will be cautious, Father."

"May we please eat our dinner? It is getting cold on the table!"

Edward's mother always had a way of bringing a conversation back to earth. The food was passed around the table. The conversation between the family members and Clara continued on lighter and more frivolous subjects. Edward still felt a need to justify himself, especially to his father, but let any further possibility of argument drop. It would upset his mother too much, and he didn't want to drag Clara into a heated family discussion—not that she hadn't heard them before.

With dinner concluded, the women cleared the dishes and took them to the kitchen while the men refilled their glasses with port and moved to the parlor.

Edward resumed the conversation with a provocative question. "Father, do you believe that everything happens for a reason?"

Thomas lit his pipe, giving the question some thought. He realized his son was about to continue the dinner conversation without the women present, and he welcomed it, but wasn't sure what his son was getting at. "Are you speaking of predestination, like a Presbyterian?"

Edward laughed. His father always had a way of bringing a discussion back to its true roots—the division of Christian denominations. In his father's eyes, every problem, every moral dilemma, every sacrilege known to man could be traced back to religious doctrine and dogma.

"Well, not in the same way as the Presbyterians, but yes! Do you think that a series of events can be set in motion—not by the Maker, mind you, but by other living men—the result of which, while not obvious during the series of events, seems extremely obvious at the conclusion? As if the resulting end was destined from the outset." Edward knew his father was a smart man, but even he doubted whether or not he had just been at all lucid.

"I am not sure that I follow you, but go on."

Edward took a sip of the port. "You raised me to think on things a certain way. Then you sent me to college. I don't regret that at all, I swear it, but I graduated not knowing exactly what I wanted to do with the education you provided for me. So I guess I have been foundering for the past few years…"

"Foundering? Yes, a good word for it."

"Yes, I suppose it is. But I have studied the law, and I think that you, and Mother, were determined that I practice law, but I wasn't exactly sure if that was what I wanted to do."

"What do you want to do? Become a member of the clergy?"

"Heavens no! Please, Father, let me finish. I wasn't sure if I wanted to practice law until today."

Thomas grew agitated. "Edward, please, don't close the door on this. I will give you more time, if you need."

"Father, I have decided to take the bar exam."

"What? You have?"

"I don't know exactly what I am going to do once I pass the exam, but this I do know. The events of this morning at church, and then again at dinner, have made me realize that there are people out there—millions of people, Father—who need an advocate. Someone who will make sure they are not used like pawns. I think it will take a lawyer to do this."

Thomas Collier smiled. "You want to be an advocate for the black man?"

"Yes, Father, I do. And I think it will take a white man to do this."

"You do realize that you are setting yourself up for many a lost battle, that you are going to be awakened in the middle of the night by the sound of a brick being hurled through your window?"

"I know."

Thomas had always been proud of his son, of his accomplishments. But this was a new side of him.

"Let's go tell your mother, then." They both stood, putting down pipe and drink as they readied themselves for the walk to the rear of the house. "I can tell you one person who will be awfully proud of your decision."

"Mr. Burleigh?"

"Him? Probably! But I was thinking more of Clara. She's been hoping for years that you would find the right way. I hope you are prepared for the hugging you're going to get."

Personal Journal Entry
March 27, 1898

This was a day of many revelations! I cannot say where this course may take me. I am not sure of the way. Mr. Morgan could be a big help, but I am not sure that I trust him. I know Father does not. I will begin tomorrow by signing up to take the bar exam. I will wait to see what happens after that. Who knows?

My father is suspicious about Mr. Morgan's intentions. I must admit that so am I.

My mother is strangely ambivalent. She cannot even mention Morgan by name without looking at the floor.

There are many poor souls living in squalor on Hester Street. Immigrants continue to poor in daily from Ellis Island. And there is a constant influx of poor blacks coming up from the South. Who will speak for all these?

I will!

Chapter 3
Fate Intercedes

Edward Thomas Collier passed the New York Bar Exam in December 1898. He had spent the late spring, summer, and fall working as a clerk in a small law office in the Wall Street area. The partners in the firm liked Edward, but it was also clear that they were not going to be willing to sacrifice their thriving practice for the sake of the poor. Edward decided not to push his agenda with them, but rather chose to go it alone.

He hung a shingle outside his family's brownstone home that read simply:

Edward T. Collier, Esq.

He had a few inquiries, but no clients.

Edward T. Collier was no Beau Brummell, but he did like to look fashionable. He was always impeccably dressed when out in public. His clothes were a humorous pun on his own name—Edwardian; slightly more elegant and slimming than the bulky Victorian style. His suits were always well tailored, but certainly less expensive than those worn by the men whose level in life he hoped to one day attain. But he was a handsome young man, with hair the color of coal and piercing blue eyes. He kept his black hair a little long for the age; more often than not it covered the tops of his ears, but he was careful to keep his facial hair groomed. He didn't like "burnsides"—at least not the style made popular by and named for the Union general. Instead, he wore them no lower than his earlobes and kept them neatly trimmed. Edward stood six foot one, tall for his age. He did not profess any particular athletic skills, although he did enjoy going to the Polo Grounds every now and again to watch that most common of sports—baseball. But even though he was not an active participant in anything that resembled Theodore Roosevelt's "strenuous life," he nevertheless had not a pound of fat on his lean body. He was as thin as a pencil.

He continued to attend St. George's, and had experienced a renewal of his faith of late. As he had discussed with his father, Edward felt he was predestined to help others less fortunate than himself. He didn't really know how he was going to go about doing this, but he felt that God would send him a sign.

Harry Burleigh sang more solos; sometimes accompanied by Homer Norris, sometimes without accompaniment. By October Harry had ventured out of the choir loft. Edward noticed that many of the members had started speaking to him—some even shook his hand. It was a slow process, but Harry was beginning to break through to them.

Edward did see Morgan every so often in church. Sometimes he sat alone, sometimes he had his wife with him, and sometimes it was the entire family.

But Edward and Morgan never exchanged words. They hadn't spoken to each other since their first meeting back in March. Occasionally there was a cordial nod, a glimmer of a smile, but nothing more.

Then, in December, just two days after Edward had passed the bar exam, he was at home, sitting in the parlor reading. There was a quiet knock on the door. The chilly air of a New York December entered the house as Edward opened the front door. A young man stood there, shivering from the cold.

"Are you Mr. Edward T. Collier, Esquire?"

"Yes. Yes, I am."

"I represent Mr. J. Pierpont Morgan. You have no doubt heard of him?"

"Yes. Yes, I have. Will you please come in before you freeze to death?"

The young man stepped inside and Edward promptly closed the door. There was a look of gratitude and relief on the young man's face.

Edward continued, "Do you work for Mr. Morgan, then?"

"Yes, sir. I am one of his clerks." The boy still continued to shiver in the hallway.

"Come inside, then. Warm yourself by the fireplace."

"That is not necessary, sir. I have been instructed not to inconvenience you, sir."

"Nonsense! You are chilled to the very core. I insist! I will have Clara make you some tea."

"That's very kind of you, sir." The young man walked over to the fireplace and warmed his hands.

"Now, what is all this about…um…I'm sorry. You didn't give me your name, sir."

"Geoff…er…Geoffrey Atwater, sir."

"Well, Geoff, tell me of your mission here today."

Edward smiled broadly at the young man, who, for the first time, smiled back at him. The young man removed his hat and muffler, allowing Edward to get a better look at his entire face. Geoffrey Atwater had a gaunt look, Edward thought, and it was due to the fact that he hardly ever ate, but quite often drank. His cheeks were sallow, his eyes slightly sunk in, and his dusty brown hair was long and unkempt. His looked like he needed a shave, as his chin whiskers—thin as they were—were coarse and straggly. Edward wondered if all of Morgan's employees worked themselves ragged to this point. But Geoff had an instantaneous infectious charm; he was a very likeable young man.

Geoff quickly produced a small white business card and handed it to Edward. It was Morgan's card. Geoff then recited the message he was sent to deliver, as if he were saying lines in a poorly directed play. "Mr. Morgan sends his salutations and greetings and wishes that you would call upon his office to set up an appointment with him as the earliest possible convenience."

"Nicely done, Mr. Atwater."

"Thank you, sir."

"Edward."

"I beg your pardon, sir?"

"Please call me Edward. I am only a few years your senior. You don't need to be formal with me. I think this kind of formality tends to keep people at a distance from each other. Don't you agree?"

"I…uh…well…I suppose it does, doesn't it?"

Edward extended his hand, which was quickly gripped by Geoffrey. "I am very glad to make your acquaintance, Geoffrey Atwater. Will you please do me the honor of sitting down?" Geoff quickly sat in the nearest wing chair. "Now then, why does Mr. Morgan want to see me?"

Geoff squirmed a little. "Well now, Mr. Collier—sorry, Edward—you don't really expect that J. P. Morgan tells me his business, now do you?"

"Come now, Geoff, you know there's always gossip around the office. Nothing is truly a secret these days. What does the old boy have in mind for me?"

Geoff smiled. "You're very clever, Edward. I can see why J. P. wants you."

"Wants me for what, Geoff?"

Geoff's smiled quickly vanished. "Sorry. I've said more than I should have said." He stood up, ready to go.

"Sorry, Geoff. I really didn't mean to make you uncomfortable on our first meeting. I will call his office and set up the appointment. You are off the hook, as they say."

Atwater nodded to Edward. "Thank you, Edward, for understanding. I hope to see you when you come downtown."

"As do I, Geoff."

The young men shook hands and then parted company. Edward wondered what the old fox was up to. He rang up a messenger and sent word of his schedule to Morgan's office. An hour later a reply came via messenger that he should be at Morgan's office at ten a.m. the following day.

Edward didn't mention the meeting to his parents that night at dinner, although he was positive that Clara had overheard the entire conversation with Geoff. He really didn't know the nature of the meeting, so there was no need to get either of his parents excited. His father would voice his suspicions of Morgan. His mother would wring her hands in worry. Better to wait until there was something concrete to report. Better to wait.

Personal Journal Entry
December 5, 1898

I cannot believe that I am to meet with J. P. Morgan in the morning. Is this a dream, or a nightmare? I cannot tell. I am aware that my father harbors some resentment toward the man, although I cannot say why this is. Possibly resentment is the wrong word—my father tends to be very tight-lipped when it comes to Morgan. My mother stays out of any conversation concerning the man altogether. I do know they want the best for my future.

I will only mention this meeting to them after the fact. There is no use stirring up a hornet's nest until there is good reason to do so.

Edward arrived at the offices of J. S. Morgan and Company at nine forty-five. Going to Morgan's office was not like getting up for church—he made sure that he was early. The company was still named for Morgan's father, Junius, who had died in 1890. J. P. eventually would change the name of the company. The office was decorated in the symbolism of a Wall Street magnate: mahogany paneling and doors, highly polished brass doorknobs and plates, and the best office furniture money could buy.

"You must be Mr. Collier," a woman's voice said, as Edward closed the door behind him. He looked up to see an attractive young lady with auburn hair sitting at the reception desk.

"Yes, I am."

The young lady smiled at him. "Mr. Morgan is not quite finished with his nine-thirty meeting. Please sit down. He will be with you shortly." Edward found one of the chairs in the reception area meant just for him, and others waiting to see Morgan. "May I get you some coffee or tea?"

"No thank you...uh..."

"Rebecca."

"Rebecca. No thank you, Rebecca." Edward could not help wondering how old the young lady was. She looked to be in her twenties, but not by much.

"Do you come from around here, Mr. Collier? From New York, I mean?"

All right, Edward thought, *it's just small talk.*

"Actually, yes, I do. I live uptown, near Stuyvesant Square."

"No! Really? I live near Gramercy Park."

"Only a few blocks away? Really? It is, as they say, a very small world."

Edward didn't mind having his mind taken off his nerves by this attractive creature; she was helping to make the waiting moments go by. But he was aware, nevertheless, that there was the sound of voices coming from behind the doors that led to Morgan's office. At first he couldn't make out if Morgan was speaking, but then the din grew louder, and it became obvious that Morgan was doing most of the yelling. Much of what he could hear was business language, but every once in a while Morgan would mix in an expletive or two for punctuation. Suddenly, the door burst open and two men quickly exited Morgan's office, followed closely by the big man himself, who gave them a parting word of advice: "And don't you come crawling back here unless he meets my terms."

Edward could almost see steam coming off Morgan's head. He seemed really angry at the two men. What terrible shortcoming were they guilty of? But worst of all, Edward was to be the next person to deal with Morgan, and now he was fit to be tied. Edward felt his stomach twist into a knot.

Morgan turned to face Edward. The scowl immediately disappeared and a broad smile broke across his face. "Young Mr. Collier is here." Morgan quickly crossed the reception area and extended his hand. "How have you been these past months, Edward?"

"I have been well, sir. And you?"

"Nothing I haven't dealt with before, my boy."

Indeed, this was the case. Morgan, for all his money, suffered from several ailments. The most obvious was a skin malady called rosacea—an inflammation of the facial skin, which causes it to redden. Consequently, Morgan often looked like he had just spent the better part of the day in a tavern drinking heavily. But as an extra bonus, and probably because of the rosacea, Morgan also suffered from rhinophyma, which caused his nose to turn purple, distort, pit, and grow appendages. The condition was a great embarrassment to him when he was out in public. He didn't like to be photographed, but if he was, the nose in the photo always needed to be retouched.

"I see that you have met my dear Rebecca. Wonderful girl, Rebecca! I don't know what I would do without her!" He gave Rebecca a wink. "Well, come in, my boy. Let's get started."

Edward and Morgan walked into Morgan's inner office. As they passed through the double doors to the office, Edward couldn't help hoping that this meeting didn't end like the last.

If Morgan's reception area had been a vision of Wall Street opulence, his office was a far more personal statement of his wealth. Almost every inch of the four walls was covered with some evidence of his personal and corporate wealth. There were at least two dozen pictures of locomotives—all symbols of the various lines Morgan now controlled. There was a picture of Thomas Edison. Morgan had given Edison financial backing and now had a major share in his business. Morgan was also proud that his home on Madison Avenue was the first house to be completely outfitted with Edison's electric lighting.

There were pictures of mines—iron mines, to be exact. Morgan was interested in getting involved in the steel industry, an industry that was now very much controlled by one of his friends, Andrew Carnegie.

But Morgan knew that Carnegie was aging and wanted to get out, so he was simply biding his time. There were steamships and boats of every design. There were three models of sailing yachts. Morgan owned the full-sized version of these models. Asked once by a curious onlooker how much money it took to pay for the upkeep on a yacht, Morgan supposedly replied, "If you have to ask, you can't afford it!"

Morgan sat down behind his desk and then gestured to Edward to take a seat. "So, Edward, I hear that you have passed the New York Bar Exam."

"That is correct, sir. Actually, I only received the results two days ago."

"Yes, I know. I also know that you have been clerking these past few months for the firm of Smith, Yates, and Roe."

"Yes, sir, but—"

"And I also know that you have a shingle hanging outside your family's brownstone on Sixteenth Street. Doing a little freelance lawyering, I imagine?"

Edward sat shocked. This was the man who had been virtually ignoring him in church for the past nine months, and yet he seemed to know every detail of his professional career. "But sir, how did you—"

"How do I know these things? I have spies, Edward. Spies! A man in my position must have them. I have more than a dozen men on retainer whose very livelihood is limited to keeping me informed of what is going on around this city—and this country."

Edward eyed Morgan, took a deep breath, and then said, "Well then, I feel honored, Mr. Morgan, that you consider me dangerous enough to have to set your spies on me." Edward waited for a response.

"Oh, very good, Edward! Very good! I knew I had picked the right man for the job!"

A job? With J. P. Morgan? Edward knew he would have to tread lightly. "A job, sir? But I already have a job, with Smith, Yates—"

"And Roe. Yes, this is ancient history."

"I was hoping to make partner someday."

"You won't make partner, Edward."

Edward went on the defensive. "And why not?"

"Because in the first place, the firm is not very solvent financially. I strongly doubt that they will last the year in this economy. And in the second place—and probably more importantly—because you really don't want to make partner. Do you?"

"Well…no."

"And the reason you don't want to make partner is the same reason that you hung a shingle on your parents' house. You want to start your own firm." Edward simply nodded. "And how do I know these things?"

"Spies?"

"Spies!"

Was he that obvious? And what was it that Morgan was getting at?

"And that brings me back to my offer of a job." Morgan pushed himself back from his desk and then swiveled his chair to look out on the financial area of the city. "Do you know why you are being offered a job, Edward?" Edward shook his head slowly. "I will tell you. We met each other in March, in a chance happening at St. George's. I know you remember that. So do I. I am a man of great wealth and power—there is no denying that—and let me tell you, there would be many a young man in just your position who would have used that chance meeting, or his membership at St. George's, or his parents' membership at St. George's, in order to win favor with me. But over these past months you have never once approached me, never had your mother badger me, never in any way tried to convince me that you were someone I should be interested in—which is the very reason that I am interested in you. And no, in this case I did not need my spies! You displayed a character trait that is sorely lacking in the men of the legal profession, and a trait that is virtually missing in the business world—integrity! You, Edward Collier, have integrity, and that is the primary qualification for the post I am going to offer you today."

Edward was taken aback, but managed to squeak out a humble, "Thank you, sir."

Morgan stood up and started to slowly walk toward the back wall of his office. "But there is more to you than integrity. The reason you hung that shingle out was so that you could start a practice that would help some of the more indigent of this city. Am I right?" Edward slowly nodded. "Very noble, Edward. My friend Carnegie came to this country virtually penniless. Did you know that?" Edward did know that fact. "He built his sizeable wealth from scratch by sheer determination. And now he wants to give it all away. Now, I have a little more money than Andrew Carnegie, but I had some help. My father was already quite wealthy, and once you have some money you can usually make that money work for you, if you know what you are doing."

Morgan stopped by a small framed certificate that was mounted on the back wall. "So you have your integrity, Edward, the very thing that we Morgans sorely lacked. And here is the proof!" He pointed to the little document on the wall. "Here! This is the disgrace of the Morgan family, and it will be forever so."

He reached up and removed the certificate from the wall and examined it, gazing at it with the same expression one might use when reading bad news for the very first time.

"Now, I know the Morgan Company made some significant contributions to the Northern war machine back in the 1860s, but my father felt that my presence was so vital to the preservation of the Union that he forbade me from serving in the Union Army. Instead, he paid for a 'substitute.' He paid the army three hundred dollars to find a man to serve in my place."

Edward almost fell off his chair. This sounded frighteningly like the other side of a Sunday dinner story.

"We were not permitted to know the name of the substitute, and that man was never to know who paid the bounty, but it happened just the same." He looked directly into Edward's eyes. "I do not know if my substitute survived the war or not. So much for spies!" Morgan let out a loud, deep exhalation. "So...I made millions of dollars when others lay dying. And what were they dying for? Among other issues, they were fighting to make all the races free in this country. And I tell you, Edward, the war may have ended in 1865, but there are still terrible inequalities up here in the North—and even worse in the South."

Morgan moved to a table near the center of the room. There was a decanter on a silver tray, surrounded by an array of crystal glasses. He picked up the decanter and poured two glasses.

"Here, Edward," said Morgan, handing him a glass.

"Mr. Morgan...it is only a little past ten in the morning, sir."

"Nonsense! It is just a little port. Besides, it's medicinal!"

Morgan proceeded to sit in an armchair across from Edward. "Now, here is the thing, Edward. Mr. Carnegie wants to be known as a philanthropist. A philanthropist? That's rich! I don't care who knows or who doesn't know what I do with my money, so I don't care if I am ever called a philanthropist! I've been called everything under the sun—and none of it very complimentary—but as soon as I publically give away a million or two, then they will call me a philanthropist. What a world!"

Morgan took a sip of the port. "So, do you remember our first meeting?"

Edward nodded.

"Of course you do. You were awestruck by Mr. Burleigh." Morgan leaned forward in his chair, as if he were going to let Edward in on a state secret. "You know, Edward, there are people in this city who would do anything to stop Mr. Burleigh from singing in public, but there are just as many who would seek to make a profit from that man's voice. Mark my words, there will be a time when that man is recognized world-wide as a singer of great ability, and the world will come knocking at his door. I am in the process of bringing an Italian publisher of music, Signor Ricordi, to this county in order to publish some of those spiritu-als that Burleigh sings. My contacts alone would be enough to place him on the stage of Carnegie Hall in a month's time. But I'm far too busy to watch over his career for him. He needs someone like you."

"Me? A musical manager? But I'm a lawyer."

"Mr. Burleigh is just the start, Edward. I have a number of projects that will require a person of sensitivity—just like you."

Edward instantly felt his father's skepticism welling up from some-where in his bowels. What was he being asked to do? Were there illegal doings to be done? Was he going to be asked to look the other way, or to keep silent? He didn't know if he could do this job. "What kind of projects, Mr. Morgan?"

"Land acquisitions, mainly. Not for me, mind you, but for people who can't afford to set themselves up and need a little help financial-ly. One of my first projects is very personal, Edward. There are a great many unwanted babies in this city. Babies who come into the world for a variety of reasons, but enter it in the same condition—unappreciated. I intend to help build a children's hospital to take care of these children, probably near St. George's. Like I told you, I don't want people to know who I am giving my money to."

"So I would be in charge of a trust fund?"

"That seems to be the gist of the idea. What do you think?"

Edward needed to give this plenty of thought, but he could also see that Morgan wasn't going to let him out of his office without a com-mitment. "We haven't discussed terms, sir."

"Terms? That's the lawyer in you, Edward! I knew we would talk money sooner or later. You had me a little worried there. All right, in addition to some stock options, which my accounting office will go over with you in detail, I am in a position to retain you at ten thousand per year."

"Ten thousand dollars?"

"You're right! Twenty thousand per year—just to start!"

Twenty thousand dollars! Edward knew the going rate for most laborers was a dollar a day. Twenty thousand dollars was well beyond his imagination. Still, that kind of money might come with a price attached. "I don't know, Mr. Morgan. It is certainly a tempting offer."

"Edward, I don't know if this will make any difference in your decision, but I promise you that you will never have to do anything illegal or immoral to earn that salary. You will be a fresh face here at J. S. Morgan and Company, and that fresh face will be one that we serve up to the world."

Edward liked J. P. Morgan. He knew the money was tempting, but he couldn't make the final decision without first consulting his father.

"I am thinking very positively of your offer, Mr. Morgan, but may I request an evening to think over my options?"

Edward expected Morgan to stand on his shoes until he gave an answer.

"That is more than fair. But I think you will be working for me in the morning. Go talk it over with your parents. I know they will give you good counsel. And if you decide to join my company, then a celebration is warranted."

Edward cast a quizzical look in Morgan's direction.

"Not with me, foolish boy. I am sure you will find my Rebecca to be very pleasant company."

And with that, Edward was free to leave.

"Are you sure about this, Edward?"

He had expected his father's reticence over Morgan's offer. He also knew that he needed to put up a very confident front if he was to convince his father that he had thought out the proposal completely. His father was not above taking calculated risks; in fact, he was all for them. He just wanted to make sure that his only child knew what he was getting into. Thomas Collier was not enamored with J. P. Morgan, but he couldn't find a strong enough argument against taking the job, and twenty thousand dollars would give his son a really strong start in life. The selling price of their four-story brownstone in the current 1898 market was just a little over four thousand dollars, and most of the furniture could probably be sold with the house at that price, so he knew that his son had a golden opportunity for advancement.

"This offer is all I have been thinking about, Father. I can't really find any flaws with the proposal. I personally think Morgan has mentally set up a kind of philanthropic competition between himself and Carnegie, and he wants me to be the trustee of the money. I think that is why I am convinced it is all legal and aboveboard."

"I think you might be correct about that." That was the phrase Edward was waiting for his father to say, but then he added, "Congratulations!"

"Thank you, Father. Mr. Morgan suggested that I plan a something to celebrate my good fortune. Nothing too lavish, you understand—I don't want to spend my entire salary before I begin work—but I would like to take you, Mother, and Clara to dinner. I was thinking of Delmonico's."

"Diamond Jim Brady, when did you get into town?" His father was laughing, but Edward was quite aware that was usually a prelude to him refusing an offer. "Mother? Clara? Come in here, won't you?" The two women were in the parlor within moments of the call. "Edward has come into some very good fortune and he would like to take us out to celebrate. We are going to Delmonico's."

"Delmonico's?" cried Clara. "Oh, Mr. Edward, I don't know if I will be allowed through the door, let alone be served dinner there."

"Well, that is a possibility, but not if they know what is good for them. I have here Mr. J. P. Morgan's card. I am his solicitor, and if they do not let you in, Clara, then you will become my first client—and woe be to them if you are." Having said this oath, Edward suggested that they plan to have their dinner at around six. The family didn't think this was unusual, as this was their normal dinner hour, but Edward also knew that the Delmonico's dinner crowd would be arriving much later in the evening, so there would be a lesser chance of a fuss. He wanted to hedge his bet.

There was, however, one aspect of the interview with Morgan that Edward neglected to discuss with his father. He did not bother to tell him about the fact that Morgan's father had paid a bounty to hire a "substitute" to keep him out of the Civil War. He knew that Morgan's father, who had died eight years ago, had arranged the deal. That was not the problem.

Times were difficult in New York City in 1863. Edward William Collier and his wife, Anne, and their son, Thomas, had immigrated to the United States in 1860. They were both English-born, but had come over on a steamship from Belfast which was packed with mostly poor Irish immigrants. When the ship docked in New York there had been a great push to enlist the uneducated Irish men into the Union Army. Jobs were scarce, especially for an immigrant, and the couple feared for the health of their son, Thomas.

Then, on a brisk January day in 1861, the elder Collier was approached while crossing Canal Street by a man who claimed to be an agent for the Union Army. He told Edward that he was looking for men for the army, and that the army was paying a special "one time only" bounty of three hundred dollars for new recruits. He told Edward that it was a regiment of special recruits that would act as "substitute" soldiers for men who were either too elderly, crippled, or mentally deficient to fight. In addition to substituting for this group of individuals, there was also the possibility that they would be taking the place of some men whose contribution to the war effort was already invaluable in other areas.

Three hundred dollars was more than a year's wages for Edward. That bounty, plus the regular army pay, would allow Anne and Thomas to live in an apartment with central heat and would put food on the table. He agreed to take the offer. He was instructed that he should not speak of the bounty to any other man he was stationed with, for fear of jealousy, and that he should never attempt to find out who the man was that he was substituting for.

Edward left for basic training in February. He saw very limited action in his first year of service. By the summer of 1862 his unit was called up. They were sent to Maryland, and he was in a regiment assigned to the Union Third Corps. The commanding general was George McClellan. On September 17 his division was brought up to fight in a battle with Robert E. Lee's Army of Northern Virginia. His regiment was ordered to capture a piece of the landscape that was characterized by having a sunken road running through it. The rebels were firmly entrenched in the natural fortifications of the sunken road. Edward Collier's company participated in the fourth wave of Union soldiers that charged the sunken road.

He took a Confederate minié ball to the head and died instantly. The battle was the bloodiest of the Civil War, at a place called Antietam Creek.

Thomas Collier was ten years old when his father was killed in the war. His mother had been educated in England, and because of this was able to find work as a schoolteacher on the Lower East Side. It wasn't easy, but they managed to get by. Thomas was able to go to school—a luxury in those days—and later was able to earn a respectable living. He first managed accounts at the fish market on Fulton Street; then, when he was eighteen, he started working for a publisher of books located on Madison Avenue. He met his wife, Elizabeth, at a social affair at St. George's Church on Stuyvesant Square. They were married in the chapel behind the high altar the next year. They remained as members of the church, and soon had enough money to purchase a nice brownstone on 16th Street, just off the park. Their first son was born the next summer. He gave them all quite a scare, as he arrived almost two months premature, but was perfectly healthy. He was named Edward, after Thomas's father.

Thomas made sure that Edward knew who his grandfather was, and that he was killed defending the Union. The word *substitute* would always come up when telling the family history, but the term was always held in the highest regard. They never tried to find out who Edward had paid the ultimate sacrifice for.

Edward knew he shouldn't bring this information up to his father. It was probably nothing, and, at best, it was an unusual coincidence.

Still, Edward thought, *Morgan has spies. He has spies everywhere.* Could he have found out who his substitute was? Could he have paid off government agencies, the War Department? And what if the substitute turned out to be a young father and husband by the name of Edward Collier? Could that cause Morgan to find a soft spot in his heart for Collier's heir of the same name? It was strange—but it was possible!

Edward wanted to find out, and yet he didn't want to know.

The dinner at Delmonico's did not go off without a hitch, but Edward had been ready—just in case. He expected that some resistance to seating Clara would be present, but he really wasn't sure how much.

The family ordered up a cab to take them to the restaurant. They all wore their best clothes—the clothes they were planning to wear to St. George's on Easter Sunday. Several times on the way to the restaurant Clara had said that if the family encountered any problem at the door she would be content to just wait for them in the cab. Edward then gently countered that he didn't expect there would be a problem—but he was apprehensive anyway.

When the cab stopped in front of Delmonico's, Edward jumped out to the curb. "Wait here, just a moment, please," he asked his family. "I want to make sure they have all that I requested for dinner." That, of course, was a lie. He wanted to go ahead of his parents and Clara to make sure there wasn't going to be a scene played out when they walked in. Edward entered the restaurant and quickly found the maître d'hôtel, a stuck-up little man with a droopy mustache and slicked-down, matted hair.

"I am going to need your best table for four, sir," Edward began. "But before I bring my party inside, I would like you to have this."

The man raised his eyebrows, thoroughly expecting to be handed a sizeable gratuity for the convenience of seating the party in a preferred place in the dining room; instead, Edward handed him an envelope. The envelope was the personal stationery of J. P. Morgan. The maître d' recognized it at once—Morgan being a frequent diner at Delmonico's. He opened the envelope and removed the note inside. The note read:

To the Management of Delmonico's,

I would greatly appreciate that you show the utmost hospitality and graciousness to the bearer of this note, Mr. Edward T. Collier, Esq., and all the members of his party. Should this not be the case, you will be hearing from me—personally.

J. Pierpont Morgan

The maître d' folded the note and put it in his pocket. "We certainly have a most excellent table for you and your guests, Mr. Collier."

"Yes, I thought you would. However, I feel I must underscore that which Mr. Morgan also underscored in his note to you—the word *all*. When I escort my party in momentarily, I would like *all* the members greeted and treated as welcomed guests of this establishment. While I am outside assembling my party, I wish for you to convey this to your staff."

The man looked annoyed with Edward. He understood the note. He could read. What more had to be said? "I shall follow your instructions, sir. Everything will be perfect this evening. Bring your party inside at your convenience."

Edward nodded to the man. He then turned and went out to the waiting cab. He paid and tipped the driver, and then took Clara by the arm to escort her inside. His parents led the way; he and Clara followed close behind. The maître d'hôtel blanched when he saw that a woman of color was one of the guests entering the restaurant. He had guessed there would be a person with an incurable disease, such as leprosy, dining there that evening—but this was worse. Who did J. P. Morgan think he was? he thought. The answer was immediately clear—he was J. P. Morgan, whose bank held the note that financed the restaurant. He smiled blandly at the group and politely greeted them. "Welcome to Delmonico's. I have a special table waiting for you. Please follow me."

Delmonico's was not particularly busy. As Edward had surmised, they were too early to see the dining room filled to capacity. As the maître d' led the party through the room Edward did see heads turn their way—as expected. He glanced over at Clara, who was walking like the Queen of Sheba, with her head held proud and high. There was an undertone of tittering going on, and Edward could tell that some of the other guests were not particularly happy at that moment. In fact, the further they walked in the dining room, the more the sound of complaint became apparent. One man became indignant, stood up, then threw his napkin on the table and headed for the door, with his wife in tow. It was clear that other guests were taking their cue from this couple and also planning a hasty departure.

But then—a miracle. A gentleman of about sixty years of age—white-haired and with a full white beard, who was having dinner with his wife and another couple—slowly and deliberately rose to his feet. He looked firmly and resolutely at Edward's party, gave them a slight nod of his head, and began to clap his hands; slowly at first, and then increasing in tempo. The others at his table soon joined him, standing and applauding.

And the world turned.

The other guests in the room stopped their complaining to re-evaluate the situation. As if watching one of Thomas Edison's motion pictures running too slowly to be real, more guests around the room stood and joined in the applause. Not all the guests joined in, but the ill will that had been felt in the room, the tension so great that it could have been sliced with a knife, had dissipated. Many of the guests wondered who the lady of color could be. They did not recognize her, but then again, there were no persons of color in New York society. She must be someone famous, but all were hard-pressed to know who she was.

The applause subsided, and all once again sat down and went back to their meals. Edward and his party were seated. Edward ordered a bottle of champagne from their waiter. He patted Clara on the hand, and she leaned over and kissed him on the cheek. Conversation turned to the menu and the choice of meal. All four wanted to have the steak that Delmonico's was most famous for serving. The champagne arrived, was poured, and Edward offered a short toast to his family.

"Excuse me," came a voice from behind Edward's left ear. He turned to see that it was the white-haired gentleman who had stood and initiated the applause.

It was Andrew Carnegie.

Edward quickly rose and faced him. "Mr. Carnegie."

"I may be mistaken, but am I in the presence of Mr. Edward T. Collier, one of J. P. Morgan's newest and brightest young stars?"

Edward was quite amazed, and almost speechless. "You are, sir," he managed to reply.

"And this must be your charming family. Your parents, no doubt."

"Um…yes. May I introduce my father, Thomas Collier, and my mother, Elizabeth." Thomas Collier rose from the table and bowed slightly to Carnegie. Then, Edward turned to Clara and said, "And this is a dear friend of our family, Mrs. Clara Watson." Carnegie took Clara's hand in his and kissed it, knowing that every other eye in the room was planted firmly on what the famous man was doing.

"Please forgive my interruption of your celebration. I hope that we will be hearing more of you in the future, Mr. Collier."

"Thank you, sir."

And with that, Carnegie returned to his table. The rest of the dinner was nothing more than a happy memory.

Personal Journal Entry
January 1, 1899

I am in love! I spent last evening, New Year's Eve, in the company of Rebecca Stimson. We have been keeping company for the last few weeks, ever since I joined the firm. I have never felt this way before. My life seems to be coming together in a whirlwind and I fear that everything is going far too fast for me to control it satisfactorily. First this job—now Rebecca!

Life certainly is filled with many possibilities!

Chapter 4
On the Job

Edward arrived at the office at nine a.m. sharp on January 2, 1899. He had spent New Year's Day at home with his parents, enjoying a ham dinner and about a thousand questions aimed at him by his father, his mother, and Clara. The questions were centered around two specific topics: J. P. Morgan and Rebecca Stimson.

Edward had taken Rebecca to a New Year's Eve gala in the ballroom of the Waldorf-Astoria Hotel on 34th Street and Fifth Avenue. All the top brass from the Morgan firm were in attendance with their wives. He had been calling on Rebecca for the past week, so he asked her to join him at this, the first of many social functions with the firm. Most of the older, more rotund members of the company spent the ball talking politics, economics, stocks, and the pleasant outcome of the short war with Spain. It wasn't that Edward didn't wish to participate in these discussions; he could do this most any day at the office. Rebecca looked radiant!

Edward had hired a cab for the evening. He was picked up at his home on 16th Street at seven thirty p.m., and proceeded to the Stimson residence on 22nd Street, by Gramercy Park. It was then a mere twelve blocks or so to the Waldorf. It seemed a foolish place to put a hotel, as it was so far north of almost everything else in the city. What really was uptown? A new railroad station that Morgan was financing. The Tenderloin district in the forties, but there were nothing but cabarets and prostitutes there. Everyone knew that life in the city was centered south of Union Square!

They arrived at the Waldorf at almost nine—just in time for the beginning of the ball. Their first stop was the cloak check. Edward was wearing a new black overcoat which had a seal collar. He was also sporting a new top hat. Underneath the coat Edward was wearing the ubiquitous black tailcoat and white tie. He would exactly match most of the males at the ball. Rebecca was wearing a cloak that enveloped her from collar to toe. When she removed the cloak Edward was able to see her evening gown for the first time. It was also totally black, with a great deal of hand beading on the bodice. She had black ostrich plumes in her hair. Edward thought she looked absolutely beautiful—and he told her so!

They entered the ballroom and found their table. They were served pheasant and lobster. They drank champagne. They danced, and they danced, and they danced.

Then, at about eleven, the doors to the ballroom opened and Stanford White, one of Morgan's best friends, entered the room, with a young lady on his arm. Edward, and most everyone else in the ballroom, had to look twice at the girl, for she was indeed a young lady. Edward guessed that she could not have been more than fourteen or fifteen years old—possibly his daughter, or a niece. But she certainly was not dressed like a girl of such a tender age. Her face was completely covered with cosmetics, including lipstick—which was considered shocking. Her gown was floor-length, but had a massive slit up the right side so that her entire right leg protruded when she walked. Were it not for her obvious age, she could have easily been mistaken for a prostitute.

Stanford White was the most prominent architect in New York. He had designed the second Madison Square Garden a few years before, and had also designed a new men's social club for Morgan—the Union Club. White, while most nondescript in looks, boasted an unusually large mustache which entirely hid his upper lip and most of his cheek area. What Edward didn't know, and may have been the only person in the room that evening who didn't, was that White had a proclivity for very young girls. His behavior outside his office was often described as scandalous. Morgan tolerated White for his talent, but that was about all.

Edward and Rebecca resumed a dance after White's entrance. Edward watched out of the corner of his eye as White and his mistress (if you could call her that) approached Morgan at his table. Satisfied that the show had ended, Edward turned his full attention to Rebecca. They were doing a waltz—not one of Edward's best dances, but he tried gamely. They were about to pass in front of the stage and orchestra when Edward felt a tap on his shoulder. They immediately stopped dancing, as was the custom if someone were to try to cut in on the partnership. Edward wheeled around to comply with the gentleman, and who should be standing there leering at him but Stanford White.

Edward didn't like White; something was very wrong with this man. Edward was about to do the socially unthinkable—refuse the cut—when he noticed J. P. Morgan charging across the dance floor.

Morgan was brandishing his walking stick, a formidable weapon that was crowned with an imperial silver handle. Just last week, Edward had witnessed Morgan thrusting that stick in the face of a photographer who was attempting to take his picture—nose and all. Now it seemed that something on the dance floor was agitating him, and that something was Stanford White. The silver handle was placed directly under White's chin.

"White, you son of a bitch! You get back to your...girl...and get yourself away from Mr. Collier and my Rebecca. They—especially she—are off-limits to you. If you want to live to see 1899, you had better get your arse off this dance floor."

"Come on, J. P., you know I didn't mean any harm. It's New Year's Eve, J. P."

"And you're drunk as a skunk, Stan. Go sleep it off!"

"But, J. P.," White whined.

"Get out!"

For a moment, everything stopped. Morgan had raised his voice and made a threatening gesture with his cane. The orchestra stopped playing, dancers came to a complete halt, and conversation at the tables ceased. The only sound to be heard was the distant clanging of trays and plates in the kitchen. Then, as Stanford White began to slink from the dance floor, the conversation and music slowly resumed. White found the girl he had escorted to the party, collected his outerwear, and left the Waldorf.

"I am sorry about Mr. White, Edward, Rebecca. He does have a bit of a reputation, and I won't have either of you getting caught up in it. He's a talented fellow, and I am sure that I will have more projects for him, but Lord, the man does have his demons!" Morgan felt the need to explain the situation to the couple, or possibly make an excuse for White's behavior. "Anyway, enjoy the rest of the evening, and the holiday tomorrow, and I will see you both in the New Year."

"Thank you, sir," was all Edward replied. Rebecca said nothing; instead, she gave a tiny smile.

Within minutes it became time to have the traditional countdown to the New Year. Edward coaxed Rebecca back to their table where they found glasses of newly poured champagne. The conductor of the orchestra took charge of the ceremony, and when he began the final countdown, however unofficial the time truly was, Edward handed a glass of champagne to Rebecca. Shouts of "Happy New Year!" filled the ballroom, but Edward never heard them. The crowd had disappeared; instead, there was only Rebecca, looking him squarely in the eyes over the rim of her champagne glass. Then she did the unexpected: she kissed him. It was a very proper Victorian age kiss—one that was brief, gentle, and placed on one of his cheeks—but she had kissed him nevertheless. He knew it would be considered improper and out of place to kiss her back—not there, not in public—even though he could glance around the room and witness all kinds of goings-on happening in the name of the New Year. Edward returned the kiss in the most accepted of Victorian ways; he raised her gloved right hand and kissed it—albeit through her opera glove—and Rebecca approved of his action with a smile. He offered his arm, which she quickly accepted, and they once again resumed their place on the dance floor.

The couple left the Waldorf at one thirty a.m. and headed back downtown in their hansom cab. The early morning air was even colder than when they had arrived at the party. Their driver accommodated them by handing them another horse blanket to help keep them warm. Edward found Rebecca's hands under the blanket and held them in his. Rebecca inched a little closer to Edward when they passed 30th Street. Edward kissed Rebecca, this time on the lips, underneath the lamplight as they passed Gramercy Park. As the cab pulled up in front of Rebecca's home, he could see that a family member was silhouetted in the parlor window—waiting up for her safe return home. After the driver stopped the cab, he hopped down and opened the carriage door. Edward alighted first, holding his hand out to Rebecca to help her descend from the cab. He then walked her to the front door.

Just before entering her house, she turned to Edward, raised her right hand and said, "Thank you for a wonderful and eventful evening, Edward. I look forward to seeing you again."

Edward kissed her gloved hand again, and she went into the house. Edward returned to the waiting cab, now ready to take him the few short blocks to Stuyvesant Square. Edward had never noticed until this very moment how quiet the streets of the city were at this time. The only sound to be heard was the sound of the horse's hooves hitting the cobblestones. It seemed but just a few minutes and they were at 16th Street.

"Happy New Year, sir," the driver said, after Edward paid him and gave him a tip.

"Yes, I think it will be. Happy New Year to you, sir."

Personal Journal Entry
January 2, 1899

I have decided that I do not care for the character of Stanford White.

I have a great deal of respect for Mr. Morgan, but I do not know why he keeps giving White such favorable commissions. I suppose he is talented, but New York is filled with talented people, architects among them. Richard Morris Hunt is a wonderful architect. The Vanderbilt family has used him on countless occasions. Stanford White is a rogue and a scoundrel.

What does J. P. Morgan see in him that I do not?

"Come into my office, Edward. I need to give you an assignment."

Morgan sounded as if his holiday had ended before it began. Edward followed him into the inner office. Morgan seated himself in one of the wing chairs. Edward followed suit by sitting in an adjacent chair.

"I think it is about time that you start earning your salary, my boy. I want you to set up a big debut concert for our Mr. Burleigh. I want you to do this in a big way, so this will take some planning. I think the late spring or early summer will do just fine."

"Yes, sir."

"It will be a public event, but there should be a private performance, as well. The masses should get to know Mr. Burleigh, but financial support can easily be coaxed from my friends."

"A concert hall, and then a large private residence?"

"You catch on quickly! It will take months for you to set all the proper wheels in motion, so plan well."

"What about expenses, sir?" Edward knew there was a trust, but Morgan had never bothered to explain just where that trust came from, or how it was to be accessed.

Morgan laughed, "You can spend anything you like, Edward."

Edward didn't quite know what that meant, exactly—or was it a test? "Sir, I need a little guidance here."

"Come over here, Edward."

Edward watched Morgan rise and walk to a large painting on the wall. He gave the frame a tug and the painting swung away from the wall, revealing a wall safe. Edward now started to rise from his chair.

Could the trust fund be kept in a wall safe in Morgan's office? Morgan quickly dialed the combination and opened the door to the safe. He reached in with both hands and removed a cloth bag. He turned back to Edward.

"This is what runs the world, Edward. This is what should run the country." He opened the drawstring and pulled out a bar of gold. Edward's eyes widened at the sight. "Never saw a bar of gold before, have you?" Edward shook his head. Morgan was already on the move, returning to the wing chair with the bullion.

"This," Morgan continued, "is what cost Grover Cleveland the re-election! Did you know that?" Edward felt that he was a little foggy on his facts, so he returned a vague expression of doubt. Morgan said, "Did you know that our U.S. Treasury was almost out of gold in 1893? Of course not, you were still in college and having a good time in local taverns. You weren't worried about the American economy. Fact is, no one was worried about it! So I convinced Cleveland that we should get some gold from Europe, a loan of their gold, so that we had enough in our Treasury to keep our currency at full value. It worked, but the Democrats didn't like our tactics. That old woman, Bill Bryan, went to war with the banking industry, which split the party. McKinley got himself elected, and he made sure that the country went solidly on the gold standard."

"But then, why do you have a bar of gold? Shouldn't the Treasury have this?"

"You are smart, Edward! Let me tell you something. Politicians will have you believe that this country is built on the backs of laborers, or on the backs of farmers, or from the patriotism of our military, or whatever else seems to sound good in a political speech. This is all horse feathers! This country is built on its economy, and the economic center of the country is right here. It's Wall Street. It's the banking industry. So I helped our government out, as I have several times in the past, but this last time I learned something more, something which I am now about to pass on to you. Are you ready?"

Edward slowly nodded his assent, but really wasn't sure that he wanted to hear what Morgan had to say.

"Money is power! I've got the money, so I've got the power! The government will tell you that they are making decisions that will run the country better, but I say that these decisions are helping to run the country right into the ground. So, I've taken steps to make sure that no matter what bonehead is running things down in Washington, I will still have enough power—enough money—to correct what they have done to the country."

Edward couldn't believe what he was hearing. Morgan was creating an ad hoc Treasury?

"I can see that look of fear washing over your face, my boy. You think that I am breaking the law, don't you? Well, Mr. Lawyer, owning gold is not illegal. People wear it all the time. Churches have thin layers of it on their ceilings and pulpits. I have a collection of gold bars."

"A collection?"

"Let's just say that I have enough to keep the government out of hock."

Edward could just about hear his father telling him that he hadn't thought the position through enough; that he was now embroiled in a banking scandal.

"Edward? What's the matter, boy? You look like you've seen a ghost! You're worried about the gold, I can see that. Don't worry! It's not a state secret. Plenty of people know that I have my own gold depository."

"They do?"

"Of course! Didn't I promise you when you took this job that I would never make you do anything illegal?"

"Yes, you did."

"And that promise still holds firm."

"But I still don't understand my role in all this, sir."

"I know. Look, I am sixty-two years old. I am not going to live forever, and who knows, maybe I will start to lose my mental faculties sooner than later. I am telling you that I have enough gold that I could buy the country. I need someone I can trust to administer that fund. My God, the interest on the investment alone is what will fund your projects, and much more."

"You trust me to do this all by myself?"

"No, of course not! You shall have an assistant. You may pick one of the office staff to become your executive assistant." Morgan stopped momentarily, and then flashed a grin at Edward. "And you shall not ask for my receptionist, Miss Rebecca Stimson, as much as you would like to have her working for you. If you don't mind me saying, Edward, it also might ruin what you are trying to build, if you get my point. I know you are very attracted to Rebecca, and what's more, I know she is very attracted to you—and for this I did not need my spies, only my eyes."

Edward understood the problem Morgan was warning him about. It was good advice.

"So then, I can pick anyone else in the office to be my assistant?"

"You have my cooperation in the matter."

Edward knew immediately who he would ask for; he also wondered how Morgan would react to his choice. Everything was a game, and now it was his turn.

"I would like Mr. Geoffrey Atwater as my executive assistant."

"Geoffrey Atwater? The clerk? He's just a boy, Edward! Is that a wise choice?"

"You mean to say that I should choose someone older than I? I don't know Mr. Atwater very well, but he is eager and sharp. I think I will grow to trust him."

Morgan was silent for a moment. "Very well, Atwater it is. You may have the privilege of breaking the bad news to him yourself, Edward. I am sure he will go instantly into a deep depression."

Edward nodded to Morgan, smiling, and then added, "Is there anything I might tell him about a rise in his salary because of his new responsibilities?"

Morgan coughed. "And now you pick my pocket, as well? Let's see…Atwater is a clerk. He probably makes about five hundred dollars a year. You may inform him that his salary has been raised to five thousand dollars a year. Now I am sure he will go into a deeper depression over this. I will have the added expense of having to bring Mr. Freud over from Vienna to open a clinic to treat my office workers."

Edward beamed. "Thank you, sir. I am sure he will be happy with the arrangements."

"Of course he will be happy. The only one around here who isn't making any money today is me!"

Personal Journal Entry
January 4, 1899

I have been awarded an assistant by Mr. Morgan. I believe he was correct in refusing my first choice, my dear Rebecca. I don't think I would have been able to concentrate on my work with Rebecca in the same room.

But I am satisfied with the alternative. I liked Geoffrey Atwater from the first moment I laid eyes on him. I think his mind and his talents are misused by the Morgan Company.

I think this will make for a good partnership.

Chapter 5
Concert Preparations

Edward, with Geoffrey's assistance, spent most of the next few days planning Harry Burleigh's debut concert. The public concert was easy—almost too easy. He would perform at Carnegie Hall, which was even further uptown than the Waldorf. The Music Hall, as it originally was named, had been built in 1891. Andrew Carnegie had provided the finances for the construction. It was renamed in his honor in 1893. It was simply the best concert hall in the city. It had seating for almost three thousand and boasted superb acoustics.

But that was not the principal reason why Edward chose Carnegie Hall for the concert. He had learned very rapidly that Morgan believed in a system of business which would, one day, be called *networking*. Edward knew that Carnegie and Morgan were associates. They were both interested in pursuing philanthropic projects in their later years. They would both like to see the other "robber barons" become equally invested in the future of the social, artistic, and cultural aspects of the country. Edward suspected that Morgan wanted to bring in other men; men such as Henry Ford, John D. Rockefeller, the Vanderbilts, John Jacob Astor, and so on. Edward was also just as sure that there was another, far more sinister plot involved with this plan. From what he already knew of Morgan, he deduced that Morgan's view of Utopia would be modeled on the United States government, but under the complete fiscal control of a few exceptional men.

But for now, it was just a concert; a concert to introduce a wonderful singer and man, Mr. Harry T. Burleigh, to the world. Edward felt he could easily put aside any misgivings he might feel about Morgan's intentions simply because he knew it was such a noble thing that he was doing.

Edward was in his office on the morning of January 10, when Geoffrey entered holding a note. "Mr. Morgan has sent a memo over for you, Edward."

"Really? A memo? Well, let's have a look." Geoffrey passed the small envelope to Edward, who opened it carefully and read the note.

"Mr. Morgan is of the opinion that the private performance for Mr. Burleigh should occur at a new summer cottage at Newport, Rhode Island. I am to speak to him about this at my earliest convenience."

This usually meant immediately.

"Edward, didn't you think the private concert was going to be somewhere in the city?"

"Actually, yes, I did. This is a surprise, I must admit. Do you know anything about Newport?"

"It's in Rhode Island." Geoff was trying to make light of the fact that their boss had just thrown them a curve ball.

"Yes, I know that. Why did he pick Newport? I've never been there. I know nothing of the place. Ever been there?"

Geoff was taken aback. "Me? Are you joking? I spend my summers at Coney Island, along with half of New York."

"Well, we need information, so while I'm in with Morgan, could you find us a map? I'm sure that I will find out why he is so anxious to have this happen in Newport when I speak to him, but what we need to find out is how practical this is going to be to pull off."

"Right." And Geoff disappeared out the door.

Edward walked downstairs to the suite that contained Morgan's office. This was the second time that morning that he had walked into this group of rooms—the first time was at 8:55 to say good morning to Rebecca. Upon his entrance into the reception area, Rebecca looked up and smiled at him.

"Ah, I see that you received the memo."

Edward laughed. "Isn't it funny that I receive a memo, in a sealed envelope, from the boss, and everyone already seems to know about it."

Rebecca just shrugged her shoulders, and then indicated that he should go right in to see Morgan.

Edward saw that Morgan was seated at his desk, but on this occasion he was not alone. A man with black hair sat facing the desk.

"Ah, Edward, what a coincidence." He gave Edward a knowing nod—meaning, *Don't say a word.* "You know Mr. Stanford White, the architect?" White immediately stood and swung around, facing Edward. He offered his hand. Edward complied with a handshake. "It's funny that you happened to walk into my office just at this time, Edward. Mr. White has been building a summer cottage for the Oelrichs family, out in Newport. That's in Rhode Island, Edward."

"Yes, sir."

"They call them 'summer cottages,' but they are anything but that. What did you say you were modeling the house after, Stan?"

"The Grand Trianon of Versailles," quipped White.

"Isn't that something, Edward? Versailles—in Rhode Island!" Morgan laughed at his little joke. "Stan was just telling me that Mrs. Oelrichs has quite a problem on her rich little hands. She has planned a big house opening party for late May, but Stan tells me that the house won't be entirely finished until the spring of next year. Whatever will she do?"

"Well, it seems simple to me, so this is probably the wrong reply. Shouldn't she just postpone the party?"

"Edward, this is Newport society. Everyone is out to impress everyone else. People spend money they don't have on houses they will live in for six to eight weeks out of the year. If Mrs. Oelrichs postpones her party it will cause her to suffer a tremendous loss of social face."

"I don't know how I can get the house finished in time, J. P. We only have a crew of twenty-five working on the place. It would require twice that many artisans to finish the detail work." White was concerned, but not as much as Morgan seemed to be about the situation.

Morgan queried, "Then why doesn't she hire more workers to speed up the job?"

And then the missing piece of the puzzle was dropped into place by Stanford White. "Because she has already convinced her husband that the entire project will cost half of what it has already cost."

Morgan raised one eyebrow in Edward's direction, as if to ask, *Do you get it now?*

Edward sat down in the chair across from White. "Mr. White, what do you think Mrs. Oelrichs would say if you were to tell her that you have found the money to finish the house on time, and that it would not cost her another dime?"

"She would be in heaven. But dear boy, I cannot afford to swallow the expense of finishing the house for her. It's not the construction— that's all done. It's the finishing. There is so much carving and marble. It is very time-consuming." White was looking at Edward as if he had absolutely no idea as to his profession.

"I realize that, Mr. White. What if this firm were to be the guarantor of the monies needed to complete the task?"

"I do not wish to take out a loan just to finish a house, without benefit to me."

"I did not say that you had to pay the loan back to us."

"What? You are saying that this money would be a gift?" He quickly looked over at Morgan, who stared blankly back at him. "You have the authority to grant this loan?" He again looked over at Morgan, who continued his stare.

"I do," answered Edward, without taking his eyes off White.

"Then I accept it! This building will be the finest of the cottages. It will be another gem in my architectural crown." White stood to leave.

"There is, however, one small stipulation to the loan," Edward calmly added.

White sank back down into the chair. "I knew it! There had to be something!" White was directing all his frustration straight at Edward, as if Morgan had nothing to do with the deal.

"All I am asking is a small favor that you are to request from Mrs. Oelrichs because of all the added expense that you yourself have had to absorb in order to finish the house in time."

"A favor? What might that be?"

"At the party there will undoubtedly be entertainment? Musicians, in all probability?"

White nodded in the affirmative.

Edward continued, "I would like a singer to perform at the party for Mrs. Oelrichs's guests. He will have already given his Carnegie Hall debut concert, so this would be a nice chance for him to perform the same concert again for, well, let's say a more cultured clientele."

"That doesn't seem unfair. What are you not telling me?"

"Well, I haven't finished yet. The singer's name is Harry T. Burleigh. He is a Negro."

White turned scarlet before exploding, "Are you crazy?"

Edward calmly replied, "No, I am not crazy. I am allowing you, Mr. White, the opportunity to be a part of introducing a new major talent to our area."

White again turned to Morgan, who was slowly nodding his head. "You agree with this, J. P.?"

"Wholeheartedly, Stan. Mr. Burleigh will be the toast of the town."

"If they don't lynch him first, J. P."

"This is not the Deep South, Stan. I advise you to offer your plan to Mrs. Oelrichs."

"I am not promising anything. I really can't say." He again stood to leave. "Didn't we meet on New Year's Eve, sir?"

Edward quietly replied, "We might have. I seem to recognize that mustache of yours."

As White was exiting the room, he replied, "Yes, it seems to have become a trademark of mine."

After the door shut, Edward answered, "Yes, that and a fourteen-year-old girl on your arm."

"Good work, Edward! Good work!" Morgan was overjoyed with what had just transpired. "He took the bait—hook, line, and sinker!"

"I am still not exactly sure what just happened, sir. Why do we want Mr. Burleigh to sing all the way out in Newport?"

"Well, I can't say that I was ever one for Newport society, but I have sailed my yachts up there a few times. I must say that it is very, very nice. But here's the thing, Edward. During the two months of summer almost everyone who is anyone in high society—especially the well-heeled—spends those weeks in Newport. Not the Fords or the Rockefellers, mind you. Newport is a place for old money."

"But sir, the debut concert is here in New York. Wouldn't it have been easier to find a nice one-hundred-and-fifty-room mansion on Fifth Avenue for Mr. Burleigh's private recital? Everyone would just take a short carriage ride to hear it."

"Someplace like the Vanderbilt mansion? Don't worry, Edward, the Vanderbilts will be there in Newport—all of them!"

"I see your point, sir. I will start planning in the event Mrs. Oelrichs agrees to Mr. White's offer." Edward started his retreat from the office.

"Don't worry," Morgan called after him, "she will."

Geoff had just returned from his errand when Edward got back to his office. "Good luck, Edward, the stationer on Trinity had a map. How did your meeting go?"

"Oh, you are not going to believe this!"

Edward then related all the details of the meeting to Geoff, who was fast becoming not only his executive assistant, but his closest friend. After he finished the details, Edward continued, "I think we need to do some research on Newport, Geoff."

"Research?"

"Something is still missing! I know why we are doing the recital there, but Morgan has something up his sleeve. There is something he is not telling me. The answer doesn't lie with Stanford White, either. He's seems to be just…a pawn."

"A pawn, Edward?"

"A pawn. Chess, Geoff. You know chess, don't you?"

"Indeed I do! Shall we do our research while playing chess?"

"You know that's not what I mean. Morgan is using White to get what he wants!"

"Well, what does he want?"

"I don't think he desires Mrs. Oelrichs. But he does seem to want to get into that house before it is finished, and then make sure it is finished."

Edward was beginning to formulate a reason for Morgan's methods. However, Geoff, not knowing Morgan quite as well, was having more difficulty.

"Edward, are you saying that Mr. Morgan wants access to White's new building?"

"I think that might be the case, yes."

"Are you a lawyer, or a detective, Edward?" Geoff laughed.

"Actually...I'm a spy!"

Personal Journal Entry
March 5, 1899

I have decided to ask Rebecca to marry me. I must speak with her father as soon as I can. No one has ever made me as happy as I am when I am with her.

As for other events, we have approved another team of six men to work on White's house in Newport. The work goes slowly during the winter months. Geoff has been in Rhode Island most of the month, carefully inspecting the house and property. When he gets back next week, we shall compare our research.

Chapter 6
The Report

Spring was late in arriving in 1899. It was already the second week in March and snow was still falling in New York City. Edward arrived at his typical punctual time of five minutes before nine on the morning of March 12. He observed his morning ritual of stopping in the reception area to wish Rebecca a pleasant day, and then hurried up to his office. He always made sure that his rendezvous with Rebecca happened before Morgan arrived at the office. He didn't think Morgan would mind, but he didn't want to test it, either. He walked into his private office to find someone waiting for him.

"Geoff! Welcome back!"

"Edward, have you any idea how much colder it is in Newport than it is in New York?"

"No idea, mate."

"I was frozen most of the time. I don't know why all the rich folks go there, anyway. It is the most tiresome place on the planet. My evenings were so boring. Luckily, the taverns are still open for business."

"The town only comes alive in the summer, Geoff. Besides, you were sent to snoop around. If there had been a big crowd you wouldn't have accomplished much."

"And I did accomplish much."

"So then, tell me." Edward wanted to know every detail of the reconnaissance, but Geoff had other ideas first.

"No, first you tell me." Edward really wasn't in the mood for one of Geoff's games. He scowled at Geoff for putting him off like that, but Geoff smiled back at him and asked, "Tell me what Rebecca said. You know…"

"Oh!" Edward smiled.

"She said yes?"

"She did. I suppose that today we will have to have a drink at the tavern to celebrate our good fortune, you and I?" Edward could hardly contain his excitement.

"Our good fortune? Edward, you're marrying Rebecca, not me!"

"I know. But when you ask someone to be your best man at your wedding, doesn't that call for a toast?"

"What? You want me to be your best man?" Geoff was getting emotional at the prospect.

"Geoff, you already are my best man." Edward clapped Geoff on the back. "Now, can we can down to work? Let's try to accomplish something before we get too tanked to think straight."

"Right! Edward, you are not going to believe what Newport looks like! Most of the town looks very middle class, but then—out by the ocean—there's this entire big section where one house is larger than the next. It's as if the owners are in competition with each other for bragging rights."

"I think that is exactly the case, Geoff!"

"There are streets and streets of these huge houses. But they call them cottages. Sure! Cottages, my bum! Some are as big as a Fifth Avenue chateau! None of the owners are there now, which was good for us because I spent time cozying up to some of the caretakers. There's a family of caretakers living in each house to watch over it during the off-season. Ha! That's forty-four weeks of the year! Anyway, I accidentally on purpose ran into these people—in the hardware store, at the market, in church—and I always was found to be so personable that I would get invited over to 'the big house' for dinner."

"The big house?"

"It's funny, isn't it? Each caretaker calls his own house 'the big house,' even though they all know there is only one really big house there."

"Really? The one that White is building?"

"No. That's a big house, but the Vanderbilts have the biggest home there."

"It figures. Go on."

"So I meet this guy, Bill, who happens to have his family working for the Vanderbilts as their caretaker, and we raise a pint or two in a local establishment. I got a few drinks in him and he really started to open up, especially about his employers. No love lost there, I can tell you. Did you know that you must be really specific when you mention the Vanderbilts in town? You can't just say, 'I am going to the Vanderbilt house tonight.' No! You must specify! You must say if it's Mr. Cornelius Vanderbilt the Second, or Mr. William Vanderbilt, or Mr. Alfred Vanderbilt."

"So which one did Bill work for?"

"Cornelius Vanderbilt the Second, son of the commodore. So Bill invites me out to see the house and then I stay for dinner. We went for a tour of the house. Edward, they have a vault in the kitchen to keep the silver place settings! The kitchen is bigger than your entire brownstone!"

"Are they the servants in the summer?"

"No. They move out of the house when the regular staff starts arriving in the late spring. Each family brings their domestic staff with them wherever they go. The house actually has a name: the Breakers. It was designed by Richard Morris Hunt, who is—"

"A major rival of Stanford White."

"You've got it! And White's house is really nice, Edward. It's not anywhere near the size of Vanderbilt's. In fact, I could see myself living in it. It's really a beautiful house. It has a name, as well: Rosecliff. It has a double staircase in the entrance foyer that is shaped like a heart. Oh, and one other thing—it is the only house there that has a swimming pool."

"A swimming pool?"

"A swimming pool. The ocean is right outside the door, and they put in a swimming pool. That was one of the details that still had to be completed. The pool."

"It's March, Geoff. They will have to wait until April or early May for the thaw so they can dig. The dirt will be like iron! No wonder they are under the gun to be ready for the party."

"No. The digging is pretty much finished. It was dug before the winter set in. Right now it's a big hole in the ground. I stood right next to the excavation. I don't get it, though. It looked like the pool was going to be about twenty feet deep, but the workers there said it wouldn't exceed a depth of eight feet. I guess they have to leave room for the concrete."

"I guess. Did you see White or Mrs. Oelrichs?"

"I saw White twice. He was always barking orders to the crew. I didn't ever see anyone from the family."

Edward nodded. "Good work, Geoff. I'm sure that there are more details that you can fill me in on. Let me tell you what I discovered so we can both start thinking along the same lines. First of all, Mrs. Oelrichs is the heiress to the Fair family fortune. Mr. James Graham Fair, her father, was one of the partners in the Comstock Lode." This did not ring a bell with Geoff. "The silver mine, Geoff! Her wealth comes from silver!"

"So?"

"I don't know. Maybe I am making more out of this than actually exists. I keep looking for a connection. I thought the connection was the silver. Anyway, they have a very closed little society up there during the summer, and Mrs. Oelrichs is one of the three major hostesses in Newport. That's why she consented to Mr. Burleigh's recital."

"I don't think she understands the seriousness of the situation, Edward."

Geoff was correct. Even though Harry Burleigh had now been a regular soloist at St. George's Episcopal Church for several years, the idea of a black man having a role of any kind, other than as a servant, in polite society was just not done. In the Tenderloin district, around 40th Street and a few blocks north, and around the area where the *New York Times* was printed, a series of burlesque houses and vaudeville theaters were springing up. Some of these houses featured minstrel shows; shows that lampooned life in black America by having the white actors put on "blackface"—a mixture of burnt cork and greasepaint. The actors then presented a loosely knit variety of acts featuring various stereotypes: Mr. Hambone, Mr. Jones, Mr. Interlocutor, and a male chorus in blackface. The shows all had their roots in the post-Civil War South, and were an outgrowth of the Reconstruction years and the Jim Crow laws. The audiences at a minstrel show were primarily white.

On the other hand, there were several houses in the Tenderloin that specialized in an African American audience. Here all the performers were also black, and these shows were very rarely visited by a white clientele. No, for Harry Burleigh to perform at Rosecliff, he would have to resign himself to expecting screams, swooning, and objects being hurled in his direction.

Edward knew they still had a great deal of work to do before this recital.

Personal Journal Entry
March 13, 1899

The plans for our upcoming wedding are proceeding quickly. I have already arranged for the ceremony at St. George's, including hiring Mr. Norris to play the organ and Mr. Burleigh to sing the solos. I hope it will not be a very hot, humid June. But I did want to wait until after Mr. Burleigh's concert and recital are finished. Rebecca agrees with this. She already realizes the tremendous pressure I am feeling.

Geoff is a good man, but I feel that I must travel to Newport in short order to check on what he has told me. I don't know when I will be able to get away from the office to do this. I have another project in the works; Morgan is assisting Carnegie in the purchase of a large piece of property in the Uptown area. It's all very hush-hush. Rebecca is busy with the details of the wedding, but I still have to find a place for us to live. Morgan has given me a lead, although it does sound a bit far from the office. I will be going there tomorrow.

Chapter 7
The Great Northern Expanses of the City

Edward was able to leave work in the early afternoon so that he could meet with an agent who was to show him an apartment for lease. Morgan had suggested the place, because he felt that many of the city's well-to-do clients would eventually make their way to the same address. Edward was leery of life uptown. He knew that Carnegie wanted to purchase property in the nineties, and that the mayor's mansion was even further uptown. In 1899, Manhattan Island was clearly divided into two major populated areas—the original old city, found at the southern tip of the island; and Harlem, which populated most of the north. Harlem, or Haarlem, as it had been called by the Dutch, was originally farmland, as the Dutch name inferred. Now it was inhabited mostly by immigrants, many of them black. North of Harlem were Washington Heights and Inwood, which were home to a very large segment of the Irish population.

In between these two populated areas was a confused landscape of housing, businesses, and strangely appropriated lands. North of Union Square was the Garment District, perhaps the most industrialized area of the city. To the north of that area was the Tenderloin district—too unsavory to even be considered by a genteel couple. To the west were the Hudson River and the docks—and everything else that went with a waterfront. A little north of the Tenderloin, but still on the west side of the island, was a tangled web of tenements known with various degrees of affection as Hell's Kitchen. But then there was the park—Central Park.

Central Park was a large but remote tract of land that had been set aside by the New York Legislature in 1853. The park opened in 1857, but was largely a simple open piece of undeveloped land. William Cullen Bryant, American poet and editor of the *Evening Post*, declared that New York City needed to develop this land into a park fit to rival the great urban parks of Europe, such as Hyde Park in London, or the Bois de Boulogne in Paris. The task was undertaken by Fredric Law Olmstead and Calvert Vaux, who designed a park that allowed people to stroll or ride through the various areas. Moreover, the park extended up the center of the island, from 59th Street to 110th Street. The area was massive. Little by little, because of the fact that Lower Manhattan was so congested, some of the wealthier residents sought to purchase land on the perimeter of the park. They wanted escape from the city streets and views of something green.

The problem was that the land was not particularly pleasant. It had large swampy areas, certainly not conducive to picnics or strolling. Loads upon loads of topsoil were carted in from New Jersey, the swamps were drained, and the unwanted growth of trees cleared. A large lake was created near the center of the park. A zoo was designed and built. The largest flat area was left as a grassy plain and was inhabited by flocks of sheep to keep the grass short. It became known as "the sheep meadow."

Fifth Avenue created the eastern boundary of the park, and Central Park West became the western boundary. Several cultural sites were built either on the perimeter of the park or on park land itself. The Metropolitan Museum of Art found a home on the park grounds in a building designed by Vaux, nicknamed the Mausoleum. The American Museum of Natural History was housed in another building designed by Vaux at 77th Street and Central Park West. Both of these thoroughfares had become valuable real estate by the end of the century. Two of the Vanderbilt brothers had large homes in the area. The Plaza Hotel sat across 59th Street from the southeast boundary. It was slated for demolition, to be replaced by another, larger Plaza Hotel on the same property. There was talk of hotels springing up everywhere, but mostly on Fifth Avenue.

Morgan was sending Edward to visit a large apartment house located at 72nd Street and Central Park West. Its owner, Edward Clark, was the head of the Singer Sewing Machine Company. Mr. Clark was, like Theodore Roosevelt, enamored with the western frontier of the country, and he named his building the Dakota, after one of the new territories. The building was completed in 1874, when the area was still considered too remote for habitation, but the population of the city was increasing quickly. Transportation had also played a part in shrinking the size of the twelve-mile-long island. Horse-drawn carriages were still popular, especially among the rich, but the largest body of citizens moved quickly around Manhattan using trolleys and the elevated railroad. Already under construction was an underground transit system, a subway that would connect the top of the island to the bottom.

Edward arrived by cab at the apartment building at about one in the afternoon. Stuck out in the middle of nowhere as it was, the structure seemed massive. There were no other buildings in close proximity, and the Dakota was at least ten stories tall. The front featured a porte cochere, an entrance for a horse-drawn carriage, which allowed passengers to embark and disembark without interference from the elements. There was a sculpture of a Dakota Indian above the entrance. This area then opened onto a central courtyard.

As Edward alighted from the cab, he was greeted by a tall gentleman.

"Mr. Collier, I presume?"

"Yes. You must be Mr. Frankel."

"Yes, sir. Please follow me." They entered a room directly off the porte cochere which was intended to be a large reception hall. "Not all our apartments are filled at this time, Mr. Collier, but I have it on good authority that you might be interested in one in particular." Frankel then nodded very knowingly. "Mr. Clark built the Dakota with the express purpose of attracting some of the most affluent members of New York society."

"Yes, Mr. Frankel, but I am not a member of New York society."

"I am well aware of that fact, Mr. Collier. Mr. Morgan seems to think you will be very suited to a residence here. That is why we are showing the apartment to you." Edward knew he had just been slighted. "On the other hand, Mr. Clark's expectations of leasing the entire building have fallen short of the mark, so many of the most expensive apartments sit vacant."

Now that was closer to the real reason for showing him the apartment. They needed money. Edward and Frankel walked slowly down a corridor while Frankel talked about the building.

"This entire building has been wired for electricity. We have our own power plant here. We also have central heating throughout the building. There are four elevators, one at each corner of the courtyard. We feel that this is an extremely modern apartment building. There is a tennis court beyond the building, and we own a very modern stable on 72nd Street to house your private carriage and horses. That, too, has an elevator."

"You stable the horses on different levels?"

"No, not the horses, the carriages. We send each carriage to a space on an upper floor to save on floor space."

"I see." Edward thought this was either visionary, or insane.

"Do you have children, Mr. Collier?"

"Children? No, not yet. I am engaged to be married in June."

"Well, when the little ones arrive, have no fear. There is a playroom on the tenth floor, along with a gymnasium."

They stepped into the elevator. Frankel closed the door and the safety cage, then pushed the control and they started to ascend. Edward did not care for elevators; he did not think they were all that safe. Then again, he had only been in an elevator a few times in his life.

Frankel stopped the elevator at the seventh floor, opened the doors, and gestured for Edward to exit. "This way," he commanded. They rounded a corner and found the main entrance to the apartment in question. "This is a four-bedroom apartment, Mr. Collier."

"Four bedrooms? That seems a bit large for us right now."

"That is true, no doubt, but take a look at it anyway. There is also a library, a study, a living room and dining room, and of course a kitchen. However, should you wish to avail yourself to it, we also offer catered meals that can be sent up on the dumbwaiter, and if you don't wish to eat in your own apartment we also have a full-service restaurant on the ground floor. All the apartments also have servant's quarters."

"You seem to have thought of everything, Mr. Frankel."

"Oh, not me, Mr. Collier. That was Mr. Clark's doing. Come, let's tour the apartment."

They left the foyer and entered an empty room. Frankel explained that this was one of the bedrooms. It was very large—bigger than any room in the family brownstone. The room was on one of the corners of the building and had windows looking out on Central Park. Frankel opened another door and gestured for Edward to follow him. They walked into another room without going back into the hallway.

"This apartment house is designed in the French system. All the rooms connect directly to the next room. There is also a corridor which runs behind the rooms so that the domestics can come and go without disturbing other rooms by passing through them."

They walked slowly through each of the adjoining rooms. The only rooms that did not adjoin were the kitchen and servant areas. Edward knew that, even on Morgan's generous salary, he could never afford to lease this space.

"Well, what did you think, Mr. Collier?" asked Frankel at the conclusion of the tour.

"It is a very impressive apartment, Mr. Frankel. Very impressive, indeed! Might I ask what the rent is on this particular unit?"

"I have been instructed to offer you the apartment for no less than...one hundred dollars per month."

"One hundred dollars a month? Did I hear you correctly?" Edward was certain that Frankel must have misplaced another zero in the number.

"That is the price, sir, and if I were you...I would take it." Frankel seemed to grimace as he said the last phrase.

"I will have to discuss this with my wife—my fiancée—naturally."

"Naturally. Take your time, but not too much time." Frankel offered a weak smile.

Edward brought Rebecca uptown to see the apartment the next Saturday. Frankel arranged to have the building caretaker let them in to see it. Rebecca was overwhelmed by the building before she even left the cab, but she was astounded by the living space.

"Edward, how can this apartment cost only a hundred dollars per month?"

"I don't think it does, my dear."

"What do you mean?" But Rebecca already suspected that Morgan had more to do with their living arrangements than a mere suggestion to look at a place uptown.

"I think this is a job incentive."

"It's a pretty good incentive, Edward. But the cost of living here would not stop at the rent. It will cost us a fortune to fill it with furniture—furniture that deserves this apartment, and this building."

"That sounds very upper crust, dear."

Rebecca hated class distinctions just as much as Edward did. "I am not saying that to be snobby, Edward. This is an opulent building, it deserves to be outfitted properly. We are more pedestrian. And then there's the problem of servants."

"Servants?" Edward had already thought about this problem, too.

"It would be expected that we have at least one domestic, maybe more. Wouldn't we have to entertain some of the other building residents? Wouldn't we have to buy a carriage, and a horse? How could we ever afford this?"

"I fully agree with you, Rebecca. We are not meant to be in this building, but you know how it is. Mr. Morgan pulled some strings, so we can't really turn it down without seeing it."

"I know. We can't afford this lifestyle even if we combined our two salaries, and that will last only so long before little ones take my salary away. I doubt we could afford this even if Mr. Morgan were to double your salary."

"Double my salary? I have only been working for him for a number of months. I haven't even had a day in court. Why would he do such a thing?"

Rebecca took his hand. "Are you disappointed, Edward?"

"No, not terribly. Maybe someday for this place, but certainly not today. The worst thing is that I will have to bring this up to Morgan on Monday."

"Why don't we speak to him together?"

Personal Journal Entry
March 20, 1899

I have the feeling that I am being controlled. Father warned me about this last year, but I don't think this was exactly what he was considering at the time. I don't think I am in over my head, but things seem to be slipping from my hands. I know Rebecca agrees with me.

I don't know if I can totally confide in Geoff, plus there is something else about him lately. I don't know what it is, but he seems to lack the concentration needed for the job. He also tends to ignore basic hygiene, which I can overlook, but it doesn't play out well at the office. Sometimes it looks like he has been sleeping in his clothes.

I have a distinct feeling that I will have to pay for this one day; perhaps not in dollars and cents, but rather in some form of servitude. I feel very ungracious; the man has given me a great deal. Why am I so damned suspicious?

My God, I have become my father.

Chapter 8
The Office

Edward and Rebecca entered Morgan's office at nine fifteen on Monday morning. Morgan was having breakfast at his desk. He smiled broadly at both of them.

"To what do I owe the honor of seeing the bride and groom together?"

"We need to speak to you about something, sir." Edward had planned out his delivery, but now hoped that his words would not fail him.

"Glad to oblige. What can I do for you two? Here, sit." He gestured to the wing chairs and rose from his desk to join them.

"I went uptown to see the apartment building that you had suggested, sir. The Dakota? It is a beautiful building and a spacious apartment." Morgan nodded his agreement. "Then I brought Rebecca to see it this past Saturday."

"It is truly magnificent, Mr. Morgan." Rebecca felt obligated to express her opinion.

"But?" Morgan was already a step ahead of them.

"But," Edward said calmly, "we don't think that we are ready to live that kind of lifestyle. In fact, we don't think we can afford to live that lifestyle."

"Why not? The rent is very affordable, isn't it?" Morgan was baiting them.

"Yes, it is, sir. Very affordable. Strangely affordable. I would have guessed that an apartment of that size would rent for hundreds of dollars more each month."

"And you think that I have something to do with the price? You think I badgered Clark into letting one of my young attorneys rent the place dirt cheap?"

"Well..."

"Maybe you think I am paying the excess rent? Of course I am!"

There, he said it. Edward looked at the floor. Rebecca had tears in her eyes.

Morgan continued. "So maybe you are worried that you can't afford to furnish the place, or that you can't afford servants, or whatever. Edward, I am putting my trust in you to handle my affairs. You know what my fortune is worth. Making sure that you are happy is one of the little joys of my advancing years."

Rebecca was the first to speak. "But this is too much, sir!"

"Why? Consider it a wedding present! Consider the apartment, and the furnishings, a wedding present. Don't you think I would have given you a wedding present?"

Rebecca broke into sobs. "You are too generous to us, sir."

Morgan spoke directly to Rebecca. "Then you will accept my gift?"

Edward allowed Rebecca to answer. "Yes, with all our gratitude."

"Then it is settled. Now, Rebecca, if you will excuse us, I need to speak to Edward alone."

Rebecca pulled her handkerchief from her sleeve and patted her eyes as she left the room.

"Edward...you have something more to add, don't you?"

Here it was at last; the moment Edward had anticipated and feared. "Yes, Mr. Morgan, I do."

"Well, spit it out, my boy."

Edward prayed for courage as he asked, "Mr. Morgan, are you using me?"

"Using you? Well, of course I am using you. I am your employer, and I am using you just as any other employer uses his staff. Is that what you are getting at?"

"It's not that I don't appreciate everything you have done for me. I have, very much, indeed! It is simply that it all has happened so quickly—like a tornado—that it is hard for me to stay focused. I suppose I sometimes have a tendency to think things out a bit too much. I get confused."

"We all get confused sometimes, Edward, but I think you are saying something more profound."

Edward was indeed confused. "More profound, sir?"

"Yes. It sounds to me as if you are about to ask me for an increase in your salary."

Edward felt his stomach pitch and roll. "No, sir, that was not my plan."

"Well, plan or not, I agree with it. I am going to raise your pay."

"Sir!"

"You make twenty thousand a year now, so let's just make it an even forty thousand dollars."

Spies everywhere!

"Sir! I have not done enough to deserve this yet!"

"But you will, Edward. You will. And tell what's-his-name that he gets five thousand dollars more for himself." That was the hook. How could Edward be selfish enough to hurt Geoff? "Now we must talk about the Newport deal. How is the house progressing?"

Edward took a deep breath to steady his emotions. "The house is progressing rapidly. Mr. Atwater has just come back from viewing the site, so my information is very accurate."

"Good. Did he run into Stan White?"

"Oh yes. He spoke to him while surveying the swimming pool."

"The swimming pool? What swimming pool?"

"Well, there's no pool there yet, it's just a big hole in the ground. White told Geoff that it was going to be a swimming pool."

"Fools! What do they need a pool for? They've got the entire ocean, and none of 'em can even swim!"

"Does it matter that much, sir?"

"It gobbles up time, and we don't have time! You need to go up there, Edward. I mean, personally. You take Atwater with you. When is the earliest you can leave?"

"I can be on a train tomorrow."

"Good. You see, this is why I hired you. I am smelling a rat here, Edward. I want to see if you smell the same rat."

Edward shook Morgan's hand and exited his office. Rebecca looked up from her desk as he closed the door behind him.

"I have to go up to Newport with Geoff tomorrow. I'll be gone just a few days, dear."

Rebecca nodded. "That's fine. I'll be busy with the plans for the wedding. I suppose I will be ordering furniture by the cartload, too."

Edward laughed. "And we were going to go in there and tell him, weren't we?"

"We surely were planning on it. So tell me, did he double your salary?"

Personal Journal Entry
March 23, 1899

Today did not go the way I wanted it to go, and yet today went exactly like I expected it to go. Why do I feel this way?

Of course Geoff is very happy with his raise, and I admit it will be entertaining to be away with him for the next few days, but if I look at this game with Morgan as being a chess game metaphor, then is Geoff also one of the pawns?

Morgan told me this afternoon that he has several new projects lined up for me to act upon when I return from Newport. One has to do with Carnegie, another has to do with a new arena at Madison Square, and a third has to do with some tortured genius I have never heard of in my life.

I may now be on the brink of earning my salary.

Chapter 9
Newport

Edward and Geoff met at Pennsylvania Station at nine thirty in order to board the train to Providence, Rhode Island. Edward had booked a private compartment so they would be able to work on the way. They had sensitive information to speak of, and the club car would be no place to do this. Besides, if Morgan had spies everywhere, then others might have them, too.

They both threw their carpetbags in an overhead storage rack. Edward removed his suit coat and hung it up in a small closet. Geoff took his cue and did the same. They sat facing each other in the compartment. Edward noticed that Geoff seemed to be unusually unkempt. His hair needed a good combing and it looked like he had skipped shaving this morning. Even though his was still the stubble of a nineteen-year-old, he didn't look much like a representative of one of the world's richest men. But, worse than that, his eyes were bloodshot.

Edward asked good-naturedly, "Out celebrating your advancement in the company last night?"

Geoff didn't seem uncomfortable with the observation. "Oh yes! It isn't every day one gets his salary raised by fifty percent—unless, of course, it's you." He laughed at the irony of the situation. The train started to move.

This really had been the first time Geoff spoke to Edward, other than greeting him good morning when they met at the station. Edward had no idea why, but Geoff was in a particularly bad mood, it seemed.

Edward didn't laugh. "I didn't mean to pry, Geoff."

Geoff's face fell. "The hell you didn't!"

Edward had never heard a cross word from Geoff's lips. "I'm sorry for asking. I didn't realize you were in such a foul mood this morning."

"Live and learn, my friend."

Edward didn't understand what was happening with Geoff, but he felt compelled to find out. "Have I done something wrong by you, Geoff?"

Geoff exploded, "Done something wrong by me? What are we both doing here, if you haven't done something wrong by me? Morgan obviously has no confidence in me. He has plenty in you, but none in me. I bring you back observations, and he sends us right back up to get another look-see. He sends us both because he doesn't want me hanging around the office while you are gone. And...and..." Geoff wanted to say something else, but decided against it.

Edward knew this was a big problem. "Look, Geoff, I believed every word of your report." Geoff smirked. "I did. I still do. I don't know why Morgan sent us back again. I didn't really care. I was actually happy to be getting out of town, and I was glad that you were accompanying me."

"You know, I've been working at the company longer than you have, Edward."

"I know."

"But I was always...invisible. Even before you arrived, I was invisible. No one there knew I existed. They all probably wished—hoped—that I would get my experience and then move on to another company. But then you came along."

"And?"

"And I'm still invisible." Geoff actually started to sob. "What do you understand about it, Edward? You are Morgan's 'golden boy.' It is very clear that you are his chosen one, his anointed. Me? I've done his dirty work since I was sixteen years old. Did you know that?"

Edward shook his head.

"No, why would you know that? I suppose I should be grateful to you, Edward, for letting me get some of the scraps that fall from Morgan's table, but I tell you, my pride is suffering from all this. I am sick to death of being treated like I don't even exist, like I am invisible. He knows I exist, Edward, so why doesn't he treat me like you?"

Edward was sure what Geoff had meant by that last remark—of course Morgan knew that Geoff existed.

Edward moved to the edge of his seat, closer to Geoff, who had put his head in his hands. "I don't think you are invisible, Geoff. I think you are my right arm." And then it hit him—like a load of bricks. He smelled alcohol on Geoff's breath. It wasn't difficult to do, as Geoff was sobbing. But it wasn't the smell of someone who had been out until the early hours carousing, then falling into bed and rising late; too late to practice the necessary hygiene before catching the train. This was the smell of fresh liquor; liquor that had been consumed recently—in the morning.

Geoff was blubbering. "I'm sorry, Edward. I don't know what is wrong with me."

Edward reached out and gently tapped Geoff on the knee. "Geoff, look at me." Geoff wiped his eyes on his shirtsleeve. "Geoff, do you have a drinking problem?"

Geoff gave a light laugh. "Do I have a drinking problem? Let me show you, Edward."

Geoff stood up from his seat, almost losing his balance and landing on Edward. He steadied himself and grabbed his carpetbag from the storage compartment. He opened the bag and pulled out an opened bottle of Irish whiskey. "Does this answer your question?" He started to pull various articles of clothing out of the bag. "Let's see...I didn't pack any toiletries, not even my razor. I didn't bring a nightshirt, so that may have dire consequences as far as you are concerned. I don't even know if I have a second dress shirt in here. No, I don't, but I do have this bottle of whiskey. I have my priorities in the right order, don't I?" He sat back down, his possessions still littered all over the compartment floor. "And I guess there is only one thing for you to do now, right, Edward?"

Edward wasn't taking Geoff's baiting. "What's that, Geoff?"

"You're going to sack me." Geoff looked at Edward just as a child might look at his parent who was about to dole out punishment.

"I'm sorry, Geoff."

"You're sorry? What do you have to be sorry about? I am a wreck, not you."

"How did I not see this happening to you?"

"I didn't think this was about you, Edward."

"I know it isn't about me. It's about you, Geoff. I have been so preoccupied by my life—the wedding, the job—that I didn't see what was happening to you."

"It's not your responsibility to watch out for me, you know. You're my boss."

"I thought I was your friend."

Geoff closed his eyes and then bowed his head toward the floor. "You are my friend. I am an ass!"

"Well, ass, it is time to get you sober. Do you think you can walk on the moving train?"

"Why? Where are you taking me?"

"To the club car, for a decent meal—and plenty of coffee."

"I think I can get there, but I may vomit along the way."

Geoffrey Atwater lived by himself in a rooming house on Bleeker Street. His father died when Geoff was five, and his mother succumbed to typhoid when he was twelve. He spent the rest of his youth living in a Catholic orphanage, and it was there that he received most of his primary education, but he had also gotten much of his education from the school of hard knocks. He had been beaten more times than he could remember, and had been the recipient of all manner of verbal and physical abuse, yet in most instances he was a very personable and happy-go-lucky young man. He hid his inner demons very well from all who knew him—even those who loved him. He had been living on his own from the time he was sixteen. He still lived in a boarding house, despite the two large increases in his yearly wage. He told no one he knew outside work what he earned, for fear that they might try to rob him. He very much wanted to move his residence, but unbeknownst to all who cared about him, he spent most of his off hours at local taverns. It had been fortunate for him that he kept his money in Morgan's bank, and that he quickly deposited his earnings directly after receiving them, or he would certainly have given away his greatest secret to his neighbors and bar mates.

Geoff did manage to get to the club car without embarrassing himself. The selection of food at this time was meager; some rolls, pastries, and coffee. Geoff took a big gulp of his coffee.

"You know, it's all because of the Irish blood I have coursing through my veins. The drinking, you know?"

"Are you being serious, Geoff?"

"I think it has already been proven scientifically. The Irish are predisposed to hard drinking."

Edward took a bite out of his pastry. How do you argue with that type of logic? "You are only part Irish, Mr. Atwater. But it does sound like a good excuse."

"Excuse?"

"Yes, to justify your behavior. Why not blame it on your ancestors? That way you can't be at fault."

"Edward, you make a very good argument for a person who has yet to stand and address a courtroom."

"And so do you, for a person who is still two sheets to the wind." But Edward felt their discussion was beginning to feel antagonistic once more, so he decided to lighten the situation. "And you showed particularly bad taste with your choice of spirits, my man. Irish whiskey? Why not a good single malt Scots whiskey?"

"Ah, little do you know, my friend. It doesn't really matter what I drink, because it all tastes just about the same. I can save my money not buying the good whiskies because the cheap ones give the same effect in the end. You could have found a bottle of rum, or gin, or even some Russian vodka. It wouldn't have mattered. I drink them all." Geoff's face continually saddened as he related his plight. "I even ventured into one of those dark cellars in Chinatown, Edward."

"What?" Edward asked. "Are you speaking of the opium dens?" Geoff nodded. "I think you need help, Geoff."

"From you?" Geoff intended that to sound like a joke; it didn't. "I am destined to die like my father before me, drunk and alone, and in the gutter. Isn't that why we have the Bowery?"

Edward rose above the sting of the last insult. "Geoff, you are too young to do this to yourself. You are only nineteen." Geoff gave him a glance. "I know, I know—almost twenty."

"I didn't know there was an age restriction on alcoholism, Edward."

"I suppose there isn't, but there are no age restrictions on other vices, either: sloth, greed, lust, gluttony…"

"Can't think of the other deadly sins, Edward?"

"No, not at the moment." Geoff sniggered at him. "That's not really the point. You are smart. You are very smart—and clever—but stupid."

"Thanks."

"You are stupid if you are going to throw your entire life down into…" He stopped.

"Into the gutter? Like my father?"

"I wasn't going to say that!" Edward knew he had just taken the conversation where he did not want it to go. Geoff was already drowning in self-pity.

"I know, Edward. You can't imagine the dark place I am in sometimes. You can't appreciate it."

"I have been drunk. I enjoy lifting a pint or two."

"Sure you do, but I go beyond a pint or two. Liquor is the only thing that works for me. When I walk back to Bleeker at the end of the day, I pass countless men with bottles in their hands. They're looking for the same thing I'm looking for. So I keep walking, past my stoop and then into the tavern. Many times I don't even bother to eat dinner. I hid it well, didn't I?"

"You did, indeed." But then Edward had a thought. "What you need, first of all, is to move out of your room. You can afford much better now, so move."

"So what? That won't change my drinking any. I'll just get drunk in a better class of tavern."

Edward smiled at his friend. "Not if I can help it. Listen, shortly I will be moving up to Central Park, you know that. My room in my parents' house on Sixteenth will be vacant. I would be willing to bet that they would love to have you stay with them."

"Are you joking?"

"I am perfectly serious. Just think of it: a stern fatherly man, and two mothers to dote on you and grant your every wish. And you would be fed constantly."

"I don't know, Edward."

"Give it some thought, Geoff. And I figure I have the next few days to wear you down."

Geoff became suddenly quiet. "Does Clara still bake her apple pies each Tuesday?"

"Wait! How do you know that she bakes on Tuesday?"

"I know quite a few things about your family domicile. I could write you a schedule of daily activities."

Edward couldn't believe his ears. "Are you telling me, that you are…were—"

"That's right, Edward. Morgan hired me specifically to spy on you."

"I don't believe it!"

"Believe it! I could tell you a great deal about life in the Collier house. I have several notebooks that I kept on the daily habits of your family."

Edward frowned.

"It's true. I could tell you what you had for dinner on a particular night in May 1897, or I could tell you when your father took sick with a fever, or when your mother normally when to the fish market. Hell, I could even tell you who in the family had regular bowel movements."

"Stop it, Geoff!"

"I'm sorry, Edward." Geoff became very quiet. "It was my job. I never would have guessed that my mark would ask for me to be his assistant. I wasn't prepared for that."

"I suppose not," Edward replied quietly.

"But you know what was worse?" Edward looked up, right into Geoff's misty eyes. "I never, ever gave any thought that my mark might actually end up being my best friend."

The train pulled into Providence in the early afternoon. They had about an hour to wait for their train to Newport, so Edward suggested they visit a barber shop in the terminal so that Geoff could be a little more groomed. Geoff happily agreed with the idea. After a shave and a haircut, they found a small store and purchased some of the things Geoff had forgotten to pack. Edward and Geoff had lunch at the terminal, and then they boarded the train to Newport. The train took them into the center of the business district of Newport and let them off by the waterfront. The scene was familiar to Geoff, but all new to Edward, who had never been in the city before this day. They took a carriage from the station to their hotel, where Edward had arranged to have a suite of rooms. It was late afternoon by the time they got to the hotel, so Edward determined that they would start their investigation in the morning, after breakfast.

Being the off-season, the hotel was almost completely deserted. The bell captain took both carpetbags and proceeded up the large staircase to the next level. He unlocked the door to Room 203 and allowed the two gentlemen to enter the suite, then followed them in with the bags. They were standing in a large sitting area which overlooked the harbor. There was a door leading to a bedroom on the right side of the room and another on the left. There was a third door that opened to a private bathroom—truly a luxury in those days.

Edward gave the bellman a gratuity and asked a few questions about the area, particularly about good restaurants, and then allowed the bellman to leave. Geoff was already exploring the suite.

"The bedroom over there has a better view of the water, Edward. You can take that one, if you'd like. I've already seen it."

"Sounds good. I am in the mood for some really fresh seafood for dinner. The bellman gave me a few suggestions. That's if you're up to eating."

"I feel much better. Thanks. After dinner I can show you the town center."

They unpacked what little they had brought with them.

"It's a good thing that we packed light," Edward called across the suite. "We will only be in this hotel for one night."

Geoff called back, "One night? I thought we were here for at least a few days?"

Edward walked to his bedroom door so that he didn't have to raise his voice. "That's correct, but we have accommodations elsewhere for the duration of our stay. I didn't know what time we would arrive here today, so I put it off until tomorrow."

Geoff now walked to his bedroom door. They faced each other across the sitting room. "Really? And where will we be staying hereafter?"

"We will have the run of Mr. William K. Vanderbilt's home."

"Marble House? Edward, do you know anything about that place?"

"I hear that it's…nice." He laughed.

"It's supposed to be the most opulent home in all of Newport. His brother's house is much bigger, but William's is…outstanding!"

"We will see it tomorrow. Are you ready to go to dinner?"

"I am starving! I am seriously considering lobster for dinner."

"I was thinking very much along the same line."

They both laughed. Order and friendship had been restored, at least for the moment, although Geoff's problems still weighed heavily on Edward's mind.

They had dinner in a quaint little tavern down by the wharf. True to their wishes, they both had a whole lobster for dinner. It was still quite chilly in the evenings in Newport, even if it was beginning to turn to spring in New York, so there was a roaring fire in the fireplace. A number of crusty locals sat at the bar, swilling tankards of ale, beer, or something they called grog. Edward and Geoff both enjoyed a tankard of ale with their dinner; however, Edward had instructed Geoff that this was their only tankard of the evening. Geoff dutifully agreed.

After dinner they took a leisurely stroll through Newport. They walked uphill on Church Street, crossed Mary Street, and then completed the circuit by walking down Touro Street. Geoff had remarked early in their walk that they were walking right by Trinity Churchyard, and then laughed because it looked nothing like the one they knew off Wall Street. Then, on their way down Touro Street, Edward pointed out that they were passing Washington Square. Geoff observed that it was missing its arch. Edward asked that he not be reminded; the Washington Square arch in Greenwich Village had been designed by Stanford White. They both had a good laugh over that fact; neither one of them cared for Stanford White. They turned right on Thames Street and headed back to their hotel. It was close to ten p.m.

Back in their suite all seemed normal, but wasn't. It wasn't easy to notice at first, but now Geoff's body was starting to yearn for the chemicals that it had been deprived of for the past few hours. Edward noticed that Geoff was getting more and more restless. They were both trying to catch up on some letters, but Geoff was having a difficult time concentrating. He kept getting up from the table and pacing the sitting room floor. Even though it was late, Edward decided to ring for some food. The front desk sent up a tray of pastries and a pot of tea. Having consumed everything on the tray, Edward suggested they turn in for the night.

As Edward stood in his bedroom, preparing to undress and put on his nightshirt, there was a knock on the door. There stood a forlorn-looking Geoff.

"Edward? Sorry to bother you. I'm not feeling all that well right now, and I was wondering if you could leave this door open tonight. I will do the same with my door."

Edward looked puzzled. "What's the matter, Geoff?"

"I know the taverns are open late. I don't want to go, but I may have to. I may need you to stop me."

"I'll try to get up to check on you during the night, old man."

"Thank you. But Edward...we never did buy that nightshirt I forgot to pack!"

"I stand warned."

Edward worked at the desk in his bedroom until quite late, mostly out of a desire to make sure that Geoff remained in the hotel room. He worked on his journal, which was still a daily habit, but didn't enter the day's entry because, in his opinion, the day hadn't ended yet. Edward reread the earlier entries for that particular year. Some entries had humor to them—or at least seemed funny in retrospect. Other entries were puzzles yet to be solved.

Around midnight, Edward heard a noise coming from the other bedroom. He rose from the desk and quietly walked to his door. He could hear Geoff's voice in the other room, but it was muffled and garbled—not clear at all. Edward couldn't understand a word Geoff was saying, but he sounded upset. Edward quietly took a candle from his room and crossed the sitting room to Geoff's bedroom.

Geoff was still in his bed. He was moving around a bit, sometimes agitated, and then he would speak.

Geoff was talking in his sleep.

Edward moved closer to the bed. The candlelight illuminated more of the room. Geoff was facing him, but fast asleep. Geoff had kicked most of the covers off his body with his nightmare, and, true to his word, was only wearing his undershorts. Edward felt a bit of a laugh beginning to well up, but choked it back when Geoff suddenly reversed his position on the bed. He now was facing away. That was when Edward saw it.

Geoff's back was a latticework of scars; some shallow, but many looked very deep, trough-like gouges that looked like much of the muscle had been removed with the skin. These marks could have only gotten there one way, Edward thought.

Geoff had been whipped.

Repeatedly.

This was something that was not meant for Edward's eyes, and yet he knew he had to talk to Geoff about it. Now he simply felt like...a spy.

Edward slowly shook his head. "Poor Geoff!" he whispered to himself. "What a horrible childhood you must have had!"

Edward crossed closer to the bed. He reached down and grabbed the comforter, pulling it up to his friend's shoulders. Geoff rotated again, this time onto his back. He momentarily opened his eyes, looking up at Edward. Geoff smiled slightly, as if Edward were the pleasant part of a dream, and then closed his eyes and went back into a deeper sleep again.

Edward blew out the candle and left the room. He sat back down at the desk and turned to the next page of his journal, and then entered his daily entry. He changed into his nightshirt and crawled into his bed, wondering if he should sleep or not.

But the bed was soft and comfortable, and Edward did fall asleep.

Luckily for Edward, Geoff slept through the night—soundly.

Personal Journal Entry
March 24, 1899

Geoff has finally fallen asleep in the other bedroom. He is snoring. I will be watching out for him. He is a good man, just a little immature.

I now understand him a little better, but I need to talk with him.

This is what I have been questioning all along—that two young men can grow up in the same city, at basically the same time period, and one gets the nurturing of loving parents while the other gets beaten and abused. This is the social injustice I thought I could right! Instead, I am in the service of the horribly rich of the gilded world.

Poor Geoff!

We will be going to the building site in the morning, and then will be talking with someone over at Marble House. I know Geoff is insulted that we have come back here so soon, but I need to be the one to sign off on the project.

I will know more in the morning.

Chapter 10
Rosecliff

Edward and Geoff had breakfast in the hotel restaurant early the next morning. While they were eating, the desk clerk arranged for a carriage and driver for the day.

The carriage ride somewhat retraced their steps from the outset of their after dinner stroll by ascending Church Street. After a few short turns, they finally turned right onto Bellevue Avenue. The avenue was lined on both sides with mansions, but in this case they were summer cottages. They arrived at their destination, Rosecliff, the summer cottage of the Oelrichs family. Edward could see that the exterior of the building was just about complete. The grounds, however, were a mess. The area was terribly muddy, and planking had been laid down to allow workers to neatly get from one part of the estate to the next. It took a bit of skillful navigating, but the two gentlemen managed to make it into the house without tracking in very much mud. They were able to locate the construction foreman quickly.

After introducing himself, Edward asked, "Is Mr. White present today?"

"Mr. White? Haven't seen him in over a week."

"Good," Edward replied. "We will just have a look around the property. No need to concern yourself with us."

The man seemed obliged. "Very well. I have more than enough to do today if we are going to finish by May." The man took the opportunity to hurry away. "Call me if you need me."

"That's better," sighed Edward. "We can't explore the place with him looking over our shoulders. Let's look at the swimming pool first."

They headed out the back of the house, toward the ocean. A large circular fountain stood just beyond the rear patio.

"Where is the pool, Geoff?" Edward thought that Geoff had said the pool had been dug where the fountain now stood. He looked over at Geoff, who stood confounded.

"It was right there, Edward. Right where that fountain is standing. Only it was a hole twenty feet wide by forty feet long and as much as twenty feet deep." Geoff pointed to a place some thirty feet away from where they stood. "Stanford White and I stood over the hole, right over there."

"Well, it's not there now."

"Are you calling me a liar?"

Edward, in fact, was not calling Geoff a liar. It was anything but that. "No. I'm saying that the plans have been altered. Altered since you were here a week ago."

"Shouldn't you have known about a change in plans?"

"Precisely my point! Would you find that foreman for me?" Geoff went to find the man, whom they knew didn't want to be questioned, in order to question him. Geoff returned with the hapless man in short order.

"Now, my good man, please tell me—what happened to the swimming pool?"

"I knew you were going to ask that question."

"Yes? And?"

"Well, we had it all dug out. It was a big piece of work, considering how hard the soil is, but it was ready for the concrete. And then, all of a sudden Mr. White tells us to fill it in. He tells us that a fountain is going there instead. But first, he says, we have to rough out a cinder-block foundation in the deep end for the pump room. He says that it will adjoin the basement of the house. So he gives me the plans and we have the thing built in a day and a half. It butts right up to the basement wall. To my mind, it looked like a…you know, like in a fancy cemetery. What is it called…"

"A mausoleum?" Geoff said helpfully.

"Yeah, that's right."

"Like a vault?" Edward asked.

"Now you said it. Because we went home on a Friday, and when we came back on the next Monday, down in the basement, right where this vault joins with the house, there's a big safe."

"What?" Geoff was astounded. "The pump house became a safe? What are they going to put in it? Their silverware?"

Edward didn't seem surprised at all. "Why not? Mrs. Oelrichs is a silver heiress."

The foreman led them to the basement of Rosecliff. There, situated in the middle of the rear wall of the basement, was a bank vault door. The door was shut. Edward tried the release, but the tumblers had been secured.

"Do you think something is in there?" the foreman asked.

"I have no idea," was Edward's response.

Geoff's mind, however, was on a different detail. "The vault door is flush with the outer wall of the basement, correct?" The foreman nodded. "The pool that was to be but is no more was located about thirty feet off the rear patio of the house, correct?" Again the foreman nodded. "Does the patio have a deep foundation, like a basement?"

The foreman thought a moment and then answered, "No, we only have to put in footings that go down lower than the frost line."

Geoff continued, "So if the back wall of the pool had the back wall of the mausoleum, and this is the back wall of the foundation of the house, I would say there is a good fifty to sixty feet of area between this door and the mausoleum."

"A tunnel?" the man asked.

"Or an extremely big vault," answered Edward. "It's a mystery."

They excused the foreman under the pretense that he needed to get back to his crew. Both knew that what they had found was a bit unusual. They continued to explore the unfinished home, marveling at how beautiful it would be in just a few weeks. Then, around noontime, they got back into their carriage and rode a little further out on Bellevue Avenue to an ever grander home named Marble House.

Marble House was built for the family of William K. Vanderbilt, but was largely the pet project of his wife, Alva. The home was designed by Richard Morris Hunt, who also designed the Breakers for Vanderbilt's brother, Cornelius II. It was reported to have cost eleven million dollars to build the house, with seven million dollars of the total spent on the purchase of marble. William and Alva divorced, and Alva married Oliver Hazard Perry Belmont and moved into another cottage, Belcourt, which was just a little farther down the road.

They were met at the front door by the Marble House caretaker, John Burns.

"Mr. Collier and Mr. Atwater?" Mr. Burns had a Scottish brogue.

"Mr. Burns? A pleasure to make your acquaintance," Edward said, shaking his hand.

"Well, come in to Marble House. I can't let you sleep in the mistress's bedroom, but I do have some very nice guest rooms made up for you."

Edward was quick to observe Burns's tone. "You mentioned Mrs. Vanderbilt's room, but not Mr. Vanderbilt's. Why the oversight?"

John Burns leaned in and whispered, "Wait until you see the master bedroom. It's hardly worth mentioning. Mrs. V. runs the show around here."

Burns led Edward and Geoff upstairs to the second floor, where the bedrooms were located. He showed them two beautiful guest rooms, each with a four-poster. Both rooms had fires lit in the fireplaces. Each had a sitting area and a desk. The rooms were joining by way of a common bathroom. The sink and bathtub had both hot and cold, fresh and salt water.

"Feel free to wander around the house," Burns advised. "There is a wonderful library, and a billiard room, and all kinds of surprises throughout the house. I am sure you will find everything to your liking. The kitchen is fully stocked for your stay. Normally it is filled with food for me and my family, but special things were ordered for you. Dinner will be at eight o'clock, but don't feel that you have to dress." Burns laughed at this. "Oh, have you heard about the Cliff Walk?"

"No, I don't believe I have," replied Edward. "What about you, Geoff?"

"I heard it mentioned, but only in passing. What is it?"

Burns smiled. "It's a pathway that runs along the seawall for quite some distance. It passes in front of each estate on the ocean side of the peninsula. It's not lit at night, so if you go down there, you best be careful or you'll end up on the rocks below."

Geoff beamed. "We should definitely look this over, Edward. It sounds interesting."

"Interesting, cold, and wet—not to mention dangerous."

"Well," Burns added, "you still have several hours of daylight and plenty of time before dinner. To find an entrance, just head out the back doors and walk to the sea. You will see it."

Edward and Geoff set off for the Cliff Walk and found it just as Burns had described. There was a short set of steps that connected the property to the Cliff Walk so that the path was almost a body length below the grade of the yard. A tall person could be seen walking on most of the walk from the residences; a short person might disappear entirely. But it was from this perspective, from the oceanfront, that Edward and Geoff could see several estates at one glance. They could also appreciate how much acreage was included in each estate. They walked north, toward Rosecliff.

"Geoff? I noticed that each of these homes has a gated entrance on Bellevue Avenue. Each one looks like a high-security prison from up there."

"I noticed that, too."

"Yes, but look. Anyone can gain access to any of these homes simply by taking the Cliff Walk."

Edward was correct. If the land assault failed, the invasion could come from the sea.

The air was turning colder by the minute, and they were being pummeled by sea spray when the waves broke on the rocks below. They headed back toward Marble House and the welcoming glow of fireplaces. They enjoyed a hearty meal of roast beef, potatoes, and gravy with the Burns family. Burns opened a bottle of claret to have with the meal. Geoff had two glasses, but refused the third.

Mrs. Burns, who instructed the young men to call her Louise, played hostess for the evening. She was assisted by their two daughters— Emily, who was sixteen, and Sarah, who was fourteen. They set the table in the dining room with the everyday dishes the Vanderbilts would have used daily. Even so, they were all etched in gold leaf. The girls were totally captivated by Edward and Geoff, who were certainly the first guests to have stayed in the house that were invited by the Vanderbilts, but were having dinner with the servants. After dinner, Edward and Geoff spent some time in the library. Edward was particularly interested in finding any books concerning the Newport area; he wished he could find building plans, maps, or other historic references. He didn't find any.

They headed up to their rooms at eleven p.m. Once again, they left the adjoining doors open.

Personal Journal Entry
March 26, 1899

I had a terrible night's sleep in Marble House. I had a recurring dream that lasted throughout the night. I dreamt that I was in a large bed, but it was swinging to and fro like a hammock on a ship at sea. Every time the apogee of the swing would get to the point where I felt as if I would tumble off the bed, that is when I would wake up. Then, I think it was around three in the morning, I had the dream again, but on this occasion I felt as if someone was trying to smother me with a wet cloth held down over my face. I struggled to get free, and when I did…I woke up.

They had breakfast in the kitchen the next morning. Mrs. Burns had prepared a hearty meal of eggs, bacon, potatoes, and toast. She brewed an excellent pot of coffee.

After breakfast, Edward and Geoff went back to the library. Edward recounted his dreams from the previous night to Geoff, who found them quite amusing. As Geoff calmed down from his laugh at Edward's expense, Edward decided it was time to ask Geoff a personal question.

He had been a spy.

"Geoff, you will, of course, remember that you told me about all your exploits—spying on me and my family?"

Geoff chuckled a bit. "Sure. I hope you aren't still mad over that."

Edward smiled an artificial smile. "No, but I must confess, my friend, that I have done a little spying on you, so I guess we are now even."

"What are you blabbering about, Edward?"

Edward closed the book he was thumbing through. This, he thought, was it. There was no turning back now. "Geoff, you had a bad nightmare the night in the hotel."

"Did I?" Geoff asked coolly.

"Yes," Edward continued, "you were talking in your sleep. I went to your bedroom to see if you were all right."

"And was I all right, Edward?" Geoff had a slightly confrontational tone in his voice, as if he could start at this point and crescendo at any moment.

"Geoff, I saw your back." There, he said it.

"Really?" asked a suddenly upbeat Geoff. "A nice design, don't you think?"

"Geoff!"

Geoff stood as if to leave.

"Where are you going?" Edward asked hastily.

"Out for some air. Perhaps the Cliff Walk."

Edward also stood up. He crossed the room in seconds and placed his hand on Geoff's shoulder, pushing downward. "Sit down, Geoff," he demanded quietly.

"Edward, don't do this! I can knock you to the floor, you know I can."

"Yes, I know, but not today, my friend. Today is one of those days when I get to find out why you hurt inside so very much."

"I don't want to talk about it, Edward."

"Geoff," Edward said, gently, as if talking to a child, "I have already seen the evidence. Why not tell me how it happened? Let me understand. Allow me into your world."

"I need a drink or two before I can talk. Better yet, I have to be drunk."

"No!" Edward countered. "You need to be as sober as a judge. Now talk to me. Don't you trust me?"

"Trust you?" Geoff laughed. "Edward, I would trust you with my life. I don't want you to know any of the things I went through when I was just a kid. I'm too embarrassed."

"And I am embarrassed for you, Geoff. That's how I felt when I first saw those markings on your back, like I had just entered a place that I had no right to be at—but I've seen it, Geoff. It's too late now!"

"I can't, Edward."

Edward sat down next to his friend. "You know something, Geoff? I'm getting married in just a few short months. I am sure you will also be getting married one of these days." Geoff muttered at this. "It's true. Someday we will both have children. What will you choose to tell your children when they ask why their father has so many ugly lines across his back?"

"I'll make something up. I'll tell them it was an accident at work."

"And what will that teach them? Let them appreciate the wonderful man their father became, in spite of his terrible childhood. Warn them that there are violent, evil people in the world, people who take out their aggressions on children, but that your children are loved. Tell them that there are many children in New York City who need help and understanding."

Geoff put his arm around his friend. "Oh, you are good, Edward. You are very, very good. You should stand before the court—you are a born orator." Geoff thought a little more on this. "Or maybe you should have a pulpit, or run for public office?"

"I am trying to help you!" Edward yelled, grabbing him by the arms.

"Get off me, Edward!" Geoff yelled back, and then very forcefully pushed Edward away. Edward reeled backward a few steps, but his left leg caught on the couch, which upset his balance. He landed hard on the floor. "See?" Geoff argued. "I warned you! You just can't leave well enough alone!"

Geoff spun on his heel, determined to exit the library as quickly as possible. Edward simply sat on his buttocks, watching his friend spin out of control. Geoff got as far as the door to the room before he turned around to see if Edward had gotten up yet.

He hadn't.

Geoff walked back to Edward and sat down next to him on the floor.

"What am I going to do with you, Edward?" he asked. "You just don't take no for an answer."

"I know," Edward replied, "my parents always called it my stubborn streak. One of my mother's favorite lines is, 'I hope your children inherit your stubbornness, just so you can understand what your father and I have been going through for years.'"

"You have your curse, Edward, and I have mine." Geoff took a deep breath. He had never really related this story before—not even to the man who saved him. He slowly began to explain his past. "You can't possibly appreciate what it was like growing up in that home for boys. If I wasn't being kicked and beaten by the older boys, I was being whipped by the matron in charge of my dormitory—or even worse, whipped by the headmaster."

Edward listened carefully, nodding for Geoff to continue.

"I would get beaten two, sometimes four times every week. Just because. They would tell me it was for my own good." He gestured to his back. "A lot of good it did me. No, Edward, my childhood was definitely not like yours. I had to scrape and crawl for everything and anything that came my way." Geoff paused. He looked over at Edward, and for a moment debated saying any more. "One day, when I was sixteen, a man approached me on the street. His name was Bill Greyson. He was an agent for the Morgan Company. He asked me if I would like to work for his company. I was brought over to the office—never met Morgan, or anything like that, not right away. I was given odd jobs to do, mostly— you know, spying. I guess they wanted me for my quickness and my street smarts. They paid me more money than I ever thought I would make, and the day after I got my first paycheck I ran away from the home. I worked for that man for almost three years before I met you."

Edward interrupted his friend. "I consider that a very good, memorable day, Geoff."

"Wait," Geoff retorted, "do you want to hear this, or not?"

"I'm sorry. Go on, please."

Geoff then continued, "Bill Greyson was about as close to a father figure, or a mentor, that I ever knew—up to now." He smiled at Edward. "One day when I was eighteen there was a commotion at the office. Greyson had gotten himself run over by a trolley and was dead. I couldn't believe my ears. Then I started hearing murmurs from the other agents that it wasn't an accident—that he was pushed in front of the thing. Next thing I know I'm hearing rumors that Greyson had been trying to extort money from Morgan over something he found out."

"That's terrible," Edward said. "Do you think Morgan had him killed?"

"I never could find out an answer," Geoff replied, "but I wouldn't put it past him! I know you kind of like the man, Edward, but he's not the man he seems. I have a few things on him, but I don't want to end up under a streetcar, so I'm keeping it all to myself—for now. That's why I write it all down in my notebooks—that's another thing that Greyson taught me—then I hide them."

"And did they ever find Greyson's notebooks?" Edward asked.

"Yep, they did," Geoff nodded, "when they emptied his apartment. They found all of them, all neatly dated. All except one!" Edward understood the significance of the missing notebook. He slowly nodded. Geoff concluded, "That's why I am so happy to be working for you now, but I think that it's also why I spent the last year or so inside a bottle. I have a hard time when people get close to me. It hurts too much when I'm alone again."

"Like a said before," Edward added, "I think our fortunes changed on the day we met. I mean to say formally met." He smiled at Geoff.

"So do I, but Edward, I want what you have. I envy how happy you are. I want to be you!"

"Why?" Edward asked. "The Geoff Atwater I know is a charming, handsome young gentleman—who occasionally forgets to shave and bathe—but otherwise is intelligent and resourceful. I consider him a very close, trusted friend."

Geoff embraced his friend. "I am humbled by you, Edward. You must have been a whiz in Sunday school."

Edward laughed. "So if you need to get me back for spying on you, go right ahead. Look in my belongings, or in my desk. Spy on me when I'm in the bathtub or on the toilet."

Geoff did not think this was funny. "I've done all that already, Edward."

"When? Here in Newport?"

"No," Geoff replied quietly, "in your house on Sixteenth Street."

"I don't believe you!" Edward joked with him. "Now you are just trying to have the upper hand." Edward raised his eyebrow. "Prove it to me."

"Well," replied Geoff, "I can tell you that you have a mole about the size of a quarter dollar on your right bum."

"What?" Edward said, shocked. "Geoff, in order for you to know that, you would have had to have—"

"Been in your house?"

Edward suddenly was very serious. "I am dumbfounded. All I can say is that I am glad you are on my side."

They laughed a bit. In the weeks to come, Geoff would slowly and deliberately unravel the stories of his youth to Edward, but for now, Edward had opened a door into Geoff's soul, and that was a good start.

It was time to get down to work.

"What did you think about the disappearance of the swimming pool, Geoff?"

"It was odd, all right, but I suppose the lady has the right to change her mind."

"I think the pool was in Stanford White's original design, and he was told to change it after the excavation was finished."

"Who would do such a thing?" Geoff wondered aloud.

"Morgan virtually exploded when he heard about the pool," Edward said, very matter-of-factly.

"Did he now? Do you think Morgan ordered White to fill in the pool?"

"I am sure he did. I think Morgan is in complete control of the entire project, but White, me, and now you are the only people who know this."

"I don't understand any of this. All this is for a recital by Harry Burleigh?"

"I don't claim to fully understand it, either. But Geoff, all this can't just be for a recital by Harry Burleigh. The expenses don't add up. He could have sung in any of the fine churches in New York—it would hardly have cost anything. Instead, we have many people jumping through hoops to finish a multimillion-dollar rich man's house so that Harry Burleigh will have a suitable venue to sing for an extremely cultured crowd."

"And your thoughts are...?"

"I have been under the impression that Morgan had something up his sleeve. I think it is something very big. Something that will shake the country." Edward had walked right up to the precipice, and now knew that it was time to bring Geoff in, or leave him safely outside. "I think Mr. Morgan is amassing precious metals in the form of ingots, gold and silver."

"What?" Geoff's eyes were wide and his jaw hung slack.

"I have had my suspicions for a while now. The vault confirmed it. I think Morgan is building safes to hide and hold his gold. I didn't know who I could trust. I didn't tell my parents how I thought. I didn't even tell Rebecca, and I didn't tell you."

"Thanks, Edward," Geoff said sarcastically.

"Please, Geoff, understand me. It wasn't so much a matter of trust—I know this now—it was out of fear of involving someone else in his scheme."

Geoff looked surprised. "His scheme? You think he's doing something illegal?"

"I don't know, but I swear to you, Geoff, I think that's why I have this job. I think that it's why my salary is so high. I think it's why I'm moving to the Dakota. And I only hope that it's not the reason why Rebecca is marrying me."

"I doubt that is true."

"I hope so, but remember, Rebecca was working for Morgan as his receptionist before I was brought in. She is privy to a great deal of sensitive office information. It's crazy, I know, and I hope it is not true because I truly love the girl."

There was an awkward silence in the room, until Geoff spoke. "And what about that vault thing over at Rosecliff? What is that about?"

"And what about the stealth used to install it? It was installed over the weekend when the crew and foreman were off. It just magically appeared, fully installed."

"What's in it, I wonder?"

That was also on Edward's mind. An invasion from the sea. Spies were everywhere.

Personal Journal Entry
March 27, 1899

I had the same dream again last night. There was a variation in the plot, however. I was protecting something of great value in the dream—something I valued more than my own life. I know that cannot be gold, or currency of any kind. This was more important to me, and to my soul.

I didn't see Rebecca's face in the dream, but the possession I was protecting was as valuable to me as she.

Chapter 11
The Concert and Recital

The young men stayed another two days in Newport; doing research, visiting more of the cottages, and speaking with the local residents. They headed back to New York the following day, basically retracing the path that had brought them a few days before: Newport to Providence, Providence to New York.

Edward met with Morgan on his first day back in the office. He told his boss about the mysterious disappearance of the swimming pool, the large circular fountain in its place, the mausoleum-type vault that was buried under the fountain, and the bank-quality safe that had been installed in the basement. He said all these things in his report because he didn't want Morgan to think he was holding out on him. Morgan probably knew all these things already.

Spies were everywhere. His conversations with Geoff had proven that.

When he exited Morgan's office, Rebecca told him that she was busy as well—successfully buying the furniture needed for their apartment at the Dakota. He kissed her on the cheek and asked to have dinner with him that evening. She never asked him for any of the details of his trip, which Edward felt was a good sign.

Harry Burleigh was scheduled to sing at Carnegie Hall on Sunday afternoon, April 16, 1899. This date was now fast approaching, as was the recital at Rosecliff, which was to be held on Saturday evening, May 27.

Edward had seen to virtually every aspect of the performances; from arranging for the venues, to publicity, to tickets and programs. Tickets were selling well for the Carnegie Hall concert. Almost everyone from St. George's had purchased a ticket or two. Edward had seen to it that the uppermost tier seats sold for prices that all people—even people of the same color as Mr. Burleigh himself—could afford. The balcony was sold out in just a few days. The orchestra section and the box seats also sold out relatively quickly. Edward surmised that this was probably due to pressure from the Morgan organization. It was the seats in the middle that were selling slower, but even these were sold after someone took out an advertisement in the *New York Times* which praised the musicality of Burleigh's voice.

Personal Journal Entry
April 15, 1899

I feel that much is riding on the success or failure of Mr. Burleigh's concert tomorrow. I have a great deal of faith in his musicianship and in the quality of his voice.

I do not have faith in the public, especially in those who are in a position of power—those who might criticize the man based solely on the color of his skin, and not the warmth of his voice.

I have done my job, but if he fails then so will I.

The day of the concert arrived. April 16 was sunny and warm—a perfect spring day. The concert was to begin at four o'clock. The audience started to arrive around three fifteen, and the doors opened at three thirty. As they walked into the auditorium, the only thing present on the stage was a grand piano.

Edward, Rebecca, and Edward's parents sat in the front row of the orchestra section. J. P. Morgan and his clan had a box. Geoffrey Atwater sat a few rows behind Edward. There were music critics from all the city newspapers in attendance; Edward had seen to that.

At 4:01, Harry T. Burleigh and his accompanist walked onstage. The applause that greeted him was a mixture of unbridled enthusiasm and cool aloofness. He began his program, not with a spiritual, but with Schubert. He sang "An die Musik"—an art song dedicated to the glory and beauty of music—and he sang it in German. And that was all it took. At the end of the lied the entire room erupted into cheers and applause.

He next performed a bass aria from *Elijah* by Felix Mendelssohn, which he sang in English. This was followed by two selections from Handel's *Messiah*—the recitative "Thus Saith the Lord" and the aria "But Who May Abide the Day of His Coming?" He then turned to Mozart and sang one of Papageno's arias from *The Magic Flute*. This was followed by three Italian art songs. He then returned to Schubert and performed the dramatic Der Erlkönig." He ended the first half of his concert with "Tit Willow" from Gilbert and Sullivan's *The Mikado*.

The audience was loud and excited during the Intermission. Edward could hear the celebration in the upper tier, but he was also trying to hear some of the comments from the people closest to him. He heard one woman remark, "I didn't know that black people could sing our music," and a man wonder, "How ever did he learn to sing in all those foreign languages? Most Negroes have enough trouble trying to speak English." For the most part, the comments were favorable and enthusiastic. But the second half of the program would be quite a new experience for most there.

For the second part of his program, Burleigh decided to sing a collection of spirituals. He took a step or two out from the crook of the piano and, without a note of accompaniment, sang "Were You There?" Most of the audience had never heard that, or any other spiritual before, and they certainly hadn't heard one as performed by Harry Burleigh. He began by singing the first verse sotto voce, a soft-voiced operatic technique:

Were You There When they crucified my Lord?
Were You There When they crucified my Lord?
Oh, Sometimes It Causes Me to Tremble, Tremble, Tremble
Were You There When they crucified my Lord?

It was only two weeks since Holy Week and Easter, but the audience was captivated by the mood of the song—not because of its religious theme, but because here was music that also reflected the pain and suffering of an entire race of people, and then mirrored it in a song. He then sang "Deep River," which, in addition to the surface meaning of the lyrics, was also a song of the Underground Railroad.

Deep River…my home is over Jordan
Deep River, Lord…I long to cross over into campground.

The Jordan River mentioned in the spiritual was not really the river in Judea, but usually was a coded name for the Ohio River—and crossing into campground indicated that by crossing the river the slaves would now be in a "free state." Edward knew this spiritual better than most—it was the first song he had heard Burleigh sing, back in St. George's a year ago.

Burleigh then sang "Go Down, Moses," a long narrative spiritual that, once again, on the surface told the Bible story of Moses asking the Pharaoh of Egypt to free the people of Israel. In the last year of the turbulent century that had seen more than six hundred twenty thousand men die in a war that, in addition to preserving the Union, had freed the slaves, the allegory was certainly recognized by most in the audience. In the earlier part of the century, however, this would have simply been a work song, sung by the slaves in the field, with the text a seemingly innocent retelling of a Bible story that had been the sum and substance of their religious and linguistic education.

Harry Burleigh sang the following spirituals at his Carnegie Hall concert:

"Couldn't Hear Nobody Pray"
"De Blin' Man Stood on de Road an' Cried"
"Ev'ry Time I Feel the Spirit"
"Wade in de Water"
"Sometimes I Feel Like a Motherless Child"
"Deep River"
"Were You There?"
"Go Down, Moses"

And then the concert was over. Many stayed longer in the hall to talk about what they had just heard, but the majority of the house filed out as best they could. The rich were going to dinner, and the less fortunate were left struggling to find a way back home.

Edward and his party ran into Morgan in the lobby. Morgan extended his hand to Edward, and then to his father. He kissed the gloved hands of Rebecca and Edward's mother.

"This was a fine concert, Edward," Morgan began. "Mr. Burleigh has made history today."

"He is completely deserving of all this praise," Edward replied.

Then Morgan met up with his party, and the Colliers met up with Clara, who had purchased seats closer to her friends from church, and everyone proceeded out the exit and on to 57th Street.

Personal Journal Entry
April 16, 1899

What a relief! What a success!

I am happy for myself, but I am even more joyful for Harry Burleigh. He deserves all the credit.

If people came to Carnegie Hall out of curiosity—just to see if a black man was capable of singing lieder, opera, sacred songs, and so on—then they exited the building with a firmer understanding that all of God's people can achieve great things, once they are afforded a proper and equal education.

I look forward to reading the reviews in the papers tomorrow.

A few short weeks later Edward was back in Newport. This time it was for Mr. Burleigh's recital at Rosecliff. It was the last weekend in May, and the official start of the summer social season of Newport. The little town was totally transformed from the sleepy oceanside hamlet that Edward had visited only a few months before. The streets were bustling with activity; there were carriages, motorcars, liveries, even pushcarts. Edward could now smell the odor of fish, typical of any harbor town, but especially in the warmer months.

Rebecca had accompanied Edward on this trip, and they stayed in the same hotel in which he and Geoff had stayed. They had made the trip on Friday, would go to the party on Saturday, and then return to Manhattan on Sunday. J. P. Morgan had left Manhattan on Monday, sailing aboard his brand-new yacht, the *Corsair*. He made landfall in Newport on Thursday, having stopped several times along the way on Long Island. Morgan was not a stranger in Newport—he especially liked the yacht races—but he did not indulge in the society events. Usually. This was an exception. He stayed with Cornelius Vanderbilt II at the Breakers.

All of Newport society had turned out for the opening of Rosecliff. That meant that all of New York society had turned out as well. Mrs. Oelrichs was ecstatic about the manner in which the cottage was finished. She had voiced her disappointment that the swimming pool had been removed from White's original plan, but was extremely happy with the fountain as a substitute.

Stanford White was also in attendance, this time with an age-appropriate woman—his wife.

The performance at Rosecliff began at five o'clock. Burleigh sang basically the same repertoire as he had at Carnegie Hall, but he sang it without an intermission. He stood on the rear patio and performed for the guests as they sat or stood around the fountain. The fact that he had become an overnight sensation in New York after his debut concert quelled any shock that might have occurred due to his skin color. He was already accepted. Mrs. Oelrichs was so taken by his performance—

"that a man of his origin" could perform the classics so well—that she would, at a future date, take on the morays of Newport society once again by bringing a Jewish immigrant—one Erich Weiss—to perform for the same people, standing in the same spot as Harry Burleigh. Erich Weiss was the most famous illusionist and escape artist the world had ever seen. His stage name—Harry Houdini.

Edward had proven his worth to J. P. Morgan. The projects would now begin to accumulate.

Personal Journal Entry
June 2, 1899

I am to be married to my dearest Rebecca in the morning at St. George's. It is my fondest desire to get a good night's sleep, but I fear this may not be—I am so excited! The ceremony will begin at ten a.m., followed by a luncheon. We will board the *Britannic*, owned by the White Star Line, at three, and depart for a European honeymoon at four. When we return in late August, we shall begin our lives together at the Dakota.

Geoff has been put in charge of watching over the office business until I return. There are so many unfinished projects on my desk—most of them having to do with Stanford White.

I have finished packing my steamer trunk; my clothes are laid out for the ceremony. Now all I have to do is get some sleep.

Chapter 12
A New, New York City

Manhattan Island was being ripped open. Since the introduction of electrical lighting and telephones, the city streets had become a morass of poles and wiring. Add to that the grid of wires used to run the streetcars and there was no longer an unfettered view up or down an avenue in the busier parts of the city. Henry Ford's automobiles, a variety of trucks, and wagons and carts of every size and capability were clogging the roadways. At the junction of Park Avenue and 42nd Street, an area that had once been thought very remote, Commodore Vanderbilt had constructed the Grand Central Depot. Trains of all purposes, passenger and freight, were using this station as the main depot on Manhattan. The soot from the locomotives choked the surrounding area, and the train yard itself stretched for blocks in each direction.

At the same time, several independent entrepreneurs had individual plans to create an underground tube, or subway, similar to the one operating in London. Over a building period that would cover several decades, the Rapid Transit System would provide a solution to moving masses of people around the city; and it was, for the most part, out of sight—unlike its older, unattractive cousin, the elevated train. Unfortunately, the independent operators of the different subway lines were in competition with each other for business, and therefore did not have a shared vision that someday the entire network of track would become one transit system. They designed different subway cars and used different gauge track.

The biggest problem was the method used to build the subway. Most of the project required complete excavation of a city avenue to the depth of the track. A section would be dug, constructed, covered over with a tunnel, and then repaved. Then the site would move further uptown. City engineers realized the potential of such massive excavations and decided to move the electrical, telephone, water, and sewer infrastructure underground as well.

The same solution was being discussed at 42nd Street. The Commodore's Depot, which had opened in the 1870s, was obsolete the moment it opened. Plans were already under way to put the entire train yard underground, allowing construction of buildings to occur above it. Talk of a new, modern terminal to replace the depot was already in progress. The structure would be called the Grand Central Terminal.

Now, creeping closer and closer to the turn of a new century, the excavation had begun. Deep in the ground, digging stories and stories below street level, workers started to prepare the area around 42nd Street uptown to 48th Street, and from Madison over to Lexington Avenues for the new terminal. It would take years to complete, but would not be without an air of mystery. The new terminal would still be a depot for passenger trains—particularly the New York Central, which was owned by the Vanderbilts—but it would also be a stop on the subway line. People could take a train into Manhattan and then hop a subway down to Wall Street. It would be very convenient, and very private, because they could do this all without ever seeing the light of day, or dealing with the teeming masses on the sidewalks above them. It would be a perfect way to bring a dignitary into the city unnoticed. Moreover, there would be sidings constructed to hide the unused trains in the below-ground train yard. These sidings would extend for city blocks. The possibilities were endless.

The White Star Line's *Britannic* took more than a week to make the crossing from New York to Southampton. The couple traveled in first-class accommodations, but even so, Rebecca spent most of the voyage seasick. Her symptoms immediately disappeared once she set foot on dry land. The *Britannic* was an elegant steamship, but she was old. New technologies in shipbuilding were pushing the White Star Line to revamp its fleet of ocean liners. It was in stiff competition with another line, Cunard. Cunard had already launched a new vessel that could make the crossing to America in almost half the time, the *Mauretania*. Talk was under way at White Star headquarters of contracting four new giant liners to compete with the Cunard ships; one of those four would be a new *Britannic*.

Edward and Rebecca proved to be an elegant newlywed couple. They became the talk of the first-class salons, especially because they were so young—most of the people traveling in that class were at least middle-aged.

Rebecca looked stunning, especially at dinner and for the evening activities. She had spent her time preparing for the voyage, and had chosen her wardrobe to complement Edward's evening clothes. Edward, on the other hand, refused to adjourn to the men's salon after dinner with the other men of the class. This was a smoke-filled room of card playing and politics. He preferred to spend the evening with Rebecca in his arms as they whirled around the dance floor. Unfortunately, the whirling would always take its toll, and Rebecca would usually suffer a bought of seasickness before the night was over.

Edward and Rebecca spent two weeks traveling through England, Wales, Scotland, and Ireland before crossing the English Channel from Dover to Calais. (Rebecca was once again under the weather during the ferry ride.) They were met at the dock by an autobus made by the Benz company, which took them to Paris. They spent a week in Paris, taking in the Louvre, Notre Dame, St. Sulpice, Napoleon's Tomb, an opera, and a cruise on the Seine. They then headed south, through the Loire Valley, and on to Spain and Portugal. The couple boarded a train at Barcelona and traveled the Mediterranean coast until they arrived at Milan. Rebecca insisted that they see another opera, this time at La Scala, and then they spent almost two weeks touring Italy, ending their circuit in Venice.

Then it was off to Vienna and Budapest, on to Berlin, and then by train to Holland and Belgium. It was truly the grand tour.

With seven weeks of touring behind them, they once again crossed the ocean—this time, fittingly enough, on a White Star liner named the *Oceanic.* Once again Rebecca spent most of the journey in the head, but upon making berth in New York, she did not find that the symptoms disappeared. The nausea continued to bother her on the carriage ride to the Dakota, and continued again the next day. Edward rang a doctor who resided on the third floor of the building and he gave her an examination.

Rebecca was suffering from morning sickness. She was pregnant.

Personal Journal Entry
August 20, 1899

I have skipped many an entry in this journal.

I have been distracted from my daily writings due to my duties as a bridegroom.

We are now back on American shores.

I have just discovered that I am going to be a father. What a uniquely joyous feeling this creates—right down to my very core! I have never felt this way before.

Rebecca had impeccable taste when it came to decorating the Dakota apartment. She was not particularly enamored with the heavy, gilded furniture that had been so popular among the wealthy for the past four decades. She preferred most classical lines—a revival of European design from the earlier part of the nineteenth century. When they had arrived back from Europe, the entire apartment had been either painted or wallpapered. New carpets had been laid, and all their new furniture had arrived and been arranged. The place was move-in ready. She had left her mother in charge of these details, and her wishes were strictly adhered to.

One of the bedrooms had been painted but not decorated. This was to be the nursery, although neither had expected to need the room in their first year of marriage.

Edward also discovered that one of their dumbwaiters did not work properly; it was caught between floors. He asked the caretaker of the building to look into the problem, and the man had reported back that the reason for the problem was that he, Edward, had ordered a large cast-iron box installed in the elevator shaft, and it prevented the rope/pulley system from working. Edward explained that he had given no such order, but the caretaker produced a document that authorized the installation, and it had been signed by Edward. Edward decided not to make a large issue of the matter with the caretaker, but he had a suspicion of who had ordered that installation. It was the same person who could have obtained a copy of his signature. He wondered what the box was for, and in addition wondered if anything was in the box. As that particular shaft was only used to transport items to the study, and not to the kitchen, Edward decided to ignore the thing completely—but he made a note of it in his personal journal.

He had started the journal when he was just out of Columbia, and had been keeping up with it faithfully for some years now. In addition to holding some of his most private, secret thoughts, he also wrote himself cryptic little phrases that referenced odd things he noticed when working with Morgan. On an entry page when he and Geoff had gone to inspect the Newport cottage, he had entered:

RC-tomb-under-ftn

On the page he was completing before bed that evening, he now added:

Dta-dw-sty-bkd

There would be others to come.

Edward returned to work on Monday, August 21, 1899. It was to be one of the hottest days that year. In his briefcase he carried Rebecca's letter of resignation. They hadn't been exactly sure how much longer she would work, the apartment and her new social status playing a big part in their concern, but her pregnancy now sealed the question. Carrying a baby to full term, even in the modern era of 1900, still had many risks—for the baby and for the mother. Very often, well-to-do mothers were confined to bed for the duration of their pregnancy. Edward, while overly concerned and nervous, did not expect Rebecca to stay in bed all day, but he also knew that a bumpy carriage ride from 72nd Street to Wall Street was not in the best interest of their child.

Morgan agreed completely. He was overjoyed for the couple.

So was Geoff. Edward let Geoff in on the news over lunch in a tavern on Broome Street. Geoff immediately called for drinks to celebrate, an action which raised Edward's eyebrow.

"Geoff! A pint is good enough. We don't need anything stronger!"

"Still worried about me, Edward? That's good, I suppose, but you've been gone for more than two months. If I was drinking heavily, I'd be dead already—and here I am. Besides, I could have taken up something far worse, you know, like visiting one of those opium dens over in Chinatown."

"Shh! Keep your voice down! I know you're joking with me, but these other people don't know you like I do."

"You always were a bit of a stuffed shirt, Edward. But now I've got something to tell you."

Edward feared the worst. When he left his home on 16th Street for his wedding, he was leaving that address as well. Geoff had made the necessary arrangements to live with Edward's parents. All seemed to look forward to the new living arrangement. Edward now worried that something had gone terribly wrong.

"What is it, Geoff?"

"Well, I had a very good time at your wedding, my man. It was a distinct pleasure for me to serve as your best man. It is amazing what that title enables you to experience."

"What are you talking about?" Edward couldn't imagine, because alcohol was not liberally served at the luncheon. Geoff couldn't have gotten that drunk!

"I am saying that after you two left the party for the boat, the real party began. The dancing continued until the evening. I needed a partner, and who should I find? The bride's younger sister, Margaret."

"Margaret?" Rebecca's sister, Margaret, was eighteen years old. She wasn't as worldly as Rebecca, but she was a very lively, attractive young lady.

"Yes. We have been keeping company together for as long as you have been away."

"And?"

"And nothing! She is a lovely girl. I like her a great deal."

"Yes? And?" Edward baited.

"And I couldn't wait until you got back! Do you really think I would do something that would be sure to upset you while you were away?"

"Like what, Geoffrey?" Geoff squinted at Edward. "Ask her to marry you?"

Geoff looked frustrated. "I think she wants me to ask her. I know her father wants me to ask—he keeps hinting. Your mother and Clara are dropping little ideas and hints, as well."

"So?"

"But that would make you and I related. We would be brothers-in-law. I couldn't do that to you without at least consulting you first."

"I thought you were supposed to ask the girl first." Edward was making the most of an already comical situation.

"Damn, Edward. You know what I mean! It could ruin our working relationship."

"Why? Morgan's son works in the company. They seem to get along fine."

"You're right, they do. But you may have objections, because of things you know about me."

Edward dropped his glance to the tabletop. "You mean the drinking? I thought you just said it was under control."

"It is! It is! I swear it to you!" Geoff was instantly agitated. "But... you know me."

Edward smiled, "I do know you, Geoff, and so does Rebecca. We both love you. You are our friend, except now we will be related."

"Then it is all right with you?"

Edward laughed at him. "I've told you already, it doesn't matter what I think. Go ask the lady." He motioned toward the bar. "And now I think we do need a drink stronger than ale."

Geoff laughed in agreement. Before long, the bartender brought two glasses of single malt Scots whiskey to the table. Edward raised his glass to Geoff and they downed the liquor.

"It's funny, though," Geoff remarked, loudly smashing his glass on the table, "that you mentioned Morgan and Jack Junior before."

"Why is that?" answered Edward, following through with his glass.

"Because even though they are father and son, and seem to get along really well at the office, Morgan had me keeping tabs on Jack for quite a while."

"You were spying on Morgan's son?" Edward gasped. It was true. There were spies everywhere.

Personal Journal Entry
August 21, 1899

Geoff!

I am happy for Geoff—I hope everything goes well with Rebecca's sister.

But he has told me things that cause me to suspect him once more.

He is my dearest, closest friend, but I pray that this friendship is not part of the chess game.

I would have been played as a fool!

Chapter 13
A New Century

Unlike the previous New Year's Eve, Edward and Rebecca did not go out for the evening to attend the Morgan and Company celebration; instead, they entertained guests and neighbors from the Dakota. Rebecca had taken on the familiar shape of a woman entering her third trimester, and her doctor estimated that she would have the baby either in late March or early April.

The nursery remained undecorated. Clara thought it was bad luck to fix up the nursery before the baby was born. Mrs. Stimson thought Rebecca was going to have a girl, because she was carrying the same way she had, and she only had girls. Mrs. Collier thought Rebecca was going to have a boy, as she was suffering from lower back pain, just like she had when she was carrying Edward. Mrs. Collier never mentioned to Rebecca that Edward was the only child of five to have survived childbirth. Edward didn't mention this fact to his wife, either.

Edward returned to work at Morgan and Company on Tuesday, January 2. Almost immediately, Morgan sent for him.

"Edward, my boy, good to see you. How was your holiday?"

"Happy New Year to you, Mr. Morgan. My holiday went very well. And yours?"

"The usual gala at the Waldorf." But Morgan wasn't interested in telling Edward about his New Year's. "How is that bride of yours?"

"She has been feeling better, thank you."

"Take good care of her." And that concluded the small talk. "Now we need to talk about your latest projects."

Morgan reviewed some of the assignments he already given to Edward, including the handling of the purchase of property for Andrew Carnegie. This, Edward reported, was already in its final stages, and building would commence shortly.

"Good," answered Morgan, "but my friend Carnegie has his hands full at the moment. There is a movement afoot that involves a bunch of radicals—anarchists—people who would like nothing more than to overthrow our form of government and set up a new one where chaos prevails." Edward knew what an anarchist was. Many confused them for socialists, but anarchists always had a flair for the violent. "Have you heard of that Goldman woman, Edward?"

Edward didn't recognize the name.

"She and the man she's involved with are plotting something with Carnegie's steel workers. They want to bring in a union. You know, except for when it applied to the government, or the Union Army, I never did like that word." Edward smiled at Morgan's use of humor. "Anyway, they are painting the picture that Carnegie, myself, and all the other leaders of industry are getting wealthy off the sweat of the lower classes."

Edward bravely replied, "Pardon me, sir, but she does have reason to make that claim. My observations in Newport certainly confirm that."

"I must agree with you there, Edward. We must be careful, though. Carnegie and I are trying to divest ourselves of our money, but there are others of our class that only want to use their money for more profit and for their own personal enjoyment. The anarchists don't see a difference. They would see us all murdered in our sleep."

But Morgan had other matters for Edward to consider.

First, he explained that the grand arena at Madison Square had become old and dangerous. He had seen to it that Stanford White had been named as architect for a replacement structure that would be built on the same site as the first Madison Square Garden. White had already finished the drawings. The façade was going to have a Moorish flair, complete with towers and minarets. In addition to the main arena, there would be a nightclub on the rooftop. White was so taken by the building's plans that he planned to create an apartment for himself in one of the towers.

Morgan went on to tell Edward that White had recently acquired a new "girl." Edward had squirmed a bit when Morgan mentioned this, but J. P. continued anyway. The new girl was a sixteen-year-old Gibson Girl by the name of Evelyn Nesbit. Morgan told Edward that he expected nothing but trouble from the relationship.

He then went on to say that he was working on a secret project with the Vanderbilts and their rebuild of Grand Central. He told Edward that he wasn't ready to bring him into the discussions, but that time was forthcoming. Edward wondered why he bothered to tell him anything at all about the matter.

He asked Edward if living in the seventies gave him an opportunity to take a ride up to Morningside Heights. Edward said he had been there several times since they moved to the Dakota. His principal reason for going uptown had been to see the new buildings of his alma mater, Columbia—now Columbia University. He mentioned that he had seen a new hospital, St. Luke's, being built. He also said that the Episcopal cathedral was at last under construction.

"Aha!" said Morgan. "This is the reason I asked you in the first place. I love St. George's, but it's about time we Episcopalians had our own cathedral. I am going to take a special interest in the building of that church, Edward. I may not live long enough to see it finished, but I want to see it progress quickly. I have already financed over five hundred thousand dollars for the building of the cathedral. Bishop Potter and I have been friends for a long time."

"It certainly seems like a worthwhile cause, sir."

"I think so, too. Tell me, did you explore any of the new construction. They started with the apse and the choir?"

"Yes, I believe so." Edward really wasn't too sure of what he had seen. "The architecture is a combination of Byzantine and Romanesque. It has been set back off Amsterdam Avenue by several hundred yards, so if they follow the traditional cathedral footprint of east to west, then the part they are working on right now is the apse and choir."

Morgan was impressed with Edward's knowledge of church buildings and architecture. "Very good, Edward! Now tell me, do you think it has a crypt?"

"A crypt? You mean a tomb for their bishops?"

"Exactly! All the European cathedrals have crypts. St. Patrick's has a crypt. Does the new cathedral have a crypt?"

"I am not sure, sir. I know they excavated quite a bit for the foundation. Why, sir?"

But Edward suspected why Morgan had asked the question.

"It's nothing, Edward. I have a fascination with the macabre."

Now Morgan turned his attention to a serious project that he had become involved in. Morgan had personally underwritten Thomas Edison and his electrical experiments. When he had done this, a young electrical engineer named Nikola Tesla had been working for Edison. But the two men had some disagreements on several key theories, most importantly a debate over the choice of direct current (DC) or alternating current (AC) as a means of powering their lighting. Edison favored DC, which had more power, but could not run long distances, and was also more dangerous. Tesla wanted to use AC, which could send electrical current over large areas at the same time. Tesla left the Edison Company and struck out on his own, eventually coming to Morgan for financial help. Morgan arranged a loan of one hundred fifty thousand dollars and personally contributed 51 percent of the money. Tesla's plan was to find a new way of generating electrical power that was safe and cheap.

Morgan knew this was a conflict of interests on his part. That was where Edward would come in.

"Tesla is building a massive electrical tower on Long Island, at a place called Wardenclyffe. He plans to take on both Edison and Marconi at the same time. He plans to prove that electrical currents can be transmitted as far as Europe."

"That's impossible!" answered Edward.

"That's what I thought, too, but the man is some sort of mad scientist. He's far more eccentric than Edison. At the time I thought he was a good investment. I even had Stan White design the building at Wardenclyffe for him. He was able to create wireless electric light in his lab in Colorado. He lit up a whole town from miles away."

"What's so bad about that?"

"It costs almost nothing! Where is the profit in that? I get the man one hundred and fifty thousand dollars and he comes up with a generating system that creates cheap energy. I asked him, 'Where's the meter?'"

Thus began one of Edward's less savory projects—the ruining of Nikola Tesla by J. P. Morgan.

Finally, Morgan gave Edward a pleasant project to begin work on—one that brought him back to their beginnings together.

Homer Norris had been organist and choir director at St. George's Episcopal Church on Stuyvesant Square for a number of years. Morgan was chief warden of the church vestry, and he appreciated Norris's playing a great deal. He also had enjoyed listening to some of the songs and sacred music Norris had composed over the years. Morgan had supported Harry Burleigh's career, which was still an ongoing project, but now he was going to help Homer Norris.

Edward was to arrange a meeting together with Norris at the musician's studio, which was located on East 16th Street, just a bit down from where Edward grew up, and where his parents and Geoff still lived.

The meeting with Morgan over, Edward went back to his office to dash off a note to Norris. He asked if Morgan and he could meet with him on Friday, January 5, at his studio. He sent the note by messenger, telling the boy to check first at his studio, and then at the church. It was far more likely that he would be at the studio because it was January and the church was not heated during the week.

The messenger boy returned within the hour, saying that Norris said he would be happy to meet them on Friday. He suggested one p.m.

Personal Journal Entry
January 5, 1900

Morgan has now asked me to investigate whether or not the new cathedral will have a crypt.

A crypt? Why would he care about something like that?

Then he asked me to oversee Nikola Tesla. I understand that Morgan feels he did not invest his money in a way that would have earned him a big return, but how could he back both Edison and Tesla, who are bitter competitors?

And then there is the Wardenclyffe tower—another design by Stanford White. That in itself makes me wonder.

Why does every other Morgan project have to involve Stanford White?

He may have his heart with Edison, but has Tesla afforded him other opportunities?

I am very conflicted.

When Friday arrived, Morgan and Edward left the office at twelve thirty and took a carriage to East 16th Street. Morgan kept his muffler unusually high around his face to hide who he was, and to protect the sensitive tissues of his nose. Upon their arrival, Homer Norris greeted them at the door and invited them inside. He was a nervous, tightly wound fellow, and found it difficult to make eye contact with Morgan, or even with Edward. He prepared some tea for his guests. His studio was nicely appointed; there was a grand piano and a harmonium. There was also a nice sofa and some comfortable chairs. A large fire blazed in the fireplace.

Edward was given the responsibility of beginning the meeting. "Mr. Norris, Mr. Morgan has long held great respect for your musicianship and your compositional abilities." And then he quickly added, "And so have I."

Norris replied, "Thank you, Mr. Morgan. Thank you, too, Mr. Collier...uh, Edward."

Edward continued. "Mr. Morgan is aware that this area of New York is getting more and more crowded. There is noise in the street almost twenty-four hours a day. He wonders how it is that you can concentrate on the writing of musical ideas with such a din about you?"

Norris looked at Morgan. "It is sometimes very difficult, Mr. Morgan. I try to write a song that imitates the call of the birds, and all I hear outside my window are shouts and bicycle horns."

Edward then added, "That is precisely why we are here today, Mr. Norris. Mr. Morgan feels that you would be far more prolific with your composition if you had a place to retreat to outside the city."

Homer's eyebrows rose to his hairline. "What do you mean?"

"Mr. Morgan has purchased a tract of land for you, and on that tract would like to build a bungalow for you to visit whenever you feel the need to escape the city."

Norris collapsed back in his chair. He had never expected to hear these words.

Morgan spoke at last. "Homer, I have acquired more than two hundred acres of land northwest of the city in Orange County. I purchased the land from the Harriman estate. When I walked the property, I immediately thought of you. The property overlooks the largest lake in the area, the Indians used to call it Long Pond. There is a high stone abutment that rises about thirty feet above the water. I think that would be the perfect place for the bungalow."

Norris looked like he was in a state of shock. "I...I...don't know what to say."

Edward answered, "Just say that you accept Mr. Morgan's gift."

"Yes, oh yes," he said, excitement showing in his eyes. "Can I go to see the property?"

Edward was prepared for the question. "Absolutely! I will arrange to take you there. I have yet to see this place myself. We will go in the spring, after the snow has melted."

Norris agreed, and then asked, "May I have some ability to design the way the house will look?"

Morgan hadn't realized that Norris also had architecture as one of his talents. "Of course you may. I want you to be happy there."

Edward noticed there were tears in Norris's eyes.

Chapter 14
The Waiting Ends

Edward Thomas Collier, Jr., was born at 5:53 a.m. on the morning of April 13, 1900. He was delivered in his parents' bed in the Dakota by a midwife. All went very smoothly, and mother and baby were in excellent health.

Edward spent the rest of April 13 handing out cigars around the Dakota. He continued this tradition the next day at the office, as well. Morgan insisted that Edward immediately set up a trust fund for little Eddie in the bank, and then dashed off a check for five thousand dollars to begin the fund.

Edward spent lunchtime at his parents' house, where he informed them that they were grandparents. Geoff was also in attendance. Edward asked Geoff to be the baby's godfather. Geoff happily accepted.

Personal Journal Entry
April 13, 1900

I am a father!

This day is the happiest day of my life—eclipsed only by my own wedding day.

Do all new fathers feel this way? I suppose that all do not, for there are many abandoned children—orphans of society—that are living on the streets of New York.

Children need nurturing. Children need healthy food. Children need to be educated. What was it that Dickens said in "A Christmas Carol"?

> This boy is Ignorance. This girl is Want. Beware them both, and all of their degree, but most of all beware this boy, for on his brow I see that written which is Doom, unless the writing be erased.

I have already pledged that my son will not suffer from these two social maladies. I have the hope that I will be in a position to ensure that other children will not suffer from these maladies also.

⚜

Geoff had indeed asked Margaret Stimson to marry him, and she had accepted. They were to marry almost a year to the day after Edward and Rebecca had married—on May 26. The Stimsons moved into the Dakota for almost a month so that Rebecca's mother could help with the baby. Edward didn't mind the help; besides, he had a great deal of work at the office, and this quelled the feeling of guilt for not being home.

All in all, the dawn of the new century had proven very happy for the Colliers and the Atwaters.

It was mid-June by the time the excursion to Homer Norris's retreat property could be arranged. It had been another harsh winter, and it had been reported that the snows had been particularly deep north of the city and in the higher elevations. But June was perfect for a hike through the woods, and so, on Friday, the ninth of June, Norris and Edward started on their journey. They needed to first get to the New Jersey side of the Hudson River, and chose to take the Canal Street Ferry in order to do this. The ferry allowed them to connect with an Erie Railroad line, which began in Jersey City and then snaked its way through various small hamlets in New Jersey—Montclair, Little Falls, Pompton Plains, Midvale—ending at the New Jersey/New York border at Sterling Forest.

The Sterling Forest station was perched atop the shore of a large and beautiful lake. Was this the Long Pond Morgan had mentioned? There was a steam-powered ferryboat tied to a dock just below the train station. Edward wasn't exactly sure which way he needed to go, so he asked a gentleman who looked like he was boarding the ferry if he knew of the Harriman estate. The man replied that Edward didn't need the ferry for the Harriman estate, that it was only a mile or so north on the same shore. He pointed them to a livery stable, where Edward could rent a carriage.

Edward already knew about the livery stable. Morgan had mentioned it to him, personally. He knew that he was close to being in the state of New York, but wasn't sure where that dividing line occurred. One gentleman pointed and said, "Stand here and you are in New Jersey. Take a step to the right and you are in New York." This meant that the hamlet of Sterling Forest was divided down the middle between the two states.

Edward crossed a dirt road to the livery stable. He inquired about hiring a carriage from the owner, a Mr. McNabb, who, when he asked Edward where he intended to go, politely explained that he would be better served by a draft horse and a wagon. He then introduced Edward to his thirteen-year-old son, Tim, who was available to act as a guide.

Tim was, to Edward's imagination, a modern Tom Sawyer type. He stood about five foot six inches tall and looked like he was encrusted with dirt. Edward guessed that the boy might be a very handsome young man, but it was almost impossible to tell through the grime. He had very long blond hair, which was so dirty that it was matted to his head. Tim had a pair of piercing blue eyes and an abundance of freckles on his face. He wore no shoes, and his pants were shredded from the shin down. His shirttail was mostly hanging out the back of his trousers, which were held in place by only one suspender. He even had a piece of straw in his mouth. But the boy was very quick-witted, and had a personality that reminded Edward a great deal of Geoff's.

Sterling Forest looked about as far away from civilization as a man could get, and still be back in New York by nightfall.

The largest horse Edward had ever seen was hitched to the wagon, and Norris, Edward, and Tim climbed onto the bench seat. Tim grabbed the reins, which Edward appreciated more than he wanted to let on. They pulled out of the livery stable and headed to the right just as the steamer pulled away from the dock. Edward could see that the boat was named the *Montclair.*

Edward spoke to their guide. "So, Tim, do you know this area very well?"

"I lived here all my life, mister. I know every rock." Tim seemed proud of his knowledge.

"What is the road that we are on now?"

"This here is the East Shore Road. It's not much to talk about, but it will get you there."

Norris was confused. "Get you where, exactly?"

Tim answered, "Any place you want to go, mister." And that was that.

The road climbed a bit for a hundred yards or so, and it looked like they were leaving the lake off to their left and heading into the woods. The dirt road was filled with holes that had been made from ice freezing, then thawing, then freezing again. The ride was bumpy and hard on their bottoms. Edward could see that they had now risen to an elevation about forty feet higher than the shore.

Edward wanted to know more about the area, since Morgan had told him really very little. "So, that lake is called Long Pond." It was more of a question than a statement, but he was hoping that it would initiate a response from their young guide.

"Long Pond? Mister, it hasn't been called that since before I was born. Heck, before anyone alive was born. Even you, mister," he said to Norris.

Suddenly Edward thought he was in the wrong place. "But I thought—"

"That was what the Indians called it. There haven't been Indians around here since before the Revolutionary War." Whether or not Tim was knowledgeable of American history or was just spouting local legend, the fact remained that the area had been home to the Long Pond Iron Works—a series of furnaces and mills run by a German colonist named Peter Hasenclever. Hasenclever imported more than five hundred European laborers to work the sites, along with their families. They used water power from the nearby Long Pond River. When the river didn't deliver enough force, Hasenclever built at dam where the river exits the Long Pond itself. This gave the ironworks better water power, but also raised and enlarged the lake. The New Jersey end of the present lake, especially in a little community known as Awosting, had been mostly farmland controlled by Hasenclever. The dam flooded this plain to a depth of about twelve to fifteen feet. The original lake also spread out wider and longer, but the dam had the greatest effect on the overall depth of the northern half of the lake. Tim had really no idea how the beautiful lake that he lived at came to be, but he did know what it was called. "Now we call it Greenwood Lake."

Edward thought the name fit very well. The lake was surrounded by hillsides on both shores, and all manner of pine, oak, and maple covered the hills right down to the shore.

Tim called out, "Look down there, through those trees. Do you see that big building there?" It was a large rectangular wooden building several hundred yards away, and near the shore. "That there is the new ice house. We had a really good winter for ice this year, we did. I worked many an hour out on the lake, cutting blocks of ice." Tim was very proud of his vocation, it seemed.

"And what about school? Do you go to school?" Edward inquired.

"Nah! Ma teaches me what she can at home. Don't need any more'n that."

Edward then noticed that they were once again climbing. The road was banking to the left and heading up steeply at the same time. He observed to Tim, "This horse doesn't seem to care that we are taking a steep hill. He keeps clopping at the same speed."

To which Tim replied, "You are going to thank him for his strength in just a few minutes, mister. Ole Ned is the best horse in these parts."

Edward could no longer see the lake. They must now have been over a hundred feet above the level of the water. But just then Tim pulled Ole Ned to the left, and the horse pulled the wagon into another road that had been roughly cut through the trees. A small wooden sign that had been tacked to a tree announced that they had just turned onto Shore Avenue—which Edward found amusing, as the road was about as opposite as one could imagine from any avenue in New York City. Edward could feel that they were descending, albeit very slowly; they were also heading back in the general direction of the water. After a few hundred yards, Tim called out, "This is when the trip gets pretty exciting."

And it did just that. Suddenly they were perched at the top of a steep grade. There were rock formations on their right side and a sheer cliff on their left. Edward heard Tim call out, "Whoa, slow, Ned," and the horse continued his measured gait, now holding back the weight of the wagon and three riders. They continued downhill for almost three hundred yards, and when they reached the bottom they were right at the lakeshore. Ned then pulled the wagon to the right.

The vista to their left was of an inlet—a cove. Several hundred yards from where they were, across the expanse of water, stood a jetty—a rock-faced outcropping. As the wagon continued north on Shore Avenue, the view beyond the outcropping opened to reveal a great deal of the southern half of the lake. The western shore seemed a good mile away. They could not see how long the northern end of the lake was, for the trees blocked their view.

Another few hundred yards and the journey was at an end. The trio hopped down from the wagon. Tim waved them toward the direction of the lake, but somehow, over the course of the last few moments of travel, they had again climbed in elevation. They were standing on an immense outcropping of rock about thirty feet above the water.

"This is it, Homer!" Edward exclaimed. "This is where Mr. Morgan wants you to place your cottage."

"It is magnificent," replied Homer, struggling to hold back his emotions.

"It's somethin', isn't it?" added Tim. "The lake is so deep here that you can jump into it right offa these rocks."

"No!" cried Homer. He didn't swim a stroke. It was a frightening prospect to him. Edward could swim, but a jump from that height was not only out of the question—it was insanity!

"Why not? I do it all the time." The men looked at him skeptically. "You don't believe me? Well, you come back in July when the water's a tad warmer and I'll show you. I'll jump in buck naked right from this ledge."

"How will you get back up? The rock face is pretty sheer!" Edward still was skeptical of Tim's prowess as a cliff diver.

"See down there?" He pointed down, out, and to the right. "Mister, you have to walk out as far as me to see what I'm talkin' about." Norris was not prepared to budge an inch closer to the edge of the cliff, so Tim turned to Edward. "There's a path right there, and when you climb it, it leads you back around, until you get back here again. You have to be careful, though. There's lots of poison ivy growing along that path."

Homer had started surveying the rest of the property. They could see about two acres of land clearly, but Morgan had said that the estate was over two hundred acres. Norris also noticed there were many large fieldstones lying around the property. "I think the house should be built incorporating the natural fieldstones of the area. Make it look like it is springing out of the cliff."

"That's a good idea, Homer. I'll bet Mr. Morgan would agree."

"I even have a name for the cottage," he said. "I will call it the Boulders."

"Very original," said Edward. "What do you think, Tim?"

"I like it," he replied enthusiastically. "But mister, after you've built your house here, can I still come over and jump from the rocks?"

"You certainly may, young man."

Edward was mindful of the time. "Homer, we have to leave now if we expect to get back to the depot to catch the last train back to Jersey City today."

They turned to get back into the wagon. Suddenly, a large black-snake, indigenous to the area, slithered across the ground in front of them, its tail brushing over Norris's shoes. Norris blanched, totally rattled by the experience. "Snakes," he puffed. "If there's one thing I hate, it's snakes. Serpents! Creatures of Satan!"

"It was only a blacksnake, mister," offered their guide, Tim. "They won't harm you, and they ain't poisonous, either. What you really have to worry about are the copperheads, or sometimes a rattler."

"Rattlesnakes?" Edward thought they were only in the Wild West.

"Oh, yeah. They come down from the rocks when it gets dry during the summer."

This did nothing for Homer Norris, who was still shaking from his encounter with the blacksnake.

They mounted the wagon and put their trust in Ole Ned again.

Edward thought of another very curious question for Tim. "Tell me, Tim, there is absolutely nothing on Shore Avenue. We haven't passed a single house, or a dock, or a boat tied up. The place looks completely uninhabited. Why is this road here? Who would build a road to nowhere?"

Tim looked at Edward very quizzically and asked, "You mean you don't know, mister?"

Edward wondered why Tim's tone meant that he should know. "No, I don't know, Tim. Tell me."

Tim smiled knowingly and then said, "It was put in quite a few years ago—before I was born. I heard tell it was paid for by the richest man in the world. He came up here to see the property that he had just purchased. You men look rich, judging from your clothes, so I figured you must know him."

Yes, Edward thought, *we know him!*

Personal Journal Entry
June 22, 1900

I have met a most interesting young man, Master Timothy McNabb. He is about as close to a feral child as I have ever seen, and yet he is an absolute delight to know.

I have been bringing Geoff up-to-date with my latest suspicions about Morgan. I know now that I am in this position because Morgan doesn't want to involve Jack Jr.

Every project that we, Geoff and I, are assigned to has something secretive buried or hidden somewhere on the property. Geoff knew about the vault at Rosecliff, of course, because he saw it. I hadn't told him until yesterday about the box stuck in my dumbwaiter shaft, about

Morgan's obsession with crypts, or my feeling that something similar will end up somewhere in the Carnegie mansion.

I also don't understand Morgan's patronage of Stanford White. The man is oily and despicable. Why does Morgan keep handing him work? I don't know if I will ever understand it.

Chapter 15
A Third Time

J. P. Morgan liked Theodore Roosevelt. He was a man after his own heart, especially because he was a tough, outspoken New Yorker—just like he was. But although Morgan agreed with Roosevelt, at least in principle, on many points, there were also just as many ideas that Roosevelt spoke about that Morgan could not abide.

Both men were Republicans, and on that point alone Morgan should have felt that he had an ally, but Roosevelt was known to speak out against trusts and monopolies. Even though he believed in big business as the key to the American economy, he also felt there should be strong regulations applied to it.

Roosevelt was an outdoorsman, a person who truly believed in living "the strenuous life." Morgan didn't have a problem with this personal philosophy, but he didn't like the fact that TR was listening to do-gooders like John Muir. Morgan felt that the country's natural resources were there to be used and exploited. Muir, and Roosevelt, felt that certain natural wonders needed to be preserved. But Morgan loved Roosevelt's dash. He thought his charge up San Juan Hill had been nothing but a massive publicity stunt, but it had galvanized the people of this country. It had put the U.S. on the world stage by the end of the Spanish-American War.

One of the chief by-products of the lopsided American victory in the war had been possession of new territories that had been ceded to the U.S. by Spain, including Guam, the Philippines, Puerto Rico, and a strip of land in Panama. Of this last possession Roosevelt was adamant. In order for the United States to become a global player, the country needed to be able to get its navy and marines from the Atlantic to the Pacific, and back again, without having to travel thousands of miles out of the way around the tip of South America. A canal was to be built in the Isthmus of Panama. The project would take years, American lives, and a tremendous amount of ingenuity, but eventually the continent would have a shortcut to the opposite shore. Morgan wholeheartedly agreed with this project.

The one issue that the two men most agreed upon was the national economy. Both agreed that the United States currency should be based upon the gold standard—that the Treasury should have a reserve of gold ingots set aside that would buoy the currency and keep its worth. Morgan had already proven his point during the Panic of 1893. He had personally arranged for a loan of gold from several European nations. Even though Democrat Grover Cleveland had supported the measure, he met with opposition from fellow Democrat William Jennings Bryant, and William McKinley was able to capture the White House.

He also knew that the Republicans had decided to silence the outspoken Roosevelt by placing him in the one position where he would fall out of the public eye—the vice presidency of the United States.

All this changed in September 1901.

William McKinley was attending the Pan-American Exposition in Buffalo, New York, in early September. On September 6, the president was entering the Temple of Music at the exposition. He was approached by a man wearing a bandage over his right hand. McKinley reached out to shake the injured man's hand, but the man shot him twice at close range. He had concealed a pistol under the bandage. The man, Leon Czolgosz, was an avowed anarchist. He was immediately beaten to the ground and then taken off to jail. When interviewed, he claimed that he was inspired by fellow anarchist, Emma Goldman. Goldman was arrested in connection with the attempted assassination of the president, for McKinley had not died from his wounds. Unfortunately, the bullet that lodged itself inside McKinley's body was never found by doctors, even though the newly invented X-ray machine was on display at the exposition. Over the course of the next few days, McKinley's health first improved, but then suddenly took a turn for the worse, as his body succumbed to infection and gangrene. The president died on September 14. He became the third president of the United States to die from an assassin's bullet.

Theodore Roosevelt had been vacationing in the Adirondacks when he was informed that the president had died. He was immediately administered the oath of office.

Homer Norris was designing his home at Greenwood Lake. His plans called for the home to rise out of the top of the rock bluff in a way that the ground floor patio seemed to almost cantilever over the cliff. There would be three bedrooms on the ground floor, plus the living room and kitchen, as well as a large bathroom complete with a sunken bathtub—a luxury item in those days. The patio would be accessed through French doors off the living room.

It was on the second floor, however, that Norris made the most dramatic design. The entire floor would have a cathedral ceiling, up to a height of over twenty feet. An immense fieldstone fireplace would rise from floor to ceiling on the south wall. The décor of the room otherwise was kept to hardwood surfaces—no carpeting on the floor, and wood paneling on the walls. This was done to create a music performance area, allowing the hard surfaces and high ceiling to reflect sound. To the right of the fireplace, a set of French doors led to an observation deck which was to be built directly over the patio. From this deck a person could be almost fifty feet above the lake surface.

To the rear of the room was a staircase that led up to a loft. Norris planned to install a small pipe organ in the loft. He planned to purchase a grand piano for the main performance area. Underneath the loft was a small closet that he planned to outfit as a movie projection booth. To the left of the entrance to the great room would be a set of French doors leading to a guest bedroom. Behind that room was another bathroom and the servant's quarters.

For some unknown reason, it took Homer Norris almost three years to complete his design, even though Morgan kept asking him to finish it. Norris complained of chronic illnesses, his schedule at St. George's, personal problems, and the like as reasons for the delay. There was however, one secret reason that kept a vigil in Norris's mind and prevented him from finalizing his plans for the house.

Morgan was a busy man, and even though he was magnanimous toward Norris, he did not feel inclined to personally hound him on the matter. Morgan placed the project on the back burner. Construction on the house would begin in 1909.

Power corrupts.

This adage has proven true throughout centuries of recorded history. Unbridled power has brought down governments, dethroned kings, defrocked the clergy, and thrown the wealthy and influential in jail.

Power can manifest itself in many ways; through position or title, wealth, fame, or even talent.

Stanford White was a powerful man. He had talent—he was one of the most sought-after architects in the country. Because of the demand for his work, he had also acquired wealth—not the kind of wealth that Morgan, Carnegie, or the Vanderbilts had, but he certainly could live a more than comfortable life.

Evelyn Nesbit was born in western Pennsylvania, in a small town near Pittsburgh, in 1884. Her family lived in virtually impoverished conditions. As she reached adolescence, she blossomed into a beautiful young girl and began a career as an artist's model. Evelyn and her mother moved to New York City in 1901. She began modeling in earnest in New York, finding work with some of the more famous photographers in the city. Her photos caught the attention of Charles Dana Gibson, an artist whose collection of hand-drawn young beauties were simply called Gibson Girls.

Gibson drew a famous portrait using Evelyn, who sat in profile, her flowing red hair shaped something like a question mark, and entitled the work "The Eternal Question." Evelyn became famous. She soon was earning in excess of two hundred dollars per day as a model.

She also attracted the attention of Stanford White, who had an eye for very young women.

At first, the relationship did not really seem more than platonic. Evelyn's mother liked White; this was helped along when White used his influence to get Evelyn's brother, Howard, placed in a prominent military school. When her mother decided to take a trip out of town, she had so much trust in White that she placed Evelyn in his care.

The new and improved second version of the Madison Square Garden had opened. The rooftop cabaret became a hot spot for well-heeled New Yorkers. Stanford White kept an office in one of the Moorish towers of the building. His studio and apartment were located on West 24th Street, above the FOA Schwarz toy store. One of the rooms in his apartment was nicknamed "the mirror room." It had mirrors on the walls and ceilings, a green velvet couch, and a red velvet swing suspended from the ceiling.

White brought Nesbit to the mirror room, got her drunk on champagne, and then deflowered her.

Geoffrey and Margaret Atwater were frequent dinner guests at the Colliers' apartment at the Dakota on West 72nd Street. Geoff had married Margaret, Rebecca's younger sister, at St. George's Episcopal Church on May 26. Geoff had spent some time living with Thomas and Anne Collier, which had made a tremendous difference in how he viewed his lifestyle. Even though they could not afford to live in the luxurious manner of Edward and Rebecca, they were able to purchase a new brownstone on East 61st Street, between Park and Lexington Avenues. Geoff was earning a very good salary, and Morgan's wedding present to the couple had provided the down payment, along with financing through the company bank. The couple went to the Berkshires for their honeymoon, which was a conservative three weeks in length. Margaret was pregnant with their first child by the time the first snow fell in November.

The two couples now lived, once again, within reasonably close proximity of each other. About ten city blocks separated them, north to south, with Central Park and a few avenues in between. It would have seemed a much greater distance if the park were not designed after the great European city parks, with roadways crisscrossing the girth of the park every so often, and fewer, but longer, carriage routes taking travelers north and south. Once Eddie was walking, his parents would take him to the park on Sundays so that he could pet the sheep in the meadow or see the wild animals in the zoo. The park designers had planned for boaters on the lake, and had also constructed an ice-skating rink and a band shell. Central Park had become an oasis for those living in the middle of the island.

J. P. Morgan was spending a great deal of his time on the cathedral project. He had used his influence, and his money, to make sure the cathedral was built in accordance with methods practiced when the great cathedrals of Europe were built in the Middle Ages.

Morgan particularly disliked the way that St. Patrick's Cathedral was designed and built. The cathedral had gone up quickly, and the building lasted only from 1858 to 1879. Even though built in the Gothic style, was constructed with the most modern techniques available to New York construction companies in the middle of the nineteenth century. Structural steel, not flying buttresses, had been used to carry the height of the walls and the weight of the roof.

It was the flying buttress that had allowed the cathedral builders of the Middle Ages to build their walls higher. The previous design, Romanesque, was based upon having thick walls and small rounded windows. It was discovered early on that, even though the medieval mindset was to build the church closer to God, every time this was attempted the walls would collapse into the middle of the nave. The solution was to lessen the weight of the wall by pulling it to the outside with an externally built buttress. With the weight off the walls, they could now be built taller, and the windows enlarged to let in more light. The added strength of the walls also supported the vaulted ceiling.

Morgan wished to see the new Episcopal cathedral built in the manner of the great Gothic cathedrals of Europe, but in a grander style. The original plan called for a Byzantine-Romanesque style. The architects for the project were the firm of Heins and Lafarge. Morgan started lobbying for Stanford White's firm, but this choice was rejected by committee. Morgan was particularly adamant about the style of architecture, and was an outspoken opponent to the Romanesque style, even after the building had started.

The cathedral footprint was to be traditional in that it would be in the shape of a cross. The top section of the cross, the apse, was completed first. The apse contained the altar and choir areas at the front of the church, plus there was an array of chapels that fanned out behind the high altar area. By 1902, most of the work in the building of the Romanesque apse had been completed.

The next area to tackle was, in cathedral geography, the crossing. The crossing was the section of the building that contained the transept, or crosspiece. The north and south transepts would be built last, along with the spire, but the crossing area in the middle of the building would have to be built in order to connect the apse to the nave. Heins and Lafarge had designed a massive spire that would sit astride the center of the building. Until it was time to add this finishing touch to the cathedral, a tiled dome would be constructed temporarily. Rafael Guastavino was brought in to work on the dome.

It seemed that, despite Morgan's efforts to thwart the design, the Heins and Lafarge Romanesque cathedral was moving forward. But in a sudden twist of fate, Heins passed away. A new architect had to be found.

Morgan redoubled his pressure on the vestry. He withdrew his earlier suggestions and began to push for a young Boston architect, Ralph Adam Cram. Cram specialized in designing in the Gothic style. The committee accepted the new architect, and the design of the cathedral was altered. The existing work was not removed, but rather adapted into the overall design.

Most importantly, it was decided that the nave would be built under the rules of the Middle Ages; that is to say, stone upon stone rather than by using structural steel. Morgan had gotten his way.

Chapter 16
Exploring the Wilderness of New Jersey

The Homer Norris house was Edward's assigned project, and even though Morgan had removed himself from the building process, pending Norris's plans, Edward felt compelled to continue the planning process in the event that Norris finally made a decision. Edward decided to send Geoff to the construction site, as his representative, in the late spring of 1904.

Edward spent some time with Geoff, explaining the route he should use in order to get to the construction site. He told him that the last stop on the train route was at Sterling Forest, and that he should see if young Tim was still available as a guide—even though a few years had passed since the boy had first taken them to the estate. Tim would probably be fifteen or sixteen, so he might still be in the area.

But Geoff had other plans.

Geoff was far more adventurous than Edward. Edward liked to plan out his every move, whereas Geoff liked to see where the road would lead him. As much as he respected Edward, he wanted to find his own way through the western woods of New Jersey. He also wanted to start making a larger mark for himself with the company.

Geoff had researched the northern part of New Jersey prior to asking for the trip to Greenwood Lake. He had discovered that the northern counties of Morris, Passaic, and Sussex were dotted with mines. Many of the mines were iron mines, but there were also zinc and copper mines. Morgan might be interested in these mines, and if not Morgan, then possibly Carnegie, or the United States Steel Corporation. He told Edward that he would be out of the office for several days, and that he would look in on the Norris house site on the same trip.

The trip began in a similar manner. Geoff took the ferry to Jersey City. He then boarded a train to Paterson, and took a Susquehanna line train north from there. The train chugged through some picturesque landscape, but traveled through little hamlets once out of the Paterson area. He found that some were named for the national origin of their settlers: New Holland, New Russia, and New Sweden. The train stopped in a whistle stop in New Sweden called, fairly enough, Stockholm. The locals referred to the area as simply Snufftown.

Geoff walked from the station until he found the Stockholm to Vernon Turnpike. He walked north on this dirt road, passing by a Methodist-Episcopal church on the right. He then reached his destination for the day, the Snufftown Hotel. The hotel was a wooden three-story structure built in the Victorian style. A fieldstone wall encircled the property. There was a large wraparound porch at ground level.

Geoff walked up three steps to get onto the porch and then entered through the door to the lobby. He had stayed in much fancier accommodations in his career, but the owners were friendly and eager to please. He arranged to rent a horse and carriage from the livery across the road for the next day, and then went to his room. His room was very simple but comfortable. He wasn't as put out as his friend Edward would have been over the fact that there was only one bathroom, and it was outside. He enjoyed a fine meal in the restaurant, and spent the evening in the tavern—never drinking anything harder than ale.

He rose early the next morning, ate breakfast, and then checked out of the hotel. He walked across the road to the livery and made arrangements for his horse and carriage. He had a map of the area, but it was not drawn to scale and looked full of inaccuracies. He asked the owner of the shop for directions. He also made arrangements with the proprietor to keep his property for the next few days, as he had many miles to cover. The owner knew the entire area and gave Geoff suggestions as to where he could rest the horse, or stable it for the night. By eight a.m., Geoff was heading north on the road. It was rough, full of ruts, and was constantly meandering through the dense forest. He saw fox, deer, wild turkeys, and a black bear.

He had gone almost three miles when he came upon a farmhouse. The livery man had mentioned this house as a landmark, so Geoff felt he was making progress. He had been told that this had been the home of Captain John Seward, a hero of the American Revolution.

Captain Seward had been a crusty patriot—in charge of the local militia in that area. The border with the colony of New York was only a few miles to the north, and New York was filled with loyalist Tories. There was talk that they wanted the captain dead. One fine day, the captain was riding his horse north on the turnpike. He approached a large outcropping of rock that had forced the road to turn to the left to avoid it. Legend has it that a Tory spy had hidden behind the rock, waiting to ambush the captain when he rode by. Evidently the man lost his nerve and ran away and the captain survived. The rock was thereafter nicknamed Tory Rock and the captain's grandson, William Seward, would become Abraham Lincoln's secretary of state, survive assassination on the same night that John Wilkes Booth killed Lincoln, and, most famously, go on to purchase the Alaskan Territory in a move that was called, at the time, Seward's Folly.

Geoff pulled the carriage to the left to avoid the famous Tory Rock, and continued his bumpy ride due north. After another few hard miles, he began his descent into a valley floor. The turnpike now rode along the face of a mountain so that Geoff had a perfect view of the valley below. He could see a small town at the bottom of the hill. He could also see farms and pastures. The view was idyllic.

His descent down the mountain began as a very gradual, easy one, but the grade of the road increased as his progressed. The last mile was extremely steep, and Geoff was worried about his ability to control a strange horse in these conditions. Another dirt road intersected on his right, which gave Geoff a small laugh, despite his caution. Someone had hung a rough-hewn board on a tree by the intersection, announcing that the name of that road was Breakneck Road. Geoff looked over his shoulder and back up from where the road came and noticed that it was even steeper than the road he was on.

He had made it to the valley floor. He passed a small mill on the right. It had taken him almost three hours of riding and bouncing to travel about ten miles. He continued straight on the road, bypassing the little town, until he found a tavern. He tied up the carriage and went inside to enjoy some lunch and to talk to some of the locals. His next stop would be over the border in the state of New York, and he wanted to check the road conditions, as well as how much time it would take to get to the next stop. He found that he was about halfway there.

After lunch, he continued on his way. His journey was almost all level with just a few minor rises in the roadway. The turnpike constantly turned right and then left. He passed through a little settlement, which Geoff didn't think could even constitute being called a town. After several more hours on board the carriage, his backside aching with pain, he entered the town of Warwick, New York. It was here that he was to bear right and take another road for what could amount to another day's journey. Geoff decided it would be better to quit for the day. There was an attractive Victorian inn, fittingly called the Warwick Inn, at the intersection of the roads. Geoff made this his stop for the day. An attendant took care of horse and carriage, and Geoff found the accommodations very comfortable—and the food and wine excellent.

Anxious to get an early start, Geoff arose early the next day. He ate a quick breakfast and asked for some rolls to take on the journey. He mounted the carriage and set out, heading now to the northeast. The road seemed better than the turnpike had been, and he was able to make better time. He passed through a little hamlet called Bellvale in less than an hour, but then the going got more difficult. Had he not been warned about the leg of the journey he was about to begin, he would have been dismayed. Horse, buggy, and rider were now ascending a steep hill. The ascent lasted for more than a mile before leveling off. Geoff pulled off the road when they reached the summit so that the horse could rest for a few minutes. Once again, the vistas from the top of the mountain were spectacular. Geoff took the time to water the horse, and to eat a roll or two.

After a break of almost a half hour, Geoff again set off, this time to descend the mountain they had just climbed. The road declined sharply almost immediately—a straight drop of a half mile before curving into a switchback. As the road curved around, changing their direction 180 degrees, Geoff caught site of their destination—Greenwood Lake. He could see the entire outline of the lake from this height. The road then continued straight to the bottom of the mountain. Geoff used the hand-brake on the carriage to help the horse hold the carriage safely back.

In another hour Geoff reached the little village of Greenwood Lake. The village was situated at the northernmost end of the lake. Geoff made several inquiries of the locals. He needed a place to stay, he needed a stable for the horse and the carriage, and he needed to find a way to get halfway down the lake. He was given information on all three of his needs, and within an hour's time he had hotel accommodations, a livery stable, and was on his way to meeting a young man that ran a steam-powered water taxi.

The young man's name was Sam Waters, oddly enough, and Geoff was quick to mention how similar their surnames were. Sam was a little younger than Geoff; he had just turned twenty. Sam was a local—born and raised on the lake. One of Geoff's first impressions of the young man was that he was very different from most of the other locals. He seemed to be restless; he looked like he wanted more than the situation he had been dealt. He had the spirit of an entrepreneur, however, and found most of his work during the summer months using his boat to ferry visitors from one arm of the lake to the other. One of his busiest days was Sunday. There was a small island just outside the east arm of the lake that held an Episcopal chapel. The chapel held regular services, and residents could take Sam's boat out to the island, hop out on its dock, and return the same way when the service had ended.

Geoff met Sam around two in the afternoon. The sun was out, bright and hot. He paid Sam fifty dollars for the use of his boat for the afternoon. The sum was more than Sam could make on the water in several weeks, so he jumped at the good fortune. They immediately set out on the water.

Sam was a good-natured young man. In many physical ways, Sam reminded Geoff of Edward. He was also impeccably thin—his clothes virtually hung on his frame. He also had black hair—but Sam's eyes were green, unlike Edward's blue eyes. He was a very handsome young man, and Geoff was convinced that, if he were living in New York City, he would undoubtedly be some sort of dandy—or rogue.

Sam was filled with curiosity about Geoff. Sam thought, here is a young gentleman, wearing nice, expensive clothes—when any fool knows that you don't dress this way to ride all day in a horse and carriage—and looks like he earns plenty of money. Who is this man? Who does he work for? He must be only a year or so older than I am.

Geoff smiled and listened to Sam's innocent small talk and constant questioning, being careful not to let too much out. Sam kept the launch moving southward along the west shore of the lake. Geoff hadn't mentioned precisely where they were headed—just that they were heading south. The boat was moving about ten miles per hour. Geoff was engaged in polite conversation with Sam, while keeping his eyes on the lake, looking as best he could for the landmarks that Edward had described for him. They passed an inlet that contained a small castle. Sam pointed out that the castle was not historic, as it had only been constructed there in 1903. A New York doctor owned the place. It was one of the few big houses on the lake.

Suddenly, in the middle of one of Sam's endless questions, Geoff spotted a landmark. "Turn left, Sam," he ordered.

"But that will take us across the lake, Geoff."

"Exactly!"

"Well then, let's hope that the lake doesn't get too choppy, because this vessel doesn't do very well in big waves."

Geoff paled a bit. "Shouldn't you have told me this before we left the dock?"

Sam replied very simply, "You didn't tell me we were going to the east shore. Otherwise, I would have crossed in front of Chapel Island. But don't you worry, there's not much wind, so it should go all right."

The lake was a mile wide at this point. As the boat changed directions, Geoff now became the recipient of the fumes from the engine. "Keep your bow aimed at that rock cliff rising from the lake," Geoff coughed.

"Yes, sir," Sam replied, with a salute.

It took almost fifteen minutes to cross the width of the lake. As they approached the cliff, it seemed to grow taller and taller. Geoff gave Sam instructions. "Stay about forty feet off the shore." He then took a look around. To the left was a small inlet. It looked like a beach, and that they would be able to bring the boat ashore, if they needed to do so. To the right was the cove that Edward had described. Further to the right Geoff saw the large outcropping of a peninsula of rock that Edward had also mentioned. He knew he was in the right spot. He turned on his seat to ask Sam to head down toward the cove, when his eye caught sight of something falling from the cliff in front of him.

It was a human body.

The body hit the water with a splash, and then resurfaced. By this time, the startled Geoff had turned to face the front of the boat again. "My God! Did you see that?"

"I didn't see a thing, Geoff. Your head was in my way."

"I think someone fell off the cliff into the lake!"

But just then, a voice called to them over the water. "Hey, out there!" It was a male voice.

The voice sounded...happy. It wasn't a cry for help. Geoff waved in the direction of the voice. He could see a head bobbing in the water, then hands, and then legs. The person was swimming toward the boat.

"Are you all right, sir?" Geoff called out, but there was no answer. The swimmer was quickly closing the distance to the launch. In just a few moments a wet hand grabbed the gunwale of the boat. A young man's face appeared, his blond hair plastered to his head.

"Hello," the young man began, "did I give you a start?"

"You did indeed. What happened?" Geoff never really thought the worst of a situation, but this was very strange.

"I jumped in, that's all. It's a hot day, so I jumped. It's a bit of a shock at first, 'cause the water's cold. Sorry if I startled you."

Geoff studied the young man. He looked to be about fifteen or so. "By any chance, is your name Tim?"

"Do I know you, mister? How'd you know my name?"

"Do you remember showing two gentlemen that land up there about two years ago?"

Tim looked away momentarily, and then back at Geoff. "Mr. Collier was one, and the older man was Mr. Norris. Mr. Norris is building the house, only right now there's no house even started, so I just come up to go swimming when it's hot. Do you work for Mr. Norris?"

"No," Geoff replied, gently, "I work with Mr. Collier. I am his assistant, Geoffrey Atwater."

Tim extended a dripping hand toward Geoff. "Pleased to meet you, Mr. Atwater."

"I was going to try to look you up so that you could show me the property, like you showed Mr. Collier two years ago, and look—you practically fell into the boat!"

Tim laughed. "If I can come aboard, I can show you where to put the boat, and then I can take you around."

Geoff nodded and extended his hand, but Tim didn't need his help. He grabbed hold of the gunwale with both hands, and then with one swift motion pulled himself into the launch. Tim would have been naked, were it not for a pair of bathing trunks that he wore—a stark contrast to the Edwardian suit that Geoff was wearing. Tim sat on a seat in the bow and let the lake water pour off his body. He started to shiver.

"Sam? I noticed you have a towel or two back there. May I have one, please?" Sam quickly found a towel and handed it to Geoff, who in turn gave it to Tim.

"Thank you, mister." Tim smiled a big, friendly smile.

Geoff remembered what Edward had said regarding Tim from their first meeting; that Tim had told them that he liked to dive from the top of the cliff, and that he would do it, as he said, "buck naked." He mentioned his recollection to Tim, with a laugh.

Tim laughed, too. "I did used to swim without these here trunks, but I'm almost sixteen, and that wouldn't be respectable anymore, if you know what I mean."

Geoff also laughed. "I surely do. I used to swim in the East River with a couple of my school friends, until one day the headmaster told me that it was time I put on proper swimming wear. I'll bet your mother told you that, as well."

Tim shook his head. "My mother died of cholera a year ago. It's just Dad and me now. I help out in the stable most days." When he finished, he turned to Sam and said, "Follow the shoreline going south. I can show you where to beach the boat."

Sam nodded and brought the launch around to the right. In a few hundred yards they were in the cove. Tim told Sam to keep following the shore and they would find a good place to stop, and they did. There was a small inlet at the back end of the cove where the water was shallow and somewhat brackish.

"Be careful to step directly onto the land. There's bloodsuckers in this area," Tim warned.

"Bloodsuckers?" Geoff asked.

"Leeches," replied Sam.

The warning was heeded. When they left the launch they were standing on Shore Avenue, the road that Morgan had constructed when he first purchased the property. They were at the bend at the bottom of the steep hill. Of course, Geoff and Sam were seeing this for the first time. They now headed north on Shore Avenue, Tim in the lead, walking barefoot, wearing swimming trunks and a towel wrapped around his shoulders.

"Tim?" Geoff asked. "Where are your clothes?"

"Don't worry, mister, they're right where we are goin'. I left them by the top of the cliff."

"Doesn't walking barefoot hurt the soles of your feet?"

"Nah! I do this all the time. My feet are like leather."

The young men would not have realized it, as they had only met the boy, but Tim had grown into young manhood. He was almost a full six feet tall and displayed large, muscular shoulders and arms.

After a few minutes of walking and pleasant conversation, the trio reached the property. Tim led them toward the edge of the cliff. Unlike Norris, both young men had no fear in peering out over the precipice, but both were impressed nevertheless that Tim had made the jump. Geoff slowly exhaled, taking in the beauty of the scenery, especially the view of the lake. He admired how different the area was from anything he had come to know living in New York. Here he could breathe deeply. For the moment, he was envious of Homer Norris.

"You like our lake, mister?" Tim had asked the question, but Sam was just as much a part of it.

"I absolutely love the lake, Tim, Sam. I wish I could live here forever."

"Really?" Sam asked incredulously. "I find that it is too small a place for me. I would love to live in a big city, like New York. Life doesn't move fast enough for me."

"And sometimes life moves too quickly for me, Sam," Geoff laughed. "What about you, Tim?"

"I don't know, mister. I ain't never been anywhere but here. This is all I know." Tim had just lost his permanent smile. It vanished from his face.

"You mean that you have never left northern New Jersey?" asked Geoff, trying to clarify his meaning, and the change in mood.

"No, I never have left the lake. My pa works seven days a week, and I help him most days. He has no reason to leave, so that means I stay here, too." He didn't sound very happy about it.

"But what about your education?"

"Boy," Tim laughed, "you and Mr. Collier both think the same." Geoff had to laugh at that comment.

But it was Sam who spoke up. "Mr. Atwater? Do you think I could make a living in a place like New York City? I have some education—no college, mind you—but I did finish the sixth grade. Are there jobs for men like me? You know, ambitious young men who are ready to make their mark in the world."

"I can't promise you anything, Sam, but I will say this. Almost every single day of the week a steamship arrives from some distant port in Europe. It stops at a little island in the Hudson River called Ellis Island. That island is right in the shadow of the Statue of Liberty."

"Hey! I heard about that statue!" interrupted Tim.

"It is a very powerful symbol of our country, Tim," Geoff gently replied. "These steamships are filled to overflowing with immigrants, people who have left the country where they were born—where they have lived their entire life—and then they picked up and came over here to America."

"Why did they do that, mister?" Tim asked.

"Many different reasons, I suppose. Many come because they are being persecuted for religious or social reasons. Some come because they have heard that America is filled with opportunity. Some come because their home is beset by famine or starvation—that's why my parents came over, because of the potato famine in Ireland. And many of them can't speak a word of English, but they work hard and they make their way. So—"

"So if they can do it, so can I," finished Sam proudly.

"That's right, Sam." Geoff gave him a pat on the back.

But Tim had other thoughts. "Sure, it's good for Sam 'cause he's got some education, but I'm trapped here. The lake only comes alive toward the summer months. The rest of the year is hard, really hard."

"But Tim," Geoff began, "I thought you loved living here? I thought you liked things just the way they are? And what about your father, and the stable?"

"As for my father, sometimes I think he would just like to get rid of me." Tim's eyes began to well up. "I just want to see—just once—what is out there. It doesn't have to be the big city. I would like to see things and to go places...and...and...I would like to be able to wear clothes like you wear."

"Really?" asked Geoff, who was perspiring heavily in the June heat. "Right now I would give almost anything to be wearing your swimming trunks instead of several layers of wool." That made Tim laugh. "Perhaps we should pull off our own version of *The Prince and the Pauper* and simply trade places?" Geoff laughed at his own wit, but neither Tim nor Sam was laughing with him. Instead, there wasn't a sign on either face that they had recognized the Mark Twain novel Geoff had made reference to. Geoff decided to change the subject. "So, has there been any work at all on the house?"

Tim pointed out the details. "Well, there's a few survey spikes over there, and there's some more digging over there, but come over here and look at this."

They walked about twenty-five feet to the right of where they had been standing on solid rock, the same rock that formed the cliff. The plans called for the house to be anchored and then built on the rock. Tim was showing them something that didn't quite fit. The top of the cliff had been carved out—quarried—and now had a perfect rectangular hole cut into the top face of the rock. It was about ten feet deep and dimensionally looked like a grave. The bottom was filled with rainwater.

Geoff was confused. "Do you know who did this, Tim?"

"I didn't recognize the men, mister. They were here this time last year. Brought in machinery. I came up here for a swim and they chased me away, but I came back after they left to see what they had done." Tim started to pull his trousers on over his swimming trunks.

Sam piped up, "Maybe it's a footing for the building?"

"I can't say I would rule that out, but I'm no architect."

As there were no answers to be gained, the three left the property and headed back to the launch. Geoff now had three matters on his mind. He knew the cut in the cliff was a subject to discuss with Edward. But his recent conversation had made him feel responsible for Sam. He wondered what he could do for him, given his fortunate position in the company. He also remembered Bill Greyson mentioning something about the McNabbs. Not Tim, he wouldn't have known Tim. It was about his father and mother.

"Sam," he began, "would you like to do a job for me for the next week or so?"

"What kind of job?" asked Sam.

"Well, I was planning to spend more time in the northern part of New Jersey, and I have rented a horse and carriage, which is now stabled at MacGilvary's in town. I was wondering if you might see your way clear to taking the beast and cart and returning them for me." Sam's eyes widened. "I will pay you well, plus I will cover your expenses. What do you say?"

Sam answered quickly. "Yes, I would love to do this." Then he added, "Not that it matters to me, but why did you change your plans?"

"I realized that I need to return to New York sooner than I expected." Geoff had dropped his line in the water and gone exploring. Now for the bait. "But if you'd like, Sam, you can really help me out by doing a little fieldwork for me in Sussex County."

"New Jersey?" Sam's eyes were watering.

"The very same. I was going to visit some mining operations in that area. Could you do this for me? I think you will be able to cover some of the distance by train, so that should speed it up a bit."

"But I don't know anything about mining, Geoff."

"That's all right, Sam, neither do I. I will give you a list of questions to ask. Be sure to write down the answers. Wear your best suit."

"This sounds like an adventure."

"I am sure it does." Now—hook, line, and sinker. "When you have finished your tour, if you still have the time and the energy, I want you to bring all the information and deliver it to me at the address on this card." Geoff handed Sam his business card.

"But…this is in New York City." Sam couldn't believe his eyes.

"Yes, it is. Do you think you can find it?"

"I'll find it, Geoff. Don't you worry about anything."

"Fine." They had just reached the launch again. After they had boarded, Geoff gave new directions to the captain. "Sam, go out past that point over there, and then head back toward the state line. Take me to the wharf where the steamers dock. I can pick up the afternoon train at the depot, and Tim can get back home." He clapped Tim on the shoulder. "Right, Tim?"

But Tim didn't answer. He stayed seated in the bow of the launch and stared out over the water. Geoff moved to the seat directly behind the boy.

"Tim?" he said quietly. "I would like the opportunity to speak with your father before I leave on the train today. Do you think that can be arranged?"

"Do you need to rent a horse and carriage?" he replied glumly.

"Let's just leave it at that for now. Your father and I have some business to discuss."

"Yes, mister. So how come you gave all that work to Sam back there?"

"Does it bother you that I offered him the work, and not you?"

"Sure it does!" Tim raised his voice a little, but kept looking straight out. "I've helped your people twice now—him, only once."

"But Tim, Sam has more education than you do. He can read well, and he can write."

"But I'm smart! Everyone says so!"

"Then think of just how far you will go in the world if you are smart and you have an education."

"But now I'm too old! I'm way too old to go back to school."

"You are never too old. Would you go to school again, if you had the chance?"

"If I could amount to someone like you someday—in a heartbeat!" Then Tim added, "Why?"

"No matter. I just wanted to hear you say it."

Sam eased the launch next to the wharf at the depot. Geoff and Tim hopped out onto the dock. Geoff pulled out a handwritten list of questions and gave the list to Sam. Geoff took out his billfold and gave Sam two hundred dollars. "That should be good to get the horse and carriage back to Stockholm, Sam. There will be an additional two hundred dollars waiting for you in New York."

Sam nodded approvingly, and then he pushed the launch off and started his trip back up to the village of Greenwood Lake.

Geoff picked up his carpetbag, walked to the ticket window of the train depot, and purchased a ticket for the four p.m. train. "Is the train full for the return trip?" he asked.

"Oh, no, sir," the agent replied, "there are plenty of seats at this time of the year."

Geoff thanked the agent and strode across the dirt road to the livery stable owned by Tim's father. It was three o'clock. A heated discussion ensued.

At three fifteen p.m., Tim's father's voice bellowed for Tim to come to the stable.

By three thirty arrangements had been made for Tim to attend school at the St. George's Choir School.

At three forty-five p.m., Tim had changed into his Sunday best, packed the few possessions he owned, and bid his father farewell. He was off to seek his fortune in the big city with Mr. Geoffrey Atwater.

At four o'clock the train pulled out of the depot. Geoff and Tim sat in the second car. Tim was smiling, although confused from the whirlwind that had just upset everything he knew in life.

Geoff knew he could square what he had just done—both with Sam and with Tim—with Edward and with Morgan. He only hoped that he was doing the right thing for the boy. But he did have a bigger concern. "By the way, Tim, can you sing?"

"Like a bird, sir. Why?"

"You will see."

What he would never, ever tell Tim was that he had just paid the boy's father three hundred dollars for the privilege of taking his son to be educated.

Chapter 17
The Crime of the Century

It really didn't matter what Edward thought of Geoff's bold plan to send Sam into Sussex County, New Jersey, to investigate the mining operations there—J. P. Morgan loved the idea. In fact, he thought Geoff had finally taken some initiative—something he had to do in order to move up in the company.

Geoff had arrived back in New York two days earlier than expected, and with a young companion. He had gone directly to his apartment on East 61st Street to see his wife and to inform her that they would have a guest for possibly a few days. When Margaret said that she needed to fix up the guest bedroom, she gave Geoff a "come hither" look and nod. Behind the closed door of the guest bedroom, Geoff quietly explained why there was a strange boy in their apartment. Margaret proved icy, until Geoff mentioned that he had virtually bought the boy from his father so that he could educate him. That turned the tide.

As it was still mid-afternoon, the Atwaters decided the best way to spend the remainder of the day was to take Master Timothy to buy some new clothing. If he was going to become a young gentleman, then he certainly had to play the part. Tim, on the other hand, could not stop looking at everything new around him—from the train ride, to the hotel stay for an evening, to eating in a restaurant, to a ferryboat crossing, to a ride in a motorcar. Most amazing of all, in his eyes, were the beautiful buildings.

The trio ate dinner in the apartment that evening, both young adults gently correcting Tim's table manners, as well as his English. After dinner, Margaret cut Tim's overgrown and straggly hair while he sat on a chair in the kitchen. He was then sent to the bathroom to take a very long bath. Geoff realized there was still much to do before he could introduce Tim to Morgan, and especially to Norris, so he asked Margaret to work with Tim the next day while he went to work and prepared the way. By the time they went to bed, both he and Margaret had resolved that, if things did not go as preferred with Morgan, Edward, and Norris, they would take on the responsibility themselves to educate the boy, and then find him employment and housing. Both were determined not to send him back to a life of ignorance and poverty.

But Morgan also approved of this action on Geoff's part, and he, too, had been taken in by the boy's personality, although Geoff seemed to note a reaction on Morgan's part when he mentioned that his young ward's last name was McNabb. Morgan suggested training Tim as a chauffeur, especially now that motorcars were becoming the popular mode of transportation around the city. Geoff expressed his thought that the boy had a sharp mind, which he might prove with an education. Edward, having met and conversed with Tim, agreed with Geoff.

Morgan then asked Geoff if he had a particular plan in mind for the young man.

"Yes, sir, I do," replied Geoff confidently. "I propose that we ask Mr. Norris to accept him into the St. George's Choir School."

"A clever idea, Mr. Atwater, but he is a bit old for a choirboy. Don't you agree?"

The traditional choir in the Anglican Church has always been the Choir of Men and Boys. This choir would sing in four parts, but the soprano and alto parts would be given to the boys. This choir was such a staple in the large Church of England and American Episcopal churches that choir schools were established to allow for the complete musical and academic training of the boys. Many of the larger churches—such as St. George's, Trinity Wall Street, and St. Thomas's—would have schools that were residential. The boys would live at the school. The usual age for a choirboy was around eight through about fourteen, or whenever his voice changed. At that point the boy might be able to stay as a tenor or bass, or he might find a place in the mixed adult choir of men and women. Still, the boy would have received a very good education—a far better and more comprehensive one than the vast majority of children were receiving in 1905. At almost sixteen years old, Timothy McNabb was older than the oldest male alto in the choir, and stood a head and a half taller than anyone. He was almost as tall as Homer Norris.

"Still," Edward suggested, "if we bring Timothy into the office here to meet Mr. Norris, I am sure we can come to some sort of arrangement."

Geoff smiled at Edward. It was as good as done. They left the office together.

"You know, Geoff," Edward began, "I was so tempted to do what you did when I was out there two years ago. You did a wonderful thing."

"Thank you. You know, 'there but for the Grace of God...'"

"I know. I am looking forward to seeing him again."

"Edward, there's more to tell you." And Geoff proceeded to tell Edward about the grave-like cut in the top of the cliff. Edward's eyes narrowed to only slits as he listened.

Personal Journal Entry
June 15, 1905

Geoff has returned from the trip to the lake with two new accomplices. One is already here. His name is Timothy McNabb. I met him several years ago when I was out there surveying the property. I liked him then, and I like him even more now that he is several years older. He is very much a ragamuffin, but he seems naturally intelligent and has a wonderful personality.

I know that Geoff brought him back to New York to save him from a worthless existence. I don't doubt Geoff's motives, but I hope this decision proves to be good for the boy, or else it will be on our heads.

Geoff mentioned that he bought the boy from his father for three hundred dollars. Is Tim now an indentured servant?

The other new face will be a young man named Sam Waters. I have not had the pleasure of meeting Sam yet, but Geoff assures me that he is a young man of unquestionable character.

We shall see.

Morgan's office was used the following morning to receive Homer Norris, who had absolutely no idea why he had been called in to see Morgan. He thought it had something to do with his house. He was shown in and realized that, in addition to Morgan, he was also meeting with Messrs. Collier and Atwater.

When all were seated, Morgan began. "Homer, we have found a new boy for you and the St. George's Choir of Men and Boys." Morgan never liked to beat around the bush.

Norris immediately started to fidget. He nervously answered, "I don't understand, Mr. Morgan. Auditioning the boys is *my* job. I don't understand what you are talking about."

"It's quite simple, really. We—and by 'we' I include Mr. Collier, Mr. Atwater, and me—have found a boy in need of education, plus room and board. We immediately thought of you and your Choir School. Is there a reason why I am unable to count on you for your assistance, Homer?"

"None whatsoever, Mr. Morgan." Homer had very little backbone for confrontation. "May I ask, can he sing?"

"Like a bird," Geoff replied.

"Might I be able to meet him first?" Homer was grabbing at straws. The deal was already sealed; he just didn't realize it.

"You already have met him, Homer," Edward answered, smiling from ear to ear.

Morgan paged his receptionist; a moment later, Margaret Atwater walked in with a well-dressed fifteen-year-old young gentleman. Edward continued, "Mr. Norris, may I introduce you to Master Timothy McNabb?" Tim extended his hand to Norris, who accepted it and shook it vigorously.

"I am very glad to make your acquaintance, Master McNabb, but I must confess, I was led to believe that we had met previously. I don't think I have had the pleasure until today."

"Nonsense, Homer!" Edward laughed. "We met him together. Don't you remember? We spent an entire afternoon with him at your property on Greenwood Lake."

Homer's eyes widened. "This...this is the young ragamuffin who claimed he could dive into the lake from the top of the cliff?"

"He can do it, Homer," Geoff added. "I saw him."

Homer looked from Morgan to Geoff to Edward, and then back to Morgan again. He was totally exasperated. His instincts told him to hold his tongue, which is exactly what he did.

Edward tried to fill in the blanks for him. "Homer, I know this is all a bit of a shock for you, but we really believe in your abilities as a musician, and as an educator. You can listen to him sing, and if his voice is too low,"—Edward decidedly did not say *bad*—"then I would suggest that you make him a docent at St. George's. Or better yet, your house assistant. He is very tall and strong. I would think he would be a big help in keeping the younger boys in line."

Homer gave it some thought. "You are correct, perhaps. I shall give him a try."

As they left the office together, Tim tugged on Geoff's jacket sleeve. It occurred to Geoff that this was an action a small child might do in order to gain attention.

"Yes, Tim?" Geoff asked.

"I will study hard, Geoff, I will. I won't let you down."

"You don't have to promise anything to me, Tim."

"Oh, yes, I do," the boy answered. "I don't want you to think that you wasted your three hundred dollars on me."

"How did you know about that?" Geoff asked.

"I came back to the stable while you and my father were talking about me. I heard you tell him, and then I saw you give him the money."

"Did you hear us talking about anything else?"

"No," he answered truthfully, "I missed the first few minutes of the discussion."

"Good!" answered Geoff. "Just do your best in school, Tim."

"Oh, I will sure try," said Tim, "'cause I know that you will have every right to whip me if I don't."

"Don't worry, Tim," Geoff gently said, putting his hand on the boy's shoulder, "that is something I will never, ever do." He patted his shoulder twice. "I swear this to you on my very soul."

Meanwhile, Sam Waters was having a wonderful time following Geoff's itinerary in reverse. He had taken the horse and carriage back up the mountain and then down again, through Bellvale and then on to Warwick. He stayed in the Warwick Inn for the evening, just as Geoff had done. He was now in totally unfamiliar territory as he headed south toward New Jersey. By the end of the second day he had reached the same hotel in Snufftown where Geoff had stayed almost one week earlier, and after returning the steadfast horse and uncomfortable carriage to the livery stable, checked in to that inn for the night. In the morning he walked to the Stockholm rail station and boarded a train heading north. The train carried him through a mountain pass, slowly descending the Hamburg Mountain into the town of Franklin. He was able to hire a carriage at the Franklin station, and after getting directions to the various mining operations he was to visit, he headed off on his mission. Sam spent three days wandering around the mining region of Sussex County, but gained enough information that he felt satisfied that Geoff would be happy with his results. He also realized that dropping the name of J. Pierpont Morgan had a very positive effect on the conversations he had with the mine managers. He headed back to Franklin and secured transportation on a southbound train. It would take him almost a full day to make the necessary connections to get back to Jersey City. He stayed a night in a hotel not far from the terminal. He hopped a ferry for New York City in the morning. Like Tim a few days prior, Sam was totally unprepared for New York City, especially the financial area. He arrived on the shore of Manhattan by eight thirty a.m., and spent several hours walking the city streets. He only had to ask one passerby for directions to the address on the Geoff's business card. He felt ready to go in at about eleven a.m.

When he walked through the doors of Morgan and Company, Sam Waters asked to see Geoffrey Atwater. The receptionist in the lobby directed Sam to the fifth floor, where he found Geoff's small office. He knocked on the door.

"Come in," said the voice inside. Sam entered the office. "Sam Waters! How good it is to see you again." Geoff was seated behind his desk. Another young gentleman was also in the office. "Sam, this is Mr. Edward Collier. Edward, this is the young man I was telling you about, Samuel Waters."

"I am pleased to finally meet you, Sam. Our friend Mr. Atwater has kept you busy, it seems, running you all over the state of New Jersey." Edward had already been informed of Sam's task, and expectations were running very high for his success.

"I really only confined myself to the most northern part of the state, but there was a great deal to see, and many people to interview." Then he turned to Geoff and said, "Thank you, Geoff, for giving me this opportunity." Geoff nodded to him.

The young men then set about discussing the findings of Sam's trip. They decided to plan a formal presentation for Morgan. Edward was extremely satisfied with the thoroughness of Sam's work, especially his note taking. The fact was that Sam had been so nervous that he might fail to jot down something important that he wrote down just about everything that had been said to him.

After the business at hand was concluded, Edward asked Sam what his plans were for the future.

"I think I would like to see more of the city before heading back up-country," was his reply—and it was a reply filled with hope.

"So you are determined to return to Orange County? Is there nothing we can do to make you change your mind so that you may set up residence here in New York?" Geoff and Edward had already discussed what to do with Sam, if and when he arrived on their doorstep. Geoff had complained that he really didn't know Sam well enough to predict his answer.

Sam, on the other hand, had prayed that he might be asked this very thing, but he decided to play the scene out very slowly and cleverly. "I certainly do not have much reason to return to my place of birth, and I would like to seek a more exciting and lucrative career than that of a water taxi captain, but I must admit that I don't have any immediate prospects that would keep me here in New York City."

Edward was impressed. "Spoken like a true gentleman, Sam. I think Geoff and I are agreed that it would be in the best interest of our company, as well as in your best interest, if you were to stay here in the city. Furthermore, I think Mr. Morgan will agree with our opinion, however, I have not spoken with him as of yet. I personally can make great use of you."

Sam's eyes lit up. "Anything, Edward. I would do anything!"

"Now, Sam," Edward interrupted, "please don't grovel. You were doing so well up to this point. I will speak with Mr. Morgan to see if there is a position in the company for a young man of your talents and personality. In the interim, I would like to ask you if you would consider being my chauffeur."

"What is a chauffeur?" Sam asked, puzzled.

"I have just purchased a Great Arrow motorcar. Mr. Morgan has mentioned that it is more dignified if I have someone drive the car for me, although I must admit that it is a great deal of fun to run the thing through Central Park. You could take me to the office, being sure to stop at Sixty-first Street to pick up Geoff along the way, and then head down here to Wall Street. You would be available if I need to travel anywhere in the city, but I am sure Mr. Morgan will also find things for you to work on when you are not taking me about. I can afford to pay you one hundred dollars per week, plus you can live in quarters in my apartment on Seventy-second Street, and you can eat most of your meals there, as well. If Mr. Morgan wishes to have you work here, that would mean additional salary. Now, how is that for an immediate prospect?"

"It sounds great!" answered Sam, almost without thinking. "But there is one problem."

"And what is that?" asked Edward.

"I've never driven a motorcar before—only carriages and boats."

Edward laughed. "Then I shall have to show you how and let you practice in the park. The driving part isn't difficult. You will master that in short order. I find that most problems occur when trying to avoid people, horses, wagons, and streetcars."

"Then I would like to try it, if you'll let me."

Sam was very sure of his prospects now.

It was decided that Tim would spend the summer with the Atwaters, as the Choir School had already gone into summer recess. Tim would be on hand when Margaret needed him most—when she went into labor at the end of August.

The day of August 28 had started like any other hot, humid New York City summer day. Geoff had gone off to work, picked up by Edward at eight in his motorcar with Sam at the wheel. Margaret had made it a habit to work with Tim on his studies during the next two hours each day. They were working on grammar when Margaret felt her water break. She asked Tim to ring her mother and then call the Morgan Company, to inform her husband of the events. There had been no answer at the office, as it was too early in the morning. Even the secretaries and receptionists would only get in around eight forty-five. Her mother did answer the phone, told Tim that she would head uptown immediately, and then asked him to get the midwife, which he was ready to do anyway. The midwife lived on East 65th Street, only a few blocks away. Tim was gone within moments, leaving Margaret alone in the brownstone.

Tim ran at top speed the few blocks uptown to 65th, and then cut to the east, toward the river, crossing the long crosstown blocks. He reached 220 East 65th Street within fifteen minutes, but no one answered the bell. A neighbor opened her door because of Tim's incessant knocking, and informed him that the midwife had been busy with another woman since early the previous evening and had not yet returned home. Not knowing what to do next, the boy raced back home.

He found Margaret lying on the kitchen floor, in obvious agony. He knew it took almost an hour to get to Wall Street, and it would take another hour for the men to return home. It would surely take at least an hour for Margaret's mother to get there, and he had no idea how long it would take for the midwife to arrive. He ran to the other brownstones up and down the street, pleading with the owners or their servants. A doctor lived in one of the buildings, but he was already out on calls. Beginning to panic, Tim ran back to see how Margaret was doing.

Margaret was conscious, but not by much. Tim could see that she was bleeding heavily.

He had worked side by side with his father from the time he was old enough to know when to get out of the way. He had assisted with the birthing of cows, horses, and cats. He knew that most animals were capable of delivering their own babies without a bit of human help, but he also knew there were times when both mother and calf, colt, or kitten would die without intervention. He ran to the bedroom and grabbed pillows from the bed. He placed the pillows under Margaret's head and upper back.

Tim knelt beside Margaret on the floor. "Margaret? I may have to help you with birthing this baby. I've called everyone I can, but you need help real soon."

Margaret closed her eyes and nodded in agreement. She reached out and took Tim's right hand. "Have you ever done this before, Tim?"

"I've helped my father with the stock. I've seen and helped lots of times, but I must confess that I've never helped with a human. I'm sorry."

"I know, Tim, but I think you're going to have to do the best you can."

"Yes, ma'am." He looked again toward the door, hoping to see someone—anyone—standing there to help, but that was not to be. He took a deep breath and spoke quietly. "Margaret? I'm going to have to lift your skirt so I can see what is going on. Will that be all right?" Margaret nodded. Tim moved her clothing, used a knife to cut away her undergarments, and saw that she was hemorrhaging badly. Something was terribly wrong and he knew it.

He had to concentrate. He knew that he had to determine where the baby was in the birth canal. He had done this with cows and horses by putting his hand inside, but he couldn't imagine doing this to Margaret.

But it had to be done.

"Margaret? I...I need to check where the baby is. Will you...may I...you know...touch you down there?" Margaret slowly nodded. Tim ran to the sink and quickly washed his hands. The kettle was still warm from the tea they had been drinking while doing his studies; he poured it into the sink so that the water he used would be hot. He didn't know why, but he knew that hot water was better than cold. He ran back to Margaret's side. "I'm going to do it now, Margaret. Take a deep breath." She did, and so did he. He very slowly and gently pushed her legs apart. He saw himself performing this same exam on a cow one time and was reminded that his arm had gone in up to his elbow. He didn't imagine that he would need to do the same thing now, at least he hoped not. He entered Margaret's most private and sacred area. He used only two fingers and moved slowly. He was feeling for the head of the baby—but instead he thought that he felt a foot. Tim removed his hand.

He remembered once, about a year ago, a mare was having trouble delivering its foal. His father said the foal was in breech position, but not much more information was passed on than that. He later learned that the colt had revolved in his mother's womb and was exiting the wrong way. The mare was already dying, and both would soon be dead if something drastic wasn't done.

"Margaret, something is wrong! Your baby has turned and is coming out feet first!" Tim started to cry.

"Tim," Margaret said hoarsely, "help me. Help my baby."

"I don't know if I can do it, ma'am. I've seen it, but I've never actually done it. I felt a foot, so I don't think I can turn the baby." Tim chose his next words carefully. "I've seen foals delivered through the flank. I think that's what I need to do for you, but I don't know if I can."

Margaret knew what "through the flank" meant. He was going to cut the baby out of her. He was going to give her his version of a Caesarian section.

Tim ran again to the sink, filled the kettle and lit the burner. He then went to the knife block and found the sharpest knives that resided there. He secretly hoped that someone would burst through the door in the time he took to make his preparations. He found a clean white towel to receive the baby. He ran to the bathroom and got a bottle of iodine, and also grabbed a washcloth from the linen closet. He found a pair of dress shears to cut the umbilical cord, and also located a fine needle and some white thread. His final stop was in the study, where he took a decanter of Irish whiskey. The kettle whistled so he ran back and doused the knives, needle, and shears in boiling water. He poured the rest into the sink and then rewashed his hands.

The "through the flank" delivery is performed on a horse or cow while it is standing on all fours in a stall. Tim realized this was not the same thing. Margaret's belly was extended with the pregnancy, so that must be where the baby was. He also knew that a person's belly button was a remnant of childbirth, so it also had to be in a related area. Tim poured a full glass of whiskey and gave it to Margaret.

"You must drink this, Margaret. All of it." Margaret did not enjoy spirits, but she downed the glass in only three gulps.

He spread the towel on the floor next to him and placed the shears on top, ready to go. He then uncorked the bottle of iodine and poured about half the bottle over her abdomen, saving the rest for later. He rolled the washcloth up and brought it to Margaret's mouth.

"Bite down on this, ma'am—and think about your baby and Geoff."

He picked up the paring knife. Tim was sweating profusely, and the sweat was running down his forehead into his eyes, burning them. He took a deep breath, picked his spot, and then firmly drew the knife across Margaret's abdomen, about halfway between the bottom of her ribcage and her navel. He tried not to cut very deep, for fear of causing harm to the baby, or to Margaret. He ignored her muted screams as he completed the first pass—then she stopped screaming. He looked over to see if he had killed her.

She had passed out.

Tim now redoubled his efforts; at least she was unconscious. He tried to pull back the flap he had just cut, but saw that there were several layers of muscle that still needed to be cut through. He remembered this was also the case with the mare. He wanted to keep his cutting to a minimum, but he also had to make enough of an opening to extract the baby.

"Dear Lord Jesus," he prayed, while cutting through a layer of muscle, "please guide my hand. Don't let me harm this woman, or her baby."

"My God! What are you doing, boy?" came a voice from behind him. It was the doctor from the neighboring brownstone. He threw off his jacket and hat, opened his bag, and quickly examined Margaret. Tim was only too glad to move aside. "I don't know how you knew to do what you did, boy, but you made the right decision. This baby is breech and stuck in the birth canal, so cutting is the only answer." Using his scalpel to finish the cut, in just a few moments he extracted the baby. It was a boy. The doctor cleared his airways and gave him a slap on his bottom. The baby cried.

"Get me that towel—are you?"

"Tim."

"Get me that towel, Tim. Put in there so we can wrap the baby in it, after we cut the cord. Are those shears sterile?"

"I boiled everything, sir."

"Good boy." The doctor prepared to cut the umbilical cord, but then stopped. "Here. You take the shears. Cut the cord....right about there." Tim cut the cord and the doctor clamped it. Just then, the midwife arrived. "Ma'am, go send for an ambulance to take Mrs. Atwater to the hospital."

The woman didn't move. "But the baby, Doctor."

"The baby is in good hands. Quickly—go!" And the woman ran. "Tim, move the baby away from here. You hold it. We can clean it up later."

Geoff burst through the door, followed by Margaret's mother. Edward and Sam stayed with the car. The doctor looked up at Geoff. "Well, sir, you have a new son. Congratulations! But your wife is in serious condition, so she is going to the hospital as soon as I get her closed up. We will know in a day or two just how strong she really is, although infection is our biggest worry. You can thank this young man here. He did a most amazing thing, he did!"

"Tim?" Geoff was confused by what the doctor had said.

"Tim diagnosed the fact that your wife was delivering breech. He decided to help her by attempting to perform a Caesarian section in the best way he could. And he would have succeeded, had I not come along and finished the job for him."

"What?" Margaret's mother only understood the fact that this strange young man had just performed major surgery on her daughter, and that she was still lying on the kitchen floor with most of her clothing from the waist down cut away.

But Geoff understood. "Tim? How did you know all this?"

Tim didn't bother to explain, he could do that later. He presented the baby to Geoff, who gazed upon his son for the first time. Geoff looked back at Tim, who began to sob deep and uncontrollable sobs. Geoff gave the baby to his mother-in-law and put his arm around the boy. "Thank you, Tim. I don't know what would have happened if you hadn't been here."

Margaret Atwater was moved to the hospital not long after. She developed an infection within a day of giving birth. She died in the hospital on the first day of September.

The baby had weighed seven pounds, eleven ounces. He was twenty inches long. He had a shock of brownish hair on his head. He came home from the hospital with his father and grandparents the day after Margaret died. It was at that moment that Geoff announced the baby would be named Timothy Edward Atwater.

Evelyn Nesbit had moved on from Stanford White. She still loved her "Stanny," but she was constantly wooed by eligible bachelors. One of these suitors was the heir to an iron fortune, Harry Kendall Thaw. Thaw was the kind of man who didn't take kindly to rejection, and was also known to have a violent, sadistic side. He wanted to marry Evelyn, and bullied the rest of her suitors until they gave up the quest. He also bullied her, and would not give up until she finally relented and agreed to marry him.

But Thaw knew the gossip; he heard the rumors, and so he relentlessly badgered Evelyn, even after they were married, to tell him about her past with Stanford White. She finally gave in and told him all about their escapade in the mirror room.

On the evening of June 25, 1906, Stanford White went to the cabaret atop his recently completed Madison Square Garden. He was seated at a table down front, enjoying the show, when Harry Thaw entered the club. Thaw walked over to White, pulled out a pistol, and shot the architect three times in the face as point-blank range. White died instantly.

The murder was called "the crime of the century," even if the century was only six years old. Thaw was tried twice. The jury could not reach a consensus at the first trial, and Evelyn pleaded her husband's case at the second, leading to an acquittal based on, for the first time, temporary insanity.

Morgan was aware of Stanford White's dalliances with young girls. He tried to get White more involved with his work, creating bigger and more lavish projects, but all that accomplished was to give White more fame, and more fortune.

Chapter 18
A Doctor in the House

The Atwater family became frequent guests at the Dakota. It was now nearing the end of 1906 and the official period of mourning for Margaret Atwater had passed, but her memory had not. Geoff had known all his life what it had been like to grow up without a mother—for that matter, without any parents—and he had resolved to make his son's childhood a little less bleak than his had been. The two families, when together at the Dakota, really became more like one extended family. There were the Colliers: Edward, Rebecca—who was expecting their second child—and Eddie, now six years old. Then there were the Atwaters: Geoff and little Timothy Edward. But in addition to the obvious, there was also Tim McNabb, who lived with Geoff, and Sam Waters, who worked for Edward.

In the waning months of 1906, another person would enter the family circle. An attractive young lady from the Morgan Company, a bookkeeper by the name of Miss Emily Jones, had become a more and more frequent guest. Sam had been seeing Emily since late summer, and now this had blossomed into a full-blown romance.

Sam had been doing very well for himself. Morgan was impressed with Sam's confidence and his ebullient personality. He had first employed Sam as a glorified office boy, and sent him on errands around Lower Manhattan. He paid him seventy-five dollars a week to keep him on retainer. But Morgan also realized that Sam's talents were being overlooked and underdeveloped. By October, Morgan proposed to Sam, Edward, and Geoff that Sam become an accountant in the firm. He would need additional schooling, but it also meant a better salary. That, and the fact that he was getting very serious with Miss Jones, convinced Edward that he would soon be losing his chauffer, and that Sam would be moving out of the Dakota, as well.

Tim, on the other hand, was excelling beyond all expectations. Homer Norris tested his voice, and while it had already broken, it was remarkably true to pitch. He lacked formal training, however, and this needed addressing before he could be allowed to sing with the other boys, even as a bass. But his personality and willingness to learn endeared him to everyone he met, and Norris knew that he had found a more than capable assistant for the Choir School. Tim took on the role of prefect, a form of residence assistant, but he acted more like a big brother to the younger boys of the choir.

It had been Edward who related the story of the birth of Geoff's son to Morgan, for Geoff at that point was mourning the loss of his wife. Edward gave his thirdhand account of the events of that day in August when young Tim took matters into his own hands and practically delivered Baby Timothy all by himself. Edward suggested, and Morgan concurred, that it would be prudent to observe Tim's progress in the school, especially academically. They would have a difficult time trying to convince Geoff that he didn't have to pay for Tim's education—not after what he had done—but they were convinced that, given the right schooling, Tim would make a fine doctor. Over the course of several years Edward would gently drop a hint, and then Geoff would agree, that Tim should consider a career in the field of medicine, until finally one day Tim came to that conclusion himself, as if it was his idea all along.

The holidays of 1906 arrived. Sam proposed to Emily Jones, who gleefully accepted. They would marry in the spring of 1907. Tim asked Edward if he could become his chauffer, to which he and Geoff in unison said, "No." Rebecca kept her eye out for a suitable young lady for Geoff. She missed her sister Margaret dearly, but she also adored her brother-in-law. She knew he was a good and honest man, and sooner or later he would need a woman's help to raise his son. Besides, she thought, he looked so lonely. It wasn't anywhere near the proper length of time after the death of a spouse to start the process again—usually a year was customary—but Rebecca wanted to be prepared. She was due in March; her time was fast approaching.

Even though 1906 was ending on a bittersweet note in New York City, there were many tears being shed on the Pacific Coast. San Francisco had been hit with a major earthquake in April. People on the East Coast sympathized with the plight of their distant neighbors and fellow Americans, but they could do little to help. By the early spring of 1907 the effects of the earthquake struck Wall Street. There had been a steady stream of money flowing from the East Coast to the West Coast to aid in the reconstruction process, which eventually put a strain on the eastern banks. To further add to the dilemma, the Bank of England was forced to raise interest rates, due to the fact that it had to pay off on so many insurance claims.

Then in October of that year, a scheme was hatched to corner the copper market by buying up stock of the United Copper Company. When this scheme failed, there was a run on the Knickerbocker Trust Company—the third-largest trust company in New York. A panic was in the making. Led by J. P. Morgan, bankers in the city realized they would be next if something drastic was not done to stave off disaster. In a meeting in the library of his mansion on Madison Avenue that lasted until midnight, Morgan bullied the other financiers to insure loans to the Trust Company of America in order to stop the bank runs. Morgan would eventually uphold the financial center of the United States by using his own money, much in the same way he had done in 1893. But Morgan was no longer the richest man in America—Standard Oil billionaire John D. Rockefeller was—so Morgan asked Rockefeller to help. Ever the businessman, Rockefeller realized that widespread panic was not good business for anyone, so he pledged to bail out the banks, using up to 50 percent of his personal wealth, if need be.

But in order to prevent such widespread panic, the United States government would have to get involved. Morgan sent emissaries to Washington to see President Theodore Roosevelt. Roosevelt was a die-hard antitrust president, so there was justifiable fear that he would not agree to the measures being proposed by Morgan and the other financiers, because in order for solvency to be achieved many companies were being taken over by stronger, sounder companies. Many in Roosevelt's administration were already crying "monopoly."

But Roosevelt did agree to the measures, and the financiers of New York, led by Morgan, were able to stabilize the economy. Morgan was a temporary hero at best, and before long there were Congressional inquests into his financial dealings. Morgan had made some acquisitions during the panic—his United States Steel absorbed the Tennessee Coal, Iron and Railroad Company. Even though he had personally lost over twenty-one million dollars in the panic, he was now forced to answer questions at hearings in Washington.

At approximately the same time as the financial pressures were mounting, a representative from the Italian music publisher Ricordi came to New York City. Morgan arranged to have the agent meet with Burleigh, who had already had several of his spirituals published by G. Schirmer. Burleigh would eventually go on to become an editor for the Italian publisher. In addition to his duties as soloist at St. George's, Burleigh had also become a soloist at Temple Emanu-El. Edward worked to broker these major career moves for his friend.

Rebecca Collier gave birth to a daughter, Alice Anne, on March 5, 1907. There were no complications associated with the birth.

Sam Waters married Emily Jones in April at St. George's. Sam was now a full-fledged accountant at J. P. Morgan and Company. Instead of working as a driver for Edward Collier, Sam now owned a Ford of his own. Sam moved out of the Dakota and rented an apartment on East 78th Street, just off First Avenue.

Geoff took Tim to see the great illusionist, Harry Houdini, at the recently completed Hippodrome Theater. The Hippodrome seated over six thousand people and was hailed as the largest theater in the world.

Rebecca Collier introduced Geoff to a young lady that she had gotten to know at church, Miss Millicent Maxwell. Geoff was particularly taken by her name, Millicent Maxwell, although she preferred to be called simply Millie. The couple would take Sunday walks through Central Park, and, when the air turned colder, spent many hours in the Metropolitan Museum of Art. Millie loved to look at artwork, and Geoff was a very willing learner. By year's end they were engaged and the wedding was set for the spring of 1908. Timothy Edward would serve as ring bearer. Millie asked Rebecca to be matron of honor. Edward, knowing Geoff's true feelings, mentioned to him that he thought Tim McNabb should be his best man. Geoff realized Edward had just done him a favor and thanked him, and then asked Tim. Tim had just turned eighteen and was now finished at St. George's Choir School. He would be attending Columbia University in the fall, majoring in medicine.

Tim received word in the summer of 1907 that his father had suffered a massive heart attack while shoeing Big Ned. He had died almost instantly. Tim went back to Sterling Forest to attend the funeral and to help settle his father's affairs. Geoff accompanied him on the journey. Tim now owned property in Sterling Forest, but was unsure how to make use of it. Geoff advised renting the stable until Tim knew where his life was taking him.

J. P. Morgan's health was now in a gradual spiral of decline. He would live another few years, but the stress that the panic and the hearings that ensued caused him had negatively affected his health. But he had projects to finish, and there was still much on his mind.

Theodore Roosevelt had an immense project of his own that he was personally overseeing—the construction of the Panama Canal. In 1907 the canal was almost half completed, and much of the credit would go to Roosevelt for making sure that money was continually flowing into the project.

Homer Norris went to Morgan's office in the winter of 1908 to ask Morgan if construction on his house could begin in earnest. Morgan agreed. The construction would start as soon as the ground thawed in the spring. Edward and Geoff were to oversee the project, but from a distance. Norris was to feel as if he were calling the shots.

Chapter 19
The Boulders

Construction on Norris's cottage began in the first week of April 1908. It took several weeks to get the construction equipment to Sterling Forest, then to Shore Avenue, and then to the property. It was all very slow going. The first order of business was the foundation. Footings had to be carved into the cliff, and other footings had to be dug in the dirt behind the cliff. The largest project of the first few months of building was the quarrying of fieldstone from the area around the estate. Not only was most of the house to be built with the local stone, but the massive fireplace in the second-floor great room was to be constructed of the same. The hearth was to be more than twenty feet tall and be three-quarters of the room in width at its base.

Homer Norris had this vision in his mind when he drew up the plans several years before. He had clearly seen the use of natural materials, such as the fieldstone, as a focal point of the home, and so it was his intention to name the house, appropriately, the Boulders. When Edward seemed quizzical about the name, Norris replied, "If Cornelius Vanderbilt can have a home called the Breakers, then I can have a home called the Boulders."

But Norris was prissy and fussy over the details of the construction and spent many days, sometimes weeks, at the construction site. The foundation was completed by June, and the walls of the first floor began rising in July. Structural steel was used to fortify the walls, but especially to create the strength necessary to build a second story, and then the large gabled roof. The need for steel presented yet another delay, as it had to be brought over the water to the site. A derrick had to be constructed at the top of the cliff to raise the girders to their destination. The house was still an incomplete shell by the time construction had to be put on hold for the season.

Work resumed in March 1909. The construction could begin earlier because the foundation was complete and they didn't have to wait for the spring thaw. The entire house was roughed out by early summer, with the subfloors in place. The rest of the summer would be spent working on the interior of the house.

On several design details, Homer Norris remained adamant and unwavering.

First, he demanded that he have indoor plumbing. This required a great deal of thought, considering where he was building. There was a lot of rock to contend with. A cesspool, or septic tank, might be installed, but either needed a drainage field. Drainage fields needed to have soft soil and gravel so that liquids could leach into the soil. Workmen had to place these fields many yards away from the house in order to find such soft soil. They then had to run lines out from the house to connect to the fields. Norris also required that everything was planned for future expansion, including the septic system, so all had to be larger than need demanded at the time. So the lines were run and the tank system dug, but that was just a beginning to the problem. Toilets flush because of gravity and water. In order for a toilet to send its contents to the septic tank and fields there had to be a sustainable supply of water returning to the tank above the toilet. His cottage needed to have running water, so a pump was installed. The pump was gasoline-powered at first, but would be replaced by an electrical pump as soon as electric service was run out to the estate from Sterling Forest.

His second demand concerned the kitchen. It was very common to have a detached kitchen in summer homes. Coal stoves were the norm, and house fires were very common because of this. Norris wanted to cook and heat his bathwater with gas, but as gas lines were not being run in the wilderness, he had to settle for bottled gas. He didn't worry about central heating—he had several large fireplaces planned for the house, and the season ran from late spring to early fall.

Edward and Geoff took an excursion out to the construction site in May 1909. Norris hadn't been pleased with the progress, but the two men felt that the house was looking very impressive. Edward even went so far as to pay the captain of the steamer *Montclair* a few extra dollars if he would take the steamer up the lake so that he could survey the effect the house had from the water side. There was a great deal of talk among the locals about the house, both positive and negative. Some thought it was magnificent and a marvel of construction; others felt it detracted from the natural beauty of the lake. Many more were just envious of the size and grandeur of the home.

As the summer of 1909 came to a close, the interior finishing touches began. The hardwood floors were installed on both floors. The wood paneling was installed in the great room, along with the installation of the great room fireplace. The windows were installed, as well as several sets of French doors. The bathroom fixtures were installed, including a sunken bathtub on the first floor. The patios, upper and lower, were both tiled with four-inch terra-cotta tiles. The trim was painted a deep forest green.

The house was completed in total by November 1909, but it was too late to bring in any furniture, so that detail would have to wait for the warmer weather of 1910. Norris was filled with anticipation, like a child waiting for St. Nicholas.

At long last, in April 1910, word came to Edward that Norris was moving into the Boulders. Edward contacted Norris at his New York studio to inform him that he would be going out to Greenwood Lake to inspect the house sometime in late May. Norris countered by saying he should come with Geoff, Tim, and even Eddie, who was now almost ten years old. Edward accepted his offer, and said they would come as soon as school was out for Eddie, and Columbia University went into recess for Tim.

They headed north to Greenwood Lake on June 1, 1910. Edward noted mentally that very little had changed in the lake area since the men from Morgan and Company had first visited the site. They did not take the train to Sterling Forest; they rode there in Edward's new Pierce-Arrow. Except for Eddie, they were all quite familiar with the dirt roads in Sterling Forest, even Shore Avenue, with its steep hill.

They arrived at the Boulders. It appeared through the trees as if by magic, like in some fairy tale. Eddie was even heard to exclaim, "Wow!"

Norris came running to their car from the lower patio. "I am so glad to see all of you here at my new home. Leave your bags in the motorcar. I will take you on a tour of the house first."

Norris had every reason to be proud of his new summer cottage. It was magnificent! The inspection party entered the house by way of the lower patio. In order to do this they had to ascend three steps into a formal English garden, which led all the way out to the cliff. It had been from this spot several years earlier that Tim had jumped into the water below, frightening both Sam and Geoff. Fill had been brought in, the grade raised, and an attractive lawn planted, with boxwoods lining the perimeter. The boxwoods even provided a bit of containment from the cliff edge. They then ascended another step and were on the lower patio. The patio cantilevered out over the cliff face by just a few feet, but that was enough to give you a sense that you were suspended above the water. There were two fieldstone columns at each of the lakeside corners of the patio, which were used to support the upper patio. There was also a wrought-iron banister and decorative ironwork extending around the three sides of the patio that came near the cliff face. The ironwork had also been painted forest green. The floor of the patio was made entirely of four-inch-square terra-cotta tiles. They had been cemented in place to guard against the cold months. Edward looked off to the right. The patio was open on the other side, as well, forming perfect symmetry, but the grade was lower on that side of the house, so there were several steps down to a pathway that led to the rest of the gardens. At this point, a fieldstone wall provided protection against falling from the cliff.

Norris guided them through a set of French doors and into the house. Upon entering, they were standing in the living area. It contained a comfortable sitting area, complete with fireplace, and an area with a table and chairs for dining. The floor was hardwood, but was covered largely by an oriental rug. Two large picture windows had been installed on either side of the French doors so that even inside you could still see the panorama of the lake.

Behind the living room was the master bedroom. It was twenty feet by twenty feet and very nicely appointed. Norris had excellent taste in furniture. But there was a single focal point in the room that made all four visitors look twice. Young Eddie tried to comment on the marvel, but was silenced immediately by his father, who simply put his hand on Eddie's shoulder.

A double bed was in the geographical center of the room, but the frame had been hung from the ceiling using four independent chains. The bed was free to swing in any direction, and technically speaking, was always in a state of perpetual motion. Norris never said a single word regarding this design oddity; he simply gave the signal to move on. They entered a second, smaller bedroom. Beautifully decorated in the Victorian style, it too had a bed suspended from the ceiling. Norris once again chose not to explain his way of thinking, but Eddie was busting at the seams to find out why he did this. His father kept him reined in tightly.

Down a short hallway from the living area was the main bathroom of the house. It had, as Norris demanded, hot and cold running water.

There was a toilet and sink, but the most elegant aspect, not to mention the largest item in the room, was the sunken bathtub. The tub was made entirely of white marble. The top of the tub was flush with the floor. There were three marble steps at the far end of the tub to allow the bather to walk in and sit down. It held a tremendous amount of water.

After they left the bathroom, they headed into the kitchen. The kitchen was large enough to eat meals in, and there was a table and chairs set in the middle of the room. There were cabinets all around, painted white, and a large pantry at one end that had already been stocked with staple items. There was plenty of work area, with counter space on three-quarters of the kitchen's perimeter. A door led to the rear entrance of the house, which also featured a little covered porch made of stone that looked out on more gardens. The gardens, as it turned out, were far more practical than met the eye. Hidden behind the boxwoods was a small wooden hut that held the pumping equipment that brought water up from the lake and into the house.

A door off the kitchen brought the guests into the third bedroom on the first floor. This was another very large bedroom, and it, too, had a double bed suspended from the ceiling.

At this point, Norris spoke. "So, what do you think of my house thus far?"

Eddie answered before Edward could stop him. "Mr. Norris, I love your house, and I love the lake. I was just wondering, though…how it is that all your beds are hanging from the ceiling on chains?"

Homer Norris laughed. "Thank you, Eddie, for asking the most obvious question. The question these other men, including your dear father, have been trying to avoid asking me."

Geoff simply rolled his eyes.

Norris continued, "There is only one reason that the beds are hanging from the ceiling, my dear boy." Norris bent forward, his face close to Eddie's. Eddie raised his eyebrows expectantly. "Snakes!"

"Snakes?" Eddie repeated.

"This area is loaded with snakes. I hate snakes. Actually, I am a bit ashamed of this, but…well…I am deathly afraid of snakes."

"The poisonous kind?" asked Geoff.

"Any kind!" answered Norris. The thought alone made him blanch. "I came up here many times during the construction phase, and every time I was here during the summer months there would be a snake or two sunning themselves out on the rocks. On one occasion, a workman uncovered a nest of copperheads. Another man killed a large rattle-snake and then skinned it and took the skin home."

"Gee!" Eddie was more than impressed. He wished he could see a snake.

"For quite a while I was arguing with myself whether or not I should thank Mr. Morgan for his generous gift, but graciously refuse it," Norris explained.

"What?" Geoff couldn't believe his ears. Over snakes?

"That is why it took so long for me to draw up the plans. The exterior was the easy part. I had that done in no time, but I needed to come up with a plan wherein I could enjoy this beautiful house and the beautiful scenery and not have to worry about the snakes."

This was too much for Geoff. "Do you mean to say that you are afraid that a snake is going to open your front door and march right in to torment you?"

"Geoff!" Edward reproached.

"No, Edward, it is quite all right," Norris said. "I know this is crazy. The workmen had quite a laugh at my expense. I have what Mr. Freud calls a phobia, a fear."

"Are the beds comfortable?" asked Tim.

"Actually, yes, they are," answered Norris proudly. "You feel as if you are floating on a cloud."

"Well then, there it is," concluded Tim. "What difference does anything else make? I'll bet they make for a really nice sleep."

"Yes, they do," replied Norris, "and you will find out for yourselves tonight."

They left the third bedroom and took the staircase to the second floor. The staircase was ingeniously designed to take as little room as possible out of the floor plan. One ascended five steps to a landing, which turned ninety degrees, and then had a switchback of ninety degrees again and another five stairs. There were a few small pictures hanging on the staircase walls, but something else caught Eddie's eye.

"Dad, look!" he exclaimed, pointing to a long rectangular board hanging on the wall.

The board was only a few steps away. Tim recognized it immediately. "That's a rattlesnake skin, Eddie. Big one, too. Must be almost three feet."

"Good joke, right?" asked Homer. "Some of my workmen thought it would be funny to skin one of those serpents and present it to me. So

I had them hang it here. I told them it was a lasting reminder of why I designed the house the way I did."

"It doesn't have a head!" exclaimed Eddie.

"Nah," explained Tim, "they cut that away. But look, here are the rattles." Tim reached out and flicked the rattles.

"Can I touch it?" asked Eddie.

"Why not?" answered Tim. "It's not going to bite you." He laughed a little at his own joke.

Eddie reached out and tentatively ran his index finger across the skin. "It doesn't feel like I expected it would."

"I must admit, Master Collier," said Norris, "that you are far braver than I am. I would never touch that thing, and I usually pass by on the staircase pressed as far into the railing as I can be. Shall we continue on?"

They entered the great room, and all eyes were immediately drawn to the most imposing feature of the room, the great fireplace.

The fireplace hearth was more than twenty-five feet wide, with the chimney exposed as it continued upward to the ceiling. Just like the exterior of the house, the fireplace was constructed of natural fieldstone. A square grand piano sat near the hearth. The walls of the room were wood paneled. Two French doors led to the upper patio, which gave one an even more breathtaking view of the lake. When the entourage returned inside, they had a really good view of the rear of the room, which featured a loft area that was built above the staircase from the first floor. It was here that Homer planned to install a small pipe organ. At this time the loft was used as a library.

Turning again to the right, the group encountered another set of French doors. These led to the fourth and final guest bedroom of the house. This room had two hanging double beds, set at right angles to each other, head to side. The room also boasted a bay window which looked out over the kitchen entrance. At the rear of the bedroom was a bathroom, but this one had only a sink and a toilet. There wasn't a tub in the room. Down a very short corridor was a small bedroom that was meant for servant's quarters.

"Gentlemen," Norris said, "these are your sleeping arrangements for the evening. I thought I would put you all up here in the big guest room."

The three men agreed to the arrangements. Edward and Eddie would take one bed, and Tim and Geoff the other.

Homer continued, "You can bring your bags up later. There is still enough daylight for you to walk the rest of the property. I have had the workmen clear quite a bit of the brush, and there are a few pathways for your comfort. I won't be going with you, of course, because—"

"Of the snakes?" offered Eddie.

"Yes, young Edward, because of the snakes."

Even though the three men had seen the estate property several times before, they all went on an excursion for Eddie's sake. The property sloped downhill on the north side of the house, until it reached the water's edge at a little cove. From that point the property ran north along the shore for several hundred yards, and for several hundred yards deep—although it really did not matter, for Norris had no neighbors. The water was quite shallow along this part of the property, as opposed to the depth off the cliffs. They could easily see the bottom.

"May I go in the water, Father?" Eddie asked. The temperature was close to eighty-five degrees, and the sun was shining and very warm.

"Are you going to run back up to the car to grab your trunks, Eddie?"

"Can't I just swim in my underwear?"

"Sure you can."

Eddie started to remove his outer clothing. Geoff and Tim went on a scouting mission to find the other surveyor's pegs.

"Put your clothes neatly on that big rock, Eddie," Edward told him.

Eddie carefully placed his jacket, knickerbockers, knee socks, tie, dress shirt, straw hat, and undershirt on the boulder that sat about ten feet back from the shore. He then timidly tested the water. "It's cold!" he said.

"Changing your mind?" Edward chided.

"No," Eddie said, looking back at his father, "it will just take a little longer to get wet."

Eddie slowly and cautiously edged his way out from the shore. The water deepened by a few inches with each step he took. He turned around to Edward with a very disagreeable look on his face.

"What's wrong, Ed?" his father asked.

"There are rocks and slimy grass. It feels funny."

"Yes, it's not like Coney Island. There's no sand to speak of, and there is seaweed growing on the lake bottom."

"I'm not sure I like it." But Eddie kept moving out further.

"Eddie, just watch what you are doing. It's shallow where you are now, but there may be a big drop-off all of a sudden."

"I can still see the bottom, Dad."

Edward liked it when Eddie called him Dad. He liked the formality of Father under certain conditions, like in public or when being referred to, as in "Father does this" or "my father thinks that." But it always made him feel good to hear Eddie call him Dad. It felt so twentieth century.

"Whoa!" Eddie yelled, and a moment later he was in up to his neck.

"Eddie! Are you all right?"

"Fine. I think I reached the drop-off." It made sense, too, because he was out far enough from the shoreline to be about equal with the cliff face. Eddie began to swim around, paddling and kicking. "Hey! The water just got warmer. Right here! It's warmer right here."

"That's a spring, my boy. The lake is fed by springs. You are swimming directly above one."

Geoff and Tim returned from their search for the property boundaries.

"Did you find the northeast boundary?" Edward asked.

"We did," replied Geoff, his face covered with perspiration. "It's way back up there. This is a big piece of property."

Tim, who was also covered with sweat, did not have his mind on the scouting report. He was watching Eddie enjoying himself in the water. He was swimming in his water. "Edward? Do you think I could jump in with Eddie?"

"Why not? It's a big lake and a hot day. Just...you know..."

"I know," Tim said, sotto voce, "I'll keep my underwear on, too."

In a few moments Tim had removed almost all his clothing and was bounding into the lake. When he came near the drop-off he dove into the water.

Eddie was impressed. "Gee! You really know this lake, Tim."

"I know this spot very well, Eddie. I grew up here."

"You are so lucky!" Eddie grinned at Tim, who grinned back.

"I thought so, too, at the time. But now I know the real meaning of the word *lucky*. Eddie, do you know how to dive?"

"I don't know."

"What I just did. I dove into the water. I put my head down and dove. Do you know how to do that?"

Eddie shrugged his shoulders. It was obvious he didn't know, but Tim wanted to be sure.

"Edward? Does Eddie know how to dive?" Tim called out to the shore.

"I hope you're not planning to take him up to the cliff, Tim," Edward half-joked, hoping that was all that was needed.

"No, sir! I would never do that." Tim answered sincerely. He turned to Eddie, who was treading water next to him. "And don't you even think about jumping from those cliffs, sir. I can teach you over time, but not this time."

"Aw, Tim—"

"Never mind that! You promise me, right now! I don't want you to get any crazy ideas in your head. You are a city boy. I have to slowly teach you to be a country boy, like me."

"So what do I have to do?"

"Well, let's see. Can you hold your breath under water?"

"I guess."

"Then let me see you do it. Take a deep breath and put your head under."

Eddie inhaled deeply and dropped down under the surface, but was back up in a moment, choking on water. Tim grabbed him by the shoulders to steady him until finally it passed.

"See, there's still a lot you have to learn. Swimming in a lake isn't like going to the beach. I've seen folks go in the ocean for hours, except all they do is stand there and get hit by the waves. Only a few know how to dive through the waves and then swim."

"I guess that's what I do at the beach, stand there."

"So, the beach is dangerous because of the undertow, and the lake is dangerous because of all the rocks."

Tim looked back to the shore, to Edward and Geoff. Neither one could be considered a good swimmer. They were both the type of person that Tim had just spoken to Eddie about—they stood in the water and were hit by the waves. Tim looked at Edward and gave a little shrug, as if to ask, *Should I continue?* Edward silently nodded. He wanted his son to be able to swim well, but he also wanted him to respect the danger of the water. He knew that Tim loved Eddie like a younger brother.

Tim McNabb spent about fifteen more minutes showing Eddie how to hold his breath and then showed him a shallow dive, like the one he had done when he entered the lake. Eddie tried the dive about six times, the last two being the most successful. He wrapped his arms around Tim in a hug.

"Eddie, you are shivering. It's time to get out."

Eddie's teeth were chattering. "Aw, can't we stay just a little longer, Tim?"

"We can swim again later, Ed. Either after dinner, or tomorrow."

"You promise?"

"I promise. Now head for the shore."

Eddie led the way, carefully positioning himself on the ledge of the drop-off, and then picking himself up and walking the twenty yards to the shore. He was followed closely by Tim, who knew exactly where he would meet the ground. As Eddie emerged from the water, he wrapped both his arms around his torso for warmth. Edward removed his jacket and put it over his son's shoulders.

"Tim, would you like my jacket?" Geoff kidded.

"I'm fine like this. I'll just drip-dry."

After a few minutes of drying in the bright sun, they headed up the slope toward the house. Eddie carried his clothes, and Edward carried Eddie, because he didn't want him walking barefoot through the undergrowth. He had visions of bringing him back to his mother covered with poison ivy. When they reached the motorcar, Edward put Eddie down and directed him to the house. He reached into the trunk and pulled out the bags, giving one to Tim, one to Geoff, and taking the remaining two himself.

As he gave the bag to Tim, he put a hand on his bare shoulder, and said, "Thank you for patiently teaching my son."

"My pleasure, Edward. Where would I be without you and Geoff?"

"Might I then suffer you to continue to teach him to swim?"

"Absolutely! We already made plans to work again."

They walked into the house via the kitchen entrance. A local woman from Sterling Forest, Mrs. Edith Case, was in the kitchen cooking their dinner. Norris had found Mrs. Case on one of his earlier trips to view the construction. Now she was his regular cook. Tim was not sure if he knew the woman, and she didn't seem to recognize him.

They went up to the guest room to drop their bags. Eddie and Tim found dry underwear and changed out of any clothing that had gotten either dirty or wet. As Tim helped Eddie retie his tie, he mentioned, "The next time we go swimming we will wear trunks, or we will run out of underwear before it's time to leave here." Eddie found that amusing.

Geoff and Edward had already adjourned to the living room for a glass of claret. Within minutes, Tim and Eddie joined them; both looked wet around the ears, but otherwise were neatly dressed. Tim also had a glass of claret, and Eddie was given a glass of apple cider. They enjoyed a wonderful roast beef dinner, courtesy of Mrs. Case, and then moved upstairs for the remainder of the evening. As they mounted the stairs, Tim gave Eddie a knowing look that indicated that their earlier plans for another swimming lesson were probably vetoed. Norris had other plans for them.

Norris invited them out onto the upper patio. Five chairs were already arranged, as if waiting for their bodies. It was close to eight o'clock, but the sun was still high in the sky. Mrs. Case brought up coffee and cake, and a glass of milk for Eddie. With the setting of the sun came fireflies, sometimes called june bugs, and mosquitoes. Norris was as fearful of mosquitoes as he was of snakes, owing to the research that had surfaced recently. Dr. Walter Reade had made a connection between yellow fever and the mosquito that carried it. Norris was a germophobe—another phobia. They moved inside to the great room.

Norris took a seat at the Knabe square grand piano. He launched into some of the more popular tunes of the day, and then some hymns, to which he invited his guests to sing along. Then he asked Tim to sing a solo for the others. Tim was reluctant; he had never performed by himself before—not in public. But Norris insisted, and before long so did everyone else.

"What shall I sing?" Tim asked Norris.

"Sing what you know best, Timothy. Sing of your Irish heritage," was Norris's response.

"Very well, then." Tim cleared his throat.

"I believe you sing it in C."

Tim nodded. Edward had no idea that Tim even knew what C was. Homer began the introduction. Tim sang "Londonderry Air," better known as "Danny Boy." This song, as well as numerous other songs of Ireland, had become wildly popular in the first decade of the century due to the perfection of Edison's phonograph. The Victor Company had taken this idea another step further by creating the Victrola, which played recorded discs. Irish tenor John McCormack made dozens of recordings for Victor and they sold very well.

Tim sang beautifully.

Mrs. Case came upstairs to listen. Edward and Geoff had never heard Tim sing in all the years they had known him, which made this more surprising, and even more special. To Eddie, Tim was his hero; a hero who could teach him to swim, as well as someone who could sing as if he had been touched by God.

The song "Danny Boy" was in the first person, sung by a father who is bidding his son farewell as the son prepares to leave for battle. The father must stay behind, waiting for the son to return—if he returns.

Oh, Danny Boy, the pipes, the pipes are calling
From glen to glen and down the mountainside
The summer's gone, and all the flowers dying
It's you, it's you must go and I must bide.
But come ye back when summer's in the meadow
Or when the valley's hushed and white with snow
'Tis I'll be here in sunshine or in shadow
Oh Danny Boy, oh Danny boy I love you so.

But the second verse turns darker, as the father realizes that, given his advancing age, he might not be alive to witness his son's return. He poignantly asks the son to stop by his grave, if that be the case, and say an "Ave"—a prayer to the Virgin Mary—for him.

But come ye back when all the flowers are dying
If I am dead, as dead I well may be.
Ye'll come and find the place where I am lying
And kneel and say an "Ave" there for me.
And I shall hear, tho' soft you tread above me
And all my dreams will warm and sweeter be
For you shall bend and tell me that you love me,
And I shall sleep in peace until you come to me.

Tim released the last note of the song. There was not a sound in the room, save for the sound of Mrs. Case, in the back, weeping into her handkerchief. Both Edward and Geoff were fighting back the tears, and Eddie sat wondering just what it was all about.

Then Mrs. Case ventured forward, and in one sweeping movement threw her arms around Tim. "Now I remember you, Timothy McNabb. You left here some years ago, and now look at you, all grown up."

"Yes, Mrs. Case."

"And did you do as you sang in the song?"

"Not this trip, Mrs. Case. But I surely have in the past." Tim had, in fact, gone to the grave sites of his mother and father.

"There's a good boy. Your father would be proud to see how successful you've become—and how handsome." Then she turned to Edward and Geoff, saying, "The McNabbs were always a handsome lot." Mrs. Case went back downstairs.

"Tim, that was very well done," Edward said. "I knew you could sing, but I had no idea how well you could express a song."

"Thank you, Edward," Tim replied. "There are just some songs that you sing from your heart. This one reminds me of my father."

"I liked it, too," added Eddie. "Do you know another one? Maybe a faster, happier song?"

They all laughed a bit. After a few more songs and some more conversation, Homer Norris bade them good night and headed downstairs.

"You should get ready for bed, young man," Edward told Eddie. "You need your sleep if you are going to spend a great deal of time learning to swim."

"You are so right, Dad!" He ran to his father and kissed him on the cheek, then he ran to Geoff and kissed him as well, adding, "Good night, Uncle Geoff." He then crossed to Tim and gave him a hug.

Tim tousled his hair and said, "Good night, Eddie."

"Good night, Tim." Eddie went through the French doors into the guest room and closed the doors behind him. The others watched the room become illuminated when Eddie switched on the light.

"Come on, my friends," said Geoff enthusiastically. "I have a nice surprise for us to enjoy before we all turn in. Shall we adjourn to the veranda? And never mind the mosquitoes—this will repel them."

The trio walked back outside. The sun had now set and it was night. A full moon was reflecting off the lake's surface. They could see every star in the sky. Geoff reached into his jacket pocket and produced three cigars.

"These represent one of the positive side effects of the Spanish-American War, gentlemen. These are from Cuba." Geoff handed each a cigar. He then produced a lighter.

"I've only smoked one cigar in my entire life, Geoff," remarked Tim, with an air of uncertainty. "Do you think it will make me sick?"

"Take it easy, then. Puff on it gently, and don't inhale."

They sat up for another hour, taking in the pleasures of the fine Cuban cigars and talking as old friends talk. When they decided to turn in for the night, they were especially careful not to disturb Eddie, who was sleeping like a rock. They changed quietly—Edward in the bedroom, Geoff in the servant's quarters, and Tim in the bathroom—so that they wouldn't wake the boy. Geoff and Edward wore the traditional nightshirt, but Tim was a picture of the twentieth-century young man—he wore the new fashion, pajamas.

They quietly got onto the swinging beds, which began to...swing. As much as they tried to avoid making noise, they had to snigger at their own plight. Eddie, however, continued to sleep.

Geoff was the last man to successfully climb onto the moving bed. No sooner had he settled down than he realized that the bedroom light was still on. He carefully got out of bed and turned off the light. He now had to go through the procedure all over again—in the dark.

Chapter 20
The Boat Tour

"Dad! Are you awake?" Eddie was shaking his father by the shoulder.

"Eddie! I am still trying to sleep," Edward said, still groggy.

"But the sun is up, Dad!"

"Why don't you go find your clothes and get dressed, Eddie?"

"Thanks a good idea."

"How did you sleep?"

"Just like Mr. Norris said, it was like floating on a cloud."

Eddie hopped out of bed. He headed immediately for the bathroom. Edward heard the familiar sound of the boy urinating in the toilet. He heard the toilet flush. The door opened again and Edward heard the returning footsteps.

"Did you wash your hands?" Edward mumbled.

He then heard the same footsteps reverse direction, and in a moment he heard the water running in the sink. He then heard the sounds of a boy searching through a bag for what he was to wear that day.

Edward looked over at the other bed. Tim and Geoff were still asleep; Geoff was lightly snoring.

"Dad, can I just go ahead and put on my swimming trunks now?"

"No, we have to see what is planned for the day first. Eddie, go to where my clothes are hanging and see if you can find my pocket watch."

Once again Edward heard the padding of ten-year-old feet, followed closely by the sounds of searching for the impossible. "I found it, Dad!"

"Good. What time is it?"

"It's almost eight o'clock." Then, "I'm hungry."

"That's why I asked." Edward sat up in the bed. The chains gave a low growl with his sudden movement. He hopped out of the bed, which sent it crashing against the other bed. Tim sat bolt upright.

"What was that?" he said, startled.

"Sorry, Tim. I have to work on my dismount. You don't have to get up yet. It's only eight o'clock."

Geoff never moved. Tim lay back down.

Edward selected his clothes for the day and got dressed along with Eddie. They quietly slipped through the French doors and walked downstairs to the kitchen. Edward was surprised to see Mrs. Case busy making breakfast. He had assumed that she had gone home after the dinner dishes were put away last evening. He wondered, though, how she fared traveling that dark—not to mention, dangerous—road in the middle of the night. He was too much of a proper gentleman to ask such impertinent questions.

Norris walked into the kitchen.

"Ah, it seems that the Colliers are both awake and ready for some breakfast."

"Good morning, Mr. Norris," chirped Eddie.

"How are you today, Homer?" asked Edward.

"Never better," was his reply. "The others still sleeping?"

"Like logs," answered Eddie, adding a laugh at the end.

"You know, Homer," Edward said, "you might have something with those suspended beds. Not because of snakes—I think I just had one of my better night's sleep."

"Aren't they just so comfortable?" added Mrs. Case.

What did that imply? Edward asked himself. *Did that mean Mrs. Case sleeps here when Homer is here?*

"Yes," Edward replied, without thinking. "The only problem in our room is that our beds just smashed together."

Mrs. Case put a large platter of pancakes on the kitchen table, followed by a plate of sausage. "Would you like some milk, dear?" she asked Eddie.

"Yes, ma'am."

They helped themselves to the pancakes and sausage. Halfway through their stack, a head with a mop of dirty blond hair stuck itself through the doorway. "I thought I smelled something cooking down here. Pancakes? Great!" Tim quickly sat down at the table.

"Is Geoff awake yet?" asked Edward.

"No, sir. He is dead to the world, and his breath smells like cigars."

"So does yours, Tim."

"So does yours, Dad."

Even Homer found that funny. "A little coffee will take that smell away. Then all you will smell like is coffee."

Geoff entered the kitchen at about eight thirty. "It was very lonely up there, men. I suddenly felt deserted. What's for breakfast?" He then had his stack of pancakes.

They sat at the kitchen table for a little while after the feeding frenzy had finished, although Eddie was still anxious to get the day started.

Edward had a question for Homer.

"Homer? You designed this house, and you were here for the building process, including the foundation. What is the purpose of a rectangular hole, cut in the cliff rock, that is about fifteen feet deep?"

Homer gave the question some thought, and then answered, "I don't know what you are referring to, Edward."

"Homer, there is this hole, and it should be under your sunken bathtub, perhaps."

"Well, maybe it's a dry well for the wastewater?"

Edward remained as calm as could be. "The hole is cut in solid stone. It can't be a dry well. The water would never drain out. It would eventually back up, or freeze."

"You must be mistaken, Edward. Did you see this with your own eyes?" There was a note of anxiousness in Norris's voice.

"I saw it, Homer," said Geoff.

"I saw it, too," added Tim.

Homer looked nervously around the table. "Does it really matter, gentlemen? The house is complete. It is beautiful. Why worry about what you cannot see?"

"You are correct, Homer," Edward continued. "Perhaps it was a simple miscalculation. A mistake. It just seemed a crazy thing at the time. The excavating equipment hadn't even arrived, so the hole had to have been cut out of the stone by hand. That would have taken a great deal of time and effort."

"No doubt," answered Homer calmly. "But I am sure that, whatever the mistake, this house is not going anywhere."

"Of that you can be sure," answered Edward. "Now, Homer, what do you have planned for us today?"

"I know that Master Edward is looking forward to swimming…"

Eddie looked up from his dish expectantly.

"But I have arranged to have you take a tour of the lake, by boat."

"By boat?" asked Eddie excitedly.

"By boat. A launch will pick up you four on our dock at ten o'clock. You will be gone for several hours, at least."

"Gee!" exclaimed Eddie.

Personal Journal Entry
June 2, 1910

We are about to take a tour of the lake by boat. Eddie is very excited to go.

I have confronted Norris about the carved hole in the rock. He evaded the question quite well—I think that he knows otherwise, but will not say.

The house, however, is wonderful.

I hear them calling me. I must go.

Homer explained that he would not be joining them on the tour. He was busy working on a new composition for the St. George's Choir, and besides, he really didn't trust the open water; another phobia.

They met the launch at the estate dock at the prescribed ten a.m. The launch reminded Geoff very much of Sam's old launch that had brought all their lives together just a few years back. The captain of the launch decided to begin the tour by heading south into New Jersey. They hugged the coastline, heading into Smith's Cove. There they saw a houseboat, a flat-bottomed craft, pulled up onto dry land as if marooned. There was a young man working on the boat. He waved to the launch as it passed. He was making it into a permanent home on land. There were no other buildings in the cove.

They rounded the stone abutment—the point. They could see the ice house through the trees. They passed the steamboat wharf and the train depot. Tim pointed out his old home and the stable to Eddie as they passed. They entered New Jersey. The boat steered clear of a small island—Storm Island. They headed into open water. Tim remarked that the lake was at its shallowest in this area. Eddie looked overboard and noted that he could make out the bottom of the lake.

The launch now passed a section of the lake called the Glens. They passed a few homes, all belonging to the hamlet of Sterling Forest. Then the launch veered a bit to the left. They were looking at the dam at Awosting. This was the dam that had created the lake.

They moved on again. Before long they were looking at the south shore of the lake, in the little town of Hewitt. The boat followed the curve of the lake around and headed north on the west shore. They witnessed the beginnings of a lake community; more homes, and more activity on the water. They could see sailboats, ice houses that had been pulled up on dry ground, rafts for swimming, and many more docks. The launch then passed a large island—Fox Island. Just past the island they could look across the lake, almost a mile away, and see the train depot again. They were about to leave New Jersey.

The boat continued on its northerly route. It passed a lighthouse, which doubled as a boathouse. They passed the steamer *Arlington* as it glided past them on its appointed rounds. Eddie shouted out when they were directly across from the Boulders. The launch continued to chug along until it reached the boundaries of Greenwood Lake Village. It was here that Geoff had taken a similar launch with Sam. They were now at the most northern shore of the lake. The captain steered the launch to the right, and they were now looking at Chapel Island and the east arm of the lake.

The little boat continued back on the east shore of the lake. The shoreline here was particularly inhospitable; rocks jutting out from the shore, exposed above the surface and hidden below it. The captain steered the launch further out from the shore. After a few minutes they approached a quiet wooded area with a very pleasant shoreline.

Eddie was looking off the bow when he exclaimed, "Look, everyone! Look there! That's where we went swimming yesterday."

And indeed it was. They were now approaching the property of Homer Norris once again.

The launch pulled up to the dock and all four passengers piled out. They walked back up to the house and had a light lunch. Eddie had only one thing on his mind.

"Dad, can I go swimming with Tim after lunch?"

"You may have to wait a little, Ed. Let your food go down. You don't want to get a cramp."

Tim was not eating lightly, and was enjoying everything Mrs. Case had prepared.

"What about Tim? Is he going to get a cramp?"

"I've never gotten a cramp," replied Tim. He then saw the look on Edward's face and said, "But I've known some who have, and they almost drowned." Tim, in fact, knew of no such person. Most of the lake folk considered the practice of waiting an hour after eating before swimming to be nothing more than an old wives' tale.

"Let's just give it a little time after lunch before we go exerting ourselves," added Edward.

"Wow! You're going swimming, too, Dad?" Eddie had not considered that prospect.

"We shall see." Generally speaking, that phrase, as many children already knew, usually meant a negative answer.

"What about you, Uncle Geoff?" Eddie asked expectantly.

"I don't think so, sport, "Geoff replied. "I'm not really one for going in the water. I like riding on top of it, but I save getting wet all over for baths."

The truth of the matter was that Geoff would not allow himself to be viewed in the particular state of undress needed for swimming. Even if the modest swimming outfit of the 1900s covered most of his torso, there would still be plenty of area where anyone, especially a curious child, could see the markings of his youth. In the case of Eddie, Geoff wasn't prepared to offer a truthful explanation to the boy of how the scars got there, and he didn't want to put it off onto Edward, either. As enticing as the cool water looked, Geoff decided he would rather suffer the heat than be put in an awkward situation.

The lunch concluded, the foursome retired upstairs for a few minutes of relaxation. Geoff lay back down on the swinging bed, and in a few minutes he was taking a nap. Eddie disappeared into the bathroom, and then reemerged wearing his one-piece swimming garb that consisted of trunks and tank top combined. It was mostly black, with yellow stripes on the sides.

Edward grabbed his journal—his personal journal—and sat down at Norris's desk and began to write an entry. He was startled by the sound of a voice from behind him.

"What are you doing, Dad?"

"Just writing something, Eddie."

Eddie had seen these journals before. His father's library at the Dakota had a shelf filled with them.

"You're writing in your journal again?"

"Yes. Perhaps someday you will begin the habit of writing down your thoughts."

"I don't know if I could ever write as much as you." Edward laughed. "May I read what you wrote?"

"I don't know if you would be able to read my handwriting, son, but no, these are my private thoughts."

"You mean there are secrets in the book?"

"Some." He put down the pen and lifted Eddie onto his lap. "You look pretty sharp in that new swimming outfit. Did you pick this out?"

"No, Mom did."

"Well, do you like it?"

"The way I look at it, it's better than swimming buck naked."

Edward was astonished. "Eddie! I am surprised at you! Did Tim use that expression with you?"

Eddie laughed at his father. "No, Dad. Why? Does Tim say buck naked, too?"

"Never mind."

Tim entered the room. He, too, was wearing a one-piece swimming outfit, but his was all black, with red horizontal stripes.

"Edward, would you mind if I took Eddie swimming?"

"I think you can manage without me. I know he loves your company, Tim."

Eddie hopped off his father's lap. "Thanks, Dad!"

"Eddie, you listen well to Tim, and be careful." He noticed that Tim, as usual, was going barefoot, so he added, "Eddie, make sure you are wearing your shoes down to the shore!"

"I'll get them on straightaway."

They went back into the bedroom so that Eddie could get his shoes. Tim had a sack with him to take the towels. They were out of the house in less than a minute.

The younger half of the house party went out by way of the kitchen door. They turned to the left and headed toward the path that led to the lakeshore. Edward Collier, Jr., was normally a very effervescent child, but he was even more keyed up as they reached the trail. He was so excited to retry what he had learned the day before that he simply bubbled verbiage. Tim quietly walked a few paces behind him, and occasionally would add a one- or two-word agreement to what the child had said. Eddie would ask a question or make a statement and then wheel around to look for Tim to give him an answer or reply. They were about twenty yards from the shore when Tim spotted something lying in the path ahead of Eddie.

It was a rattlesnake sunbathing on a flat stone that had been warmed by the sun. The snake was coiled. Its tail was already rattling.

Eddie was turned facing Tim and couldn't see the snake. He was talking and didn't hear the rattle, but he probably wouldn't have recognized the sound, having never heard it before. Tim knew he would be within striking distance in another step or two.

"Eddie! Stop! Don't move!" he yelled.

The boy stopped moving. He was still facing Tim. "What?"

Then he took another step backward with his left foot. Tim realized that he was now within the snake's strike zone. He broke into a gallop, quickly closing the distance between himself and the boy. Without another word, he hoisted Eddie up to his chest just as the snake lunged at the child.

Tim felt the snake bite him on the leg. He let out a yelp of pain and hopped on the other leg, carrying Eddie until they reached the shore. The snake slithered into the brush.

"Tim?" asked a surprised Eddie, who never saw the snake but saw the expression of pain on Tim's face. "What happened?"

"Rattlesnake, Ed." He put Eddie down and leaned against the big rock. "It got me."

"It bit you? Where?"

"On my leg...in the back...above my ankle."

Eddie crouched to the ground to see the bite. Tim lifted the bitten leg and rotated it out slightly. The snake had bitten the lower calf of his right leg. There were two puncture marks visible and he was bleeding from the wounds.

Eddie's response was immediate. "I'll go get help. I'll get my dad." He started toward the path.

"No!" Tim shouted. He didn't want to send the boy up the same path where the snake might still be hiding. He knew that snakes could recoil and strike several times. "I'm going to need your help here, Eddie."

"My help? What can I do?"

"First, you need to stay calm, because I need to stay calm. If you panic my pain could get a lot worse. Do you understand?"

"Sure, Tim." Tears were already rolling down Eddie's cheeks. He quickly wiped them away. "What do you want me to do?"

"I need you to find me a stick about eight inches long and about an inch thick. Don't go away from the shore."

"I can do that."

As the boy started to go, Tim said, "Wait! First look in the sack. Take out the towels. There should be a pocketknife in the bottom. Give me the knife." Eddie removed the towels from the bag and found the knife. He handed the knife to Tim without opening it. "Now you can go find the stick."

While Eddie was looking for the stick, Tim opened the pocket-knife and used it to cut the tank top of his swimming outfit. He cut away the shoulder strap from his left side, but he could not remove the entire piece of cloth without exerting a great deal of energy. He had to wait for Eddie to come back.

"How is this?" asked Eddie, holding a stick.

"That's good." He handed the knife carefully to the boy. "Now, I need you to cut away the rest of my top. Be careful. Don't cut yourself!"

Eddie started to carefully cut the upper part of the suit. He was more concerned with avoiding Tim's skin than anything else.

"Eddie, you have to just cut and then rip it. But you have to work fast!"

"All right."

Eddie cut and yanked, pulling off a sizeable piece of the suit. Tim took the cloth and the stick and fashioned a tourniquet out of them over the upper part of his calf. Eddie watched quietly, never saying a word.

"Eddie, remember the story about how I helped with the birth of your cousin, Timmy?"

"Yes."

"Well, now it's your turn to be brave."

Eddie looked up at Tim and thought Tim didn't look very good. Something was happening to him.

Tim continued, "I need you to take the knife and make two cuts into my leg—one below the bite, and the other above the bite."

"You want me to cut you?" Eddie shook his head in disbelief.

"I need to get some of the poison out of me, Eddie. I need to remain as still as possible, so you have to do it."

"Are...are you going to die?" Eddie started crying again.

"No. Very few people die from snakebites. But they can cause permanent injury, so you have to act fast. You have to be brave."

Eddie knelt down, knife in his hand. Tim's lower leg was covered with blood. He had stayed upright, leaning against the rock, so that his head would be elevated higher than his heart.

"I can't see where to cut because of the blood."

"Take a towel and wipe the blood away." Eddie followed Tim's instructions. "Now, cut the bottom one first, about an inch and a little more across. You don't have to go too deep."

Tim put a piece of his shredded tank top in his mouth and bit down. Eddie drew in a breath and then cut. Tim rotated his leg and examined the incision.

"Good, that's good. Now do the other one." Eddie placed the knife on Tim's calf and then looked up for approval. "Yes, do it there." Tim bit down again on his top.

But Tim knew the worst was yet to come for the boy.

"Now, Eddie, this is going to be bad. I need you to put your mouth right over the bite and then suck out the poison."

"What?" Eddie asked, very confused. "What?"

"You need to suck out the venom. Suck it out, but don't swallow it. Just spit it out onto the ground. Do it a few times."

"Will it taste bad?"

"I don't know what the venom tastes like, but it will certainly taste like blood."

Eddie nodded slowly. He bent down and gently lifted Tim's leg a bit. It was a mess of blood, cuts, and matted hair. He wiped away the excess blood. Eddie placed his mouth over the bite marks and started to suck out the venom.

"Suck it out as hard as you can, Eddie. Try to reduce the amount of poison in my blood."

Eddie sucked out the poison and spit it out five times.

"Now go into the lake and rinse out your mouth really well. Don't swallow until it's all out."

Eddie ran into the lake a few feet, knelt in the shallow water, and used his hands to scoop the water to his mouth. He then returned to his injured friend.

"Now I need you to wrap a towel loosely around the leg."

Eddie obeyed the order. After he did this, he stood up, facing Tim. Tim held out his arms and embraced Eddie.

"Are you safe now?" asked Eddie.

"No, not yet, I'm afraid. I really have to get to a doctor. Now you have to go get help."

Eddie looked at him quizzically. "But I could have gone before!"

"I know, but this had to be done first," he answered, gesturing to his leg. Then he looked back up the path toward the house. Had the snake gone elsewhere, or was it still near the path? he asked himself. It was a risk he was not willing to take.

"Exactly how well can you swim?"

"You saw me swim yesterday."

"I saw you hold your breath and do a shallow dive in about five feet of water. Can you swim for a distance, say, from here to the dock?" It would mean a swim of at least fifty to seventy-five yards in deep open water. Tim looked at the ground, knowing it was too much to ask of the child.

"To the dock? I don't know." Eddie had never had to swim that far before. "So, I swim to the dock, then I run up to the house, is that it?" Eddie turned toward the lake, ready to go.

"Wait!" said Tim. "Come back wearing pants and shoes, and don't forget to tell Mr. Norris that his instincts were correct."

Eddie looked puzzled. "About what?"

Tim gave Eddie a small grin and answered, "About the snakes."

"Right!" Eddie agreed, and then ran into the water.

When he approached the drop-off, he executed a very passable shallow dive that made Tim smile. He swam into the deeper water, cutting to his left and out at the same time. There was a slight breeze that day, so the water was a little choppy—certainly not like the waves of the ocean, but then again, Eddie never really swam in the ocean. Eddie started to tire as he approached the cliff rock. He could see the dock, but it was still about twenty yards away. He stopped swimming and tried to catch his breath. As he was treading water, a bigger wave suddenly washed over his head. He held his breath.

He began to swim again. He kept thinking of Tim. It seemed to take forever, but in reality he reached the safety of the dock in only ten minutes. He climbed the ladder to the deck, and then ran for the shore. He ran up the sloped path to the house. He ran to the lower patio.

"Dad! Dad! Uncle Geoff! Mr. Norris! Anyone!" he called out.

He heard several voices answering him at once. He focused on his father's voice, which came from the upper patio. "Eddie? What's the matter?"

"It's Tim, Dad. He was bitten by a rattlesnake. He needs help!"

The household became a flurry of activity. A large blanket was found to act as a stretcher. Mrs. Case pulled out the first aid kit. Homer went to start the Pierce-Arrow. Eddie put his clothes on over his swimming suit.

"Where is the nearest doctor?" Edward asked Mrs. Case.

"There is one in Hewitt, near the south shore. Doc Sherwood."

There was no communication to or from the house, as the telephone line had yet to be run. The quickest way to get help was simply to take Tim there by car.

The three men headed back down the path toward the lake. Edward demanded that Eddie stay with Mrs. Case, which did not meet with his approval. Homer had a large walking stick in his hand which he used to check for snakes by sweeping it to and fro, from side to side. They quickly reached Tim.

"Glad to see you, gentlemen," Tim smiled.

"How does it feel?" asked Edward.

"My leg is tingling a little. It probably could be worse." He then added, "How is Eddie?"

"Eddie is fine. I had to chain him to the motorcar to prevent him from coming back down here."

Tim nodded.

Geoff and Edward lowered Tim onto the blanket, which was spread out on the ground. With each man carrying two corners, they lifted him and carried him to the car, with Norris clearing the way of any possible snakes. They placed him in the backseat of the Pierce-Arrow and wrapped the blanket around him. Eddie jumped in beside him. Geoff rode up front with Edward, who drove the car. They headed out of the estate and onto Shore Avenue as quickly as they could go, given the amount of ruts. It took almost a half hour to ride to Hewitt, and another ten minutes to find Dr. Sherwood's home. Geoff hopped out of the motorcar and ran into the doctor's office to apprise him of the situation. The doctor came out to help get Tim inside.

"How long ago did this happen?" the doctor asked.

"A little over an hour ago," Geoff answered.

"If that's the case, he should look worse than he does."

The men and Eddie brought Tim into the examination room. Doc Sherwood untied the towel from his leg and examined the wounds. "Who did this first aid?" he asked. Eddie was afraid to answer.

Tim answered proudly, "Young Edward over there did the procedure. I told him what to do."

"Well, young man, very good work." The doctor smiled at Eddie, who grinned back. "I think you may have saved your friend from any really serious harm."

"Really?" asked Eddie, who was still holding Tim's hand.

"Yes, really. Most snake bites are not fatal, and defensive strikes sometimes don't even have much venom in them, but you never can tell. Can you?"

Edward mentioned to the doctor that Tim was actually at Columbia studying to become a doctor.

"That isn't where I learned how to treat snakebite," inserted Tim. "I grew up in Sterling, and we had many a rattlesnake in the barn. I've seen bites treated before today."

"Yes, well, that method of first aid has pros and cons. Lots of us doctors out there think the cure is sometimes worse than the bite."

The doctor then treated the wound. He asked the rest to step outside to the waiting room while he took care of the patient, but Eddie shook his head, saying he had to stay. The doctor relented. Doc Sherwood dressed the wound and gave Tim an extra supply of dressings. He warned him about infection, especially on the cuts made by the knife. He also told all of them that Tim might still suffer from a variety of symptoms over the next day or so, including vomiting, diarrhea, and swelling and bruising at the wound. He then suggested that they return if those symptoms became severe.

"But," he said, "a healthy young man of your size should fare pretty well and make a good, quick recovery. It's far worse when a child is bitten. Their bodies are smaller, so the poison is more deadly, and it's hard to keep a child calm after they are bitten, so the poison moves faster in the bloodstream."

Eddie recalled the series of events leading to the strike. "That's why you picked me up, Tim. You knew it would be worse for me than for you."

"Snakes usually eat rodents and birds," Tim answered gently, "the smaller the animal, the more deadly the venom. I just acted out of instinct."

"You saved my life," Eddie replied quietly. "You saved my life."

Tim recovered completely within a few days, but had some scarring on his right leg that would remain with him for the rest of his life.

It was the second time he had saved the life of a member of the Collier-Atwater family.

Personal Journal Entry
June 2, 1910

This is the second entry for this day.

My son, Eddie, has just saved the life of Tim McNabb. I am very proud of him.

Tim was bitten by a rattlesnake. A timber rattlesnake.

I suppose Homer will now feel vindicated, that snakes do abound on the property and that he needs a home that offers him a degree of protection.

Never mind that; my son is a hero.

Chapter 21
Homecoming

Edward, Geoff, Tim, and Eddie returned to Manhattan Island two days after Tim had been bitten by the snake. He seemed to be on the way to a quick recovery.

Edward decided to take a slightly different route to get home. He followed the East Shore Road out to the intersection with the Greenwood Lake Turnpike and then turned left. He followed the road for about a half mile, until he came upon a collection of old houses, a tavern, and a church. He pulled the Pierce-Arrow over by the entrance to the tavern.

"Do you know where we are?" asked Tim.

"Do you?" asked Geoff.

"Certainly! This is what is left of the settlement of Monksville, the place where Hasenclever had his mining community," Tim explained.

"These building don't look like they date back to the Revolution, Tim," Edward replied.

"No, these are newer buildings, but if you take a walk back in those woods you will come across the furnaces and remnants of the mills."

"Can we go take a look, Dad?" Eddie had forgotten about Tim's leg and was ready for a new adventure.

"I wouldn't, if I were you," cautioned Tim. "I hear that the locals around here don't take kindly to outsiders."

"Outsiders?" asked Geoff.

"People who don't belong," answered Tim, with an air of hesitancy.

Eddie was busying himself looking all around the area, so Tim took the opportunity to tacitly shake his head "no" to Edward and Geoff. He knew this was not a place to go exploring—snakes or no snakes!

"Who lives here now?" asked Eddie.

"Well, I suppose someone runs the tavern, and there's a minister for the church, but the other folk are just plain mysterious."

Edward peered into the distance, past some trees, to a small grouping of houses. There were children and a few adults standing on the front porch of one house, staring at them.

"I see what you mean," said Edward, who put the motorcar in gear and pulled away.

This was a community where fact and legend mixed ambiguously together. When Peter Hasenclever was removed as manager of the Long Pond Iron Works in 1767, many of the workers he had imported from Europe eventually returned home, but some did stay in the area, setting up small businesses, farms, and schools. Within ten years there was more turmoil as the Revolutionary War began. The iron furnaces in the area were busy working for the war effort, particularly the manufacture of an immense forged iron chain that would be used to blockade the Hudson River from the British Navy. The chain was forged in nearby Ringwood. The war was not the short skirmish that the English had expected, and before long they began to hire mercenaries from an allied province in northern Germany, Hesse-Kassel. The Hessian soldiers were some of the most highly trained professional soldiers of the war, and they were feared by the colonists because of their brutality.

But the Hessians were fighting on foreign and unknown soil. As the Americans fought on, many of the Germans became disenchanted with their lot in the war and deserted. As the punishment for desertion was death, they fled into the hinterlands and attempted to get as far away from the fighting as possible. Legend has it that these deserters came upon the remainder of Hasenclever's imported ironworkers, who just happened to speak the same language. The Hessian soldiers were amalgamated into the community.

But the legend became further convoluted by claims that the communal gene pool was also mixed with that of Native Americans, runaway African slaves, and a population of Dutch immigrants who originally settled in the area. Edward and his retinue had been looking at a small group of Ramapo Mountain People, at the turn of the century called simply "Jackson Whites."

Edward continued to drive toward New York. He passed by the large lake that the train route took him over several years ago. In just a few years, the lake would become, in fact, a reservoir. It would become the largest part of the water system that brought water to New Jersey's biggest city, Newark.

They entered small town after small town, consistently following the rail line, through towns like Wanaque, Haskell, and Midvale. The road signs eventually told them that they were riding on a road called Ringwood Avenue, but Edward knew that Ringwood was already miles behind them. They arrived at the intersection of the Paterson-Hamburg Turnpike, a road with which Geoff had some earlier experience. Here was situated a lovely church in the Dutch Reformed Tradition, built in 1812. They were in the town of Pompton Lakes.

Edward turned the Pierce-Arrow to the right. He did not want to take the turnpike to Paterson. He stayed northbound for less than a mile, until he came to the intersection with the start of the Newark-Pompton Turnpike. He turned onto this route.

The travelers rolled on, passing through the New Jersey towns of Riverdale, Wayne, Mountain View, Lincoln Park, and Totowa. They eventually met up with the Paterson Plank Road, which they stayed on until they hit the streets of Jersey City, ending up at Communipaw Avenue and the ferry terminal.

They crossed the Hudson with the Pierce-Arrow as they had a week prior, landed at Liberty Street, and then proceeded north toward their apartments near Central Park.

Edward's father, Thomas, enjoyed working in the small piece of yard that was found behind the brownstone in which he and his wife lived. He was working in his garden on the afternoon of September 20, 1910, when he suffered a massive stroke. His wife, Elizabeth, found him lying on the ground, and with the help of Clara and one of the neighbors was able to bring him into the house. He lay quietly and motionless for several days, his brain extremely damaged by the stroke. He passed from this life on September 25, with his family gathered around him.

Edward stayed away from the office until the middle of October; Geoff covered his duties for him. J. P. Morgan seemed very much affected by the passing of the elder Collier. Edward surmised that Morgan was increasingly aware that his own was approaching quickly.

Morgan insisted that he be permitted to donate a beautiful cemetery plot at St. George's to the family. He mentioned to Edward that he had originally purchased the plot for himself, but had changed his mind since and planned to be buried elsewhere. Edward went to the churchyard to examine the grave site. The plot contained a mausoleum. Written above the doorway was the name Morgan. The tomb was empty and unlocked. Edward never really cared for this form of burial, as it wasn't being buried at all. There was room for multiple caskets, enough for an entire family to spend eternity together.

But Edward knew his mother would have to give her approval, as she would then end up in the tomb as well. Edward also shivered at the thought that he and Rebecca, and maybe even their children, would eventually reside there.

He doubted his mother would agree to anything as ostentatious as this—but he was wrong. His mother very quietly told Edward that he should tell Mr. Morgan that they were most grateful for his kind thoughts. Edward was flabbergasted.

The funeral took place in the nave of St. George's on September 28, with interment in the tomb directly following the service. As was the custom, everyone in attendance wore black. Harry Burleigh sang several pieces during the service. Homer Norris played the organ.

Thomas Collier was not quite sixty years old. He had died far too young.

At the time of the interment, Edward noticed that the name Morgan, which had been so prominently displayed above the door of the tomb, had been changed to Collier. Once again, Morgan had proved that he was capable of getting people to do things very quickly.

Edward also noticed something else. When he had first viewed the tomb he had seen that there were shelves, or niches, for multiple caskets. Now there were sarcophagi—empty shells to hold the casket after interment—placed throughout the tomb. His father would be placed in one of these, and the others stood ready for the future as empty, silent sentinels.

J. P. Morgan attended the funeral service, but sat removed from the immediate family by quite a few rows of pews. When the service ended, he quickly exited the church, remaining just long enough for Edward to know that he had indeed attended.

Edward asked his mother to move in with his family at the Dakota, but she declined the offer. She explained that she enjoyed living in the hustle and bustle of Lower Manhattan, and did not take to "the country life." That explanation was just her way of saying that she didn't want to be a bother for Edward's growing family, and that she and Clara would be just fine. She even mentioned taking in a boarder or two so that life could remain a little interesting. Elizabeth Collier was already sixty-five; she was older than her husband by over five years.

They had met in one of Morgan's Trust Company branches. They courted very briefly and then plunged right into marriage. Elizabeth became pregnant, it seemed, on their first week of marriage, and then delivered the baby so very early. In less than a year's time, the couple went from single, to married, to parents.

Personal Journal Entry
September 28, 1910

I have just buried my father. I have wept with my mother.
I cannot write any more on the subject, or any other subject, today.

New York had always been known for its tall buildings, but in the beginning of the twentieth century the word *tall* became synonymous with the term *skyscraper.* Originally, the term referred to tall-masted sailing ships, whose rigging seemed to scrap the very sky. With the advent of structural steel, construction could stretch buildings to previously unheard-of heights. One of the first skyscrapers had been the Flatiron Building, which was found at the end of Madison Square, at the intersections of Fifth Avenue and Broadway.

In 1910, the talk centered once again around a new construction project, this one in Lower Manhattan. It was the Woolworth Building, which at fifty-seven stories tall would hold the record for tallest building until 1930.

Uptown, the new Episcopal cathedral was ending one phase of construction—that of the apse and choir—and beginning another, the nave. The nave was the longest section of the Gothic cathedral; it stretched from the main entrance up to the crossing, or transept. The plans being drawn up by architect Cram called for an unusually large nave; in fact, it would make the church the largest Gothic cathedral in the world. The church was to measure 601 feet in length.

The Collier-Atwater family was growing once again.

Edward and Rebecca welcomed their third child—a son, Jacob Henry Collier—into the world on January 24, 1911. He joined Edward

Thomas Collier, Jr., who was eleven, and Alice Anne Collier, who was almost five.

Geoff and Millie Atwater had their first child as husband and wife. On October 21, 1909, they had welcomed a daughter, Barbara Marie Atwater, who was now a toddler. By early 1911, Millie was expecting again. Timothy Edward Atwater was four years old.

Sam and Emily Waters, while not official members of the extended family, were always invited for family gatherings. Emily had their first child in June 1910—a daughter, Sarah Jane Waters. In February 1911, Morgan called Sam into his office to ask him if he would consider relocating to the company's London office. Sam jumped at the chance, and in May, he, Emily, and baby Sarah were loaded onto a steamship bound for England. Everyone cried, promised to write, and hoped to see each other very soon.

Timothy McNabb graduated Columbia University in May 1911. He had graduated with highest honors and had been accepted into medical school.

Chapter 22
A Nice Old Uncle

Like most other eleven-year-olds, Eddie loved going in to work with his father. It wasn't a regular occurrence, so it was special when it happened. Eddie loved riding the elevator up to his father's office. He loved gazing out on the financial district, especially from one of the higher floors of the building. He especially liked lunchtime, because his father would always take him to a Lower Manhattan restaurant, usually accompanied by his Uncle Geoff.

If someone had actually taken the time to ask Eddie about his earliest recollections of going to the Morgan Company, he probably would have been able to recall visits back to when he was five or six, although he had been to the office for the very first time when he was only a few months old.

Everyone knew him around the office, and not in a negative way, as could have easily been the case. Eddie had an infectious laugh and a personality that could claim an entire room upon entrance. He was always well mannered and polite. Eddie was also as sharp as a tack and extremely intelligent. His father was very, very proud of him.

When he visited the office after the summer of 1910, he would be asked to relate how he saved the life of Tim McNabb at Greenwood Lake. Eddie would not embellish the story, but would usually give a very accurate play-by-play account of the events of that day. He would relate this story whenever asked.

J. P. Morgan had also fallen victim to Edward Junior's personality. Morgan had taken a very special interest in Edward's family. He had always liked Rebecca—she had been his receptionist, after all—and now there were three children. But he also showed great interest in Geoff's family, and in Sam's, and there was a special place in his heart for Tim McNabb. This was not the man that the world knew as J. Pierpont Morgan. He had even told the children and their parents that they should look upon him as a "nice old uncle."

But he had gone so far as to tell Eddie that he was welcome in his office at any time of day, and that he had permission to barge in and disrupt any kind of meeting that was going on. The receptionists and other office workers found this somewhat odd, especially because his grandchildren, including those of Jack Jr.—heir to his empire—did not have a similar proviso.

Edward wisely ignored this order—however good-natured and uncharacteristic—and always made sure that the boss was not busy before he would bring Eddie in to see him. The scene was almost always the same: Morgan would ask if Eddie would like to sit on his lap. Eddie always sat on his lap, until the snake incident, and then Edward prompted Eddie that perhaps he was getting too old to do that. Edward didn't think that way because of Eddie's growing size; it was because of Morgan's growing infirmity.

Morgan would always send for cookies and other sweets. Eddie and Morgan would devour the entire tray.

Morgan would always have a conversation with Eddie, and he would never talk down to him, especially after he turned eight. He would often joke with Eddie about Theodore Roosevelt, a person Eddie admired a great deal, saying that he was going to arrange to send Eddie to Africa or South America after Roosevelt left the presidency. Eddie would then respond by saying, "Bully!"

Edward had known for years, possibly since the day Morgan hired him, that there were certain secrets that Morgan intended to keep from his son, Jack. Edward also realized that the elder Morgan was beginning to slip away, and once he was gone that his own security in the company might come under scrutiny. It had always been Edward's opinion, feeling, speculation, and conundrum that Morgan was keeping funds hidden from the company, and therefore also from Jack.

But Morgan knew that Edward was a keeper of secrets, and he would often bring up this matter when Eddie was in the office. One such conversation went like so:

"Eddie?" Morgan asked.

"Yes, Mr. Morgan?"

"Does your father still write in those journals of his?"

"Oh, yes! I think he writes something every single night before he goes to bed."

"He does? And what do you think he has so much to write about?"

"I think he likes to write about you, Mr. Morgan." Eddie laughed.

"About me?"

Edward rolled his eyes heavenward.

Morgan instantly dismissed this and continued the questioning. "How do you know that he is writing about me?"

"I've seen your name written in the books," answered Eddie innocently.

"Really?" Morgan nodded to Edward. "Have you read his journals, Eddie?"

"No, sir!" Eddie answered vehemently. "I know they are Dad's private property."

That would be the type of questioning Eddie might receive when he was nine or ten, but in late June 1911 the questioning was similar but different. Morgan even asked Edward to leave him with the boy—"as a favor to an old man." Edward excused himself from the office. He was not worried at all about what his son might tell Morgan. The boy was smart enough to know when Morgan was playing him.

The conversation began similarly to prior occasions, but there was a different spin on the content.

"Edward, you look like you are just about on the brink of manhood. I need to ask you a few delicate questions. Questions that you must promise me you will not talk to your father about, until…" Morgan stopped, thinking how to finish the statement.

"Until what, sir?"

"Until I am gone, Eddie." Morgan said that with a great deal of emotion.

"Do you mean dead, or just out of the office?"

"I mean dead! I am not a well man, and I am old."

"Aw, Uncle Pierpont, you're not that old!"

"You are a kind young man, Edward," Morgan replied, smiling. "Do you promise on your very soul? I mean no harm to your father, Eddie. I love him, like he loves you."

Eddie found it almost funny to hear a man as powerful as Morgan using the tender word *love*, and especially in connection with his father.

"I promise not to tell," Eddie began, and then added wisely, "unless you do something that hurts my dad."

"I accept that, Edward." He shook Eddie's hand in solemn agreement. "Now, does your father keep all his personal journals somewhere?"

Eddie blanched. He didn't know if he should mention this. He remembered the solemn promise. "He keeps them all in the library of the apartment."

"Are there many volumes?"

"Sure are! There is a new book for every year. I think the first is dated 1898. That's a really long time ago."

"Yes, it is." Morgan fished a piece of paper out of his coat pocket. "Now, here is our secret. I am going to give you this paper, Eddie. I want you to go to his library and I want you to hide this piece of paper in one of the volumes of his personal journal."

"I should hide it?"

"Yes. Don't let him see you do it! Can you do that for me?"

"I suppose so." Eddie didn't really think it was such a big deal.

"Good. I think you should hide it where you can remember it easily, so you can find it again. Let's see, I think you should hide it in the journal for 1910, at the page where he talks about your rattlesnake story."

"Gee! That's a really good place!" Then he asked, "How do you know he wrote about the snake story in his journal?"

"Because it was such a big event." Eddie nodded. "Here! Put it in your pocket before your father comes back in." Eddie neatly put the paper in his jacket pocket. "You don't have to worry about reading it, Eddie. You won't understand a word of it."

"So then what?" Eddie had a feeling that there was more to this.

"Let's say a day arrives when your father goes looking for something he can't find. You may be in school—in Harvard or Oxford—"

"Or Columbia?"

"Or Columbia." Morgan knew the son would follow in his father's footsteps to his alma mater. "Of course, the thing is, I must already be dead. I must be dead. Do you understand?"

"You are dead!" It sounded like a joke, so Eddie smiled.

"Well, don't look so happy about it!" Eddie's face immediately fell; then Morgan smiled and Eddie realized it was a joke. "So we have established that...I am dead. One day, your father starts pulling his hair out, because there's something he thought he knew, but he doesn't have the right answer. Something is missing. Something like—"

"A clue?" Eddie asked.

"That's it exactly, a clue!" Morgan gave Eddie a big all-knowing wink. "That's when you go to your father—your dad—and you say, 'Dad, have you tried looking in your 1910 journal under the key word, *snakebite?*'"

They both laughed at the prank. Eddie thought it was clever, whatever it was.

Morgan reminded him, "So, not a word?"

Eddie nodded. "Not a word!" And then he crossed his heart.

Morgan reminded him again, "Don't let anyone see you hide the paper."

Eddie nodded again. "I won't let anyone see me hide the paper." And then he added, "So help me, God!"

Eddie kept the piece of paper hidden in his own desk drawer for over a week, waiting for the perfect opportunity to steal into his father's library to conceal the little scrap. It wasn't that he couldn't have easily gotten away with it before then, it was just that he wanted it to be perfect, and when there could be no chance of being caught.

One day, his mother went upstairs to the playroom with Alice and Jacob. His father was at work, and the cook was busy in the kitchen. Eddie was reading a book, so his mother left him in the apartment with the cook. Eddie quickly stole into his father's office and took down the blue-covered journal that had 1910 written on the spine in gold lettering. He thumbed through the pages until he found the entry that spoke about the rattlesnake bite. He was very tempted to read the passage, because his father would have mentioned him in it, but he knew the longer he stayed there, the better chance for being caught.

He put the scrap of paper in the book, closed it and replaced it on the shelf. He never mentioned a word about it to anyone.

Personal Journal Entry
June 25, 1911

I have the suspicion that Morgan is now using my son for something. I do not know what this may be, but they seem to have secrets.

Eddie is such a trusting child—I do not want to see him hurt.

What could the old man possibly be thinking?

Chapter 23
The Voyage

Personal Journal Entry
November 6, 1911

Happiness has come to our ever-growing family once more. Geoff and Millie are parents again. Millie gave birth to a daughter, Penelope Margaret Atwater, at 8:05 this morning. Mother and baby are doing fine.

This brings their children to a total of three: Timothy Edward, Barbara Mary, and now little Penelope Margaret. I think it is very touching that Millie suggested giving the baby the middle name of Margaret.

Now he has three and I have three; three boys and three girls between the two of us. What could be more perfect?

In November 1911, Morgan called Edward into his office for an assignment. Edward had become increasingly concerned over how J. P. looked—his physical condition was worsening.

Morgan quickly dismissed any inquiries from Edward regarding his health. His mind was on quite a different set of thoughts.

"Edward, when was the last time you went to Europe?"

"Mr. Morgan, I was there in 1899 for my honeymoon."

"That's right! I should have remembered that!" There was a momentary silence in the office. "Well, we are going back!"

"What, sir?" Edward was aghast that Morgan would even consider a long sea voyage in his condition.

"I intend to go to Europe for a few months—maybe forever, if you get my point. I would like to take you along with me, in your capacity to do whatever it is that I pay you to do."

Edward was totally surprised by this demand. "What about my family, sir? I don't know if I can leave them for so long."

"Nonsense! It's work, Edward! Your wife will understand. Besides,"—he paused, ready to drop the other shoe—"I want you to bring your son, too."

"Eddie?" Edward asked.

"No, not Eddie! Jacob!" He laughed. "Of course, Eddie! The boy is almost twelve years old. He should see Europe, and with me he will see it in style."

"That is very generous, sir. I will need to discuss this with Rebecca, of course."

"Of course." Morgan knew Rebecca would not turn down such a wonderful opportunity for her son's education.

Rebecca did agree to the trip, and for Eddie to go along. They would leave before Thanksgiving, because winter travel across the Atlantic was far too bitter, and far too dangerous. To say the least, Eddie was tremendously excited about going across the ocean, and even more excited that he was going to see many of the places he had read about in history books. He wrote a very nice note to Morgan, thanking him in advance for thinking of him. Morgan was truly touched by the gesture.

Edward was put in charge of making the arrangements. Most of them were quite easy. When J. Pierpont Morgan traveled everything was always the best to be had. As Morgan had an interest in the White Star Line, Edward booked passage to England on a brand-new superliner, the *Olympic*. *Olympic* was launched in 1911, and had really made her name in just as few short months. Edward made sure that they had the biggest stateroom suite on the highest deck of the ship.

With telephone cables strung across the bed of the Atlantic Ocean, and wireless transmissions routine, it was even easier to book accommodations at the five-star hotels in each of the European cities they would visit. They would also need to hire a motorcar, but that could be done either once there or just before.

Edward spent a week preparing the itinerary and then had it approved by Morgan. Morgan added a cryptic line to the itinerary in each city. It read simply: time for shopping. Edward knew that Morgan never went shopping, certainly not for souvenirs. He wondered if the trip actually had a mission, and was not just for relaxation.

Rebecca, in the interim, worked with Eddie, teaching him important phrases in French, German, and Italian. She reviewed proper table manners with him, and instructed him constantly on the upkeep of his wardrobe. She cautioned him that Morgan would have servants along for the ride, but Eddie was not to expect their help.

Rebecca took Eddie shopping to purchase new clothes for the trip. He had just experienced a growth spurt and had shot up more than an inch. She wanted to dress him in long pants, especially for formal occasions, instead of the customary knickers for a boy his age.

The entire family of Collier-Atwater came down to the docks to see the *Olympic* off on the Saturday before Thanksgiving. They enjoyed a sumptuous bon voyage reception in Morgan's suite, which was situated on the same deck as the bridge. The suite was larger than most hotel suites and included servant's quarters, a sitting room with a piano, and several bedrooms. Edward and Eddie were going to share a bedroom on the crossing. At three thirty p.m., all passengers and their guests heard the announcement: "All ashore who are going ashore." This was the signal that guests should head down the gangway to the pier. At four o'clock, the whistle gave a mighty blast, the ropes were cast off, and the ship began to back into the Hudson River, with the aid of a few tugboats. An hour later it was headed into the open water of the Atlantic.

Morgan, Edward, and Eddie were seated for dinner that night, and for all subsequent meals, at the captain's table. Rebecca had suspected this would be where they would dine, considering Morgan's stature in the world. There were other prominent guests aboard, as well, and a few managed to get to sit in the company of the captain and J. P. Morgan. The first night's dinner would be Eddie's initial test of manners. The mood and conversation were very formal, which Morgan hated. Edward made sure he addressed his son as Edward, or sometimes even Ed, avoiding the childlike "Eddie," which annoyed Eddie and frustrated Morgan. Later, in the stateroom, Morgan asked Edward to drop the formality and let the boy be a boy. Edward relaxed and agreed.

Personal Journal Entry
November 29, 1911

We are at sea. Eddie is having a wonderful time!

He is a real charmer at dinner, and seems to know almost every guest on board.

I am still not entirely sure why he was invited to go to Europe by Morgan. For that matter, I am not sure why he invited me. I can't really complain, because it is such a great opportunity for Eddie. I must remember to chide Rebecca that he doesn't seem to feel the roll of the waves like she does.

⚜

Life at sea agreed with Eddie, and he never felt the pangs of sea-sickness. He enjoyed playing shuffleboard, and became very competitive at the game. He took advantage of the Turkish bath, but had to get a lesson on physical discretion from his father. He was not allowed to play cards, smoke cigars, or drink cognac with the other men, but he did learn to enjoy getting his young muscles un-kinked by the masseuse. He especially enjoyed the food, and he learned to enjoy many new tastes. Of course, there were some foods he avoided completely, like frogs legs and snails.

By the third day he was well-known by all the first-class passengers, and most of the crew. As the ship was English, he didn't quite understand the class distinction on board, and could not understand why most of the children were not allowed to come up to his deck. His father tried to explain it as best he could, but finally gave up, telling him that this was one of those things best understood with age. Eddie always loathed being given that reason.

Morgan made sure that he put Eddie in a position to play his trump card—his array of stories, which he always told with great expression. Many of the guests had never had an encounter with a deadly snake, so Eddie's story was particularly dramatic, especially when he came to the part where he demonstrated how he had to suck the venom out of Tim's leg. It made quite a hit.

The boy stayed up late each night, going to bed around eleven thirty or so. Edward and Morgan would enjoy a Cuban cigar and a glass or two of cognac before turning in, usually around one a.m.

On the fourth night out, Morgan had something important to relate to Edward. He dismissed the servants from the stateroom, telling them to come back around two a.m. He brought an entire bottle of Napoleon brandy to the table with two snifters, and poured a hefty glass for each of them. Eddie was already in bed and sound asleep. The sound of the ship's orchestra could be heard through the windows.

"I have to tell you something, Edward. Something very important." Morgan looked to the bedroom door. "Are you sure that he's asleep?"

"Yes. He is out like a light."

"Good." Morgan paused, not knowing how to start the conversation. This was uncharacteristic for him, as he never held back anything he wanted to say. "I have several things to say to you that may cause you to get very angry at me, Edward."

"Sir?"

"I hope this is not the case, but I am just warning you. You may find that you wish to return to New York as soon as we reach Southampton, although I daresay that would be a pity for Eddie."

"Yes, sir." Edward agreed with the fact that Eddie would miss out on the tour, but was unsure of the rest of the statement.

"You have been in my employ for, what, fourteen years now?"

"That's correct, sir. I started with the company in 1898."

"Do you remember when I called you in for an interview back in '98?"

Edward laughed. "Yes, I do. I was very nervous." But what had made it funny was that it was also the reason he had met his best friend, Geoffrey Atwater, who had been sent as a messenger to his brownstone, and then, when he entered the reception area, he had the pleasure of meeting Rebecca, who would one day become his wife.

Morgan took a long drink of cognac. "Do you remember me showing you a certificate?"

Edward certainly remembered, as it still hung in the same spot before they left for Europe. "You are referring to the certificate that explained how you were exempted from the Union Army during the Civil War, and that your father had purchased a substitute to serve in your stead."

"Exactly! You remember very well, Edward." Morgan was stalling. He took another sip of brandy. "Now, do you remember what I called that thing?"

"As I recall, you said it was a spot on the integrity of your family, or something of the sort."

"Quite right, again. Do you remember anything else?"

Edward couldn't think of anything else, and shook his head.

"I told you that it was the policy of the War Department that—"

"That no substitute should ever know who paid the fee, and no one who paid the fee should ever know his substitute."

"You did remember!" Morgan paused, looking down at the table. "But I lied to you."

"Pardon me?"

"I lied to you, Edward. I told you about my spies." There are spies everywhere. "You know the power I can exert, that I can be a bully, that I can be ruthless, even cruel. I know the name of the man that substituted for me in the Civil War, and I knew his name back then."

"Why are you telling me this, sir?"

There was silence. Morgan looked up at Edward. There was one large tear in his right eye.

"Oh no!" Edward gasped. He now looked toward the bedroom door. "Oh my God! Are you saying that...that—"

"That the substitute was Edward William Collier. Your grandfather."

Edward took a gulp of the cognac and rose from his chair. He walked to the window and looked out over the ocean. He wasn't exactly sure how to feel about this. He had never known his grandfather, so it didn't feel like such a personal loss, but why did Morgan need to burden him with this now, after all these years? Was he just trying to smooth the way for his own departure from this life?

"What makes you so sure of this?" Edward asked. "How did you find out?"

"I had a man in my service a while back," answered Morgan. "A man named Greyson." Edward remembered hearing that name before,from Geoff. "Bill Greyson was just a street urchin—someone I knew I could control—but he had absolutely no fear of anyone or anything on this planet. He broke in...er...he did very good research for me. I started using him in around 1860." Morgan took a sip of brandy. "Anyway, he found the information I needed." He looked over at Edward. "Are you angry at me, Edward?"

"I am not angry at you, Mr. Morgan. You didn't handpick my grandfather and send him off to battle to die. You made a significant contribution to the Union war effort by staying out of the army, and the custom of buying a substitute was, at that time, perfectly acceptable."

Morgan let out a great sigh. "I went against the wishes of my father in order to find out who my substitute was. I figured that he might also be from New York, but I never imagined that his family would attend the same church as I did. After I discovered who he was, I kept tabs on where he was deployed—what battles he saw action in, if he was wounded, you know. I found out that he was killed at Antietam before your grandmother was notified."

Morgan took another slug of brandy. Edward continued to stare out the window at the sea. He continued, "I decided that I had to help your grandmother in any way I could. I made sure she found a teaching job. I made sure that her son—your father—had a good education by arranging for a scholarship. There were times when money mysteriously appeared in her bank account. All this was possible because of my position—but I carried the guilt of my actions for so, so long."

Edward turned to Morgan so that he could face him when he asked the next question.

"Is this also why you sought me out and created the position I now hold? Have I been working for you these fourteen years because you felt compelled to see that the Morgan family did not inhibit my future?"

"No, not exactly."

But Edward continued, "And are all the gifts you have given me— the Dakota, the huge salary, the honeymoon trip, and the rest—were they also given as atonement for your guilt?"

"Not at all, Edward!" Morgan said this calmly, but firmly. "Edward, would you please come back to the table and sit down again? There is more that I must explain."

Edward slowly walked back and sat down.

"Are you very angry at me, Edward?"

"No, not angry. I think I now feel...like a pawn."

"A pawn? As in chess?" Morgan asked, realizing the implications.

"My father warned me about you, years ago, when you first offered me the position. I can still see his face and hear his voice. He used that exact word. He told me that I should beware that you didn't use me like a pawn."

"I see."

"No, I don't think you do, because I have been wary of you all these years. I always second-guessed your motives. I wasn't sure why you were doing all these things for me, and for my family, but I felt, deep down inside me, that there was something else that was motivating you to act."

"Edward—"

"Let me finish, please! I thought that I had abilities. I thought that I worked for you in earnest. I thought that I helped make the company better, even more human. Now I feel like a political appointee—or worse. I feel like the relative that gets a job through nepotism."

"Jack works for the company. He will inherit it soon, very soon. Do you think he got where he is through nepotism?"

"Well...yes! But Jack is talented, brilliant even."

Morgan was silent for a moment. He once again checked the bedroom door, half expecting to see Eddie standing there listening to them.

"Edward, I have more to tell you."

"I don't know if I want to hear any more, sir."

Morgan paused. "You will hear this sooner or later, so it's just a matter of when."

Edward considered if he wanted to ruin the entire tour at this moment, or put it off until another evening. Either way, the old man was determined to burden him with something.

"All right, say your piece."

Morgan didn't seem relieved by Edward's decision. He had just taken the shortcut to the inevitable. "I am not surprised your father warned you that I might use you like a pawn." Edward raised an eyebrow. "I watched your father like a hawk while he was growing up, albeit from a distance. He would catch me looking at him in church, or staring at him on the street. He was always suspicious of me."

"That's exactly how he would speak of you at home."

"You see. But I watched him grow into a fine young man. If you were to go back in time, he struck me at twenty-two years old the same way that you struck me." Morgan paused again.

"I imagine there is more?"

"Oh, yes. I have been married twice, Edward. You know my wife, Fanny—uh, Frances?"

"Yes."

"She is my second wife, and the mother of my four children. But before I married Fanny, I had married Amelia Sturgis. Everyone just called her Mimi, as in *La Boheme*."

"In *La Boheme* Mimi dies of consumption."

"Yes, she does. My Mimi died of mysterious causes in the first year of our marriage. My father arranged for me to meet Fanny, and we were married the next year. I must say that most of my years with Fanny have been very happy, and we do have four wonderful children, but…"

"But?"

"Our youngest child, Anne, was born in 1873. Frances became very distant after her birth, and I looked for solace elsewhere. I even had intentions of divorcing Frances. I met a young woman. We became very close. She was—"

"Your mistress?"

"No. That has a terrible sound to it. We were in love." He took a big swig of brandy. "Anyway, my father, who also believed strongly in spies, found out about our indiscretion. He threatened to disown me if I didn't go back to Fanny, and he also said that he would drag the poor girl through the mud as a common gold digger—which I know she wasn't."

"I don't think I would have liked your father very much," Edward replied.

"He was a tough man, let me tell you, but I had some tenacity myself. I couldn't just abandon the poor girl, not after we were intimate." Morgan poured himself another full glass of brandy. "A week later we met in the narthex of St. George's and she told me...that she was pregnant. I told her there was no future for her with me, since my father had seen to that, but I might be able to help her and the baby in the best way I could." Morgan stopped and took another drink.

"Go on," pushed Edward.

"I arranged to have her meet a young man, a wonderful young man, at the bank. She was standing near him and accidently—but on purpose—dropped her purse to the floor. He was very much a gentleman and came to her aid. He was a reserved young man, so the young lady had to be a little more aggressive to get him to take her out."

Edward was becoming very agitated by the story at this point.

Morgan continued, "They began to spend time together and their romance blossomed very quickly. So quickly that they were married within a month."

Edward leaped to his feet. "Stop! Stop this instant!" He was a deep shade of scarlet.

"Edward, you must listen to me."

"I can't listen to any more of this, because I've heard it so many times when I was growing up, so you are either playing on my sympathies based on what you know of my family, or you are telling me something that cannot possibly be true."

"Edward," Morgan said, sotto voce, "keep your voice down. Eddie, remember?"

"You're right! If he heard any of this we'd have to take him to Sigmund Freud." Edward sat down again.

"You need to think of this logically, Edward," Morgan said calmly. "You have always believed that you were born a full two months premature, and yet you were delivered healthy and unbelievably large."

"How do you know that?" asked Edward.

"Have you been listening to me? I know it all."

Edward looked Morgan directly in the eyes. "You are telling me that you are my father."

Morgan smiled weakly at Edward. "That word is the problem. Father. Your mother and I may have produced you, but Thomas Collier was, and still is, the man who raised you, and it is he who deserves that title—not me. And Edward, this is a regret that I have harbored for much of my life."

Edward put his head in his hands and shook it. "Did he know...you know...that I wasn't his?"

"I am not one hundred percent sure, but knowing your mother, I doubt it. Not that it would have made much of a difference. Your father would have raised you like his own even if he knew you weren't—and you never would have been the wiser, either."

"You have just changed my entire world in a matter of minutes," sobbed Edward.

"I know."

"I don't think I know who I am anymore."

"Nonsense!" said Morgan, a little louder than he meant to. "You are Edward Thomas Collier, son of Thomas William Collier. You are a wonderful amalgamation of both your parents."

Edward gave Morgan a look that begged the question, *How?*

"I know what you are thinking, Edward. How can this be if you carry my genes and not your father's? I can tell you, as sure as there is a God in heaven, that you are every inch your father's son. He lives and breathes in you as much as you live and breathe in Eddie. Where was I when you ran into trouble at school in the sixth level? Where was I when there was a discussion at the dinner table about equal rights for all human beings? Where was I when you told your parents that you had asked Rebecca to marry you? I may know about all these things, but your character, your morality, and the trait I love the most about you—your integrity—all came from Thomas Collier."

Edward had dissolved into a puddle of emotion. Morgan held out Edward's glass of cognac to him. He took a swallow of the liquid. "But my mother...?"

"Your mother and I had an agreement about this. We made this bargain long ago. I was never to inform you of this unless Thomas had passed on. It is my opinion that she never told Thomas because she never would have wanted to hurt him, or cause him disappointment. If he knew that you were not really his, he would be very disappointed, because he loved you so very much, and he was proud of everything you did—and what you stood for." Morgan then added, "You may now speak of this with your mother. She will corroborate my story. You see, I am not telling you to lift the burden off my soul. I am telling you all this for a very practical reason."

Edward looked up from his glass. "Practical?" It sounded…calculated!

Morgan began to explain. "Just a few minutes ago we were talking about my son, Jack Jr. How he is going to inherit the company when I am gone. We also spoke about relatives in the company and nepotism. Do you recall?"

"Yes."

"I brought you into the company when I felt you were ready—although Thomas was suspicious."

Edward couldn't believe it. "You knew he was suspicious of you?"

"It was part of his nature. He was always suspicious of me."

"So you gave me a job in the company, just as you had for your other children?"

"That's right, except of course they don't know you are related to them, so…" Morgan stopped to ponder his approach on the next topic. "If I died right now, how much do you think you would inherit as one of my heirs?"

"Absolutely nothing. I would imagine there is no scrap of evidence that links me to you, other than the fact that I work for you."

"Precisely! You, and your mother of course—are the only living people who know anything about this matter. If you were to put out a claim on my estate you would have an impossible time in court, especially when you consider that you would be attacking the Morgan family. You wouldn't have a chance."

"Thanks!"

"Edward, I am not attacking your skill as a lawyer. You know the law."

"I know. I couldn't prove my accusations."

"Correct!" Morgan smiled at Edward. "So the best course of action is to do nothing at all."

"Suits me!"

"It shouldn't suit you!" Edward looked surprised. "Since the moment you were born I have schemed in every way possible to make sure that when I leave this earth you would get your share of my estate. This is my most diabolical scheme!"

"You don't have to do that. You've given me so much already."

"Do you have any idea the kind of money we are talking about here?"

"Of course I do! I work in a very sensitive area of your company, don't I?"

Morgan looked off in the distance. He needed a new tactic.

"I have given specific instructions in my will that you, Geoff, and Sam are to retain your positions in the company for as long as you see fit. There is also language about salary, benefits, stock, and so on."

"Thank you, sir."

"But you know as well as I do that the moment my body is cold in the ground you, and your associates, may easily be let go—and no one will care. Where will you be then?"

"I would have worked for fifteen years with the best firm in the city. I think my resume will get me another job."

Morgan slammed the table with his fist. Edward jumped back, startled. "God, man, are you listening to me? You are dealing with the Morgans! If they see to it, you may never work in the country again. You may find yourself accused of all manner of nasty dealing, and you were working privately for me all these years, so they could twist anything they find to suit their wishes. Where would you be then? Where would Rebecca be, or your children?"

Edward didn't look at it that way. Morgan was trying to protect his family. His family?

"Wait a moment!" Edward ventured. "My children...my three children are also...your grandchildren!"

Now it all made sense. This was why Morgan was so outwardly fond of Eddie. This was the reason for the Dakota, the salary, and everything else.

He wasn't a pawn after all!

"At last the dawn!" joked Morgan.

"You have something more in mind, I know you do," Edward said.

"Indeed I do, but I am not going to tell you about it. Not now! Not ever!"

"I don't understand."

"Of course not, but you will figure it out—in time."

Edward drained his glass. "I guess I will turn in. I don't know if I will get much sleep tonight. I have a great deal to think about."

Morgan grinned. "I know. I'm sorry, but I had to say it."

Edward nodded. "I understand." He turned toward the bedroom, and then suddenly turned back to Morgan. "I was just thinking...now that I know who you really are, how do I address you?"

"That's easy," laughed Morgan, "you may call me Mr. Morgan."
Edward nodded slowly. He understood. He went to bed.

Personal Journal Entry
November 30, 1911

Am I to believe that which Morgan has revealed to me?

Am I his long-lost illegitimate son? Is Eddie his grandson?

And what does that make Thomas Collier? A figurehead?

And my mother? What about my mother?

All this must wait until we return to America, then I shall confront her about it.

I need to know the truth.

But Morgan said there is more. What else is he keeping from me?

Chapter 24
Southampton

If Eddie had heard anything of the conversation of the evening before, he never said a word about it to his father. Edward and Morgan didn't have another word about their talk for the rest of the voyage, and within a few days the ship was entering the port of Southampton, England.

As the *Olympic* rounded the harbor, she passed the White Star Line berths, where her three sister ships were being built. They passed a ship which looked to be a carbon copy of the *Olympic*; however, in truth she was slightly longer. The ship was not ready for service quite yet. Her interior was still being finished.

Edward pointed out the liner to Eddie and Morgan as they stood on deck. "Over there is the new White Star liner that is almost ready. She is supposed to be even more lavish in her appointments than this ship."

"Really? Morgan asked. "When will she be ready to cross the Atlantic?"

"In a few months," answered Edward. "She is scheduled to enter service in the first week of April 1912."

"That might be perfect for us, men," Morgan replied. "That should be about the right time to go home. Edward, please book us the best stateroom for the voyage home."

"Yes, sir." Edward nodded to Eddie. They were going to take a maiden voyage home to New York. That was very exciting.

"By the way, Edward," Morgan asked, "do you know the name of that ship?"

"I believe it is called the *Titanic*, sir."

In an hour or so, they were making their way from the ship onto the pier. Edward had arranged for a car and driver to get them around England, because he knew that the English had some crazy notion about which was the correct and incorrect side of the road for driving. He feared that if he drove he might have a head-on collision.

J. P. Morgan, Edward Collier, and Edward Collier, Jr., spent two weeks in England and Scotland. They were the guests of King George V at Windsor Palace, and spent a night in Holyrood Palace in Edinburgh, Scotland. All their other nights were spent in five-star hotels, where they always enjoyed the best suite in the house. On their final day in England they drove to Dover, and just as Edward and Rebecca had done a dozen years before, took the ferry to Calais. They took a train north to Brussels, and then to Amsterdam.

Morgan made several "shopping" stops in Brussels, and again in Amsterdam. In both cases he sent Edward and his son sightseeing through the historic cities, with the excuse given that he didn't want to bore Eddie. Edward suspected that he was, once again, shopping for gold—although Amsterdam was also well-known for its diamond industry.

They took another train east to Hamburg, and then on to Berlin. They were anxious to be in southern Germany by Christmas, so they pushed on, staying only a day in each city. Morgan had promised Eddie that they would celebrate Christmas in the little Austrian village of Oberndorf, where the carol "Silent Night" had been written and first performed. Trinity Church on Wall Street had been the first American church to have the beloved carol sung, and by the turn of the century it was the most popular Christmas carol in the world.

As they traveled so far south for Christmas, it was now easier for them to visit Munich, the capital of Bavaria, and then go on to Salzburg, the home of Mozart (Eddie's favorite composer), and reach Vienna. Edward had arranged to take in the Vienna Philharmonic on New Year's Eve—a Viennese tradition. Despite the cold of winter setting in, Edward and Eddie took a trip to the Prater Amusement Park to ride the immense Ferris wheel, while Morgan went to the financial district to do more shopping. Morgan never carried any boxes or bags, nor was anything ever delivered to their hotel—his purchases were simply shipped to America.

Winter was now firmly in charge of the climate, so they traveled south into Italy. They went first to Milan, where they saw a Verdi opera at La Scala. Then they headed farther south to Rome. Eddie was particularly interested in two sites: the Colosseum and the underground labyrinth known as the Catacombs. They also traveled a bit west to see the recently uncovered village of Pompeii. The gravity of being consumed by a volcanic eruption made for some sparkling dinner conversation. When they returned to Rome, Morgan arranged to have an audience with the pope.

The itinerary was specifically designed to allow them to be in Venice in early February, very near the start of an early Lent—which meant Carnival. They all participated in a masked ball, although Edward was mindful not to let Eddie overindulge in the merrymaking.

After Venice, they crossed into Greece and toured Athens. Rebecca and Edward had skipped Greece on their honeymoon tour, and Edward had particularly wanted to see the Acropolis; Eddie couldn't understand why—to him it just seemed like broken-down buildings. The trio, plus their entourage, then boarded a steamship and took a cruise on the Mediterranean Sea, heading back toward Western Europe. The ship passed by Cyprus and skirted the northern coast of Africa. Eddie was able to see Gibraltar as the ship headed north, and then it docked in the French port of Marseilles.

The final leg of the tour was spent entirely in France. They visited the Loire Valley and the wine country, but spent most of their time in Paris. Edward and Eddie spent two full days in the Louvre. Eddie compared the former palace to the Metropolitan Museum of Art, which J. P. Morgan had given sizeable contributions, saying that, just like the museum in New York, many of the people in the paintings and sculptures were buck naked. He found it amusing, but he had had enough schooling that he wasn't in any way shocked. If Edward felt the need to explain the art, then he explained it, but for the most part, he let his son experience it for himself. The last full day on the Continent was spent at the palace at Versailles. Father and son were able to take in this ornate baroque palace alone, as Morgan had begged off, saying that he had work to do in the city.

The company departed for England and their passage home on the following morning. It was April 4, 1912. They crossed the English Channel and spent some time touring around Wales. Morgan had decided to skip going to Ireland, as the country was lately in a time of political unrest and upheaval. They needed to be in Southampton by April 9, as the *Titanic* would set sail to America the next day. This gave them plenty of opportunity to relax and tour at their own pace. They spent the evening of April 7 on the Welsh coast, in Cornwall. There were many nice tourist-class hotels, but only one hotel that suited Morgan, so they stayed there. They had dinner that night in the hotel restaurant. Not surprisingly, seafood was the major choice on the menu; however, there was also lamb, beef, and pork. Morgan chose the rack of lamb—he asked the waiter to make sure it wasn't mutton, but lamb. It was, in fact, lamb. Edward chose the fresh catch of the day, which was some form of English halibut. It was served pan-seared. Eddie decided that he would have the loin of pork.

The dinners arrived and the trio ate ravenously, barely saying three words for the first few minutes after the plates were set in front of them. Finally, Edward asked, "How is your meal, Mr. Morgan?"

"I must say, the lamb is excellent! Perfectly cooked! And yours, Edward?"

"It is a very tender fish, flaky and dry. It's very good. Eddie, how is your pork?"

Eddie had a mouthful of meat, which he was chewing quite vigorously, so he declined an immediate answer—which made Morgan smile. Edward spied the portion of food on Eddie's plate, but noticed something out of order.

"Eddie, does your food taste all right? It looks a little underdone."

Eddie swallowed the mouthful. "It's a little chewy, but I guess it's good." He had already consumed several of the slices of pork.

"That meat isn't underdone, Edward, it's mostly raw. The boy shouldn't eat it. I'll send it back." Morgan signaled for the waiter and complained about the pork. The waiter quickly agreed and removed the dish. He asked Eddie if he would like something else in its place. Eddie had already eaten most of the pork, so he wasn't interested in another main dish. His eyes had already been set on the dessert tray.

After the main course was cleared, Morgan and Edward enjoyed their nightly cognac and cigar—Morgan had brought along several cases of his favorites, which he called Havana Clubs—and Eddie enjoyed a slice of cake with some vanilla ice cream. Eddie had barely gotten the final forkful of cake into his mouth, when he complained to his father that he had a stomachache. This was odd for the boy, as he had exhibited a cast-iron stomach throughout sea, train, coach, and many different cuisines. Eddie excused himself from the table and headed for the restroom. Edward wasn't overly concerned at that moment, but became so when Eddie did not return after ten minutes.

Edward put down his cognac and cigar and went to look for Eddie. He found him in the men's room, sitting on the toilet in one of the stalls, doubled over in pain.

"My stomach hurts really bad, Dad! I threw up, too!"

"Do you have...um...diarrhea?" Edward didn't know how to ask his son about his bowel movements. He had never had to before, so it was awkward. Still, he looked to be in pain.

"Yes. Can you give me a few minutes, Dad?" He looked up and gave his father a weak smile.

"Certainly. You are entitled to your privacy." Edward returned to the table.

"Is the boy all right?" Morgan asked.

"He doesn't look very good. He's on the bowl doubled over in pain." Edward thought about what Eddie had eaten. "I wonder if it was that pork dish."

"Could be, Edward. I hope he doesn't have a case of food poisoning."

"God, no!" Edward began to worry. He knew nothing of Cornwall. What if Eddie were really sick? "Excuse me, sir, I am going to ask at the desk if there is a doctor or hospital near, just to play it safe."

"I'll wait for Eddie." Edward nodded at the plan.

Eddie didn't venture out of the restroom for almost an hour. He spent the time either vomiting or on the toilet. He had now taken on the appearance of a wet dishrag. His father had found a doctor in the vicinity, and they ordered a cab to take him there. Morgan stayed behind. He told Edward that his presence might make matters worse, in that he was not a good patient, or a good father of a patient. He didn't mind, however, telling the chef in the restaurant what he thought about his ability to cook pork thoroughly.

Edward carried Eddie into the doctor's office. The doctor thought, at first, that it could also be his appendix, but then dismissed this scenario. He finally agreed on food poisoning, and not a mild case. He recommended bed rest for a few days, and plenty of clear liquids, but no solid food until the nausea and vomiting had passed.

They returned to their hotel suite, with Eddie holding a paper bag which had been used along the way. It was a very long, sleepless night for father and son. Eddie finally fell asleep at about three thirty a.m. and slept until around seven o'clock. He had nothing left in his stomach, but still had the dry heaves. His sides hurt from the retching. He was also as pale as a ghost.

Personal Journal Entry
April 7, 1912

I have never been so frightened. I thought I might lose Eddie.

He has a strong will, but food poisoning doesn't choose strong or weak.

I am so very happy that we will be returning home in a few days.

Eddie is looking forward to taking the new ship home. I hope that he recovers enough to fare well on the open sea; otherwise, the journey will be a torture.

❦

It was April 8. Edward knew they had two days for Eddie to feel seaworthy, because if he didn't feel better, the high seas were no place for him. They stayed put in the Cornwall hotel another day and night, allowing the boy maximum bed rest. Edward coaxed his son to drink the broth that he had room service deliver. Eddie would swallow a tablespoon or two and then dash into the bathroom.

He was not appreciably better on the morning of April 9. They had to be in Southampton that evening, because the ship was departing the next day.

Morgan was relaxed. He didn't push either father or son to get up and get ready to go.

Edward was worried about Eddie. He looked dehydrated, and that was his chief concern.

Eddie, on the other hand, only worried about missing the ship.

"Dad," he said weakly, "we have to get going soon or we're going to miss the ship."

"There's always another ship, . You need to get better first. You are in no shape to travel."

"Come on, Dad, I'm not that bad," Eddie whined.

"We will leave as soon as you can keep down a full cup of broth."

But that was not going to happen, and Eddie knew it.

"Edward," Morgan said, quietly, "I shall ring ahead and have them take our belongings off the ship. We shall take a later voyage after Master Eddie feels better."

"Mr. Morgan, you should go ahead without us. You don't want to miss this voyage. It will surely be exciting!"

"I don't need excitement at my age, Edward. Besides, how can I leave this boy alone in your care?" Morgan patted Eddie on the head and smiled. Eddie forced a small laugh.

The reservation on the *Titanic* was cancelled. Morgan did miss the excitement of the voyage, but not the way anyone would have predicted.

It took another day before Eddie could keep down a full cup of broth, and another day before he felt he could stand the motion of a train or motorcar. They were able to check out of the Cornwall hotel on April 12, and reached Southampton the same evening. Edward arranged passage on the *Olympic*, the same ship that had brought them to Europe weeks before. The ship would be departing in a few days.

Morgan suggested that they simply relax in the Southampton hotel for the interim. He wanted to let Eddie completely recover. Eddie was already eating solid food again, but somewhat slower and cautiously.

They were enjoying their full English breakfast in the hotel restaurant on the morning of April 15, when a buzz started to circulate through the room. The *Titanic*, which had been considered one of the most modern and safest liners ever built—even called "unsinkable"—had struck an iceberg the previous night and sank to the bottom of the ocean. Early reports said there had been a tremendous loss of life.

The seaport was in a state of shock. The White Star Line, which belonged to a company that Morgan had a controlling interest in, was swamped with cables, calls, and questions. The ship had carried many members of English and American society, as well as second-class passengers, and a full roster of third-class, or steerage, passengers. There was also a very large crew on board. Most wondered how such a disaster could even occur.

A list of the missing was wired from New York to England on April 16. Among them were several of Morgan's closest friends, including John Jacob Astor, and Isador Straus and his wife.

Edward and Morgan didn't have to note the irony that they were to have been among the passengers, although Eddie did verbalize it.

"Gee! If we had been on that ship, where would we be now?"

Edward, seeking to ground his son, answered, "Eddie, the standing order is always that women and children get into the lifeboats first, and if there is any more room then the men go. Which would you have been: a man, or a child?"

Eddie thought for a moment, then put his arm around his father and said, "I would have been a man, Dad. I would have stayed with you and Mr. Morgan."

Edward nodded. "That would mean, Mr. Collier—since you say you are a man—that you would now be dead, along with more than a thousand other people. Most of the men went down with the ship."

Eddie fell silent, and then started to quietly sob.

"Sometimes there is a time to decide when you should go and when you should stay," Morgan counseled. "In this case, I chose to stay."

They boarded the *Olympic* the next day. Due to the fate of her sister ship, the *Titanic*, the captain of the *Olympic* steered his ship far more southerly to avoid the icebergs. This was a much longer route. They arrived back in New York in the last week of April.

Rebecca and the children met them at the pier. Rebecca had been concerned. Edward had sent her a telegram on April 6, stating that they were coming home on the *Titanic*. With Eddie's illness, he had completely forgotten that he had sent that telegram. She had gone to the docks on April 16 to find her husband and son. Her only relief came when she read the complete passenger list and saw that they were not on it.

Edward did remember to wire his wife when they reached Southampton. She received that telegram an hour after she walked back into the Dakota after returning from the pier.

She embraced Edward, and then smothered Eddie with kisses and hugs. She even gave Morgan a kiss.

Edward watched for their luggage to be unloaded from the hold of the ship. As he waited he noticed that large black steel boxes with the name Morgan stenciled on the side were being wheeled off the boat. He knew those boxes were not part of Morgan's luggage, so therefore they must be the results of his secret shopping ventures. He watched as the longshoremen labored to lift each box into a waiting truck. They were working very hard, so the boxes were obviously full, and very heavy. Morgan, and others in his class—the so-called "robber barons"—had made many a crossing to Europe in the last decade or two. The great art treasures of Europe were being purchased and carted back to the United States. Some would end up in museums, like the Metropolitan Museum of Art, but many would remain in the buyers' private collections.

The truck then disappeared, heading toward the downtown area.

Edward could only suppose what those boxes held.

As they walked from the pier arm in arm, Edward turned to Rebecca and said softly, "My dear, I have much to tell you."

Chapter 25
Elizabeth

Edward Collier went to the home in which he grew up, the brownstone off Stuyvesant Square on 16ᵗʰ Street, to visit his mother, Elizabeth.

He didn't really doubt J. P. Morgan's tale about his relationship with his mother—it all seemed to fit—but he did want to speak with her about it, if for no other reason than to let her know that he still loved his father, Thomas Collier.

Elizabeth told Edward that she fully expected Morgan to speak of this sooner or later, now that Thomas was gone. Edward was mostly confused as to how the entire matter began.

"I had a schoolgirl's infatuation with J. P. Morgan. He was so handsome in those days, you know," she said, and then pointed to her nose, "before he had this problem."

Edward nodded. He understood what she meant.

"He was a powerful man, and I guess I fell under his influence," she continued. "I made a terrible mistake. So did he. He took the proper steps to correct the situation without hurting me, or the baby I was carrying."

Edward shook his head. "But that was deceiving Father, then. Wasn't it?"

"Yes," she answered. "It was. But I honestly fell deeply in love with your father at just about the first moment we met. He was such a wonderful man." She smiled. "He was a bit stubborn sometimes…" That made Edward smile. Edward had a stubborn streak, as well. "If I was infatuated with J. P., then I was devotedly in love with your father, and I will continue to refer to him as your father." Edward nodded in agreement. Elizabeth continued, "When I saw you talking to J. P. in church that day, my heart skipped a beat or two. I knew that one day he would seek you out. I knew he would do right by you."

"You never let on—"

"That I was in favor of you working for him? No, I wanted to stay as neutral as I could. I wanted to let your father counsel you. If it was to be, then it was to be."

"But Father was suspicious?" Edward asked.

"Your father was always suspicious of the entire Morgan family. It had nothing to do with me, and especially not you. He never had any idea that you were not his child. He was a progressive, and did not approve of the fact that a handful of men controlled so much of the wealth in this country."

"Then why didn't he object when I went to work for Morgan?"

"I suppose for several reasons. First, he knew it was an excellent opportunity for you. That was the most important reason, Edward. It was always about you. Didn't you know that?"

"Well…"

"Didn't you realize how proud he was of you?" Edward's mother had tears in her eyes.

"I know he did, Mother, but if he didn't like Morgan—"

"Oh, I didn't say that he didn't like him, Edward. Your father respected him a great deal. He thought he was a brilliant businessman, and that he used his money to help save the economy—twice!"

Edward wanted to ask his mother if she knew about Morgan's war record, and if she had knowledge that his grandfather had been Morgan's "substitute," but he was afraid she might not know this and that it would upset her. His mother might feel that she had been used in a chess game; that she was just another pawn.

Some things are better left unsaid.

Geoff, Millie, and their children came over to the Dakota for dinner several days after Edward and Eddie returned from Europe. Their dinner ended, Millie and Rebecca enjoyed coffee in the living room, in the company of the two youngest children. Eddie took Timmy, Alice, and Jacob upstairs to the playroom on the tenth floor. Edward and Geoff escaped to the privacy of Edward's study, with cigars and brandy.

Edward started speaking about some of the upcoming projects at work, especially Tesla's Wardenclyffe Tower, but Geoff seemed preoccupied with other thoughts.

"Edward?" he interrupted.

"You have a thought on Mr. Tesla, do you?" Edward asked.

"No," he replied. "I'm sorry. I haven't really been paying attention to what you were talking about."

"Is anything wrong, Geoff?"

"I'm not sure." Geoff poured himself another glass of brandy. "Edward, what did you and Morgan find to talk about on that long trip?"

Edward felt the question was asked in a very knowing way. "What do you mean, Geoff?"

Geoff shifted in his seat. "Edward…I know."

"You know what?" Edward calmly avoided eye contact with Geoff.

Geoff quietly answered, "I know he told you…secrets, Edward."

Edward was still skeptical. "Secrets that you have known yourself for years?"

"Yes."

"Such as?"

It was time for Geoff to take a sip of liquor. "That your grandfather was Morgan's Civil War 'substitute,' for starters. That Morgan and your mother—"

"Stop!" commanded Edward. "Stop right now!"

Geoff did stop. He had never seen Edward so angry at him before. Edward got up from his chair and walked to the other side of the room. "How do you know this, Geoff? Better yet, as we are friends and, for lack of a better word, family, why didn't you tell me any of this before now?"

Geoff's face saddened. "I didn't tell you because I didn't think it really mattered. You were happy being who you were, and for once in my life, so was I—and most of my happiness was because of the fact that I was working for you. I didn't want to hurt your feelings, or Rebecca's, or hurt the family, so I kept my mouth shut. I figured, hell, what difference does it make?"

Edward glanced over. "Is that all?"

"No," replied Geoff, "there really was a time when I almost spilled the beans. You remember it, too, Edward." Edward seemed puzzled. "It was when we were going up to Newport, and I was so drunk on the train. I was so angry at you, Edward, that I almost told you. I almost told you. But I didn't. I couldn't."

Edward turned to Geoff. "But that was years ago, Geoff. You have known for a dozen years?"

Geoff shook his head. "Longer than that, I'm afraid." He walked over to Edward and put his hand on his shoulder, guiding him back to his chair. "Sit down. Let me tell you a story."

Edward sat down. Geoff paced.

"Do you remember me telling you about Bill Greyson?" Geoff began.

Edward nodded. "Morgan actually mentioned his name on board the ship the night he told me...you know."

"Yes," Geoff added, "he knew him very well. Bill Greyson was Morgan's 'clean-up man.' He was always around to clean up the messes Morgan got himself into. Morgan plucked him off the streets when Bill was around twelve years old. Morgan was a regular Fagin, he was. He knew that he had a willing subject in Bill, especially when he tempted him with money."

Edward certainly understood the Fagin reference. Fagin was one of Charles Dickens's most memorable characters, from *Oliver Twist*. Fagin would recruit boys to rob and pick pockets for him.

"Bill was the one who found out about your grandfather being Morgan's substitute soldier. After that, Morgan used his contacts in the War Department to keep tabs on his whereabouts and his health. I can't lie...Bill did say that Morgan was racked with guilt over the whole affair."

Edward gave a little nod. Morgan really wasn't the guilty one, anyway. It was his father.

"Bill was put in charge of keeping his eye on your father after your grandfather was killed. He reported back to Morgan every once in a while. Bill kept all his notes in his residence. He was going to report in to Morgan one day when he came upon him and...your mother."

Edward squirmed in the chair. He didn't want to hear any more, but had to.

"Bill recorded the date in his notes, but never told a soul. When your mother married your father two months later, and you were born seven months after that, Bill put it all together."

Edward felt as if he were being handed a cleverly concocted story. "How did you—"

"I am getting to that, Edward. Please be patient." Edward nodded in agreement. "So Bill takes to following Morgan, more or less. He knows that Morgan likes to step out on the town every so often. He knows that Morgan has a taste for women other than his dear wife, Fanny. So he follows him one night down to the Bowery, where he picks up a young lady. He plies her with alcohol and takes care of business in the back of his carriage. What he doesn't know is that Bill has ridden along on the back bumper. It's 1879."

Edward recognized the year. He was five years old. That meant...

Geoff continued, "Bill doesn't do a thing except write it all down in his notes. He doesn't tell Morgan, out of fear of what he might do. But he does track the girl. He finds out that she is pregnant. He keeps an eye on her progress. She gives birth toward the end of that year. She has a son."

"My God!" sighed Edward. "There's another out there?"

"Oh, yes, Edward," Geoff confirmed, "there's another out there. Morgan doesn't know about this new baby. He only knows of the one Elizabeth Collier had—you! Bill continues to keep an eye on the mother and child, every once in a while slipping the mother some money. She thinks it is coming from Morgan, so she keeps her mouth shut!" He stopped momentarily. "Take a drink, Edward." Edward did as asked. "Don't interrupt me now. I know you are going to want to, but please don't. This is as hard for me to tell as it is for you to hear."

Edward agreed with a nod.

"The mother of the child died in 1885, and the child was sent to an orphanage."

"No!"

"I asked you not to interrupt, damn it! Bill still continued to watch out for the boy, even though life in the home was not very rosy all the time." Tears began to roll down Geoff's cheeks. "The boy was whipped soundly—over and over. But he was smart, Edward. He was smart. He fought back. He learned how to survive. When he was sixteen he ran away from the home, never to go back, with only the clothes he was wearing on his back at the time. He was standing on the street, outside Trinity Church, when he was approached by a stranger."

"Bill?"

"You have it. Bill took him in and fed him, bought him some better clothes, and taught him a few things, too. Then he took him to Morgan."

"What?"

"Don't interrupt, Edward! He took him to Morgan and told him that, as he wasn't getting any younger, he needed an assistant. So Morgan hires the boy as an 'agent.' His first assignment? Watch the household of Thomas Collier on Sixteenth Street—particularly Thomas's son, Edward."

"Oh my God!"

"You said a mouthful, my friend." Geoff took a drink. "But it doesn't end there. How could it? Bill isn't satisfied with the arrangement. I mean, he knows valuable stuff, doesn't he? He's doing all right, but figures he can do better, so one fine day in 1895 he goes and has a talk with Mr. Morgan. He tells him what he knows, and tells him that he has everything written down in a very concise account. He wants money—big money. He gives Morgan his demands, and then leaves him to think about it. He goes back to his home and tells his apprentice what he has done. He tells him so that he knows, just in case something should happen to him. He tells him where all his notebooks are hidden. The next day Bill is run over by a streetcar." Geoff wiped a tear from his eye. "Morgan's men searched the apartment for his notebooks. They found them all."

"Geoff, I had no idea!"

"I know you didn't, Edward, but Morgan knows about me."

"What?"

"I am convinced that Bill told Morgan that his new apprentice was the poor, lost son of his. Someone had Bill killed—probably Morgan, but it could have been anyone in the family. That's why I kept my mouth shut about you. The fewer that know, the better, right?"

Edward slowly nodded.

"Besides, there's no proof. Even if they found Bill's notebooks, they're not official documents. He could have written down anything. He could have figured out the appropriate dates and created the book at any time. And Morgan knew this, too."

Edward didn't follow Geoff's point.

"Don't you see? Don't you understand, Edward? This is Morgan's diabolical scheme! He has me tail you. I started when you had just finished college—I guess it didn't matter anymore about your parents—at that point it was only about you. I was the one that told him that you still attended St. George's. I was the one who told him that you had yet to take the bar exam, and I was the one who told him when you did! That's why he sent me with the invitation to come to his office."

Edward was confused. "Slow down, Geoff!"

"I can't slow down. I tell it, or bust! Don't you see, Edward? He controlled everything! He controlled your future and he controlled mine. He knew that you would ask for me to be your assistant. He gave you so many great things—the apartment, the honeymoon, the furniture, your great salary—but at the same time he gave some of those things to me. He wanted to take care of us both, and he did it without his family getting wise to it. At first, I admit it, I was jealous of you. You were older, but so what? But you had the education, and I didn't, so it made sense after a while how his mind was working. Besides, I knew he was having me watched. He knew about my drinking, and I know he knew about my visits to Chinatown for laudanum. Hell, I wouldn't have trusted me much in my condition."

Geoff finally sat down in an armchair next to Edward.

"Well," said Edward, after a bit of thought, "I suggest that we still keep this a state secret. I have already spoken to Rebecca about my talk on the ship with Morgan, but I know she will say nothing to anyone else. Does Millie know?"

"Millie loves me, and trusts me," Geoff said with a sad expression, "but she also knows that I carry many secrets in my mind, that I am tormented. She discovered this on our wedding night when she first laid eyes on my back. I told her certain bits of information, but asked her to be satisfied with that until I could tell her more. I don't think I lied when I said that the safety of her children depended upon her keeping quiet."

"I hadn't really thought along those lines, Geoff, but perhaps you are correct."

Edward took a long swig from his glass and then looked at Geoff. "I have a brother."

"I know, Edward," Geoff answered, "but when you think more about it, you're already my brother-in-law and friend. We've been family for years."

"Yes," replied Edward, "but now it feels better. It feels right!"

Geoff smiled, but then his face darkened again. "But Edward, there's more."

J. P. Morgan had no sooner landed back on American shores than he was once again subpoenaed to appear before a Congressional subcommittee to discuss his role in the recent Panic of 1907. Accusations were flying all around the committee chamber, as congressmen attempted to claim that Morgan had taken advantage of the panic in order to buy out weaker companies and strengthen his monopolistic hold on the economy. There were very few who wished to point out that it was Morgan, and Morgan's personal fortune, along with that of John D. Rockefeller and other financiers, who had saved the day by stabilizing the banking system and halting the runs on a dozen or so banks.

Morgan was tired of the way things were being handled, so by the end of 1912 he was once again on a steamship bound for Europe. He was worn down and beleaguered, and thus did not invite anyone else to accompany him, with the exception of his servants.

J. P. Morgan was staying at the Grand Hotel in Rome on March 31, 1913. He died quietly in his sleep in the middle of the night. He was seventy-five years old.

Personal Journal Entry
March 31, 1913

My benefactor is gone. How I will fare in the company is now left up to Morgan's heirs, particularly Jack Jr.

My future, and the future of my family, is at a questionable cross-roads.

Morgan's body was returned to the United States soon thereafter. Flags on Wall Street were flown at half mast, and the Stock Exchange ceased activity for two hours on the day that his body was carried through it.

His estimated net worth at the time of his death was in excess of sixty-eight million dollars, but that is based upon the 1913 economy and at a time when there was no income tax. He had an art collection that was valued in excess of fifty million dollars. He was buried in his home-town of Hartford, Connecticut. His son, John Pierpont Morgan, Jr.— Jack, as he was better known—inherited the business, as expected.

Jack called Edward into his office shortly after he had taken charge of the company. He now occupied his father's office. Jack was a person-able gentleman, but he was not as aggressive a businessman as his father. He was easy to like.

"Edward, my father made provisions in the corporate will for you and your assistant, Mr. Atwater," Jack began. "My father thought a great deal of your abilities, and that, sir, is good enough for me."

"Thank you, sir," was all Edward could reply.

"You are free to stay in your position here until the time comes when you feel you must leave us," Jack continued.

Edward thought his wording left much to be desired. Jack was inviting him to stay, but wasn't sounding very happy about it.

Edward knew he had to play his cards well, and he had to know how to bluff.

Sam Waters brought his family home from England for the funeral of J. P. Morgan. Sam had headed up the accounting department in Morgan's London office. Unlike Edward and Geoff, Jack Morgan did not have a use in New York for Sam's skills as an accountant. Sam quickly found work at the National City Bank of New York.

The bank was faring well in the international markets, and decided that Sam, due to his vast experience working for Morgan, was the perfect choice to send to London to head up its office. Sam and his family prepared to move back to England in the summer of 1915.

Timothy McNabb graduated from medical school in May 1913. He was now Dr. Timothy McNabb—a title he never would have considered tacked on to his name just a few years ago. He was set to become an intern at St. Luke's Hospital in Morningside Heights, near the new cathedral.

As this was on the west side of Central Park, Tim spent his off hours at the Dakota, visiting with the Colliers—particularly thirteen-year-old Eddie.

Geoff and Millie dearly loved Tim, but their apartment was becoming crowded. Timothy Edward was already almost eight years old, Barbara Mary was four, and Penelope Margaret was eighteen months. Tim felt more comfortable staying with the Colliers in the rambling Dakota apartment. His odd hours tended to disturb the Atwater children.

Homer Norris used his cottage on Greenwood Lake for the purpose J. P. Morgan had intended—as a retreat to compose music.

He also used it to entertain.

He never forgot the incident with Tim McNabb and the rattle-snake, but that did not prevent him from hosting the members of the St. George's Choir at the house during the summer months. He was particularly accommodating to his Choir of Men and Boys, who frequently made the trek up to the lake.

In spite of all this, shortly after Morgan died Homer decided that he would sell the lake home. He had been given the property a half dozen years previously, had patiently waited several years for the construction to begin, and then several more for the construction process to be completed. By the end of 1913 Homer was in the market for a buyer. The fact that the home had been a gift from J. P. Morgan would carry some prestige.

Edward managed the sale of the property in 1914. The house was sold to a well-to-do family from Paterson, New Jersey—the O'Dea family. They turned the Homer Norris house into a family compound.

By the middle of 1914 the world had changed.

On June 28, Archduke Franz Ferdinand of Austria, the heir to the Austro-Hungarian Empire, was assassinated, along with his pregnant wife, Sophie, as they drove in a motorcade through the streets of Sarajevo.

Europe was plunged into World War I. United States President Woodrow Wilson kept the United States out of the war for a year. On May 7, 1915, the Cunard Line ship *Lusitania* was making a regular voyage from New York to Southampton. The German submarine *U-20* fired one torpedo into the starboard side of the ship. The Germans had warned all travelers that an Atlantic crossing was a hazardous undertaking, and there was more than enough evidence to suggest that the *Lusitania* was also carrying military supplies in her hold. This would make the passengers human targets.

The torpedo caused a massive explosion. The great ship sank in only eighteen minutes. The *Lusitania* was just off the coast of Ireland, near the end of her journey.

There were almost two thousand souls on board the *Lusitania*; nearly twelve hundred died when she sank. The Broadway theatrical impresario, Charles Frohman, went down with the ship, as did Alfred Vanderbilt—one of the world's richest men.

Sam and Emily Waters, and their children, were on their way back to England so that Sam could take up his post at the London office of the National City Bank of New York. They had booked a second-class cabin on one of the lower decks on the starboard side of the ship.

They all died, too.

Personal Journal Entry
May 8, 1915

This is a day of tremendous loss. So many souls lost their lives yesterday when a German submarine sank the *Lusitania*—but among those lost were our friends, Sam and Emily Waters, and their children.

Tim and Eddie are very much affected by the loss of Sam. The Waters family had been at the Dakota apartment many times within the last few years. Geoff must be overcome—he was so close to Sam.

Tim is confused about his next course of action, but I am more worried about Eddie, as he has taken the loss very personally. I know he is fuming over the war.

The United States had taken an isolationist policy regarding the war in Europe. President Wilson knew it was only a matter of time before the country would be called upon to assist its allies in Europe, but this would be unpopular in the States. The sinking of the *Lusitania* allowed President Wilson a reason to ask Congress to declare war on Germany.

The Collier-Atwater family was shocked by the news of the death of their friend, Sam, and of his entire family. Particularly affected by the news was Dr. Tim McNabb. He was now completing his residency at St. Luke's Hospital.

When war was declared, Tim wanted to enlist, but Edward and Geoff sat him down and strongly suggested that he finish his residency first. Edward counseled that he would be of better use to the army as a field surgeon than as a doughboy. Tim did not agree, but largely because he was still grieving over the violent death of Sam.

On the evening of June 20, Tim was spending the night at the Dakota. Edward and Rebecca had gone out to dinner with Geoff and Millie, downtown to Delmonico's. They had originally planned to go for

German food at Luchow's, but Tim had been unhappy with their rather unpatriotic choice. Edward explained calmly that Luchow's served German food, it didn't sink ships. The Luchow family were all patriotic Americans. They went to Delmonico's anyway.

Alice and Jacob were in bed by nine p.m. The housekeeper had been given the night off. Tim was put in charge of the apartment, with Eddie as his assistant. Eddie planned to stay up all night talking with Tim, for he had much on his mind. They set up a makeshift camp in the library, so not to disturb the other children.

"What are your plans for the war?" Eddie asked, lying on his stomach and facing Tim.

"Haven't quite decided that yet," replied Tim, who was sitting on the floor, his back propped up against the couch.

"But you want to kill Germans, don't you?"

"Sometimes I do, and sometimes I don't."

Eddie didn't care for the ambivalent answer. "What do you mean?"

There was a note of outrage in his voice. Tim realized that he was not the only one in the room hurt and confused over the death of their friends. He leaned to the right, allowing his upper body to slide down the front of the couch, until he was almost face-to-face with Eddie.

"Eddie, I'm a doctor. I am supposed to heal people. I actually took an oath that forbids me to do any harm to a person. I don't think that shooting or bayoneting someone would be acceptable."

"I know," said Eddie, calming down. "But aren't you mad about Sam?"

"Of course I am," Tim replied. "I am very mad. I don't know what to do, Eddie."

Eddie lay quietly, and then said softly, "I wish it was still like it was a few years ago, Tim. Remember?"

"When?"

"When we went swimming, or sailing."

"At the lake?"

"Uh-huh."

"It's sad, isn't it?" Tim said. "Nothing ever stays the same. We all have to grow up."

"That's right! So why is it that I still feel like I'm a little kid?" Eddie asked. "I'm not an adult yet, but I'm no longer a child. I'm…in between."

"I remember what that was like," Tim answered, smiling at Eddie.

Then, a silence fell over the room.

Something occurred to Eddie which he hadn't considered. "Tim? If you go over to Europe, your ship might get torpedoed."

"It could happen."

"But you could die!"

"Nah! I'm a good swimmer, sport. I would swim the rest of the way to Europe."

"I'm not joking, Tim!" And Eddie wasn't joking. As angry as he was at the loss of Sam, he hadn't counted on raising the stakes by putting Tim's life on the line as well.

"I know, Ed," Tim gently answered. "This is what happens in war. There are casualties. People die. All kinds of people. There were so many innocent people who died on the *Lusitania*. Did you think they planned to die that day?"

"No."

"Of course not."

More silence. Then Tim thought he heard sniffling.

"Eddie?"

Eddie rolled over and embraced his friend. "I don't want you to die, Tim!"

"I know, Eddie. Believe me, it's not what I want either."

Eddie sobbed for a while, his mind flooded with memories of all the experiences with his older friend. Tim patted Eddie on the head, but thought deeply about the decision he needed to make—to fight or to heal.

"I think that your father and Geoff are correct, Eddie. It would be better trying to save Americans than kill Germans."

"You've decided?"

"Yes."

"What made your mind up?"

"You did."

"I did?" Eddie pulled himself up so that he could look Tim in the eye. "What did I do?"

"I don't know if I can tell you."

"Yes, you can."

Tim took a breath. "As I lay here, listening to you sob for me, I asked myself what I would rather do under a certain circumstance."

"Yes? Go on!"

Tim hesitated, and then continued. "I asked myself to imagine that we, you and I, were both soldiers in the army together."

"Gee! In the same platoon?"

"Sure! In the same squad." Tim stopped.

"Tim?"

He began again, "I asked myself where I would rather be if you happened to get shot."

"I get shot?"

"It's hypothetical, Eddie."

Eddie already knew what the word meant. "So, go on."

"Would I rather be next to you in the trench, watching you bleed to death, or standing over you in an operating room, putting you back together again—and saving your life."

"Oh!" Eddie looked over at his friend and gave him a smile, but noticed that there was a big tear streaking down his right cheek. He had never seen Tim cry before, not even when the rattlesnake bit him. But Tim had just brought up something.

"Tim?"

"Eddie?"

"If you won't go to fight, maybe I will join the army."

"No!" Tim answered sharply.

"Don't say that I'm too young. There are boys in my school who already are enlisted to go, and they're just a little older than me!"

"How old is that? You're fifteen, so they are...sixteen?" There was a strong note of sarcasm in Tim's voice.

Eddie picked up on this. "So? Don't you know that boys are lying about their age just to get in?"

"You are supposed to be eighteen years old, seventeen with your parents' permission. Do you think your parents will allow you to join the army at fifteen years old?"

Eddie became angry. "Of course not! You know they wouldn't allow it! I would have to run away!"

"Are you out of your mind?" Tim yelled.

"I could pass for at least seventeen. I've grown a great deal in the last year." Eddie sounded triumphant.

"Sure," Tim chided, "and you're shaving every day and you've got hair on your chest, too."

"Big deal!" Eddie shouted. "You think you know it all!"

Eddie was working himself into a rage. He began to flail with his fists, which Tim abruptly grabbed with both hands.

"Let go of me, Tim!" Eddie struggled to get free, but Tim was much bigger, and much stronger.

"No, not until you calm down, Eddie." Eddie stopped his squirming, but Tim still held him by the wrists. "Now, my young friend, you are going to listen to me—and you are going to listen really well. I wasn't making fun of you…well, I guess I was a little…but can you actually hear yourself? You'd better go to church and read your Bible again. In Ecclesiastes it says that to everything there is a season, a time to live and a time to die. I'll be damned if this is your time to die, because at fifteen, you haven't even started to live. I am almost ten years older than you, and I can tell you, there's a lot more that you will learn about life in the next ten years."

"Like what?"

"Never mind that! We can talk about those things after I convince you not to run away to join the army. And don't think I wouldn't put it pastd you. I know you really, really well."

"And I bet I know you well enough that now you're going to tell my parents that I told you about it."

"Don't you think I should? Don't they have a right to know? If you run away and get yourself killed on some foreign battlefield, it will kill them! It will kill them!"

"No, it won't. They will be proud that I did my duty."

"Perhaps they will be proud, but they will have lost their son, and that leaves a wound no time can heal. I see it in the hospital all the time when a family loses a child. It's heartbreaking."

"I don't want to hurt them. I want to get back at the Germans for killing Sam."

"Revenge?" Tim asked. "You can't help Sam now, Eddie. You will only hurt your parents. They will be worried sick until you return—if you return."

"Worry isn't the same as 'kill them,' Tim."

"You are so stubborn! Do you know that?" Tim stood up.

"What are you doing? Where are you going?" Eddie asked.

"I'm going to bed. I'm angry at you, Eddie."

"But we were talking about this. You can't just leave!"

"All right!" Tim replied, turning back to Eddie. "Let me put this in terms that you will understand, just so we are clear." Tim paused, thinking of the words to say. "Eddie, I love you like a brother, but if you ever do what you just hinted you would do, then our friendship has come to an end."

"What?" Eddie didn't accept this at all.

"You heard me! I will never speak to you again, and if you get yourself killed, I won't come to the funeral!"

"Tim!"

"I will give you until the morning to think it over and give me your response." Tim then added, "And you will only join the army when you are of legal age, if the war is still going on—which I pray to God that it is not."

Eddie nodded, but did not reply. Tim left the room. Eddie sat in silence, tears running down his cheeks, debating the alternatives to Tim's ultimatum. He thought about it for fifteen minutes, and then he stood up and went to his room.

He crouched down next to his bed and pulled out a valise. He went to his dresser and began to sort through his underwear and socks, throwing the cleaner and less worn sets into the valise. He was sure that he wouldn't need anything else. *Don't they give you a uniform to wear?*

He then went into his father's study. He sat at his father's desk and turned on the lamp. Eddie found a piece of his father's stationery, and in a very relaxed hand, wrote out a bogus permission for Edward Thomas Collier, Jr.—aged eighteen—to join the army. It was June 20, 1915, so he stated that he was born on May 30, 1897.

He forged his father's signature, folded the letter, and put it in one of the envelopes.

He took the letter back to his room, and placed it in the valise.

He put the valise under his bed.

Eddie pulled back the covers, undressed and changed, and went to bed.

Tim arose at the crack of dawn and quietly stole down the hallway to Eddie's room. He gently tapped on his door and, not hearing a sound of any sort, slowly opened it. Even in the semi-dark room he could tell that Eddie's bed was empty.

An alarm immediately went off in his head. He bolted from the bedroom and began to search the apartment. He checked every room twice before knocking on the master bedroom door.

Tim gave Edward and Rebecca the gist of the previous night's conversation, and also told them of his ultimatum to Eddie. It was quickly decided that they would go out to look for Eddie. Rebecca would stay behind, in case the boy decided to come back home. Tim ran to his bedroom to get dressed. Edward did the same, while Rebecca phoned Geoff. Geoff woke up his oldest son, Timothy, so that he could help.

Edward took Tim in his Pierce-Arrow and headed downtown on the west side; Geoff and Timothy would take Geoff's Ford and go downtown on the east side. The recruiting office was on Chambers Street. The men knew this; they weren't sure if Eddie did, but the boy was extremely resourceful and could ask questions, so he was bound to find it—sooner or later.

Geoff happened to get to the recruiting office first, and luckily so, because Eddie showed up, valise in hand, within the next few minutes.

Geoff could always play a scene very coolly. There was also the advantage of not actually being the boy's parent. "Good morning, Eddie."

Eddie, startled, answered, "What are you doing here, Uncle Geoff? Hi, Tim."

Timothy did not have a grasp on the situation and merely echoed a hello.

"I was just wondering what you were doing all the way down here in Lower Manhattan at eight thirty a.m.—especially by yourself, and with a suitcase."

"I suppose I should expect to see my father any moment?"

Geoff smirked, "I suppose that would be a good guess."

"And I suppose that Tim is with him?"

Geoff nodded. "Another good guess, my boy."

Eddie contemplated the situation for a moment. "So that means Tim must have turned me in."

Geoff shrugged his shoulders. "I have no idea about that. Your bed was empty. I got a call. We headed downtown, and here you are."

"And you are stalling me until my father gets here. Aren't you?"

"Yep."

"If I just push past you right now, are you really going to stop me, Uncle Geoff?" Eddie almost sounded threatening.

"Oh, you bet I will." Geoff nodded, his eyes giving away a fair amount of anger. "Even if you scream and cry bloody murder at the top of your lungs, I will prevent you from doing anything until your father gets here."

Eddie looked down at the floor, and then quickly tried to fake to the right. He was blocked hard by Geoff.

"Don't even think of it, Eddie. Your father is my best friend, and he will be the one who decides how you are going to ruin your future."

Geoff didn't have to say any more, for at that moment Edward and Tim arrived at the office.

"Eddie! Thank God we are in time!" Eddie did not reply, but simply hung his head glumly. "Thank you, Geoff. Thank you, Timothy."

Tim McNabb stood slightly apart, out of the picture. He was silent.

Edward gestured for Eddie to follow him over to a bench that was sitting by the window. Eddie reluctantly followed his father, carrying his valise. Edward then pointed to the bench, requesting that his son sit. Eddie looked up at his father, and then sat on the bench in a huff. Edward then sat down next to him.

"Eddie, look at me." Eddie didn't move, and continued to look at the floor. "I said, look at me, damn it!" Eddie lifted his head quickly and looked directly at Edward. He had never given his father cause to use any form of profanity at any time previously.

"Dad, I—"

"No, don't speak! I don't want you to speak! I want you to listen!" Edward blistered with anger and disappointment at his son. "This stunt of yours is very out of character for you, so I imagine you are very upset about something, or you are just being very stubborn." Edward knew that he also had a stubborn streak; that he could be very unreasonable at times. "Well, which is it?"

"I just wanted to be able to do something, Dad!" Eddie began. "I need to be a part of this war—not like some people I know."

"If you are referring to Tim, then I must tell you that I have never been as disappointed in you in your entire young life as I am right now. That was a terrible thing to say."

"Fine! Well, I am disappointed in him, too!"

Edward glanced around the recruiting office. "Well, we are not going to talk about this here. We will go back uptown to the apartment, and you, your mother, and I will have a discussion. I have never struck you once in your life, but I have the urge to give you the back of my hand across your cheek right now."

And then Eddie stuck out his chin to his father, as if to challenge that threat.

Edward was shocked. "How dare you tempt me?"

Edward reached out with his right hand and grabbed Eddie behind the neck, pinching his neck with his thumb and forefinger. He purposely dug his fingers in hard, in order to make an impression with the boy, and to leave a mark as a reminder. Edward stood up, with Eddie in tow, and headed toward the door. He nodded to Geoff on the way out, signifying that he had things under control for now. Geoff took Timothy home.

"Get in the car," Edward commanded, pushing Eddie roughly into the backseat. To the boy's chagrin, Tim got in the other door and sat next to him in the backseat. His father jumped into the driver's seat and started the car.

The ride uptown was silent and icy. Two blocks after starting home, Eddie gave a slow glance to his left to see what Tim was doing. He was surprised to see Tim watching him. Eddie quickly turned away.

Eddie attempted the same bit of spying every few blocks, and was always met with the same result. Tim was staring him down. Tim was trying to make him feel guilty.

They reached the Dakota. Edward got out of the car and opened the back door on Eddie's side. He reached in and pulled his son from the car. At the same time, Tim opened his door and then changed seats with Edward. Tim parked the car while Edward brought Eddie upstairs.

The scene in the apartment was anything but pleasant. Rebecca had been pacing in the living room. Edward marched Eddie into the apartment and shut the door. He pointed to an armchair in the living room. Eddie took himself to the chair and sat down, looking at the floor.

"Eddie," Rebecca began, but Edward held up his hand, silencing her for the moment. Not a word was said for several minutes.

The apartment door opened and Tim walked in. He nodded to Edward, who silently nodded back. Tim then left the room and headed toward his bedroom. They all could hear him doing something down the hall, but no one spoke. Edward did, however, give his son a nod which indicated that Tim was not happy at this moment.

Tim returned to the living room carrying his things. He put his bags down on the couch. He walked to Rebecca and embraced and kissed her, and then he shook Edward's hand and embraced him, as well. He then walked several paces toward Eddie. Eddie looked up at Tim, as if to question his actions. Tim gave him a glassy stare, shook his head slowly, and turned to exit. He picked up his things and headed for the apartment door. Edward opened the door for him, and patted him on his shoulder as he went out.

Edward walked back into the room. "Well, that's it. He moved out. He's going back to the hospital."

"I've lost him as a friend?" Eddie asked.

"No, my boy," Edward replied, "you will never lose him as a friend. He lost you as a friend."

"What?"

"He told me about his ultimatum to you. You took him up on it. You called his bluff. He is a man of his word. He has integrity. As much as it hurts him, he will not speak to you again."

Eddie sat resolute. "I don't think that will last. You'll see."

"Don't be so sure. He could be on a troop ship headed for Europe within a few weeks. If he doesn't speak to you before that happens, it could be a very long time before you see him again—if ever."

Eddie hadn't really considered that it would go this far.

"We will talk about your punishment tomorrow," his father continued. "But for now, let me just say this. I have contacts all around the city, Eddie. I will go back to the recruiting office with your picture and instruct them that if you show up again they are to contact me. Your mother and I both believe that you are an individual and that we are giving you opportunities to help guide your path. When the time is right, you will make that decision, but not until the time is right. I will not give you permission to join the army at seventeen. If you are going into the war, you will have to wait until your eighteenth birthday. If the war is still going on at that time, we would be proud if you exercised your duty to the country—but not until then."

Edward suddenly felt one word flash through his mind—*substitute*. *Substitute!*

Substitute!

Was he doing what Morgan's father had done to him in his youth? *No!* he thought. *This is not the same! This is not yet his time!*

"Am I clear on this?"

"Yes."

"Yes, what?"

"Yes, Dad!"

"And furthermore, if you pull another stunt like trying to run away from here so that you can sign up at another recruiting office, I will drag you back here and I will chain you to your bed for the duration of the war."

Even Rebecca was surprised to hear her husband speak this forcefully, especially to Eddie, but she also understood that Edward needed to create a boundary for Eddie to respect.

Now all they had to do was wait to see if Edward's plan would work.

Chapter 26
A New Beginning

Tim departed for England by year's end, 1915.

Edward and Geoff did not hear from him for months. Communication was very slow. He had left for Europe with the rank of second lieutenant. By midyear 1916, he had achieved the rank of captain. After those first few silent months, Edward began to receive weekly letters from Tim. He always received two letters in the same envelope; one for Edward and Rebecca, and the other for Eddie. In his instructions to Edward, he asked that Edward keep the letters from Eddie if he had the slightest idea that the boy might bolt.

He did share, in great detail—especially in Eddie's letters—the horror of what he was experiencing on the front. He was stationed in France, working in a field hospital.

Meanwhile, on the home front, Edward and Geoff sat down to plan their future. They both realized that their time at Morgan and Company was extremely limited. It was Edward's contention that they should leave of their own choosing, rather than wait for the axe to fall. Geoff agreed.

Edward decided it was time for him to open his own law office. Geoff would join him as his assistant. He would do basically the same type of job he did in the Morgan office; that is, snoop. Within a few days of submitting their resignations at Morgan and Company, Edward had several retainers from other residents of the Dakota. He was also able to sign the Archdiocese of New York, St. Luke's Hospital, and the new Columbia Presbyterian Hospital as clients. In the next few weeks Edward's practice had blossomed.

With the Morgan Company out of their lives, the rental of the Dakota was now theirs to pay in its entirety. The real cost of the apartment was somewhat of a shock, but Edward and Rebecca had sizeable savings, and this money cushioned them until the practice paid for itself.

Edward was still conscious of the fact that Eddie really wanted to fight in the war. As Eddie constantly reminded him, he had two schoolmates who had lied about their ages in order to enlist, and they were now fighting in France.

Edward and Rebecca both wrote to Tim on a regular basis—so did Geoff and Millie, and even Timothy. Occasionally Alice would also write a note to Tim, which would get inserted into her father's letter. His parents constantly asked Eddie if he wanted to include a note to Tim. His mother would remind him that it would mean a great deal to Tim if he wrote. His father told him that writing would ease the tension between them; the silence had already lasted more than a year. Whether it was stubbornness or simply that the silence had gone on too long, Eddie never could get a letter started. He refused to begin his letter with, "Dear Tim...I'm sorry," so he chose not to write at all. Days turned into months, and then into more than a year.

This is not to say that he didn't care how Tim was faring; he was always interested when his father received news from abroad, and he always managed to find out if Tim was in good health. He looked forward to the day when he could enlist so that he would be able to look him up in France, dressed in a doughboy's uniform. Then, he thought, they would both be in the right.

Instead of writing letters, Eddie decided to take a cue from his father and begin keeping a daily journal. He asked his father to purchase a similar blank book, which he titled, *Personal Journal of Edward Thomas Collier, Jr.* It was here that he wrote his deepest, darkest thoughts—especially his regrets concerning his friendship with Tim McNabb.

In late 1916, one of his classmates came home to the United States—in a flag-draped coffin. His other friend came home in early 1917—but without one of his legs and missing a hand, courtesy of a German grenade. Even though these sights did not dampen Eddie's resolve to fight the enemy, he did see how his friends' parents had reacted to each of the boy's return. They were devastated beyond belief—just as Tim had said Eddie's parent would be.

Personal Journal of Edward Thomas Collier, Jr.
June 18, 1916

This is my first entry. My father likes to write in his journal, so I shall see if I like writing in mine.

I can't write to Tim. I can't start the letter, because I know that I will send it and then he will read it. He won't read this journal.

I can pour out my deepest thoughts in this book, and no one will ever know.

When we first had our argument, I thought I hated Tim; I especially thought so after the scene downtown. But the months have made me realize that I made a mistake. I want him to return home safely, even if he doesn't wish to speak to me again.

Captain Timothy McNabb was in charge of a surgical unit for the United States Army. He had been trained to close wounds in medical school, but the types of wounds he was seeing on a day-to-day basis were far in excess of anything that remotely compared to the sterile environment of school. To his mind, the surgical unit seemed more like a butcher shop than a hospital.

As 1916 turned to 1917, Tim was becoming more and more detached from his patients. He stopped looking at faces; stopped using his bedside manner; became dehumanized to the experience. He was becoming a skilled technician, and the severity of the wounds and their life-threatening nature allowed doctors to invent new procedures in order to cope.

Just as occurred in the Civil War, military battle tactics hadn't changed to keep pace with a more modern war technology. In the Civil War, troops on both sides continued to use the same tactics that had been used in the Napoleonic Wars, even though rifles and other weapons had become far more accurate, and far more deadly. The result: whole brigades would line up, facing each other, and fire into the opposing ranks. The death toll was staggering. By the end of the war in 1865, more than six hundred twenty thousand Americans had lost their lives.

The same was true in World War I. Generals and their staffs could not estimate the difference that a new mechanized form of warfare would make on the outcome of a battle. Now both sides had tanks, airplanes with bombs, submarines, land mines, machine guns, and chemical weapons, including the favored weapon—mustard gas.

By late 1917, Tim was treating many Americans, French, and English for the effects of the deadly chemical. In reality, mustard gas amounted to about two thousand deaths of Americans, but over sixteen thousand were wounded in some way by the chemical. But there were also terrible wounds—wounds made from machine-gun fire, or from land mines, or from grenades. It was all too horrible to consider, and yet Tim worried about the day when Eddie would be old enough to enlist; old enough to become more human fodder for the killing fields of France.

He had Edward's letters, and they always contained a line or two regarding Eddie; that he was still planning on enlisting when he turned eighteen, but that he also hadn't tried to run away to do it on his own. He also knew that it took months for letters to reach the front, or to be sent home. Many letters would never make it to their destinations, and this would cause Tim more concern.

Edward or Rebecca would make sure to mention how much Eddie missed Tim, even though he didn't hear so in a letter. Tim would write back, telling the writer how he looked forward to the day when they would be reunited again—*all* of them.

Then, one evening in late 1917, a new group of wounded soldiers was delivered to the field hospital. The soldiers had all been casualties of a recent German offensive. An orderly brought the first patient to Tim, who had prepared the operating table. The nurse, an attractive blonde from England, administered the chloroform to the doughboy, who was writhing in pain. He had been wounded in the abdomen. The medics had tried their best to contain the wound, but he needed surgery immediately. Tim removed the bandages and packing to see that the soldier had lost most of the lower part of his torso, and that his intestines were, for the most part, hanging outside his body. He knew there was nothing he could do for the young man, so he gave him a large dose of morphine and prayed he would not wake up again.

His next soldier was missing the lower portion of his right leg. It had been blown away by a grenade. The soldier had already been given some morphine, but he was awake and talking—making jokes about needing a peg leg. Tim explained that he had to amputate his leg below the knee because gangrene had already started to set in. The soldier nodded that he understood, the nurse administered the chloroform, and Tim performed the amputation.

Tim worked through the night, along with the blonde nurse from England. Her name was Evelyn—just like Evelyn Nesbit, but she was Evelyn Smith, a native of London.

Together they worked on more than a dozen soldiers in the course of about three hours. Some died on the operating table; some would die later that night, or the next day. Others would survive the war.

They were still working at a feverish pace around three a.m., when a new soldier was placed on the table. He was already unconscious and in a state of shock. He had a blanket placed over his upper body and his face was partially obscured. His wounds were to the lower half of his body, but were so serious that the medics had not the time to cut away any of his uniform. Tim performed this operation, cutting away his trousers—what was left of them—to reveal the fact that his left leg was shattered and his genitalia all but completely gone.

Upon taking a closer look at the soldier's body, he realized that his build and degree of maturity indicated that this was no more than a boy—a boy who was going to bleed to death in a matter of minutes.

Tim had developed a policy that he would converse optimistically with soldiers who were awake and lucid—soldiers whose wounds were within the boundaries of repair. As of late, he had decided to avoid look-ing at a soldier's face, especially if he was mortally wounded—most of all if he was already unconscious.

Now he would break his unwritten policy.

Tim pulled back the blanket to see the soldier's face.

It was Eddie.

Tim recoiled from the operating table. "No!" he cried.

"Doctor?" the nurse asked, concerned for his welfare, as well as the patient's.

"No! No! No!" was all Tim could utter.

"Do you know this soldier?" the nurse asked.

Tim wiped his eyes. He had begged him not to enlist. He had warned him. Now he was hurt so badly that Tim doubted he could save him.

He heard the nurse ask again, "Doctor? Do you know this soldier? You can step away and someone else can work on him."

Tim turned back to the operating table and looked down into the face of the soldier. He realized that, in fact, it wasn't Eddie. There were many similarities—the hair color, his eyes—but it wasn't Eddie!

"No," he finally replied, "my mistake. Let's fix up this boy, quickly."

They worked on the boy for over an hour, patching him up as best they could. They put a stop to his bleeding and cauterized the wounds. Tim worked as one inspired.

It would not be enough. The young soldier would be dead by morn-ing. Tim's final act at the operating table was to pull the surgical cloth over the boy's face.

As Eddie's eighteenth birthday grew closer, Tim would repeat the scene at the table several more times, each time worrying Nurse Evelyn even more.

Personal Journal Entry
November 25, 1917
I have had the nightmare again. The same nightmare I had years ago.
I am lying on a bed—sleeping. I feel a presence in the room, but I cannot see who it is.
Suddenly something covers my face. I feel as if I am being smothered.
But now there is a new part to the dream.
I wake up and the cloth falls away. I look into a mirror. It is not my face I see, but...
I cannot even write this down.

The war had dragged into 1918, but the Germans had lost their strongest opponents, Russia. The Russian Revolution had taken place in October 1917. This enabled the Kaiser to pour all his strength into the Western Front.

But even this would fail.

By the time Eddie Collier prepared to turn eighteen, the war seemed to be winding down. Edward and Rebecca had feared the day for years.

On the day of his birthday, Edward drove Eddie to the recruiting office on Chambers Street. Edward, in spite of his feelings about war in general, did tell Eddie how proud he was of his resolve to serve the country. They entered the recruiting office.

Eddie was not permitted to enlist. The sergeant at the desk informed them that peace talks were already under way, and that an armistice was in the making. There were already so many American soldiers abroad that the War Department had curtailed enlistments, subject to the outcome of the peace talks.

Eddie was both frustrated and relieved. His parents were just plain relieved.

The Armistice was signed on November 11, 1918. The war had ended. The troops would be coming home.

Tim wired Geoff to tell him that, as there were still many badly wounded American soldiers who were too weak to move, he would not be able to return to New York until early 1919. Geoff mentioned this to Edward, who hatched a plan.

Edward arranged for the entire Collier-Atwater clan to book passage on the *Mauretania* to sail to Europe. They would cross in March 1919. Geoff wired Tim of the plans. They would have liked to have surprised him, but didn't want to chance him leaving prior to their arrival. Edward contacted the War Department, using some of his influence from his Morgan days, to ensure that Tim would be decommissioned in March, so that he would be able to return to New York with them. He also secured a letter from St. Luke's Hospital, asking that Tim be allowed to return so that he could resume his duties as one of its surgeons.

The *Mauretania* was one of the fastest liners of her day. She was part of the Cunard Line, and the sister ship of the ill-fated *Lusitania*. Edward booked several large staterooms for both crossings. Everyone in the two families would be going—including the children. Eddie had now entered Columbia University, but he was granted a leave of absence in order to make the trip. As much as Eddie wanted to go, he was anxious about seeing Tim. He was afraid that Tim would still refuse to speak to him, and that their long friendship truly had ended.

On the third night of the voyage to Europe, Eddie remained behind in the stateroom while the family went up on deck to take in the evening air. Just as his father had done, Eddie had brought along his journal and had finished writing his thoughts.

Personal Journal of Edward Thomas Collier, Jr.
March 19, 1919

What am I to do? I will be seeing my old friend Tim McNabb in just a few days, and I have no idea what I am going to say to him—if anything at all. I am so afraid that he will not have anything to do with me.

I do not know if I will be able to withstand that!

My parents have spoken to me about this. They have both agreed that everything is going to work itself out; that Tim is such a good man that he will not hold a grudge. But I am skeptical.

I keep asking myself how I would feel if our positions were reversed.

I am not entirely sure.

Eddie began to agonize over the upcoming meeting with Tim. He wanted to find something to say to Tim to break the tension. He wanted to apologize, but couldn't find his own words. He put the journal bag in his baggage. Opening the drawer of the small table next to his berth, he found a copy of the Bible. He started to thumb through the book, first in the Old Testament, and then in the New. His eye caught sight of some of the parables of Jesus, as they were listed in the reference on the upper corner of each page. He thought there might be a corollary in one of the parables that he could use.

Finally, he found a parable in the Gospel of Luke. In chapter 15 of that Gospel, he found the parable of the prodigal son. He knew the story very well from church. He read it again. Eddie read the story slowly and carefully, until he came to the following line:

> *When he came to his senses, he said, "How many of my father's hired men have food to spare, and here I am starving to death! I will set out and go back to my father and say to him: Father, I have sinned against heaven and against you. I am no longer worthy to be called your son; make me like one of your hired men."*

He had found his opening line, of sorts. He decided to paraphrase the text, finally settling on, "Tim, I have wronged you beyond all human patience. I am not worthy to be here, and I am not fit to be called your friend. I am truly sorry for what I have said and done, but I will not blame you if you never speak to me again—although I hope that you will."

Eddie memorized his statement. He opened his journal and wrote it on the inside front cover, directly across from his first journal entry.

Then he practiced it. He muttered it to himself whenever he found himself alone on deck. He said it softly under his breath as he stood in front of his bathroom mirror, watching his facial expressions; judging the sincerity of his manner of delivery. He edited himself several times, until he was convinced that what he would say and how he would say it would be believable—and heartfelt!

But he still wasn't sure he could look Tim in the eye and say it.

Edward and Geoff wanted to show England to the other children, but would delay the sightseeing until they passed that way again on their way homeward. The families immediately set out for the Dover Ferry after disembarking from the *Mauretania*. They arranged transportation from Calais to Paris. The families spent one evening in Paris before heading out with a hired driver to the field hospital.

Edward and Eddie were shocked to see the effects that the war had had on the French countryside. There were shell holes everywhere. They saw burned-out barns, churches without their steeples, whole towns that were in ruins. This was not the France that they remembered.

The driver brought them to a military encampment. It was largely deserted—the bulk of the army had already boarded troop transport ships for home. The driver directed them toward the hospital tents. They spied several tents emblazoned with large red crosses signifying their use. But, they wondered, which one was Tim's tent?

The entire group of adults and their children stood there in confusion. When a nurse passed them on the way to her duties, Geoff decided to take action.

"Excuse me, Nurse," he asked, "we are looking for Dr. Timothy McNabb. Would you know where we might find him?"

The nurse immediately stopped and turned to Geoff. She was a beautiful young lady. "Major McNabb?" she asked.

"Oh," replied Geoff, "so he's a major now, is he? Do you know him?"

"Oh yes, sir," she smiled. "I work in Major McNabb's OR. My name is Evelyn. Evelyn...uh...Smith. I will take you to his tent, if you'd like."

"Thank you, Lieutenant," Geoff replied, making sure that he pronounced her rank with the proper British *f* in the middle of the word.

Lieutenant Smith led them through the middle of the array of hospital tents until she arrived at one in particular. She lifted the flap to see if the doctor was in, and indeed he was. Edward could see past the flap. Tim was seated on the far end of the spacious tent. He was at a field desk immersed in paperwork. He was in uniform and not wearing his lab coat.

Evelyn placed her finger to her lips and cautioned the family to enter quietly. She led the way across the tent.

Eddie was not in the tent. He had been bringing up the rear and was too nervous to enter with the rest of the family.

"Oh, Major McNabb, my dear," she said in a singsong voice, "it seems you have some visitors."

Tim raised his head from his work and then quickly turned around. "My God!" he exclaimed, as he bolted from his chair. He looked older than any of the family remembered him, and he had grown a very distinguished-looking mustache. He ran to Geoff first and embraced him, then turned to Millie and did the same to her. Edward was next, followed by Rebecca. Then he knelt and gave kisses and hugs to all the children, including Timothy—the boy he had helped deliver into the world back in 1907. Timothy was now twelve.

Tim was hugging little Jacob Henry Collier, when he looked up over the eight-year-old's shoulders at his father, his eyes asking the obvious question. Edward's answer was a slight tightening of his lips, followed by a gesture sideways with his head, indicating that the object of the question was still outside the tent. Tim patted Jacob on the head and released him. He stood up and slowly walked toward the tent flap.

Geoff thought it was a bit odd that Nurse Evelyn had stayed in such close proximity during this emotional family reunion. As Tim walked toward the tent opening, she began to make light conversation with the family, as if to break the tension in the air—as if she already knew what Tim was leaving to do.

Eddie was standing several paces from the entrance to the tent, rehearsing his lines. He had walked a bit away from the tent, but he could clearly hear the excitement that was going on inside. He tried to put it out of his mind and concentrate on what he wanted to say, but faced with the moment of the task he was becoming more and more emotional.

Tim pushed back the flap and walked out of the tent. The young man he had known so well had grown substantially. He now stood over six feet tall and had acquired broad shoulders. He had become a man.

Tim didn't say a word, but simply cleared his throat.

The boy wheeled around in an instant. In a moment he recognized his old friend, even with his new mustache. They locked eyes.

Eddie took three deliberate steps toward Tim. It was time to say the lines he had rehearsed and rehearsed for the past week. "Tim, I have wronged…"

But his voice ceased working at that point. Emotion welled up in him and he broke down into uncontrollable sobs. He used his sleeve to wipe away his tears, still knowing that he had failed to say what he needed to say. Tim was just standing there, watching him cry like a baby. Eddie's lips were moving, he was trying to speak—he had to speak—but nothing came out.

Jacob heard his brother crying just outside the tent and wanted to see what was going on, but Edward stopped him from leaving. The family attempted to have a polite, but meaningless, conversation with Nurse Evelyn.

Tim decided it was time to end the torture that was unfolding outside the tent.

"Mr. Collier," he began, "it's a good thing you never bothered coming over here. You would have been totally useless. There are no rattlesnakes in France."

Eddie hadn't been the only person who had been rehearsing a line of reconciliation. It was, after all, Tim who had made the oath never to speak to Eddie again.

Then Tim walked forward and embraced Eddie. For the instant, the only thing that Eddie could say as Tim held him was his name, "Tim!"

After he gained his self-control a bit, Eddie pushed himself away from Tim and, straightening up, delivered his address.

"Tim, I have wronged you beyond all human patience. I am not worthy to be here, and I am not fit to be called your friend. I am truly sorry for what I have said and done, but I will not blame you if you never speak to me again—although I hope that you will."

Tears began to roll down Tim's face. He reached out and held Eddie's forearms, and said, "Eddie, you are like a brother to me. We had a family argument, but we are still brothers, and we will always be thus. I had to be sure you would stay put in America, and I had to resort to a very drastic ultimatum to get you to stay, but I only did it because I love you. I fully intend to speak to you again, but first I hope you will forgive me, too."

"Of course I will," Eddie replied, and then he threw his arms around Tim again. But then he added, "Nice mustache, Tim. You look like my father."

They laughed. Tim broke the celebration. "You know, we should go inside. My men will lose all respect for me if they see me blubbering out here."

He put his arm around Eddie and together they entered the tent. The air of tension quickly dissolved as soon as the adults noticed them entering as friends.

"Tim—I mean, Major McNabb," said Nurse Evelyn, "I see you have found another guest. I am just imagining that this must be Edward."

"Present, ma'am." The family laughed. Rebecca, however, was suspicious of the nurse. There was something about her; she seemed too familiar with the family.

"Doctor?" Evelyn continued, "Don't you think it is time for more formal introductions?"

"What?" asked Tim, not quite getting her drift.

She gave him a wink, which Rebecca caught her do. Now she understood.

"Oh," Tim said, "I need to introduce all of you, my family and my dearest friends, to Lieutenant Evelyn Smith—McNabb—my wife. We were married in Paris right after the armistice was declared."

The tent erupted into shocked happiness for the couple. Hugs and tears abounded. Everyone was truly surprised, with the exception of Rebecca, who asked, "And is there anything else you would like to tell us, Tim? Evelyn?"

Tim and Evelyn glanced at each other. Tim burst into a wide grin. "We are expecting."

To which Rebecca added the wry comment, "I hope, Evelyn, that you know what to expect on the crossing to America?"

Evelyn stared at Rebecca blankly.

"Don't worry," Rebecca said, "Millie and I will be there to help you, especially in the mornings."

∘✖∘

As per Edward's advance preparations, Tim was decommissioned in Paris the next day. The problem now concerned Evelyn, who was an English subject and still commissioned in the British Army. Evelyn was able to get leave to go with the family to England.

The family spent just over three weeks in England, Scotland, and Wales. Geoff took charge of the sightseeing expeditions, as Edward was busy sending wires to Washington, and taking in meetings to secure Evelyn's visa to immigrate to the United States. He was thankful, once again, for the years he had spent in the service of Morgan, for those contacts came through for him.

They boarded the *Olympic* and set sail back to New York at the beginning of April. It was a very smooth crossing, and the seas were not very rough. This made the passage bearable for Evelyn, as well as for Rebecca, who never enjoyed traveling on water.

Evelyn would spend part of her day below decks, occasionally coming up for fresh air. Tim would stay dutifully by her side, but she would send him out to spend time with the family, as well. These times afforded Tim and Eddie some time to spend together. Eddie would ask questions about the war, but Tim would table some of his answers. He explained to Eddie that some things were too recent to talk about comfortably; he wanted more pleasant topics.

Tim asked Eddie about school. He was not surprised at all to find that Eddie had chosen a premed major at Columbia.

Tim asked Edward and Geoff about some of the other people and places in his life. He asked about new buildings in Manhattan. He inquired about the new law firm. He asked about the new cathedral. He asked Eddie about a young lady that his father had mentioned in a recent letter. Eddie smiled, but refused to comment.

The ship pulled into New York Harbor after almost a week at sea. A ship-to-shore wire was received as the liner passed the Statue of Liberty. The wire was delivered to Edward.

Elizabeth Collier had died peacefully at her home on East 16th Street.

Chapter 27
Answering the Questions

Elizabeth Collier's funeral was held at St. George's Episcopal Church on April 20, 1919. The service was attended by a small group of people, largely family members. Her only son, Edward, delivered the eulogy. In attendance were Edward's wife and children, Geoff and his family, Tim McNabb and Evelyn, and Clara, who was with Elizabeth when she passed from this earth.

Following the service, the casket was taken from St. George's and brought to the tomb that stood in the churchyard—the same tomb that held the remains of Thomas Edward Collier, her late husband. Her casket was placed in the large sarcophagus that was directly across from her husband's. Edward glanced briefly at the rear wall of the tomb. There were still two empty vessels, dark and foreboding, standing ready for the next two bodies. He could only assume that those were beckoning to him and Rebecca, but he felt obliged to put this macabre thought out of his mind for the moment.

Edward watched as the groundskeeper locked and secured the entrance to the mausoleum. Rebecca had, on several occasions, said that she didn't like the idea of spending eternity on a shelf, and Edward had been inclined to agree with her. Eddie thought that the tomb was very ostentatious, and he would have preferred to see his grandparents buried in the ground, like everyone else.

Edward agreed with his son, but reminded him that the tomb had been a gift from his Uncle Pierpont. It had been a generous gift to their family.

The great organist-composer, César Franck, had met his demise by being accidently struck by a horse-drawn trolley while walking in the streets of Paris in 1890. At first the injury seemed minor, just a concussion to the head—he was even able to still work and compose, writing his last three major compositions. But as time went by, Franck's health began to deteriorate, and he finally succumbed to the injuries he had sustained.

Franck had been a great influence on Homer Norris, who played his compositions for the organ quite often.

After selling the Greenwood Lake estate, Norris would spend a few more years playing organ at St. George's Episcopal Church, but would leave that position during the war. In June 1920, Norris was crossing the intersection of 57th Street and Seventh Avenue, right outside Carnegie Hall, when he was struck by a cab.

He suffered a broken leg at the knee, which in and of itself was not life threatening by any means. But the leg developed an infection which Norris's body could not fight off, and he died on June 20.

Like his influence, Cesar Franck, Homer Norris lingered for a few days, and then died of injuries suffered while crossing the street.

His funeral service was held at St. George's Episcopal Church.

Sometime after attending the funeral service for Homer Norris, Edward went to survey the progress on the new cathedral, which was going to be named St. John the Divine, after the writer of the biblical book of Revelation.

Edward was able to walk freely around the construction site. He marveled how the nave walls were ascending, and without any use of structural steel. The nave was far from complete in 1920, but Edward was able to walk down the planned structure, stopping every so often to look up and out of the building into the sky. He could only walk as far as the crossing, and there a temporary wall had been erected to close in the finished sections of the cathedral, the apse and the choir.

He remembered a question that the church's chief benefactor, J. P. Morgan, had once asked him. "Do you think the cathedral will have a crypt?"

He ventured into the completed section of the great church and began to look around.

"May I help you?" a voice asked from behind him. It was a young priest of the parish.

"I am sorry, sir," Edward replied. "I used to work for J. P. Morgan. I worked for him at the time he donated money for the building of this cathedral. He once asked me if the cathedral would have a crypt. I was hunting for it."

The young priest laughed. "Come with me," he said.

In a few moments the pair rounded the back walkway of the apse, passing several of the large chapels. When they reached the center of the apse, the priest pointed up and behind the high altar area. "See there?" There was a large sarcophagus in a niche about their heads, with an effigy of someone lying on the lid. "That is the resting place of Bishop Potter, the man who worked with so much determination to see that this cathedral was built." Edward nodded. He remembered Bishop Potter from his youth. The priest pointed into the Chapel of St. Columba, one of the Chapels of the Tongues, and indicated the presence of another sarcophagus. "That is Bishop Manning. He coordinated the building efforts after Bishop Potter died."

Once again, Edward nodded. He knew all this already.

The priest continued, "These were the most important bishops of the Archdiocese of New York. If we had a crypt, these men would most certainly already be in it. Bishop Manning will find his final resting place in a niche that will be built in the nave—when it is finished."

Edward again nodded. "But is there no basement or other excavation beneath the church?"

"For a crypt?" the young priest answered with a laugh. "Yes, we shall have a basement beneath the cathedral. We shall have a basketball court, and, perhaps someday, a crypt."

Edward also had to laugh. It had been a ridiculous quest, but he had only undertaken this mission because of the gnawing feeling that Morgan had constantly put ideas in his mind over the years in which he had worked for him.

He didn't think that Morgan was leading him to buried treasure, but he did have the feeling that Morgan had been holding out on the Federal Reserve.

Edward returned to his home in the Dakota. He adjourned to his study and pulled down half a dozen of his blue journals; journals which dated back more than a decade. He began to read his own writings, looking for a clue to a mystery that he wasn't sure even existed.

He remembered that Morgan was particularly cryptic about all things buried. He found his 1900 journal where he noted his suspicion over the mysterious vault in the Newport home of Rosecliff. But that vault had been found empty, holding only the family china and silver service. Moreover, the Gilded Age of Newport society had now ended, and the Newport summer cottages were already beginning to fall into disrepair.

He closed the book.

He opened the journal he had written when he moved into the Dakota with Rebecca. He found the entry about the strange blockage in the study dumbwaiter. He had the large box removed right after Morgan died and found that it, too, was empty.

He closed that book, too.

He found the book that he wrote in 1907. Here was a description of the excavation that had been cut into the stone face of the cliffs on the Norris estate. The coffin-sized fifteen-foot-deep hole in solid stone which Homer Norris himself first denied existed, and then dismissed it as a dry well.

Edward then reviewed a more recent volume—the one that he had written on his last trip with Morgan—the one he took with Eddie in 1912. The trip when Morgan told him...

Just then, Eddie entered the room. He had returned home from a day of classes at Columbia. He plopped into an armchair across from his father's desk.

"Tough day, Eddie?"

"Very tough, Dad," Eddie complained. "Chemistry especially!"

"Yes, I remember it well," Edward commiserated, "but don't ask me anything about it. I couldn't possibly help you."

Eddie laughed. "So what are you doing with all your journals out, writing your memoirs?"

"My memoirs? No, I'm not that old, and I am certainly not that famous."

Eddie surveyed the pile of blue books, wondering if his journal writings would someday amount to something like this. "Then what are you doing, Dad?"

"Oh, I don't know, Eddie," Edward replied. "I am confused about a few things, and I thought I might find the answers by reviewing things I wrote years ago."

His father's words caused something to click in Eddie's brain. "Like a puzzle, Dad?"

"Yes, Eddie, like a puzzle."

"And you can't figure it out?"

"No."

Eddie studied the journal books on the shelf. The volume marked 1910 was still there.

"Have you searched for your answer in the 1910 volume, Dad?"

"No," Edward answered. "Should I?"

"I believe you should," Eddie replied, feeling very sure of himself, "although I really don't know why."

Edward eyed his son. What could he possibly know? "Any particular entry, Eddie?"

"I would try the place where you wrote about the rattlesnake, Dad."

"How did you know that I even wrote such an entry, son?"

"Just a guess. It was a momentous day, wasn't it?"

"Yes," Edward agreed, "it was momentous. I was so proud of you that day, Eddie."

Edward removed the 1910 volume from the shelf. He thumbed through the book until he came upon the entry from the beginning of June. He started to read it, but then spied a small piece of paper, folded and placed in the crease of the binding.

"Did you put this here, Eddie?"

"Me?" Eddie smiled blandly at his father.

"Why?"

"Uncle Pierpont gave the paper to me years ago. He told me to put it in a volume of your journal, in a place I was sure to remember."

"He did?" Edward asked.

"He said I should reveal it to you when you were puzzled over something—something you couldn't solve."

Edward fingered the paper. He folded back one of the edges to see what had been written inside. There was a one-word inscription.

Collier

That was all it said.

Edward placed the piece of paper on his desk.

"Why would he give me a piece of paper with our own name on it, Dad?"

"I don't know, Eddie, but I will give it some thought."

The family enjoyed a good dinner that evening, and then the children, including Eddie, turned to their studies. Edward returned to the study. He looked at the paper again.

Collier

Edward was sure he had seen the name before, not just his surname, but the way it was printed. He was sure he had seen just that typeface somewhere before, but…

And then he remembered where he had seen it.

Edward ran down the hall to Eddie's room.

"Eddie, we need to take a trip downtown tomorrow. Can you miss a class or two?"

"I suppose I could, but—"

"Good! I need to phone Geoff and Tim."

And then he was gone.

The following morning, Edward, Geoff, Tim, and Eddie headed downtown in the Pierce-Arrow. Edward refused to talk about their trip and just said that he was acting on a hunch.

Edward parked the car outside the entrance to St. George's churchyard. The foursome walked slowly through the cemetery until they arrived at the tomb containing the remains of Edward's parents.

Eddie grabbed Edward's arm. "Dad!" he exclaimed.

"I know, Eddie," Edward said calmly. "It came to me last night. I remembered where I had seen that particular printing of our name."

Above the tomb entrance was engraved:

Collier

The caretaker appeared from around a corner in the cemetery. He nodded to Edward and then unlocked the mausoleum. The man nodded again and left them alone.

The four men entered the tomb. Nothing seemed different from how it looked since the day Elizabeth Collier was laid to rest.

Edward walked several steps to the rear of the tomb, where the two empty sarcophagi lay awaiting their contents.

"I may need some assistance here," said Edward. He grabbed the lower sarcophagus and pulled on it. The coffin gently slid toward him. The shelf it was on was set on bearings, and pulled out until it was fully exposed in the middle of the floor.

"What are you doing, Dad?" Eddie asked.

"I am going to need some help to open this thing. That's why I brought you all along."

"Dad!"

"It's supposed to be empty, Eddie!" Edward said. "It's meant to hold me, you know."

The men positioned themselves at the four corners of the lid. On a count from Edward, they lifted the lid and placed it on top of Edward's father. A dark blanket covered the contents of the vault, and an envelope lay on top of the blanket. Edward grabbed the envelope and opened it. Inside he found a note addressed to him, and a packet with Geoff's name on it. He handed to packet to Geoff and opened his envelope, reading the note to himself.

Dear Edward,

If you are reading this, then you have solved my riddle. Congratulations! Enjoy your inheritance. If my calculations are correct, then Mr. Atwater is probably at your side, and I wouldn't doubt if Dr. McNabb is there, as well. Three is an odd number, so I will also venture a guess that young Edward is also there.

If this is the case, then I am overjoyed to see that my diabolical scheme has reached a successful outcome.

J. P. Morgan

Edward tucked the letter inside his jacket.

He looked over at Geoff.

"It's the missing notebook of Bill Greyson," Geoff said.

Edward nodded. He gently pulled the blanket back. The vault was filled to capacity with various items of wealth. There were stacks of currency. There were gold coins—mostly Dutch Krugerrands. There were stocks and bonds, all from companies throughout Europe, some of which were worthless because of the war. There were also silver ingots and gold bullion. From the look of it, the cache had been built up over many years of collection.

The upper sarcophagus contained more of the same. It was a fortune.

"We need to move this," said Geoff.

"Right!" answered Edward. "We need to do it over time, and in broad daylight. We will need containers."

They replaced the vaults as they had found them, making plans to return to secure the find, then they locked the tomb and left the cemetery.

"I don't understand, Edward," Geoff asked. "How did all that find its way into your parents' tomb? Morgan couldn't have done it. He was too old."

"He must have had help, Geoff."

"Then someone else knows that it exists."

Edward realized that Geoff had an excellent point. Morgan had wanted Edward to receive his share of his inheritance without anyone in the Morgan family or company knowing about it, but in order to carry out his wishes someone else had to know. Morgan had to have an associate.

They returned to the sanctity of the Dakota, and to Edward's study. The subject of their discussion would be the accomplice.

"Any suggestions, gentlemen?" Edward asked.

"It would have to be someone Morgan trusted," answered Geoff.

"True," responded Edward, "or someone he had something on."

"Yes," added Tim, "but Morgan is long dead and that would free up this person to talk."

"Yes," Edward agreed, "so it had to be someone Morgan knew would never speak of it."

Eddie simply listened. He had no idea what the other men were talking about. He only knew that his father was fabulously rich.

"What about Stanford White?" Geoff asked. "He dug the vault at Rosecliff."

"I think White may have been used," answered Edward.

"Like a pawn?" Eddie piped up.

"Exactly like a pawn," replied Edward. "But he died in 1906, so he's out of the picture."

"The person would have to have access to the tomb at St. George's," Tim pointed out.

Edward and Geoff looked at each other and said, "Homer Norris!" simultaneously.

Eddie was confused. "Mr. Norris? Why would he be involved?"

"Because Morgan gave him the house," Edward said. "That was what bought his silence."

"That's why he played dumb about the hole cut in the rock," added Geoff.

"But he was an old man," Eddie said. "He still would have needed help."

"Whose loyalty, besides ours," Geoff wondered, "was Morgan absolutely confident of?"

They racked their brains. Edward thought back to his earliest days with Morgan. Who had he known in those days? He looked over at Geoff. Of course, Geoff! But Geoff was here now, so no, it couldn't be Geoff, could it?

It had to be about Morgan...

And Norris...

And St. George's...

And...

And then he knew. He knew who it was that owed something to Morgan. He knew of someone who would never speak a word of it to anyone.

Edward looked back at the other men. "It was Burleigh. It was Harry Burleigh."

"Burleigh?" asked Geoff.

"Yes," replied Edward. "He owed his entire career to Morgan."

Edward saw it all very clearly now.

"Morgan may have used all those burial sites for a while, but he needed a final spot, one that I could get in, eventually. He used Norris and Burleigh to move the goods around, and he especially needed Norris because of his connection to St. George's. It was perfect."

"Almost perfect, Edward," Geoff said cautiously. "Have you given any thought to how you are going to make use of the money, considering that much of it is in ingot form? You can't just walk into a bank with gold bars and ask to have them deposited! And if the Morgans get wind of the fact that you have gold bars, they will immediately figure that J. P. must have given them to you, and then you will really have problems."

"I know. I know," replied Edward. "But this is what I propose." He gave each of his fellow conspirators a wink. "We shall keep the ingots exactly where they are, for now. We will remove anything in those vaults that is liquid, such as the currency, or in paper form, such as the stocks and bonds. We shall take a trip to Europe sometime in the next year, and we will bring the gold back to where Morgan acquired it, cashing it in for currency."

"You will have to be very careful, Dad," warned Eddie.

"Yes," agreed Edward. "We can't go flashing our new wealth around."

"Our new wealth, Edward?" grinned Geoff.

"I mean exactly that, my closest of friends. I mean there is more than enough in that tomb to keep all of us very happy, as well as our children, and our children's children."

Tim was puzzled; puzzled to have been included in the newfound wealth. "I don't understand, Edward. The fortune was given specifically to you, not to the rest of us."

Edward seemed to ignore the comment. "Eddie, do me a favor. Would you take the decanter on the sideboard to the pantry and refill it for us, please? I think we need to have a little celebration."

"Now, Dad?" His father only had to give him a reproving look, which sent the young man quickly from the room with the decanter.

"Now," said Edward, "while he is gone. Geoff, you have Greyson's notebook, which is proof of what you had suspected for many years, that Greyson discovered that you were fathered illegitimately by Morgan. You've known about it for years, haven't you?"

Geoff nodded.

Tim laughed. "Then that would have made you one of Morgan's heirs!"

Geoff nodded again. "As is our Mr. Collier, Tim. We are both Morgan's sons."

Edward now laughed. "And that's another thing you have known for years, isn't it, Geoff?"

"It seems like forever," he replied. "Remember, Edward, I didn't want to end up under a streetcar."

Tim sat amazed. "But this means that you are…half brothers!"

Edward and Geoff looked at each other, their expressions tacitly asking, *Should I tell, or should you tell?* Finally Edward spoke. "But there is another, Tim."

"Another?" Tim asked. "Another?" They nodded. "Are you saying that Morgan had another illegitimate child?"

"You, Tim." Geoff replied. "Eddie will be back soon, so I don't want to go into great detail at this moment, but you are also one of us. The man had many little indiscretions. We are the three that he actually knew about and followed throughout their lives. I found out about you when I was arguing with your father in the stable at Greenwood Lake the day I brought you to live in New York."

"The day you paid him the three hundred dollars?" Tim asked.

"The very same. He told me that you weren't really his boy, although he said he loved you as if you were. He also realized that he could never give you an opportunity like the one I was offering him. He only took the money to pay off the mortgage on the stable. That's how you inherited it."

"Yes," added Edward. "This is his diabolical scheme. This treasure is also meant for you."

"I am so confused," sighed Tim, "and yet, when I think about it, it all begins to make perfect sense. No wonder Morgan took such an interest in me and my career."

Eddie returned to the study with the full decanter of port and placed it back on the sideboard. He rejoined the other men.

"How much do you think is down there, Edward?" asked Tim.

Edward thought for a moment. "I would say about one quarter of his entire estate, or roughly twenty million dollars."

Jaws dropped to the floor.

Edward still wished to be heard, and on this he had done some thinking. He had been thinking about this ever since he met Morgan way back in 1898. "I would like to propose, gentlemen, that we give a large portion of the money, perhaps that which we get from cashing in the gold bars, to several charitable organizations."

The others thought about it and slowly nodded their assent.

"The donations must be completely anonymous!"

"Of course," agreed Geoff. There was no sense in sending up a flare to the Morgan family.

"Where will we donate the money, Dad?" Eddie asked.

Edward already knew his response. "We are going to donate a good deal to the new Columbia Presbyterian Hospital, Eddie. We are going to donate it in memory of the Samuel Waters family."

Eddie nodded enthusiastically. "That is a great idea, Dad."

Edward continued, "And I think another place I would like to donate money to is Howard University. I think it is about time that people not of our race should have an equal opportunity to get a fine college education."

They all agreed.

"And one more thing," Edward continued. "I would like to see that a new form of orphanage is established in the city, one located in the country, so that underprivileged children don't have to live on the streets, or compromise their godliness in a life of crime—"

"Or have themselves subjected," Geoff added, "to senseless beatings, violence, and abuse." Geoff stood and removed his jacket, and then pulled his shirt from his trousers—showing Tim and Eddie his back.

"Uncle Geoff!" Eddie gasped.

And from Tim, in unison with Eddie, "Geoff!"

Geoff lowered his shirt. "I've wanted to get that off my chest for years."

Edward moved to the sideboard and set four crystal glasses next to the decanter of port. He filled the four glasses with the deep crimson liquor, and then handed each one of the men a glass, including Eddie.

"Gentlemen," Edward announced, raising his glass, "a toast."

"A toast," answered Eddie.

"To our benefactor, J. Pierpont Morgan."

"Here, here!" was the reply from the other three.

"And to a new and better world."

"Here, here!" came the response again.

They all drained their glasses and Edward refilled each one.

"A toast," repeated Edward, again raising his glass.

"Father?" interrupted Eddie.

"What is on your mind, my boy?" asked Edward.

"I don't understand, Dad," Eddie replied. "Why would Uncle Pierpont leave you all that money?"

Edward laughed.

"Well, Edward Thomas Collier, Junior...let me tell you a little story."

Truth Is Sometimes Stranger Than Fiction

Most of this novel is based on actual events, places, and people—
only the principal characters are of my imagination, with the exception
of one:

J. Pierpont Morgan

Here are some facts about the man. All dollar amounts represent
the money spent at the time and are not adjusted for inflation in today's
economy.

Morgan's father did, in fact, hire a "substitute" to fight in his place
during the Civil War.

There is a popular theory that Morgan did father an illegitimate
child, and that he gave money to the New York Children's Hospital out
of remorse for that act.

Morgan gave a substantial sum, more than five hundred thousand
dollars, to help build the Cathedral of St. John the Divine.

Morgan was chief warden at St. George's Episcopal Church on
Stuyvesant Square.

Morgan cast the deciding vote which confirmed the hiring of Harry T. Burleigh, an African American, as a soloist at St. George's.

Morgan used Stanford White as his architect of choice on many of
his building projects.

Morgan did give the organist at St. George's Episcopal Church,
Homer Norris, a tract of land on Greenwood Lake, adjacent to the Harriman estate, and allowed Norris to design a retreat cottage on the property overlooking the lake. He also paid for the construction. It was a
lavish gift, and cost Morgan over thirty thousand dollars.

Morgan invested heavily in Thomas Edison's electric light, but also
had a large financial stake in Nikola Tesla's Wardenclyffe Tower. Tesla
had once worked for Edison, but during the time the story is set, they
were rivals.

Morgan did save the United States economy twice; once when Grover Cleveland was president, and a second time during Theodore Roosevelt's presidency, the so-called Panic of 1907.

Morgan was later vilified for his role in the Panic of 1907. Critics called him "opportunistic."

Morgan actually did have the finest stateroom booked for the maiden voyage of the *Titanic*, but canceled his reservation at the last moment.

Homer Norris

Homer Norris was, in fact, the organist at St. George's Episcopal Church.

Homer Norris was deathly afraid of snakes.

Norris designed the Boulders and made sure that all the beds in the house were suspended by chains from the ceiling, out of fear of snakes.

The house still exhibits marks in the bedroom ceilings where the beds were once attached. In the upstairs guest bedroom—where Edward, Eddie, Geoff, and Tim slept—the two beds still hang in their original state.

Homer Norris was run over by a cab near Carnegie Hall, and died later from infection of these wounds.

Stanford White

Stanford White designed many of the most beautiful buildings in the New York area, including the second Madison Square Garden. He also designed the Newport mansion, Rosecliff.

White did have a penchant for young girls.

White did have a room that was covered with mirrors and featured a red velvet swing and a green velvet couch.

White did have an affair with sixteen-year-old Evelyn Nesbit.

White was shot to death by Nesbit's husband, Harry T. Thaw, in the rooftop cabaret at Madison Square Garden.

Harry T. Burleigh

Harry T. Burleigh was once hired by composer Antonín Dvořák to assist him with themes that later became part of his *New World Symphony*. It is said that Burleigh's singing of the spiritual "Deep River" inspired Dvořák to write the famous theme used in the second movement of that symphony, sometimes called "Goin' Home."

Burleigh's position at St. George's Episcopal Church, a post which he held for over fifty years, was considered groundbreaking at the time.

Burleigh went on to work for the Italian publishing house of Ricordi, where several of his own compositions and many arrangements of African American spirituals were put into print. His works are still in print today, and his choral arrangements of spirituals are performed often, especially his arrangements of "My Lord, What a Mornin'" and "Ev'ry Time I Feel the Spirit."

When Burleigh died, he was buried in an unmarked grave. He was later exhumed and brought back to his hometown of Erie, Pennsylvania, where he was reinterred.

The Places Mentioned in the Story

All the places mentioned in the story actually exist. Very little literary license was used, either in their description or in the timeline to enhance the story.

Actual places that still do exist include:
- Rosecliff, Newport, Rhode Island
- Marble House, Newport, Rhode Island
- The Breakers, Newport, Rhode Island
- St. George's Episcopal Church, Stuyvesant Square, New York City
- The Cathedral of St. John the Divine, New York City
- The Metropolitan Museum of Art, New York City
- The American Museum of Natural History, New York City
- Carnegie Hall, New York City
- The Boulders, Greenwood Lake, New York

The residence known as the Dakota, located at Central Park West and 72ⁿᵈ Street, was home to many famous New Yorkers during its history, including Leonard Bernstein, Boris Karloff, Judy Garland, Lauren

Bacall, Neil Sedaka, John Madden, Connie Chung, Gilda Radner, and John Lennon and Yoko Ono.

It was in front of the porte cochere that John Lennon was assassinated by Mark David Chapman. The memorial garden to Lennon, Strawberry Fields, is across Central Park West and in the park.

The rest of the places mentioned in the story are to be found in areas of Manhattan Island, as well as in northern New Jersey, particularly western Passaic County and southern Sussex County. Parts of Orange County, New York—particularly Warwick and Greenwood Lake—are included in parts of the text.

The areas in and around Greenwood Lake are particularly true to how they were at the beginning of the twentieth century.

The train station at the state line of New Jersey and New York did exist in Sterling Forest, a community that straddles the state line. The station would have been located on the property of a marina on the Jersey side, called Happy Landing. The steamboat ferries would have docked just below that. There were three large steamships, named the *Clairmont,* the *Montclair,* and the *Arlington.* One of these ships was left to rot between the Castle Tavern Restaurant and the Greenwood Lake Boatworks. The tavern still exists, but the place that held the derelict steamer is now a parking lot.

The ice house was in full operation for several decades, from 1864 through 1945, when the building was torn down. The processing plant was located between Cove Road and West Cove Road.

The Greenwood Lake Boatworks was a boat-building operation for many years. Its owner was also the stuff of legend, as it was said that he made baseball bats for Yankee slugger, Babe Ruth. Ruth was a frequent visitor to Greenwood Lake, and pictures exist of him standing or sitting on a diving board that was affixed to the end of the rocky promontory mentioned in the novel—the point.

Beyond the point lay Smith's Cove, which was almost barren in the early part of the twentieth century, save for the home of Henry Logan, who had dragged his flat-bottomed houseboat onto dry land. Logan was a New York lawyer. He became one of the longest summer residents of the lake, passing away in 1985. He left more than one million dollars to Dickenson College in Pennsylvania.

Just to the north of Smith's Cove is Shore Avenue, which ends at the estate once owned by Homer Norris. The estate was indeed owned for many years by the O'Dea family, and was sold by the family in 2000.

The Boulders still exists, and stands as it did when it was in the O'Dea family.

The Castle, or Tiedemann Castle, is a set of large buildings on the west coast of the lake, built in 1903. The house was recently purchased by another Yankee slugger, Derek Jeter.

Made in the USA
Charleston, SC
04 October 2011